. . . Without words they undressed and sought the bed, Billie flinging the covers back impatiently. The pent-up eagerness created by their absence from each other burst its bounds and neither of them felt any constraint. Billie covered her with her more ample body, kissing her ears, her breasts, exploring the soft spots of her body, searching for the expectant center of her desire. Time lost its definition. They were aware of each other only in the heat of their conjoined bodies, each other's quick breathing, the energy that flowed between them. When Billie sank back on the pillow, Helena leaned over to look into her eyes. The love she saw there overwhelmed her and she pressed her face into Billie's breasts. Billie clasped her to her with a frantic grip.

Keep To Me, Stranger

by Sarah Aldridge

The Naiad Press, Inc.
1989

Printed in the United States of America
First Edition

Cover design by Pat Tong and Bonnie Liss
    (Phoenix Graphics)
Typeset by Sandi Stancil

Library of Congress Cataloging-in-Publication Data

Aldridge, Sarah.
    Keep to me stranger.

    I. Title.
PS3551.L345K4   1989   813'.54   88-29126
ISBN 0-941483-38-X (pbk.)

TO

TW

I
Rosenstein's

It was broad daylight out in the street but inside the big store the hundreds of lights were on in the ceiling, in the showcases, on the countertops. This was always the case on the ground floor, visible through the wide windows to the passersby during the night hours. Helena looked critically around, trying to evaluate the details that went to make up the overall effect. She was always the first to arrive in the morning, except for the early shift of the security personnel. The appearance of this showroom of the Rosenstein store was its hallmark, the distinctive difference between it and the other fine stores on Fifth Avenue that specialized in women's apparel and luxury appurtenances. It was often photographed and the photographs displayed in fashion exhibits and reproduced in the glossy magazines of the fashion world.

She felt uncertain in her grasp of the elements that went into achieving this distinctiveness. She must learn — she must school herself in the perceptions demanded by this unfamiliar, so far uncongenial world — so that she would acquire confidence in her own judgment of what went into creating and maintaining this image of luxury, brilliance, softly muted elegance. This was the realm of women who used these expensive dresses, perfumes, cosmetics, intimate furnishings to attain and hold dominating positions in the private and public worlds of wealth and privilege. A year ago it would not have occurred to her that her working life would be preoccupied by such concerns.

She looked around again. This apparently effortless elegance was compounded of soft lighting ingeniously placed to give full visibility while maintaining a muted radiance, of showcases sparsely set with objects that seemed to gain in value from the subtle care with which they were placed on the folds of satin — yes, even the background music, which would shortly be switched on, was exactly pitched to create a suave sense of luxuriousness to go with the perfumes and silken fabrics. All of this must be watched over with unrelenting vigilance, to see that the lamps were not set too high, the music too loud, that the saleswomen, carefully trained to flatter, made sure that all discord was excluded from the selling process. She was thankful that the oversight of the daily operation of the store was not her responsibility. But as manager of the Rosenstein Company it behooved her to understand its functioning.

A sound reached her ears. It came from behind the doors that shut off the working areas of the store from the showroom. The sound was repeated and grew in volume. She interpreted it as the arrival of the first employees, entering for the business day. She walked quickly across the showroom to the elevator that would take her directly up to the offices on the top floors of the building. She did not want to meet the flow of talkative, curious saleswomen in the corridors downstairs. She had come down from her office for this quick tour of the showroom when she would be unobserved. The saleswomen knew she was in the habit of arriving very early and leaving well after the store was closed. She supposed the watchmen had reported this and it provided fuel for the speculation about her, the new manager and the first woman in the executive offices.

As she stepped off the elevator she realized that in her preoccupation she had gone directly to the top of the building, the twelfth floor on which the board room was located. Her eyes went at once to the group of large portraits in oil that hung on the wall opposite. The day she had been invited for an interview she had been shown over the store by Daniel Rosenstein, the executive vice-president. He was a slim, dapper man, no taller than she, past middle-age, whose grey hair lay close to his head and

3

whose quick bespectacled eyes had seemed to observe every nuance of her own reactions as he pointed out not only the characteristic features of the store but also the incidental happenings that caught his attention, as if these were details integral to the scene which she should note. When they came to this floor and the portraits they had stood before them and he had explained. The middle one, of an elderly Jewish woman of great dignity and presence, he said, was the Leah Rosenstein who had founded the Company and created the store.

"Or perhaps I should say it the other way round," he said, his quick eyes watchfully on Helena. "She was my grandmother. It was her skill as a needlewoman and her great determination that brought the store into being. Those" — he pointed to the other portraits, two on each side of the founder — "are her sons. They are all dead now. My father was Aaron Rosenstein," — his long finger pointed again. "All but Moses, the eldest — that's the one on her right hand — founded their own businesses, with capital provided by their mother. Moses stayed with the store."

Helena had murmured polite responses. She was strongly aware that what he was telling her had some importance that she could not then understand but which perhaps would become clearer to her later. He had stood there with her for a few minutes in silence, as if he wanted to emphasize something. It was only later that she realized that he was subtly calling attention to the fact that these were Jewish people and that she was not a Jew.

She had not given any particular thought to this fact until some of her friends and acquaintances,

4

curious about her choice of a new departure in her business career, had pointed it out to her. Someone had said to her that there were always special problems when you worked for a family-controlled company: you were an outsider; and in her case, she was doubly so. But then her friends had not understood why, when she had decided that there was no further opportunity for advancement in the company she was with, she had chosen to accept the offer from Rosenstein's. It is retailing, they pointed out; you have no experience in retailing. Rosenstein's is the acme of the fashion world; you have no interest in haute couture. She had stubbornly resisted their negative advice. She was trained to be a manager, she said, and in the modern business world management was a distinct field. She should be able to manage any company and this offer was otherwise very attractive. It would enable her to skip two steps up the corporate ladder — and there was the prospect that she might become a vice president.

As she walked into her office her mind went back to the phrase: she had been invited to join the company. Certainly she had joined it but she now realized that behind that polite phrase she felt there was a strong sense that she had been permitted to join. From what she had come to learn in day-to-day dealings with some of the older employees, she was aware that there was some motive behind the cordial welcome she had received. Certainly it was not usual for Daniel, the effective executive officer, to escort a young prospect like herself around the store. There must be something he had wanted to learn about her that would not be apparent from the data the computer could provide. This was a new position —

5

manager of the Company — and she was the first woman to join the executive officers since the death of the founder twenty years before. Daniel himself had explained that the board of directors had decided that, in response to the demands of modern business requirements, they needed a manager to carry some of his own burden. The store's operations would continue in the traditional manner. What was needed was someone who could understand the pressures of competition in the modern world. A few days in the office had revealed to her that she had accepted a real challenge whose dimensions she as yet only dimly perceived.

But why had they wanted a woman? And why had they wanted her — a young woman who had risen to the top job in a regional office of the corporation for which she had worked since leaving business management school — where she knew she was stuck. She had soon found that they knew every detail of her working career. They had chosen her with their eyes open.

She got up from her desk and walked over to the window to look down on the thronged street below. The building of the Rosenstein store was not very tall, compared to its neighbors. It was twelve stories high, of which the top three housed the business offices. The tenth floor contained the credit office, the complaints department, the personnel manager's office, the advertising and procurement people. Her own office was on the eleventh, with those of the vice-presidents and department heads. The president's office and the board room were on the twelfth, a hushed domain where there were also a few chiefly unoccupied rooms that were occasionally used as offices by some of the directors. Right next to her own office was that of the head buyer, who was not called a vice-president but had the prestige of one — a dark-haired, thin-faced middle-aged woman, whom she had met once or twice and who had stared at her with bold black eyes. She was called simply Rachel, as if this was enough to identify her anywhere. She was seldom in her office and was often in Europe or elsewhere.

There was little activity on the eleventh floor. It was the end of summer and not the busiest season in the store. The peculiarities of this segment of the retail business — the seasonal changes, the habits of its customers, the demands of preparation for peak business periods — all these things she had to learn and she knew she would learn them quickly. She had become a familiar sight to the office staff and even to the saleswomen on the floors. The people in charge of advertising, procurement, the floor managers seemed to accept her as a matter of course. Otherwise she felt isolated. She had met few of the chief officers of the Company. Those she encountered in the elevators or corridors greeted her cordially but went no further. She supposed she was being left to orient herself before she was called into the inner circle. Most of them seemed to be away. Daniel, she was told, always took his vacation at this time of year. It was he with whom she would have most to do.

The personnel manager, an energetic woman in her forties, came to see her in her office. It was the saleswomen she wanted to talk about, she said. There was in each department a certain proportion of saleswomen close to retirement or even beyond retirement age who had been with the store for most of their working lives. These women were transmitters of the traditions inherited from the founder. The store would never discharge them. It had never suffered under this policy; the intense loyalty generated in these women compensated for other failings.

Helena asked, "Is this policy still accepted by the management?"

The personnel manager sat forward in her chair as if this was the heart of her reason for the interview. "You might as well know. Some of them — some of the officers — are impatient with this policy. They say it is old-fashioned, doesn't fit modern conditions, that it was created in the days when working-women did not have the protection of workmen's compensation laws, unemployment benefits, social security and so on. It is a sentimental inheritance from the past. They say the store has to revamp its methods of hiring. The accountants hammer away at this all the time. We need new blood, new concepts." The personnel manager paused and then added, "That's why you are here, I suppose — to bring in new methods."

Inwardly astonished, Helena answered, "I am not here to reorganize the store. My business is to manage the Company, to improve profitability. Perhaps it is true that new methods are necessary for that purpose."

The personnel manager's expression showed that she did not entirely believe Helena. "Well, they created this position just for you, I think."

Helena wanted to say, "How do you know that?" but did not. Instead she said, "You wanted to talk about the saleswomen."

8

"About a couple of them in particular. These women reached retirement age last spring but they've been kept on through the summer. I still don't have definitive word on when they will be separated and put on pensions."

"Do they want to stay?"

The personnel manager gave her a derisive smile. "Don't you know? Nobody ever wants to leave Rosenstein's."

"Do they have personal problems?"

"No. It's routine. It's not for compassionate reasons that they've been kept on. I'll give you an example. We have to hire some new saleswomen for the fall season. We have to try them out, no matter how experienced they are in other stores. They have to acquire the Rosenstein finish. The old ones help there. But it increases the overhead and that's what the complaint is about. Do you spend money maintaining the Rosenstein mystique?" The personnel manager stared at her with a quizzical expression.

When the woman had left her office, Helena sat for a while assimilating what she had said. Since there had been no board meeting or interoffice meeting so far in which she could observe the senior officers, she had no yardstick for judging the seriousness of her veiled warning. The next meeting of the board of directors was to come soon, when they had all returned to New York. There must be some discord among the officers and directors concerning the store's policies and this would necessarily affect the Company. She could sense danger ahead. She must not become a pawn in an internecine struggle.

There was another unspoken comment the woman

9

had left in the air behind her: that she saw an obvious reason why the Rosenstein Company had chosen to hire Helena as its new manager. Reluctantly Helena made herself face this recurring problem in her pursuit of a successful business career. She knew people said she was beautiful and she was often envied, for it was assumed that she had a powerful natural advantage over less good-looking women. This annoyed her, since she had come to think of personal beauty — outside of aesthetic appeal — a dangerous thing on which to base success in life and the pursuit of happiness. She had also realized at an early age that it had serious disadvantages: it made her more vulnerable to attentions she did not want from men. The result was that she had cultivated a reserve, a coolness of manner that she knew was not as unshakable as it seemed to others. She had made a habit of not looking at herself except to comb her hair or see that her clothes fitted. When she walked into a shop or restaurant with mirrored walls or along a street with highly reflective show windows she deliberately ignored the image of the tall, slim, long-legged young woman with soft brown hair that fell so naturally and becomingly over her forehead like a wing. But she could not ignore the response she saw in other people's eyes — Daniel's covert glances, the sudden widening of Rachel's eyes when they first met, the calculation in the personnel manager's appraisal of her.

Her defense against these intangible worries was her usual one: to forget them by redoubling her concentration on conquering the unknown factors in her new world. Walking through the store now she paid particular attention to the saleswomen. She came to recognize the way in which they alertly and yet unobtrusively watched everyone on the floor, herself included. It was a hallmark of Rosenstein's, she was told, that no customer must ever for the briefest period be allowed to feel overlooked or neglected. Obviously this meant a larger staff of saleswomen than other similar stores would hire.

So one day, as she strolled about, she was surprised to see that, whenever saleswomen were unoccupied, they were gathered together here and there, in clusters of three or four. When she came to the floor where nightwear, negligees, lingerie were sold — an all-important feature of Rosenstein's — she noticed that one corner of the floor had been partitioned off to make a small room decorated as a boudoir. The walls had been painted a rosy pink, draped with swatches of gauzy white curtains. There were a couple of satin-covered chaise longes, one in apple-green, the other in pale yellow. In the corners were large urns filled with real plants. The subtle scent of an expensive perfume hung in the air. Helena, bemused, stood in the doorway and watched the saleswomen as they arranged the filmy garments over the chairs. She knew they were acutely aware of her presence, that their light chatter was carefully censored for her ears.

Finally one of them — she recognized her as one of those due for retirement — came over to her and said, her eyes glowing with pleasure as she looked up at her, "Isn't it lovely?"

Nonplussed, Helena nodded, feeling very much the outsider. The saleswoman, short, rosy-cheeked, white-haired, was too taken up with her own delight to notice Helena's lack of enthusiasm. She pointed out the various details of the decor, minute touches in the decorations that Helena would never otherwise have observed. Then the saleswoman burst out, "Miss Billie will love it! Wait till she sees how we've used all these little ideas she told us about! I can hardly wait for her to see it!"

"Miss Billie?" Helena repeated the name. She had never heard it before. It was certainly not that of any of the floor supervisors.

The little saleswoman looked at her brightly, flushed with anticipation. "Yes. She is just back from Europe. She has been there all summer and she's bringing back all sorts of things from Paris."

Helena did not want to ask, "And who is she?" Obviously Miss Billie was someone everyone knew. Instead she said cautiously, "Will she be in the store this morning?"

"Well, sometime today. We'll all be so happy to see her."

Helena walked casually away, aware that the saleswomen were watching her intently.

She forgot the incident in the pressure of the business details that absorbed the rest of her morning. At lunchtime she often did not leave her office, eating from a tray that was brought to her from the elegant restaurant located on the fifth floor. Halfway through her lunch there was a knock on her door — it always stood partly open. Sherry, her secretary, had gone to lunch and the outer office was empty. She looked up to see a woman whom she knew to be the secretary to the board of directors standing there. Esther was a bustling, middle-aged woman with darting, observant eyes. She was short

12

and dumpy but dressed with the chic that proclaimed her sense of Rosenstein elegance. Helena had been told that she was the secretary to the board of directors not only because of her professional competence but also because she was a Rosenstein. Helena had first met her during the interview with Daniel Rosenstein. From that beginning she had shown an unabashed curiosity about this outsider. She had in fact become the person with whom Helena had most to do.

Helena said now, "Hello, Esther."

Esther dropped down into the chair opposite. "You've heard the news, haven't you? Billie is back." As usual when they talked she was watching Helena closely.

"Billie? Somebody mentioned her to me."

"It must have been one of the saleswomen. They adore her — especially the older ones. You should know who she is before you meet her. She is a great granddaughter of Old Leah, our founder. But she is special. Old Leah had no daughters, only sons. Billie's mother is the daughter of Moses, the oldest son. She is an only child. So is Billie. Old Leah didn't have any granddaughters except Billie's mother."

"I suppose you mean that Billie's mother was a favorite of old Mrs. Rosenstein."

Esther smiled at her. "We always call her Old Leah, you know. Nobody is in doubt who you are talking about then. Yes, Billie's mother was her favorite. A lot of us think that Billie has inherited something from her great grandmother, some special gift for preserving the traditions of the store."

Helena glanced at her sharply. "Is she an officer of the Company? I hadn't been aware of that."

13

"Oh, no! Billie doesn't hold any sort of job with Rosenstein's. But she is a director of the Company. She is the only one of the present generation who has any interest in how the store is run. You must have noticed her name in the list of directors. Of course she isn't called Billie there. She's the only woman on the board."

Helena made a wry face. "I'm afraid I haven't noticed. I haven't got that far."

Esther accepted her explanation. "There's a lot to do, coming in new like this, isn't there? You'll meet her, of course, now that she's back. So are the other directors. You'll have more to do with them than you realize now. They keep very close control of the Company. Old Leah taught her sons that and they taught their sons. We are a very close family."

Instinct told Helena that there was considerable value in listening to Esther. Was Esther warning her? Or genuinely interested in enlightening her? None of the men she was likely to deal with would take this informal discursive way of telling her things of importance. To the men in the Company she was an interloper. It could not be otherwise, no matter how cordial they might be on the surface — the first woman to break into their club. Except for Billie. But Billie was a Rosenstein.

Helena said, "Reorganizing the Company is not part of my commitment. My job is to improve profitability. That may require the implementation of some new ideas."

Esther nodded. "Yes, some people think Rosenstein's has become hidebound. But there are signs that things are changing." She laughed and added, "You're one of the changes."

14

An echo of the personnel manager's remarks, thought Helena. "Nothing has been said to me about this."

"Oh, no! That's part of the strategy. You're not supposed to know that they're thinking about changes in how the store is run. They want to see what you can do without being hampered by preconceived ideas. And you're a compromise."

A sudden sense of danger made Helena's skin prickle. Esther's information could only come from personal knowledge of what happened in the board room. If the directors did not know that she was talking this way to the new manager, it must be a breach of trust on Esther's part. But she was sure that Esther would not commit such a breech. She opened her mouth to voice some sort of protest but Esther was ahead of her.

Esther said with a smile, "Oh, I'm not telling you things I shouldn't! They are not in agreement, you know. You'll find that out for yourself tomorrow, if not today. I'm just being a little previous. They've been watching you, you know. They want to see how you make out. Everybody is back now. Things will get more interesting — especially with Billie back."

"You say she is especially popular with the saleswomen. Is there a particular reason?"

"Oh, Billie is everybody's favorite! But the saleswomen think she is their special friend, that she will look out for them if there are decisions made that will affect them — wage increases, pension changes, that sort of thing. They seem to think of her as a reincarnation of Old Leah and Old Leah is revered at Rosenstein's. That's why it is so hard to modernize things, to make changes, because she isn't here to approve them."

When Esther left, Helena turned back to the problems on her desk, but Esther's remarks cropped up in her mind from time to time. Her afternoon was too crowded for her to leave her office till she went out for a late snack, wanting a breath of outside air to ease the headache that had developed from the tension of her day. When she came back into the softly shining brilliance of the ground floor showroom she was preoccupied and unaware of her surroundings. But halfway to the rank of elevators at the back her attention was caught by some influence outside herself. The store was fairly crowded with customers but across the wide expanse she saw a woman standing behind one of the counters, leaning her elbow on the glass case, talking to two saleswomen. The thought came to her at once: this was Miss Billie — a young woman with a mass of red-gold hair, clear, translucent skin and a high-bridged nose, smiling at the laughing, flattered middle-aged women looking up at her with delight in their faces. Large earrings flashed in her ears when she moved her head. Without thinking, Helena hurried to reach the elevators, anxious not to be accosted in the thronged space.

Sometime later, when, preoccupied with the substance of the papers she held in her hand, she opened the door of her office to step out to her secretary's desk, she stopped abruptly at the sight of someone standing talking to Sherry. The same woman. Miss Billie. In her surprise she stared straight into the mild blue eyes.

Smiling at her, the woman said in a throaty,

beguiling voice, "How do you do? I'm Billie Rosenstein."

"Yes," said Helena, dismayed at her own lack of readiness. "I'm Helena Worrall." Which was a silly thing to say, since who else, under the circumstances, could she be? "Won't you come into my office? If you'll excuse me just a second. I must explain something to my secretary."

Billie nodded and strolled across the room and through the open door into the inner office. Helena was aware that she had exchanged a glance with Sherry, whose fascinated eyes stayed fixed on Billie's back until she disappeared.

When Helena went back into her office she found Billie sitting in the chair beside her desk. She sat with her legs crossed, evincing no sense of hurry, intrusion, apology, yet not giving the least impression of arrogance.

Helena sat down at her desk and said, "You're just back from Paris."

Billie nodded. Paris was written large over her from the many-stranded necklace around her throat to the high-heeled, fragile slippers on her feet. She must weigh, thought Helena, ten or fifteen pounds more than she should but perhaps that plumpness accounted for the luxurious softness of her pink-flushed skin. It occurred to Helena that no one had said anything about Billie's being married, at present or in the past. There was one ring on her white, exquisitely manicured hands, a large, brilliantly cut diamond on her right hand middle finger.

Billie's throaty voice was saying, "I always enjoy my first visit back to the store when I've been away for a while."

17

"You've been away all summer?"

"Two months. Every year there is always this business in Paris and Milan, preparing for the fashion shows."

Since she did not entirely understand what Billie was talking about, Helena kept silent.

"It takes up so much time and I can't let my attention wander. Everybody notices if I do. If it just didn't happen every year." Billie looked at her and seemed to notice that Helena was at sea. In a patient voice she explained. "Of course, you're not used to retailing — not our kind of retailing. Every September we bring over a sampling of all the new fashions from the Paris couturier houses. This has been going on for years. We're the only New York store that has this arrangement. We're the only one they trust. It is one of the legacies from my great grandmother." She shot Helena a bright blue flash of her eyes.

"There is a showing here of the Paris fashions?"

"Yes. On the seventh floor, which is completely redecorated for the show each time. Attendance is by invitation only. This means that everybody in the fashion dress business tries to get in. We have to have extra guards — all kinds of extra security."

Helena, who had been listening with her eyes cast down, looked up when Billie fell silent. But Billie was not looking at her and seemed preoccupied. After a few moments Billie turned her gaze on her again and said in an untroubled voice, "I don't suppose anybody has told you anything about this."

"No. It really doesn't come within the scope of my job — except for the expense involved."

Billie nodded. "Of course. We need a manager for

the Company. But it won't hurt to know something of the store operation. I'm told you pay quite a lot of attention to what goes on here."

Helena was wary. "I knew that alterations were being made on the seventh floor but I didn't know why. Who is in charge of this?"

"Rachel — Rachel Leventhal, our head buyer."

"I have met her, but just for a moment. She also has been away, I understand."

"I have been with Rachel," said Billie gently. "She is the one who deals with the French couturiers. When she was quite young she was trained by my great grandmother. I only act as her assistant. A great deal of Rosenstein's reputation rests on what Rachel does."

"I did not know that. I suppose that is something I should have acquainted myself with." Helena was annoyed at herself for apologizing. Then she realized that she would not have apologized to anybody but Billie.

Billie seemed to dismiss the subject. "There was no one to tell you, was there? The show is next week. It will be one of Rachel's best. Old Leah would be very pleased." She noticed the expression on Helena's face and added, "We always call her Old Leah. You must get used to that. We have to distinguish among all the Mrs. Rosensteins, there are so many of them. We use their husband's names — like royalty. My mother is Mrs. Alfred. Have you wondered why my name is Rosenstein, since it is my mother's maiden name? That is because my father took her name when he married her. Rosenstein was much more important than Liebermann." Billie's eyes, dwelling on her, twinkled.

19

Helena, at a loss, murmured, "Thank you for telling me."

Billie got up slowly from her chair. "You're quite new to the women's garment trade, aren't you — even as a customer?"

"I've never had any interest in women's fashions. My business experience has been strictly in management —"

"In large manufacturing corporations. Yes, I saw your resumé before I went abroad." She had reached the door and Helena was standing beside her. "Do come to the fashion show. You'll find it more interesting than you think." She smiled as she took another step. "You can't know all the details of a job like this right away. But don't apologize to anyone."

Billie lifted her hand in a farewell gesture as, still smiling, she walked through the door and passed through the outer office, saying, "Good to see you again, Sherry," to the girl sitting at the desk.

It was true. Up till now she had been oblivious of fashion shows except for fleeting glimpses of pictures seen in magazines and on television, showing models walking with exaggerated stances about a stage. For herself she paid little attention to clothes except as an important element of her image as a successful businesswoman. As part of her business training she had learned that the uniform worn by the businesswoman of an earlier generation — the neat suit in muted colors, the low-heeled shoes, the matching accessories in quiet harmony, a feminization of the image of the conservatively dressed businessman — no longer was what was expected of the modern successful woman executive. So she had been forced to consider the changing styles that

20

appeared in the better shops. Her handsome figure and natural taste made the task of maintaining a smart appearance easy. But she had never looked for clothes in Rosenstein's. She supposed she had been put off because Rosenstein's, in her mind, had the image of a store that catered to the very wealthy, the leisured, the frivolous. She saw now that she had been mistaken. There was something in Rosenstein's for any woman with a sense of her own potential. Suddenly she realized that a day ago she would not have thought in this way, would not have considered such things in relation to herself. Why did she now? Was it the encounter with Billie that had sparked it off?

Now every newspaper that she picked up had some mention of the Rosenstein fashion show. It was an event obviously looked forward to by many people, an annual cycle of such shows with a reputation established over the years. For some time now she had studied the advertisements that appeared for the store, as an exercise in business awareness, to acquaint herself with the characteristics of the sort of advertising copy Rosenstein's public relations people created or approved. On the Sunday before the show there was a long article in the New York Times, covering the celebrities and notables who were expected to attend. She learned from this item that Rachel was a woman of renown in her field; her opinions and approval were sought after by the most famous of the fashion world.

The day of the show, as she was coming back from lunch on the outside, she had difficulty getting into an elevator. The big elevator was packed with chattering women and when it stopped at the seventh floor she was forced to get off to allow the crowd to emerge behind her. As she stood aside she glanced around the floor, already thronged with people, some of whom filled the rows of chairs lined up facing the platform at the far end, while others stood in ranks behind them. She spotted Billie sitting in a corner on a small sofa by herself. Billie saw her and patted the empty space beside her. Helena's first impulse was to make a dash back into the now empty elevator but her impulse was checked by the sudden warning within her: you don't decline an invitation from Miss Billie.

She made her way slowly through the crowd to the settee where Billie sat and dropped down beside her. As Billie looked up and smiled at her, she noticed the barest flicker of Billie's eyelashes as she glanced up and down to see what she was wearing. The crowd pressed around them. There were only a certain number of seats, for the invited guests. Everyone else stood around at the back of the floor and around the walls. But Billie's view of the platform and the ramp where the models paraded was unobstructed.

Billie did not speak at once. Her attention was on the line of models parading back and forth. They were surrounded by television crews and cameras. One of the women on the platform was speaking into a microphone and her voice dominated the floor. It was Rachel and her angular figure and jet black hair drawn back from her sharp-featured face into coils at the back of her head made a striking focus for everyone's attention. Her eyes roamed constantly over the models moving before her. Her strident voice, full of authority, penetrated into every corner of the crowd. Helena glanced at Billie and met Billie's eyes on her.

Billie said, softly, "You recognize Rachel," and looked back at the show. Then Helena noticed that Billie held a printed program and a note pad on her knee and that occasionally she made notes.

As each group of models appeared, paced up the ramp and retreated, Rachel's dominating voice described the features of each costume, pointing out the novelties, the touches that identified each designer's creations. While she spoke the crowd was silent and intent, even those standing around the walls hushed by the tense concentration of minds and eyes that filled the floor. Only occasionally there was a communal sigh as some particularly flamboyant ensemble appeared. After the brief patter of applause when the next group of mannequins came forward there was a buzz of voices and the rustle of paper as people turned the pages of their programs and note pads.

Billie said, in one such pause, "If you look over there, on the other side of the platform, you'll see the visiting representatives of the overseas designers." Helena looked where she indicated and saw a group of men and women seated in armchairs, their alert, carefully maintained expressions of polite boredom masking the intent interest they felt. She realized that these were some of the people foremost in the world of haute couture, who would rarely be seen gathered together in one place. Billie said in her ear, "They come because we invite them and we invite them because this is what Old Leah did. They have a tremendous regard for her memory even now."

"She must have been a powerful personality."

Billie's eyes came round to her again. For the smallest moment Helena was conscious of the fact that her own words were far from adequate, but all Billie said was, "Yes," and looked back at the new groups of models strutting before the cameras. Presently Billie said, "Some of these girls have international reputations as models. That one there, for example." She made a small gesture with her pencil and Helena looked up to watch the tall thin girl with finely shaped head on which the hair had been cropped close.

Rachel's voice carried over to them. "You will see this designer's emphasis is on showing legs, bosoms — very sexy, but discreetly, with a hint of a Spanish look. You will notice also that colors and fabrics are adapted to each type of dress — pinks and greens, chiffons, organza and taffeta for evening wear —"

Helena said, "This whole operation must be extremely expensive."

Billie seemed to find this statement funny and laughed softly. "Of course. It is part of the essence of Rosenstein's."

Their attention was drawn back to the show by a ripple of laughter among the spectators. Helena watched a small mannequin walk indolently up the ramp alone with an exaggerated air of indifference. On her head was an outsize hat with a tall crown and enormous brim. Her skirt consisted of big swags of a soft material. She carried a long-handled parasol with a tiny ruffled shade. She wore white sequined mittens on her hands. The laughter grew louder. Helena looked at Billie, alarmed. But Billie touched her hand and said softly, "Listen."

Rachel's voice reached them. "You are enjoying a

24

fine example of Nadja Bizondi's sparkling wit — her satirical comment on some of the season's trends. Do you see the buttons on the gathers of the bouffant skirt? Do you see the little boots with side splits? And the hat? It is wired inside of course to fit the head." As Rachel went on describing each outrageous detail of the costume, the laughter continued, good-humoredly. Helena said to Billie, "Is anyone going to buy such things?"

"Oh, yes — for a joke." Billie gave her a laughing glance. "There are jokes in this business, too, you know."

Nonplussed, Helena sat silent until Billie, who seemed to sense her restlessness, murmured, "You want to leave, don't you? Bye bye."

Helena got up and stepped behind the people standing closest. As she left the floor she realized that at the very back of the crowd there stood a number of Rosenstein's saleswomen, enthralled by what they saw.

Though the fashion show was confined to one floor of the store and the number of store employees concerned with it was small, it had a pervasive influence during the several days it lasted. The saleswomen were alert and watchful and the store seemed unusually full of patrons who spent a good deal of time examining merchandise while they eagerly observed the comings and goings of the celebrities and fashion experts headed for the seventh floor. Helena found herself reading with even greater assiduity the news items and advertisements that appeared concerning it in the media. She began to wonder about the store's history, her interest whetted by Billie's comments.

She knew the arms and legs of that history —
that the store had had its humble beginning in the
efforts of a Russian Jewish immigrant woman in the
early years of the century. The details of Old Leah's
achievement were unknown to her. In the brief
moments when her attention was not fastened on the
daily business of the Company, she wondered. It was
difficult to learn more, especially since the Rosenstein
Company was still privately owned and nothing was
said about it in trade journals and business magazines
beyond superficial articles intended chiefly as
advertisements.

She knew more about the Company's financial
background, since she had researched this when she
was debating whether to accept the Rosenstein offer.
In the business directories and stock exchange
analyses the group of companies known as the
Rosenstein Enterprises were described at length. They
were public companies and their assets, financial
histories, the names of their officers, were readily
available. But the Rosenstein store and its Company
was mentioned only in a brief note appended to this
information, along with Aaron Rosenstein and Sons,
the investment bankers, founded by Old Leah's second
son. The only other information she was able to
gather from these sources was that the same names
appeared in the lists of officers and that large blocks
of shares in them were owned by Rosensteins.

Slowly she built up a picture of the
interrelationships between the public and private
Rosenstein companies. Lionel Rosenstein, now the
senior partner of the banking firm founded by his
father, was also the president and chairman of the
board of Rosenstein's. His brother Daniel, besides

being executive vice-president — the effective manager of Rosenstein's — was also a director, but he held no office in any other Rosenstein enterprise. She learned, by discreet inquiry, that it was Daniel who voted the shares of most of the family members holding stock in the store's company. Lionel, she also learned, paid little attention to Rosenstein's. He was chairman of the board because he was Old Leah's oldest surviving descendant. The shares in the Company had never been sold or exchanged. They were all held through inheritance.

So then who were the people who wished to reorganize Rosenstein's? Who were those who were restive with the old, closely held control of the Company? It was important for her to know.

One day, in her preoccupation, alone in the elevator, she again missed her floor and found herself stepping out into the silent, dimly lit foyer of the twelfth floor, face to face with the big oil paintings Daniel had showed her. There was Old Leah. She studied the portrait more carefully. This was no ordinary woman, yet in her formal appearance nothing of the radical nature of her achievement showed. She was the epitome of a matriarch. Helena wondered how successful the painter had been in capturing not only the likeness but also the characteristic expression of his sitter. There was nothing in the portrait that spoke intimately of the woman portrayed.

Helena glanced at the other portraits. The one on Old Leah's right hand was Moses, her eldest son and therefore Billie's grandfather. The one on her left hand was Aaron, the father of Lionel and Daniel. The silence that surrounded her was undisturbed except

27

for the faint hum of the elevators in their shafts, so she was startled when Esther's voice said at her elbow,

"This is an unusual portrait gallery, isn't it? You won't find another like it — in New York, at least."

Helena made an effort to recover from her surprise. She had forgotten that Esther's office was on this floor, a small room next to the big doors of the board room. Esther was aware of this and smiled at her.

"You mean," said Helena, "because the founder is a woman."

"Yes, and honored as the founder. Jewish women of her generation were often powerful within their families but they weren't brazen about it."

"Brazen?"

"Oh, well, not exactly brazen. But you don't see her husband here, do you?" Esther gestured toward the portraits.

"Was she a widow when she founded the store?"

"Oh, no. But he had nothing to do with the business." For an unusual moment Esther seemed at a loss to explain. Then she said, "I'm afraid you wouldn't be sensitive to our feelings about things like this."

It was the second time Helena was aware of a barrier between herself and the Rosensteins. She said earnestly, "You might try me."

"Well, the traditional place for Jewish women is in the family, especially back then when Old Leah was a young woman. But her husband was not a business man. He was a scholar and despised business dealings. But his family had to live somehow, when they arrived in this country penniless, like so many

28

others. Old Leah was the one who had to earn money to keep them. Later, when she became a successful businesswoman and dealt with men in the business world like a man, the excuse was made that this was simply the means by which she protected her husband so that he could pursue his studies. She was after all being the good Jewish wife." Esther was watching Helena as she gave this explanation.

"But, surely," Helena protested, "you couldn't expect anything else, if she had the gifts for a successful business career. Why should anyone think she should give it up?"

Esther shrugged. "These are old-fashioned ideas. But you'd be surprised how many people still cling to them. You'll hear some members of the family still apologize for her."

"Even though they all live in luxury because of her capacity and her determination?" Helena's tone was ironic.

Esther laughed. "Oh, some of them think it would have happened anyway, especially when her sons grew old enough to go into business. All of them were successful. Of course, she subsidized them."

Impulsively Helena asked, "Esther, how did she establish this store? I know that she started out in a very small way and built up her business till she achieved this building. But I don't know any of the details."

Esther looked gratified at her interest. "It's a romantic story. Someday it should be written up. Maybe Billie will do it sometime — if she gets over being so lazy. Old Leah came here from Russia in 1898 — the time of the pogroms, you know, in Russia and Poland. She was twenty years old then, married for about a year and had a baby — that was Moses." Esther pointed to his portrait. "She did not grow up in Russia but in Germany and she went to Russia as lady's maid to a Russian princess. That's how she learned about how wealthy women liked to dress, how they lived. She had a gift as a needlewoman — that's probably why she became the princess's maid — embroidery, lace-making, all that sort of thing. The man she married was a rabbi's son and dedicated to a scholar's life. She must have been the one who managed to bring them all to New York but when they got here things weren't easy. There wasn't any way that her husband could earn a living except as a street peddler and he couldn't do that. They were starving, living in one room in a tenement with other people like themselves and she was pregnant again — that was Aaron." Esther pointed again. "So she started to do needlework — piecework for a man who farmed out work to women like her, paid them a pittance for it and sold it in his store to well-to-do women for a much better price. There was quite a demand for that sort of thing in those days. Have you ever looked at the old pictures showing how women used to dress then — all those sweeping gowns with embroidered blouses and dripping lace from their sleeves and skirts?"

"Yes," said Helena. "I know the history of dress reform."

"You can't imagine going to work in corsets and long skirts, can you? But of course there was the other side of it: all those elegant gowns and trailing draperies —"

"For those who could afford them."

30

"But they made work for a lot of women. That was the reason for Rosenstein's."

"How did she get beyond the piecework stage?"

Esther looked at her with a smile. "It was just like her. When she found out about the exploitation — how this man who paid her for her work made so much more money when he sold the goods — she got angry and decided to do something about it. She hadn't had an opportunity to learn English. She didn't even know how to get around the city except to walk from her tenement to this man's shop. She couldn't afford to ride and she didn't know even how to select the right el or subway. She knew there were other women in the same situation. Some lived in the same tenement. She thought she could get them to join with her in a protest. If the shopkeeper found he couldn't get the kind of goods he needed, he might be forced to pay them better. But nobody was willing to go in with her. They were frightened that they would lose what little money they made. After all, there were an awful lot of immigrant women in the same situation."

"So she was discouraged."

"Certainly. But you couldn't keep her down for long. One day she was in this man's shop, waiting to be paid for the work she had brought in — he always made her and the other women wait while he took care of customers. Though she did not understand much English, she heard him talking to a German-speaking woman and she realized, from what she overheard, that he was charging a premium price for her work, more than he charged for the other women's work, because of the quality. I told you she had a gift for needlework. But he wasn't paying her any more than the others. She flew into a rage — Old Leah always had the reputation of having a fiery temper — right there in the shop. She attacked the shopkeeper, who called the cop in off the street and had her turned out — without her money."

Esther's eyes were bright and her sallow face was flushed. This is a favorite story of hers, thought Helena. "So then?"

"Well, you have to have backbone to face things like that and that's what Old Leah had. This turned out to be the best thing that could have happened to her. Because the German-speaking woman who witnessed what happened followed her down the street. When she caught up with her she told her she would like to order some baby clothes made and she wanted to deal directly with her. Old Leah said she did not have money to buy the materials and the woman said that if she would come to her house, she would furnish the materials. She told her how to reach her house and that was the first time that Old Leah traveled anywhere in Manhattan outside the journey from her tenement to the man's shop. The woman who ordered those baby clothes was just her first customer. She had friends who wanted the same sort of work done. It wasn't long before Old Leah was hiring girls to sew for her. So of course she had to have a workplace and she rented a small shop with living quarters at the back, where she could watch her babies. But you know she never forgot that lesson about the weakness of women who could not join together to get a fair wage. That was the beginning of Rosenstein's."

Esther beamed at her. Helena said, "That is very interesting. And what about her husband?"

"Oh, she indulged him. Sometimes she found him useful. He had to sign the lease for the first workplace, because in those days a married woman couldn't act for herself. He was always annoyed when she interrupted him to do something like this for her, but he didn't interfere. He had no head for business. He despised money-making."

"But her boys weren't that way."

"Oh, no. Moses stayed with her in the store. He helped design this building. And of course Aaron founded the banking firm. The other two went into manufacturing. They founded the companies that are now the Rosenstein Enterprises. Of course their mother provided them with their original capital. Now Rosenstein's is dwarfed by all these offspring, you might call them. But it is still the heart of the Rosenstein empire."

"Which is now in the hands of her grandsons."

"Yes, the grandsons still control a lot of it, like Lionel and Daniel. But I'm afraid the younger generation doesn't have the same interest — except Billie. The family is not as closely knit as it used to be in the business. We've even taken in quite a few Gentiles now." Esther smiled at her as if to disarm any hint of disapproval.

"Do you think Old Leah would approve of this?"

Esther hesitated before answering. "It's hard to say: Nobody could ever really be sure what she thought and how she would decide any problem. Even Moses said he was never certain about his mother. Take the question of her religious feeling. She was careful about appearances. She was very generous to a lot of charities and to Jewish causes. But she didn't keep the holidays or observe the dietary laws. I don't think she ever went to the synagogue. I know she objected to the way Jewish women were treated — having to sit behind a screen and that sort of thing."

"Her descendants are the same?"

"Some of them have become more pious — because of the terrible things that have happened to Jews in the last fifty years — the Holocaust, you know. Daniel is the most strict. You'll find that out. Old Leah was a good hater. She gave a lot of money to help track down Hitler's henchmen." Esther paused again, as if debating whether to say anything further.

Helena said, "I'm not a religious person myself."

Esther nodded. "Some of the older women in the family don't like to hear a lot about Old Leah when she was a young woman."

"Why not?"

"Well, they find her embarrassing, you know. She was really a rebel in a lot of ways. They think she should be remembered only as the matriarch, as an enabler, as they say, a woman who did not step out of her role as wife and mother except under dire necessity. That is ridiculous, because she always acted for herself. She was quite open about being the founder of Rosenstein's, the owner of the business, and she told her sons what to do, even in public, as if she was the father and not the mother, the husband and not the wife. And they all obeyed her."

Helena looked up at the portrait. "I find it incredible that they should be embarrassed by her."

"It's just that they wish she had been more

34

conventional. But you know, she was always very strict about behavior. You had to do things in the proper way. They can't complain about her in that way."

The sound of the elevator nearest where they stood came closer but it stopped at the floor below. They could hear the soft sound of the door opening and closing. It seemed to bring their conversation to an end. But before they parted Esther said, "Some of the Rosensteins say that Billie is like Old Leah. Usually they say this when they don't like what she is doing."

"Billie?" said Helena.

"You'd have to be a Rosenstein to understand."

Helena had pressed the elevator button and now in response the door opened before her. As she moved to step in Esther put her hand on Helena's arm. "I like you," she said as the door began to close.

The next morning Helena was surprised to see a strange woman come into her office unannounced with Sherry on her heels. Sherry stopped in the doorway and said in a desperate voice, "This is Mrs. Bachrach."

The woman, middle-aged but fashionably dressed and with elaborately coiffed hair, said immediately, "Yes, I'm Mrs. Bachrach — Mr. Lionel Rosenstein's secretary. We've not met."

Gathering her wits together — she had been immersed in reading the file of papers on her desk — Helena gestured silently to the nearest chair.

"I'll stay just for a moment. You're very busy, of course, and so am I. Mr. Lionel wanted me to come and tell you that the board of directors is meeting this afternoon and they want you to be present for a brief moment. They wish to meet you and welcome you to Rosenstein's. Mr. Daniel will introduce you."

"Oh, yes." To Helena her own voice sounded meek in contrast to the overflowing self-confidence in Mrs. Bachrach's. Mrs. Bachrach wore large spectacles in jeweled frames and her eyes were fixed on Helena in an intimidating stare.

"All the other officers of the Company will be present also."

Helena, annoyed at the peremptory manner in which Mrs. Bachrach spoke and the shortness of the notice, managed to say politely, "I shall look forward to meeting them and the directors."

"Then we'll see you at two o'clock," said Mrs. Bachrach, getting up. "I'm glad to have met you, Miss Worrall."

Helena watched her disappear through the doorway. Sherry, who had obviously been hovering just out of sight, came back into the room. "I couldn't stop her. Mrs. Bachrach doesn't like to wait when she comes downstairs on an errand for Mr. Lionel."

"That is apparent." Helena's tone was short. "Well, never mind. It's a good thing you've been here long enough to recognize people like her, so that you can tell me about them."

"She's been Mr. Lionel's secretary for years and years. That is, she's his secretary here at Rosenstein's. He doesn't spend much time here at the store and he relies on her to keep him up-to-date on what's going on. The girls are all afraid of her — except one or two who have been here almost as long as she has, like Mrs. Nathan, Mr. Daniel's secretary."

"Sometime — after I've met all the men — you

36

will have to tell me who their secretaries are. Of course I know that none of the officers are women."

"You're the only woman in management. There's been a lot of talk about that, when it was announced that you were joining the Company. I think that's why Mrs. Bachrach came to bring you the message herself. She wanted to see what you looked like."

At five minutes to two she got off the elevator on the twelfth floor. The big double doors of the board room were standing open. A buzz of voices came from inside. Nervously she stepped just inside the room. It was very long, with big windows all down one side. A long wide table filled the center, its polished surface gleaming in the light from the windows. There were tall-backed chairs ranged around the table, perhaps a dozen to a side, and half of them were occupied. A number of men stood about in small groups. Esther and Mrs. Bachrach sat together at a desk in one corner near the door. Then she saw that Billie was sitting at the far end of the table. She seemed unaware of Helena's entrance.

Daniel came forward to greet her and led her forward to introduce her. She was aware of the scrutiny of many pairs of eyes. The handsome elderly man with white hair and an air of studied but cheerful boredom was obviously Lionel. He gestured to a chair beside him. He proceeded to make a little speech, saying in a graceful manner that he spoke for all present when he said he welcomed her to the management of Rosenstein's. At his bidding each of the men in the room bowed as he introduced them. She tried to concentrate on each face and name, anxious to fix in her mind what each of them looked like. When he got to Billie, Billie merely nodded.

Then Helena was out in the foyer once more, surrounded by a throng of men, the officers and minor executives of the Company, who clustered around her for more conversation, all of them curious about the only woman to have a place among them.

Daniel came out of the board room, closing the doors behind him. He said, "Come with me, Helena. We had all better get acquainted."

He walked with her at the head of the group into an elevator and down to the eleventh floor, into a conference room whose furnishings gave it a work-a-day air. Here also there was a large table in the center and they all sat down, Daniel indicating where she should sit. The others sat silent, their eyes still intently on her, while he described the routine of these business meetings. They took place, he explained, once a week, "and now that you are familiar with Rosenstein's operations, naturally you'll join us. As manager we shall need to have your evaluation of our ongoing problems."

The session that followed was intense and noisy. Frequently a question was shot at her — "Have you had any experience with that?" — "What's your background on this?" Through it all she was aware that these men were not hostile but their aggressive attitude towards what they were doing and their instinct for competition among themselves overrode all other considerations.

When she got home to her apartment that evening she was exhausted and her head ached. She understood clearly now what it would mean to be manager of Rosenstein's. She dropped her jacket, poured herself a drink and sank into a chair. Never before in her brief career had she arrived at the end of the day with just this degree of fatigue nor had alcohol proved a restorative instead of a social relaxation. Mulling over the pressures of the day she realized that part of the reason, beyond the tension of confronting new responsibilities, was that now she must deal much more with people than with business abstractions. Before this she had sheltered behind problems that were chiefly confined to paper and machines. This would not be the case at Rosenstein's. There was obviously a need in the Rosenstein Company for someone to confront and coordinate the operations and ambitions of many different people.

It was clearly apparent to her that the decision to hire her had been made by the board of directors. The men she had met this afternoon had certainly not had anything to do with it — except for Daniel. Whatever the reason, Daniel seemed to be entirely behind her. He gave no hint that he was acting reluctantly or with reservations. Several times in the free-for-all of argument among the officers and heads of departments he had come to her support, pointing out that in certain matters they must await what she as manager would in due course have to say.

The men were not all Rosensteins, either by name or relationship. She thought she could recognize those who were. The Rosensteins were all volatile, pugnacious, outspoken and extraordinarily self-assured. Those who were not Rosensteins were less of all these things, more wary and watchful. She warned herself that she must be vigilant and careful not to speak her thoughts until she knew more. And also she must be wary how she threaded her way through the jungle of male-female relations. As the sole female the attention of the men was fixed on her. They were bound to try her out, until they had seen enough of her in professional terms to respect her as their equal. There must never be any hint on her part that any action of hers was to be interpreted as a resort to feminine manipulation.

She entered her office the next morning, early as usual and before Sherry arrived, aware that there had been a change in atmosphere overnight. After the events of yesterday afternoon she could no longer feel that her office was a bastion into which she could retreat. The isolation she had felt during the two or three weeks previous, an isolation that she knew now was illusory, no longer existed. She was the manager of the Rosenstein Company, aware now that she had a team of subordinates who were still largely unknown, whose real feelings towards her were unproved. She began to feel the strength of her position rather than its weakness.

Sherry came into the office apologizing for breaking into those first few moments of the business day, which Helena had indicated she wished to have uninterrupted. Sherry was a very pretty girl, blonde and fresh, who made good use of the clothing discounts that Rosenstein's granted its employees. She was soft-mannered, tactful and seemed quite willing to be the handmaid of a woman boss. Helena had wondered more than once how she had been chosen to be the secretary of the new manager. Sherry had been with Rosenstein's for a year or more.

Now Sherry said ingratiatingly, "I'm so sorry to interrupt. It's about Mr. Barton." Quick to see a slight uncertainty on Helena's face, she hurried on, "He's the vice-president for corporate interrelationships. He's been out of town. He called yesterday evening, just before I left. You were out and I didn't know whether you were coming back to your office. He said he was so sorry to miss the meeting yesterday. He wants to meet you. He's been travelling on company business."

Helena wished she could ask a few simple questions: Was he related to the Rosensteins? How long had he been with the Company? What exactly did corporate interrelationships mean? But even under Sherry's sympathetic eye she knew she could not seek information of this sort in that way. Instead she asked, "What does he want?"

"Well, he said he wanted to welcome you to Rosenstein's. He wants to come round and see you in about an hour."

Annoyed, Helena said, "That's impossible. I have a meeting with the advertising people this morning and it will absorb a lot of time. You'll just have to tell him that I will call and let him know when I'm free."

When Sherry had gone out of the room she remembered that among the large volumes in a bookcase in a corner of her room was a leather-bound loose-leaf compendium with the Rosenstein Company printed in gold letters on the spine. She had already consulted it and knew among other things that it contained an organizational chart of the Company's structure. She had looked at this several times in the first days after her arrival but without the experienced eye that she now felt she possessed. When Sherry left the room she got it down and carried it to her desk, turning to the organizational chart. It was as she remembered it: A line of boxes across the top of the page, representing the board of directors; below that a single box for the president; below that a single box for the executive vice-president; and then a row of boxes for the other vice-presidents. Below this array, with lines raying from the appropriate vice-president, were the departments — public relations, procurement and so on. There was no chart for the store itself, but a long, straight vertical line leading from the executive vice-president to the bottom of the page ended in a box that said simply The Store. Nowhere was there a box for manager. She rang for Sherry and when she appeared, asked, "Is this loose-leaf volume up-to-date?"

Sherry craned her neck to look at the page. "Oh, yes! I put the new sheets in as soon as they get to me."

"But there is no new sheet for this?" Helena pointed to the organizational chart. "The date in the corner says it is five years old."

Sherry screwed up her face. "I haven't received a new one since I've been here. They don't change very often."

"For whom did you work, Sherry, before I came?"

"I was a floater. I worked wherever they wanted me. For a while I was assistant to Mrs. Bachrach and sometimes I worked for Miss Billie — that is, whenever she needed somebody."

"Does Miss Billie have an office here?"

"Well, not exactly. She uses one of those rooms up on the twelfth floor. Mr. Lionel has an office there. That's where Mrs. Bachrach is."

Helena looked back at the chart. "I see this sheet has Mr. Barton's name on it. It's dated two years ago. Has he been here longer than that?"

"Oh, no. He came after I did. I called him with your message. He didn't like being put off, but he said he'd like to come around this afternoon. He said he'd just check to see if you had the time to see him."

Something in the manner in which Sherry spoke warned Helena and she nodded. At odd moments thereafter, when her mind was not entirely absorbed in the problems in which she was involved, she wondered about Barton and why he was making a point of calling himself to her attention. Did he wish to establish a personal relationship, to place himself on a special footing with the new manager?

In her short working life since leaving business administration school Helena had quickly learned that the technical aspects of any job she undertook would hold very little difficulty for her. But the human relationships involved would be far tougher, for she was a woman invading the world of men. It had been pointed out to her that business organizations had from time immemorial been created and run by men, that men had decided the rules of behavior, the style of communication when they dealt with each other. These methods were based on the experience of men as they grew from boys to adulthood, learning along the way the support networks that men traditionally created in their competition with one another. Women played no part in this traditional conditioning, for women were relegated to another sphere altogether and were not expected to compete with men. Now she was one of those who were challenging this scheme of things. She knew that there were still powerful and subtle forces that limited a woman's action in this, to her, new world. Laws and regulations requiring equality for women in the workplace could never achieve a real change for women until women themselves brought it about.

At the end of the day, when the pressure of work was decreasing because most people had already left their offices, she was called away from her thoughts by a soft knock on her half-open door. Sherry had already gone home. She looked up to see a tall man, whom she judged to be in his forties, standing there with an ingratiating smile. He was handsome, in excellent physical condition, expensively and elegantly dressed. His head of abundant hair was turning slightly grey and she supposed he did not darken it because he believed it contrasted more strikingly with his still-youthful face.

He said, "I'm Jim Barton. How do you do, Helena? May I come in?"

She said, "Yes, of course," and gestured to the chair opposite. He came in and sat down, crossing his legs. She saw his up-and-down glance, assessing her looks, her clothes.

"I'm sorry I couldn't be present yesterday, when you were introduced to the board. In fact, I didn't know until I got back this morning that they had held a meeting."

She murmured a polite response. He went on, "There's been a great debate, you know, about you before you arrived."

"Really?"

He leaned back comfortably in his chair. "There's been no doubt for some time that Rosenstein's needs some sort of new management. I don't know how much you have been able to absorb since you arrived, but it is ridiculous how little adequate supervision there has been over the corporate functions. Oh, they're all clever people and they run their own departments well, but there is no overall coordination. It's all hopelessly beyond Daniel. Somebody came up with the idea of a manager, new style. So here you are."

Helena said cautiously, "I understand that the effective management of the Company and the store has been in Mr. Daniel's hands. Are you saying that this is not satisfactory?"

"Oh, well, nobody is really complaining about Daniel. But after all, he's getting pretty old. He's way beyond retirement age, though the Rosensteins don't pay much attention to that. It's a question of the future. Rosenstein's is at a crossroads. Some people don't want to abandon the old way of doing things, though it seems to me that it's pretty apparent that this is leading only to a dead end. Some of the others want to modernize. Personally I am glad to see you here, since you represent a new viewpoint." He smiled benignly as he said this.

Groping for a safe reply Helena said, "It's nice of you to say that. However, I was not given to understand that reorganization of the Company was in prospect or that I was expected to have a part in that."

"Well, one thing you'll learn is that the Rosensteins are not going to be frank with you. But I'll tell you that ever since I came here I've heard arguments pro and con about the hiring of a manager. Just before I left a few weeks ago for a tour of the Rosenstein Enterprises things were very fluid, though there was talk even then of getting a woman. That was for the sake of image, I suppose. A

45

woman in your slot would look like quite an up-to-the-minute step, wouldn't it?"

Helena did not respond. She was thinking: they are all women who run the store, from Rachel down, but each in her own little niche. And none of them in the Company.

Barton went on talking. "If I had known when I left that they were so close to a decision, I would have postponed my tour. I had no idea they were so close. I was amazed when I heard about your appointment — in the business news. But that's like the Rosensteins. They don't warn you ahead of time. Now don't get the wrong idea about my attitude. I'm entirely in favor of this change and I must say I'm impressed by your qualifications. All except your lack of experience in the garment trade, that is, to put it flatly."

"I wasn't hired on the basis of my experience. My training is in management and that, I understood, was what Rosenstein's wanted."

"Oh, yes, certainly. Anywhere but here I'd say your point of view is the correct one. Management is a field of its own. Under modern circumstances that is the only sensible approach. But I'm afraid you'll find Rosenstein's is a different sort of place. The real opportunities here are with the Rosenstein Enterprises. There is no problem in those companies with a conflict between modernity and tradition. Of course, the Rosenstein Company can be a stepping stone."

Is that why you're here? Helena wondered. Aloud she said, "I'm sure you have a much broader acquaintance with things than I have. Corporate interrelations — that means liaison between the Rosenstein Enterprises and the Company?"

"Exactly. I've found it a very illuminating slot. Here in the Company you are bound by the hand of the past. The store is unique. There is no question about that. But its day is past. You can't keep it as a museum. Museums don't make profits."

"Is that what some of the Rosensteins want to do — preserve it regardless of its profitability? I should think they would be more concerned about it as a source of income."

Barton shrugged. "They are all wealthy enough from the income derived from the other companies — and other investments, of course. There is a lot of Rosenstein capital invested in the Enterprises, you know, and the return is fabulous. You must have noticed that, if you've researched them."

"Oh, yes," said Helena.

"But I'll say this." He looked at her with a sly smile. "I don't think any Rosenstein could bear to run a business that wasn't profitable. That's the rub. Even the diehards want to make the store profitable again."

Helena was silent. She disliked his patronizing manner, his half-contemptuous phrases. But she realized that he had crystallized into words the vague doubts and questions that had assailed her during the last few weeks. She had indeed been brought in to a situation of conflict — to act as what? a catalyst? a buffer? She did not want to ask him who were the individuals to whom he referred so anonymously. It would make it seem that she had become, at this short notice, his ally.

47

She said, "My undertaking was pretty clearly defined when Rosenstein's offered me this opportunity. I am to improve the profitability of the Company. It needs new management — new methods — new approaches. Obviously these cannot be achieved without some changes in the store. I shall need much more information before I can act."

He looked away as if he was dissatisfied with the result of the conversation. "You'll come to see what the situation is. You'll find, as I have, that the Rosensteins can be pretty difficult to deal with, especially when they hang together in a difference of opinion, and they always do that when they're dealing with an outsider. Tribal instinct, I suppose you'd call it. This store is a sort of idol to them. I won't say they're superstitious about it but they consider it a special creation, something a little larger than merely the creation of a gifted woman. You know, of course, that in the business world such an attitude is sentimental nonsense, but there is a basis for it. The store was the genesis of the Rosenstein fortune. It provided the springboard for Old Leah's sons — you've learned that they call her Old Leah, haven't you? — into the financial world. Her four sons were all real chips off the old block. They knew that to expand their personal fortunes they had to create new enterprises and that's what they did, encouraged by their mother. All except Moses, who found his place in the store. He was his mother's principal heir, so to speak."

Helena said carefully, "I gather you don't think much of the idea of preserving the store. What is your solution?"

"Of course I don't have to tell you that it isn't sound business to preserve the store as a sacred cow — untouchable, so to speak. Even if the financial reports and analyses don't show it, the store is losing ground. There is no growth. Without growth a business cannot thrive. The store cannot be self-sustaining for much longer. You know what that means, don't you?"

"I'm afraid I don't see what you mean."

"Why, it's obvious! The day of the single, independent specialty department store is over. Chain stores are the normal necessary mode of operation today — multiple units. All the other big stores have gone that way — Saks, Lord and Taylor. It's Rosenstein's turn now. It's overdue, in fact."

"Then it's your opinion that Rosenstein's must become a chain?"

He gave her a speculative glance. "There are two choices: to go public, to transform Rosenstein's from a family-controlled company into a public one and expand into numerous retail outlets; or sell out to an existing conglomerate. I'll be frank with you. I'm all for a change, the latter one preferably."

"But the directors are not united in this matter?"

"No, they're not. Some of them hesitate because of the implications of the change. I don't think they would suffer financially because of it. The Rosensteins would retain a large interest in whatever deal they made. But some of them are diehards on the question of the store. It must stay as it is."

"But some of them are wholeheartedly for a change?"

"Oh, yes! Moishe is all for it. He's Lionel's

49

youngest son. I think he could persuade his father easily enough. I'm very friendly with Moishe." Barton said this with a carefully casual air.

"Then you have a channel for making your opinion felt."

Barton did not at once agree. "It's sometimes a problem dealing with the Rosensteins, as I said before. You think you are dealing with one of them and then you find out that what you've said in confidence has become common knowledge among all of them. This is a complaint I've heard from others — the newer people who are not related to the Rosensteins. You and I are both officers with somewhat comparable authority. That makes us natural allies, doesn't it? Of course, the fate of Rosenstein's doesn't affect me too deeply. I see my current position as a stepping stone into another of the more modern, more progressive Rosenstein Enterprises. I don't think that is any secret to anyone."

And, thought Helena, if I become your ally and help you bring this scheme about, I'd be left behind in the wreckage. Aloud she said, "I really don't have an opinion about all this now. It is after all speculation and I must learn a good deal more about the situation before I can form one."

She saw he was offended by even this gentle rebuff. She braced herself for his taking revenge.

He turned sideways in his chair and leaned his arm on its back. "I'm pretty sure you are not aware of the sort of scrutiny they gave your personal life before they offered you the chance to come here."

"I've no idea," said Helena candidly.

"When they investigated your background they did

50

not confine themselves to your professional training and experience. They wanted to know what sort of person you were — specifically, what sort of woman. Of course I know that nowadays we all have to pass all kinds of tests for promotion in the corporate world — whether you can take pressure, stress, whether your wife can take it — that wouldn't apply to you, of course — but that sort of thing. They were especially anxious to evaluate you as a woman. Daniel made a point of this."

"Of course I know that women are more carefully scrutinized than men by would-be employers and the higher the level the more severe the scrutiny. That is not new to me."

"Oh, yes, yes." He shot her an unfriendly smile. "Well, they know that you have gained a reputation, in your prior employment, as being a hard case — not especially friendly to male pressure or seduction. Shall we put it that way? Daniel was very interested to learn this. What they found out about you weighed heavily with him in your favor. He didn't want a scarlet woman flaunting around Rosenstein's."

Trying to suppress her indignation Helena said, "I'm sure that was not the criterion that determined their offer to me."

"Oh, of course not!" He was pleased at the reaction he had provoked. "Certainly not. They — we — were all very impressed with your record, especially since you're such a young woman. That was a point that worried Daniel — how young you are. He was afraid of getting somebody who had got ahead by sleeping around. Forgive me for being blunt, but we've got to look things in the face in the business world."

Helena said coldly, "My private life and my professional life don't mix — never have."

He looked at her out of the corner of his eye and said, smiling, "No exceptions?"

She returned his look steadily and said, "No exceptions."

He burst into a loud laugh and stood up. "It doesn't hurt to find out where you stand, does it? Well, Helena, I've enjoyed our talk. Don't forget. If you need a friendly shoulder any time, you can call on me." He nodded to her and walked out of the room.

It took her a while to regain her usual even temper. The next morning she asked Sherry if Barton was married. Sherry answered in surprise. "Oh, yes. He's been married twice. He's still with his second wife. But he doesn't let that stand in his way. The girls all know that."

The days always seemed to build in intensity as the afternoons wore on, until the close of business came in a frenetic burst of activity, a hopeless effort to catch up with the unfinished problems of the earlier hours and the preparation for the day to come. Rosenstein's stayed open for customers until six o'clock, except for Thursday, when it opened at noon and stayed open until nine. The people in the business offices were unaffected by these hours, but they tended to be gone by six-thirty. Helena lingered beyond this. The abrupt cessation of sounds within the store was noticeable in her office. The hum of the elevators gradually faded away. The visit of the night watchman making his first check of the offices told her that the store was empty except for one or two workers like herself and perhaps the crews that dressed the windows. The charwomen came later.

She needed this quiet time to sort out the mass of new impressions that had crowded upon her in the last week or so. Ruefully she admitted to herself that it was partly her own lack of experience that gave these impressions such impact. Someone who had worked longer in this segment of the business world would have been prepared for the tensions and personal antagonisms that she realized must lie beneath the surface of the relations of the people she found herself among.

She thought of Old Leah. Old Leah had fought her way into the world of men single-handed, had by boldness, wile, and an iron will established her store. She had evidently been a radical, unfettered by the strictures either of the society into which she had been born or that into which she had moved as a mature woman. She had had the perspicacity to use men, including her own sons, to consolidate and expand her little empire. The scope for women in business had widened in the seventy-odd years since she had made her first assault on tradition but certain basic elements were still present for women to deal with — in fact, the ones hardest to succeed against: the solidarity that men automatically displayed whenever they perceived a woman as a threat, their instinct to use women's weaknesses, the weapon of sexual harassment.

A slight sound from her outer office caught her ear in spite of her preoccupation. Surely it was not time for another visit from the watchman. She looked toward the door, about to call out, when she saw that Billie stood there, smiling at her.

"You keep late hours." Only some desk lamps were on and the soft light caught the reddish gold of Billie's hair. She was wearing a dress of a fine, soft clinging wool with a deeply draped neckline that emphasized the gentle swell of her breasts. She must be wearing a bra, thought Helena, unable to take her eyes away, but it doesn't show.

"It's easier to work when there are not so many interruptions."

Billie came into the room and sat down. "You're finding it difficult to get used to. It's quite different from what you've done before."

"Well, yes. My time is not so rigidly organized."

Billie raised her eyebrows and then said, "Oh, I see. You're not used to working with so many people coming to see you. But that's what we need you for, you know."

Helena looked at her in silent inquiry. Billie smiled. "All this was getting too much for Daniel, even though he has several assistants. I convinced him that a woman could handle it better. She'd have more patience and more insight."

Helena sighed. "He's had a lot more experience than I've had."

Billie said sympathetically, "You must not get discouraged. You'll learn to manage it after a while. There's a lot you can't put in management manuals — at least, in a business like this."

"So I've discovered."

"Well, come and have dinner with me."

Helena glanced down at her desk. Billie said, "Put it all in neat piles and clear the space in front of you. That makes it look as if you have it all under control."

Smiling weakly Helena did as she said. When she got her hat and coat she saw that Billie had left her own on a chair in the outer office. She must have come with this intention, she thought.

When they came out of the office suite into the lobby Billie led the way to the small elevator beyond the rank of big ones. It was one that was used by the company officers and had stops only on the top floors of the building and the ground floor. The door opened to a combination, which Billie punched mechanically on the series of buttons. She said nothing as she led the way to the street, nodding briefly to the security guard standing within the darkened entry to the store.

Helena, uncertain about what was expected of her, was also silent. They traveled in a cab to an apartment building in the east seventies. She followed Billie through the lobby into an elevator that took them to an upper floor, then down a softly carpeted corridor to an apartment in a corner of the building. When Billie unlocked her door they found the lights already on. There was a large living room with windows facing two directions, one overlooking the dark, light-pricked expanse of Central Park and the other the lights of taller buildings. Before these latter was set a table ready for dinner for two people.

Billie said, "Put your hat and coat there," pointing to a closet in the vestibule. Billie herself disappeared through a doorway in the further corner of the room. Doing as she was told, Helena found herself standing alone in the middle of the big room, surrounded by expensive furniture and glowing floor lamps. There were paintings on the walls and a second look told her that they were not reproductions but the actual work of French Impressionists, even a Mary Cassatt. Beguiled by what she saw, she was startled when Billie's voice said close to her ear, "Come and have a drink."

Billie went to a cabinet set against the inner wall and lowered a drawer-front which became a table. There were bottles and glasses ranged inside and an ice container in the small refrigerator. She glanced back at Helena and asked, "What do you drink?"

"Why, anything, really."

Billie's expression was quizzical. "Then scotch with seltzer, perhaps?"

"Yes," said Helena.

Billie poured the drinks and brought them over. She said as she put them down, "If you want the bathroom, it's through there." She pointed to the door through which she herself had passed earlier.

Helena walked through the bedroom. It was very large, with a queen-sized bed covered in a heavy cream-colored brocade bedspread. There were only a few cosmetics on the dressing table. A fleeting thought passed through Helena's mind: Billie did not use eye-shadow or false eyelashes or pluck her eyebrows. The bathroom was large and luxuriously fitted. She puzzled for a moment over the impression the whole apartment made on her. There was a sense of great luxury about it — a sense that whatever was visible was only a promise of much more to be had. At the same time, there was simplicity, a very expensive simplicity. There were no frou-frous on the dressing table, no swags of fabric draping the windows or the furniture. Instead, there was an elegant plainness emphasized by the contours of the

56

chairs, of the bedstead. The floor was covered by a pale yellow silk Chinese rug. With her new sensitivity, she was struck by the feeling that this was a room that might be on display in Rosenstein's bedding department, exquisite, a perfection that seemed unobtainable in life, an ideal. Her glance, traveling over the scene, searched for what it was that was an anomaly. Of course. She finally realized that it was the bookcase. There were several built-in shelves recessed along one wall — not something one expected to find in such a sensuous lady's nest. When she went back into the living room she noticed a low table covered with piles of periodicals and newspapers — financial journals and the magazines of haute couture.

Billie was sitting in a deep armchair, gazing into space. When Helena came in she brought her gaze down to her and said, "I didn't invite you here to talk about Rosenstein's, but if you want to talk to me about it, I'm ready to listen."

Helena answered her gaze but said nothing.

Billie went on, "You haven't any confidantes, have you? You're in a pretty isolated position. Besides, you're not used to discussing your personal problems, are you? You've not been in a situation like this before."

Helena stared at her, captured by the candid, direct gaze of Billie's blue eyes. There was nothing of criticism in Billie's manner or tone of voice.

Helena said, "It's my own ignorance, really. This is an entirely new experience for me. The bad thing is that I had no concept of how ignorant I am when I accepted Rosenstein's offer."

57

"Do you regret that you did? There was no sharpness in Billie's voice but the question reached into her.

Helena hesitated for a while. "Sometimes I wonder if I have made a serious mistake."

"Why a serious mistake?"

"Because this is all so foreign to my own background. I wonder if I have made the right choice as a step forward in my business life — in the kind of business life I have projected for myself."

"You didn't think it was out-of-line when you were considering our offer?"

"No, really I didn't. Management is my field. The problems of management are similar everywhere."

"And what you manage doesn't much matter. Any business is answerable to management. Yes, I see. But Rosenstein's is a much more personal kind of business than the average." Billie paused for a moment's thought. "At least, it still is. But for how long?"

The question seemed said more to herself and Helena did not respond to it. After a moment Billie said, "Of course, the store can be a stepping stone to employment in the Rosenstein Enterprises. Did you have that in mind?"

"That was pointed out to me, when I was considering your offer, before I knew anything about the Rosenstein Enterprises. But I really didn't think about that. I think that if I had wanted to go that way, I would have sought a more direct route. But then I would have had to stay on the same level I was on or even take a demotion. That is a serious matter for a woman in the corporate world. No, when I first received your offer, I more or less dismissed it, or rather, put it aside to consider some others I had. But then my mind kept coming back to it. You see, it has meant two steps up for me. Then I began to feel intrigued. I knew nothing about retailing, nothing about women's fashions, nothing about a store like Rosenstein's. I was really tantalized by the idea that this was something I could learn, make my own —"

Billie suddenly smiled. "The lure of the unknown. Not a very businesslike basis for a career decision."

Helena, now uneasy that she had betrayed a very private feeling, frowned.

Billie saw her unease. "Don't worry about that. Don't you know that all great successes in life — in business life, as in any other — are made by people with just that sort of spark? That is just what Rosenstein's needs. It was founded by a woman who had that sort of spark. It will die — it is dying — because no one seems to have that sort of feeling now."

Alarmed, Helena stared at her. "You're not looking to me to save it, are you?"

"Don't be frightened. You could certainly have a hand in saving it." Billie glanced at the little gold clock on the tabouret beside her. "We've time for another drink. I've ordered dinner from the caterer. They'll be here soon."

She did not go back to the subject of Rosenstein's future, and Helena, her thoughts in a turmoil, was glad to let it drop. When the caterer's men arrived and set the food on the table in covered dishes and left, Billie turned off the indirect lighting around the walls. The room was then lit only by the pools of light around each lamp.

When they sat down to eat they were chiefly

silent for a while. Helena, beguiled by the gourmet food and the softly seductive surroundings, found herself hungrier than she had expected. Billie seemed preoccupied. When they were finished they carried the dishes to the kitchen — as large and well-furnished as the rest of the apartment, Helena noted — and returned to the living room.

Would she like some music? Billie asked, and went to a stereo system that was installed in the wall. The music of Beethoven filled the air, not too loud. Billie came back to her with a glass in each hand. "You'd like another, I'm sure."

Helena hesitated but took the glass. She was not used to so much to drink and set the glass down on the little table beside her. She was aware that Billie had had three scotches to her two before dinner and most of the bottle of wine while they ate. But Billie showed no sign of the effect of alcohol.

Billie sat down opposite her. She said nothing and Helena supposed she was listening to the music. It came to an end but Billie made no move to renew it. Instead, she said, "So you decided you wanted to work for Rosenstein's. When did you begin to think you had made a mistake?"

Helena hesitated a long time before answering. Ever since she had first met Billie she had felt this impulse to speak to her as if she were a friend of long standing. She could not put a finger on what it was about Billie that produced this effect and she reminded herself that it was a dangerous impulse and that she was, in fact, talking to someone who should be treated with the greatest caution. Unbidden, Barton's remark came back to her: You never know how safe it is to talk to a Rosenstein, that what you say to one may become common knowledge to the rest of them.

Billie, leaning back in the end of the big sofa where she sat, looked at her and said, "You're speaking only to me."

Helena, startled by what appeared to be Billie's divination of her thoughts, replied hastily: "I don't really think I have made a mistake. Your offer seemed to be a challenge to me — a challenge to do something I had never done before. My feeling is simply that I must make every effort to meet it."

Billie's gaze was on her and then drifted away. "It's early days. You have not had time to orient yourself."

"What bothers me most is that I don't really know the people with whom I must deal."

"In other words, the problems don't frighten you but the people do."

Helena was indignant. "Frighten me?"

"How would you describe it, then?"

"Well, as you know, I have met the board of directors, the officers. I am not finding any difficulty dealing with the people in the departments under my management, even though they know I am new to retailing and must learn as I go. I would have expected some resentment there, but I've noticed very little. It is simply that everyone here — with some exceptions, I know — has worked with everyone else for so long that they cannot help seeing me as an outsider. You said that Rosenstein's is still a more personal sort of business than most. That's part of what you meant, isn't it?"

Billie nodded. Helena added, "And the store is still a mystery to me. It must run itself, because there is

61

no coordinator, is there? Each department head operates as she always has."

Again Billie nodded and drank from her glass. "It's the mystique, the tradition, that the founder created. It has outlasted her by twenty years."

"But it can't go on forever."

Billie gazed at her again. "If it goes on the way it is going, no. We do have a number of new people. After all, the old ones retire or die off — half of them since Old Leah died. The new people — you are one — see Rosenstein's as simply a prestigious women's specialty department store that is falling behind the times because of antiquated methods. Some of them write it off as finished already."

"So why was it decided to bring me in? The more I realize this the more it puzzles me."

Billie looked at her with a faint smile. "Does it really? You don't know anything about Rosenstein's, so you won't be hampered by preconceived ideas in changing things. You're to bring in the modern way of doing things. As you have said, you're a manager, trained to manage anything."

Helena looked at her in doubt. She was uncertain what Billie really meant. Was there some ironic twist to what she was saying? Was this what Billie really believed?

She said aloud, "You know, you have the advantage of me. You know all about me — my age, my marital status, past and present, which college I went to, my family background. I know practically nothing about you except that you are a Rosenstein and that you're a director of the Company." Really, thought Helena, it must be the scotch that's making me say all this.

62

Billie laughed and got up to cross the room and pour herself another drink, having glanced to see that Helena's was barely touched.

Billie sat down again. "What do you want to know? I'm thirty-two years old — a confirmed old maid in the eyes of my mother's friends, which they consider a scandal for a good Jewish girl. I went to Smith. I'm not gainfully employed. What else?"

Responding to her smile, Helena laughed. "I suppose that is enough." There are other questions I'd like to ask, she thought. For instance, it doesn't look as if you have a live-in lover.

Billie said, "You haven't been married. Otherwise I know nothing about your private life. That intrigues me."

"I keep my private life and my business life separate." Helena thought, I said that to Barton.

Billie nodded. "A proper professional approach — especially for a woman. But sometimes you'll have to have an escort for social functions. Do you have a suitable candidate or candidates?"

"Of course."

"In the eyes of your employer you're supposed to be utterly respectable, the soul of propriety. But on the other hand you can't be seen as a frustrated woman who takes out her thwarted sexual drive by thinking of nothing but business. It's like walking a tightrope, isn't it?"

Again Helena wondered what lay behind Billie's remarks. "Every woman in business has that problem — or in the professions."

Billie did not answer but got up again and went to the liquor cabinet. She returned with two more glasses and placed one in Helena's hand. She raised

63

her glass and said, "Join me. To the future of Rosenstein's."

Helena, astonished, responded to the toast with the glass in her hand, aware that she had not yet finished the one on the side table.

Billie smiled down at her and leaned over to touch the collar of her suit jacket. "You must buy your clothes from Rosenstein's. Rachel will know just how to dress the new manager." Then she lay down full length on the sofa, pushing a cushion up behind her head.

Neither of them spoke for a moment. The music, which Billie had turned on again to play softly, had turned itself off. Then Helena, realizing that Billie had lost all sense of the passage of time, said, "It's getting pretty late. I'd better go home."

Billie did not protest when she got up to fetch her hat and coat. Instead, she sank back further into the cushions, the last glass of whiskey on the small table near her hand. Helena stood hesitating. She longed to go over and take the glass out of Billie's reach. But after all, she reminded herself, she was not on intimate terms with Billie. What Billie did was beyond any control she could exert. She paused in the doorway to look back at Billie, saying Goodnight.

Billie raised a hand in a vague gesture, without a word.

All the way home in the cab and during the night she thought about Billie. Was this a usual thing with her? Or a special occasion? It was obvious that Billie had come to her office to invite her to dinner, the evening had been planned, the meal ordered. If Billie did have a drinking problem, was this something known to her family, her friends? Or did she conceal it?

When she went to bed she found it impossible to sleep. She herself had drunk far more than she was used to. Instead of making her drowsy, the alcohol seemed to have stimulated her to the point of uncontrollable restlessness. Her mind went round and round the question of Billie. But too much to drink was not the only reason for her jumping nerves. Billie herself seemed to have an unsettling effect on her. Everyone she met at Rosenstein's seemed to have a special feeling for Billie. Barton had not mentioned her by name, but he had talked about those who would stand in the way of a transformation of the Company. Did he mean Billie in particular?

The next day, at the lunch hour, tired of struggling with the fatigue created by a sleepless night and the uncertainties she felt in trying to dominate the day's problems, she decided to take a break and visit the art exhibition that was showing on the seventh floor of the store building. Sherry had told her about it. Every year, at this time, overlapping Thanksgiving and running up to the Christmas holidays, Rosenstein's put on an art show. It was an event of the New York season, an exhibition of paintings and antique furniture gathered on loan from private collectors, a rare chance for the ordinary public to view things otherwise not to be seen in any museum or gallery. The show had been initiated by Moses Rosenstein, Billie's grandfather, Helena noted. It was he who was credited with having added a showroom for art and antiques to Rosenstein's other departments. The exhibition took the place vacated by the fashion show. It was an area of the store reserved for unusual events.

She stepped off the elevator into a small lobby that had been created by the erection of partitions that reached three-quarters to the ceiling, forming small rooms. On the walls thus provided were hung paintings — Italian Renaissance, French, modern abstractions, the surrealists. There were clusters of people wandering through, some expensively dressed, some obviously office workers who had come in during their lunch hour, a good many people speaking in foreign languages. Helena stopped in front of a Berthe Morissot — a woman in a long-skirted white dress standing in a garden surrounded by masses of green trees and shrubs.

"Marvelous, isn't it?" said a voice at her elbow. "Marvelous that we can see these things!"

She looked around to find Rachel beside her. Rachel said, "Rachel Leventhal."

"Yes, of course," said Helena, chagrined that Rachel thought it necessary to remind her who she was. "How are you, Rachel?"

"Oh, fine. Is this your first sight of this? I've come every day since they hung the pictures."

"I don't have much opportunity to get out of my office."

Rachel's black eyes sparkled. "You must not let them make you a prisoner. Oh, I know! Everybody finds an excuse to come and consult the new manager. The novelty will wear off after a while."

Obeying an impulse, Helena asked, "Are you going to lunch? Will you join me?"

Helena saw the faint blush come into Rachel's sallow cheeks. "Why, yes!" As they walked toward the elevators, Rachel asked, "Have you tried the Elysian Room? I usually eat there when I am in the store. It's much better than anything in the neighborhood."

Helena knew that Rosenstein's had its own restaurant where lunch and afternoon tea were served. She knew from the financial reports that it had a French chef, a lavish budget for premium food supplies, a large staff, and that it did not pay its way.

Rachel pressed the button for the fifth floor. "We have a perennial joke here, because the restaurant shares the fifth floor with the health spa and the beauty salon. All the essential services in one easy stop." She laughed at her own statement and Helena smiled.

When they stepped into the restaurant the hostess came to them the instant she recognized Rachel and seated them at a window. Rachel said to Helena, "This is Monique. Monique, this is our new manager."

Helena saw Monique's eyes suddenly flash as they looked at each other. Monique, Helena saw at a glance, bought her clothes at Rosenstein's. Rosenstein's generous policy of discounts to its female employees was an important element in its hiring method. She was beginning to realize that this was a deliberate encouragement to the women to maintain their share of the Rosenstein image.

As they sat down and Monique went away, Rachel said, "Monique is valuable to us. She has a phenomenal memory for people's names and faces and she can recognize anyone who is important here. We have many customers who are important, at least in

67

their own eyes. You'd be surprised how touchy some of them are if they are not immediately recognized and treated accordingly."

Helena looked around the room. Its decor spoke of the same kind of elegance as Rosenstein clothes, Rosenstein jewelry, Rosenstein furnishings. There were thick carpets, lavish white tablecloths, glossy, satin-like drapes at the tall windows, sound-proofing in the ceiling that efficiently muted the buzz of voices. Rachel, she observed, blended into this background completely, a perfectly groomed, highly sophisticated woman whose attractiveness came more from the skill with which she achieved elegance than from her natural physical endowment.

She noticed that Rachel's vigilant eyes raked the room systematically. She guessed that Rachel kept watch, wherever she went in the store, for the most valued of Rosenstein's patrons.

Rachel said, as they studied the menu, "If you want a light meal, the quiche is very good. It is a specialty of the chef's."

"Then I shall order that," said Helena. She had skipped breakfast that morning, having been unable to face food when she got up.

"It's very light. He has a marvelous touch with food."

As they ate Helena let Rachel do most of the talking. Rachel was energetic, knowledgeable, with a constant vivacity. Helena judged her to be in her fifties. Her raven hair was probably touched up with dye and her skin had a smooth quality like doeskin that did not show wrinkles. No doubt she patronized Rosenstein's salon de beaute regularly. Her manner toward Helena was slightly critical. It's my clothes, thought Helena, remembering Billie's gentle comment of the night before. But there was an unmistakable undercurrent of friendliness, of goodwill, that surprised her.

Presently Rachel said, after a brief silence, "Billie is very happy that you have joined us. She was the one who suggested that Rosenstein's should have a woman manager."

"Really?"

Rachel gave her an appraising glance that said, You're no fool. "Well, I can't speak for the decision-makers. It was Daniel, of course, who made the decision. He is the real boss of Rosenstein's. Lionel is not active in the Company. But they all listen to Billie. They have an instinct, the Rosensteins, for spotting the elements of success. If they think you have potential, they give you every chance."

"You've been with Rosenstein's a long time, haven't you?"

"Since I was fifteen years old."

"Then you knew the founder."

Rachel laughed. "You mean Old Leah. You're embarrassed to call her that. You shouldn't be. She knew that was what she was called and she never minded. If you have a lot of Leahs in the family, you have to make a distinction. Her granddaughter is Leah and so is Billie. Yes, of course, I knew her very well. She was a second mother to me. I was fifteen when I became an apprentice here. She seemed to guess my potential and she assigned me to the head buyer, who was then a woman of the age I am now. That woman had been with Old Leah back in the days before this store was built — back when Old

Leah just had a small dress shop. Old Leah began, you know, by making babies' clothes and wedding gowns. She was a beautiful needlewoman. That was what her reputation was founded on. Then she began to make all kinds of women's apparel — luxury items for wealthy women. She'd go to Paris to judge the new fashions for herself and come home and supervise the making of good imitations, usually with her own adaptations, not straight copies. You could always tell the dresses Old Leah produced. A lot of women who could afford to go to Paris to order from the dress houses there came to prefer her creations. Her shop was housed in rented buildings until this store was built, after Moses had joined her. He was the one who expanded Rosenstein's into the store you see now. He was a very good son. He understood what she wanted to do and helped her achieve it."

"You knew him, too."

"Oh, yes. She outlived him by a year. He was the one who suggested that in the new store they should have a men's department — neckties, socks, shirts, men's cosmetics — the sort of thing women would want to buy for the men in their lives — husbands or lovers. Oh, yes! The Rosensteins were strict in those days, strict about people behaving as they should. but they were also practical. There is a legend to the effect that in the earliest days, when she was building up her business from nothing, Old Leah made dresses for the more spectacular of the public beauties of the day — you remember, this was the turn of the century, the days of the Stanford-White-Elinor Nesbitt and other sex scandals, the days when keeping a flamboyant mistress was a

70

sign of financial success. Moses also put in the jewelry and antiques. These were hobbies with him."

"He was Billie's grandfather."

"Yes. He married late and had only one child, Billie's mother, Old Leah's only granddaughter. And was she spoiled! Old Leah had no daughter of her own, only boys."

Rachel broke off while her eyes scoured the room again. "There's Princess Santini, over on the other side. She is as old as the hills. She was an American railroad heiress who married an Italian. She probably remembers more about Old Leah than most of us. And over on the right —" Rachel pointed out various women of social prominence. "I could write a society gossip column about the famous names eating lunch here today. You know, it is amazing how some of these elderly people cling to Old Leah's memory. She insisted on attending personally to her special old customers and their daughters and daughters-in-law, almost up to the time of her death. She has left a legacy of friendship for the store among many people. It is of enormous value even now."

Helena listened attentively. Rachel had the justifiable arrogance of a brilliant professional but she gave no hint of disdain for Helena's ignorance of high fashion. The friendliness that Helena had noted at the beginning of their encounter endured.

Helena said, "It must be. But there are those who consider all this behind the times, something that should not be perpetuated."

"Oh, that!" Rachel dismissed the idea scornfully. "They don't know what they're talking about. Rosenstein's isn't Woolworth's. You can't duplicate what is here."

"But, nevertheless, Rachel, there is a question whether there is a place for Rosenstein's in the modern world."

"Is there a place for value — real value, not advertising rubbish? Is there a place for integrity and sound judgment? I don't believe you can abolish that. Anyhow, I wouldn't want to work for a store that did not place such things first. Yes, I know there are some people who want to make changes. Well, they can make changes but they must keep the character of the store. There is one Rosenstein who really has a wonderful idea of rightness in judging how things should be done. That's Billie, of course. I enjoy every moment when I am working with her. She has her great grandmother's touch. She understands, right down to the ground, what Old Leah did and why she did it."

"She must get it from her mother."

"Ah, Mrs. Alfred! Well, that is hard to say. Mrs. Alfred never pays any attention to Rosenstein's. As far as she's concerned, Rosenstein's exists and always will, to provide her with everything she wants, to gratify every whim. But she has absolutely no interest in the business. Billie is not like her at all. Mrs. Alfred is very excitable. Billie is as calm as can be. This isn't just my opinion. Even Daniel doesn't see any resemblance between them — in temperament, I mean — and he dotes on Mrs. Alfred. He's always acted as if she was his little sister and he had to look after her. He finds excuses for her when she is being her most outrageous."

"Why did Daniel stay with the store? He doesn't seem to be interested in the other Rosenstein companies."

"Because he has a feel for it — like Moses and Billie. He tried working with his brother for a while in the banking firm and decided he liked this better." Rachel paused to gaze about the restaurant again and then said, "Daniel is a very good man to work for. He's very fair. But you'll find he can be a problem sometimes."

"How?"

"Well, he's very strict — in religious and moral matters, I mean. Most of the Rosensteins are not observant Jews. They're what we call twice-a-year Jews; they keep Rosh Hashanah and Yom Kippur and that's it. They are good Jews but they don't keep the laws. They contribute heavily to Jewish charities and causes — and a good many that are not Jewish. And they have a very strong family feeling. You have to remember that. If they respect you, they will treat you very well, but they'll never forget that you're not a Rosenstein. Old Leah started them on that path. She was not a religious woman, though she was married to a Talmudic scholar. But Daniel is strict. He keeps the Sabbath. He's a pillar of the synagogue. You can depend on Daniel to be absolutely honest in everything he does. The trouble is that he can be puritanical. I've known him to interfere when we've had some particularly daring new fashions — extreme necklines, for instance, deeply split skirts, that sort of thing. He has banished some things from Rosenstein's showrooms, dresses he thought too scandalous. Yes, that's true. I know it is scarcely believable. But it's logical. The sort of clothes Rosenstein's specializes in are, like all high fashion, made for seduction. Old Leah understood that very well. It was a basic principle in her creation of Rosenstein's as the source

73

of the most alluring, most dazzling gowns and costumes a woman could wear. Daniel has never understood the true nature of his grandmother's achievement. He is like most men of his temperament: he fears the seduction of women's bodies. He is a true Hebrew of Biblical tradition. He thinks of Jezebel, you know, and Delilah. You've never really been on the third floor, have you? The Boutique?"

"I've walked through it. I must admit I was daunted."

"Daunted? Oh, I see — by the luxury, the rarified atmosphere. Well, that's the heart of Rosenstein's. It is there that you find Old Leah's true legacy — the ball gowns, the wedding dresses, the deceptively simple robes de chatelaine. Do you know that there are families, even here in Manhattan, that hand down some of her creations as heirlooms?" Rachel suddenly broke off to ask, "Are you married? Do you have a husband to please?" When Helena shook her head, she went on. "Nor I. Do you know, marriage is a trap for a woman like me and I have the sense to know it. As you probably have heard, that idea goes against the basic premise of Jewish life — that you must marry and have children. That is what Mrs. Alfred keeps nagging Billie about. She keeps telling her that she is a disgrace to the family, that she should pick out a nice Jewish boy and marry him."

"I suppose she wants grandchildren."

Rachel shrugged. "I don't think she cares much about that, really. In fact, she detests small children. She had Billie soon after she married and that's as far as she would go. She's done her duty. Oh, she loves Billie! After all, Billie is her child. Poor Billie."

74

"Why poor Billie?"

But Rachel only shrugged again and ate the rest of her lunch. Then she remarked, "As a matter of fact, Daniel gets some of his basic notions from Old Leah. She wasn't prudish about women's dresses, naturally, but she was very strict about any of the men in her family having anything to do with the women who worked in the store. There was no such thing as sexual harassment when she was in charge. The women all knew they could complain to her."

Helena laughed. "But how on earth could she enforce her prohibition?"

"Well, I've told you, she came into the store every day and you never knew when she might come walking by. And she talked to everybody. There wasn't much that could escape her. It was no joke."

Helena glanced at the ornate, four-faced clock that hung free in a cage of intricate metalwork over the center of the restaurant. Rachel caught her glance.

"It's time to go, I know."

They walked out into the lobby to the elevators. As they stood together waiting Rachel put her hand with its long brilliantly painted nails on Helena's arm. "You know, I have a brand-new shipment of suits and dresses arriving today in the Executive Woman's Suite on the fourth floor. They're clothes designed and created for the career woman, just a few produced by a small company that works just for Rosenstein's. This was Billie's idea, to offer a select wardrobe for the corporate woman on the rise. It has become very popular with women who are really successful. You won't meet yourself in any board room meeting. Why don't you be there at five o'clock? There are some things I'd like to show you."

Rachel's snapping black eyes looked intently into hers. Fascinated, Helena looked back. So Billie was behind this. She found herself unable to say No, to excuse herself on the grounds that five o'clock was the busiest time of the day.

"Well, yes —" she began reluctantly.

Rachel smiled and gave her arm a squeeze. "All right, five o'clock. I'll be ready for you." She turned her head at a sound behind her back. Opposite them was the doorway embowered in a trellised archway that led into the beauty salon and health spa. Esther came through it. When she caught sight of them she looked each of them up and down.

"Why, hello, Rachel," she said. "How are you, Helena?"

"Fine, Esther," Helena responded.

"Hello, Esther," said Rachel, eyeing Esther's freshly dressed hair critically. The elevator door opened and Rachel sprang forward to enter it, saying over her shoulder, "This one's for me."

As the elevator door closed on her Esther said, "Have you seen the art exhibit?"

"Just a glimpse. I walked through it when I was coming to lunch."

"Is it your first time to have lunch in the Elysian Room? I've not seen you there before. Rachel lunches there all the time. She likes to watch some of our more spectacular customers."

There was a trace of malice in her voice so Helena said blandly, "I expect she finds it useful professionally."

"Well, I suppose you could say that."

The up elevator came and they got on. Helena was grateful that it was crowded with people going to the art exhibit so that there was no further opportunity for Esther to continue.

She realized, when five o'clock came and she was in Rachel's hands, that a new era had arrived in her career. At first she felt acutely self-conscious in the garments Rachel insisted she should wear. Rachel rejected the precept that the rising young businesswoman must wear only conservative suits, blouses without frills, discreet clothes that were to project an image of conservatism, reliability, sobriety, sexlessness, an imitation of the businessman's uniform, with a skirt instead of trousers. Watching as Rachel brought out garments and fitted them to her, she saw that in fact Rachel did not depart from these concepts, but there was a subtle emphasis in the way she was dressing her on her own individuality, projecting the idea of a reserve of self-confidence and latent strength of will.

Nevertheless, she found the Rosenstein style somewhat breathtaking, a far cry from her memory of her early role models — the first woman vice-president of a bank she had encountered as a teenager, and the first woman manager of an insurance office. Yet she did not protest but meekly accepted Rachel's positively made choices. She was bemused by the success with which Rachel seemed to achieve a sort of sublimation of the traditional, and though she examined the clothes with care, she could not exactly fathom how it was that Rachel did this. When she had the clothes on they did not seem flamboyant at all. The statement they made must be in the slight variations of cut, fabric, exactness of fit, in the discreet ornamentation. And her jackets had pockets, cunningly contrived to be there and not

77

show. This last touch made her realize that Rachel's sense of fashion was soundly based on reality. A modern executive woman did not encumber herself with the large, voluminous handbags Helena remembered as inevitable appendages of the businesswoman of the past, part briefcase and part feminine accessory, considered to be obligatory for any woman. So the pockets were essential. When she looked in the full-length mirror she saw that she did not look like a female version of a typical corporate male executive and yet there was no hint of frivolity in the ensemble, only chic. And she smiled to herself when this thought entered her mind — only chic. That in itself was a measure of the triumph of Rachel's art.

She rebelled only at the shoes that Rachel wanted her to wear, shoes with heels as high as those Rachel herself wore — or Billie, Helena remembered. Giving in, Rachel found a suitable pair with three-quarter heels.

In the dressing room — a spacious chamber suitable for the display of Rosenstein's garments — when at last she stood in the complete outfit for Rachel's appraisal, Rachel had suddenly come close to her, placing her hands on Helena's breasts and looking straight into her eyes.

"You're a lovely woman," she said. "You must not hide that loveliness under ugly clothes. You have the correct tailleur — long legs, flat stomach, good posture, and these beauties —" Rachel grinned as Helena felt the featherweight touch on her breasts. She blushed furiously and Rachel, seeing it, laughed, while the attendant saleswomen and seamstresses giggled. Obviously they were used to Rachel's tactics.

When the session finally ended, Rachel stepped back and looked at her critically and carefully. At last she said, "Now Old Leah would approve."

That outfit, she said, must be ready for her in the morning. The seamstresses would finish the alterations and it would be delivered to her apartment in two or three hours' time. The other things could wait.

When Helena walked into her office the following morning she cringed a little at what Sherry's reaction would be. Sherry was delighted and jumped up from her chair to walk around her in admiration.

"Why, it's lovely!" she exclaimed. "Wow! You just watch how people are going to act when they see you! I'm so glad you decided to buy your clothes here in Rosenstein's."

"You'll have to thank Rachel," said Helena, going into her office, anxious not to betray even to Sherry the elation she felt — absurdly, she thought. But even Sherry had obviously been aware that she fell short of the Rosenstein standard. She wondered how many comments Sherry had received which she had good-naturedly not passed on to her, even in innuendo.

In fact, she was astonished at the ease with which she got used to the wardrobe that Rachel had created for her, how quickly she accepted the image it projected. True, once she was in her office the pace of the working day was such that she had very little time to give to a consideration of what she was wearing. She was only reminded when she observed the surprised or admiring gaze of the people who came into her office or when she encountered one of the big mirrors placed in various strategic angles of the corridors.

On one occasion, preoccupied by a problem involving the Rosenstein hiring policies, she almost ran into Barton. He stood in her path to attract her attention.

"Now, now, Helena, you can't walk by me that way," he said, noting the automatic annoyance in her glance before she was able to erase it. "What's the matter? Rosenstein's troubles getting you down?" Then he made an elaborate point of looking her up and down and whistled, "What have we here? The complete Rosenstein fashion plate? The eternal feminine, eh?"

Angry, she tried to hide it. "Rosenstein's troubles keep me very busy."

"Ah, but you shouldn't let them make a hermit of you. That's the mistake you earnest women make. How about having lunch with me?"

Realizing that she was courting trouble, she answered, "I'm afraid it can't be today."

Of course he was offended. It showed in his face. "All right. Another time. I'll give you a ring."

She nodded and walked on. Why was it, she wondered, that in going around the store she met everyone except the person she most wanted to meet, Billie. She wondered if it was possible that Billie purposely avoided her. She knew Billie was often in the store. She heard plenty of comment from everyone else about her. Was Billie perhaps embarrassed by the fact that she had ended their evening drunk?

But the next day, coming in from the street when she had gone for a brief noon walk to break the strain of the day's demands, she saw Billie sitting at a counter chatting with a saleswoman. For a moment she hesitated, but Billie turned and looked her way and beckoned. When she reached her she saw that the glass counter contained a display of costume jewelry; the real jewelry was kept safely on the second floor, away from the danger of thieving hands that might come in from the street. She also saw that Billie held in her hands a fragile necklace of gold-washed links which she twisted gently in her fingers to see its effect.

"Aren't these pretty?" said Billie, indicating the tray on the counter before her. "They have just arrived."

Helena, captivated by the grace of Billie's delicate fingers draped with the gold chain, said absently, "Yes, very pretty."

She noticed Billie's glance, taking in her new costume, and that the saleswoman followed Billie's glance covertly and that a faint smile was exchanged between the two women. Then Billie turned back and apparently became completely absorbed in a discussion of the trinkets in the tray. Baffled, Helena said, "Glad to see you," and walked away as Billie nodded without turning her head.

At odd moments of quiet in the rest of the day Helena's mind reverted to this brief encounter. Billie was not shy about mingling with the employees of Rosenstein's. This was the secret of her popularity. She had the common touch and the gift of making anyone feel that her interest was real and particular, not merely a general good will.

When the evening came and Helena went home, she realized that her mind had been running on Billie more than ever. And Billie, she thought, had probably forgotten the chance meeting. But had she forgotten the evening they had spent together? There was still the doubt about Billie's possible alcoholism. And whether her family knew and why she gave in to the lure of alcohol. Billie had traveled in Europe with Rachel and Rachel had known Billie since a child. So it followed that Rachel must know a good deal about Billie's private life and personal habits. But certainly she could not question Rachel about Billie.

She was finishing washing up the few dishes left from her supper when the phone rang. Her first thought was that one of her friends was calling to persuade her to join in some social activity. Most of her friends, women she had known in college, were now married. They frequently called to persuade her to go out and leave behind the preoccupations of her job. These occasions were inevitably parties consisting chiefly of couples, or girls involved in affairs or living with a current boyfriend. They were all convinced that she needed liberation from the demands of her career-oriented solitude.

Or perhaps, she thought, walking across the room, it was her mother. Her mother lived in Texas and seldom wrote letters. At least twice a month she called. But this seemed unlikely, since it had not been long ago that she had called — unless something was wrong.

But when she lifted the receiver it was Billie's soft, throaty voice that said, "Are you busy tomorrow — Saturday? Will you come to my apartment?"

Breathless as a schoolgirl, Helena said eagerly, "Why, yes. What time?"

"Whenever you're finished at Rosenstein's. How are things going?"

"Oh, fine."

"Well, we'll talk then," and Billie hung up.

Helena put the phone down with a sense of disappointment. Perhaps this was just Billie's way. She could not say exactly why she was disappointed, what more she expected or why.

Rosenstein's was open on Saturdays until one o'clock. The sales force and the credit office were on duty. The office staff was not and the offices were empty unless there was extra pressure of work, sometimes in only one department, sometimes in all, as with the approaching Christmas season. Normally, Helena spent Saturday morning alone in her office, glad of the opportunity to catch up without interruption. Saturday afternoons she usually went to the health club to which she belonged, where there were indoor tennis courts and a swimming pool. This Saturday, by the time she cleared her desk and reached for her hat and coat, the store was quiet and deserted, except for the coming and going of the one elevator in service, bringing people to the art exhibit, which was crowded and buzzing with the sound of voices. The security guard checked her out at two-thirty. If she walked — the day was sunny and mild and the idea of outdoor exercise tempted her — she would reach Billie's apartment in half an hour.

She went slowly, hampered by the crowd in the street and also because she lingered at each store window, examining the displays. She had taken to doing this, teaching herself to assess the techniques used in dressing the windows and comparing them with Rosenstein's. She had come to realize that there was a sense of opulence, of aristocratically muted grandeur about Rosenstein's windows, which, she knew, implied the existence of a world that really no longer existed. Yet this offered to the crowds in the street the appeal, she supposed, of a fairy tale.

At Billie's apartment house she gave her name to the receptionist who waved her toward the elevator. Billie stood in the open door of her apartment when Helena got off the elevator. She was dressed in street clothes, as if she herself had just come in.

"You're a little late," she said, as she took Helena's hat and coat from her.

"I walked here. I'm learning to look at shop windows."

Billie laughed and led her into the living room. A quick glance around told Helena that there was no sign of a whiskey bottle or glasses. Billie seemed as always unruffled, slow-moving. In the daylight the big room was bright. The paintings on the walls glowed in the natural light.

"You have some wonderful things," Helena said.

Billie looked at them and said, "They belong to my mother." Then she turned an obviously critical eye on Helena herself and added, "Rachel has done a very good job."

Helena said ruefully, "I've never owned so many clothes in my life."

"You've never worked for Rosenstein's before," Billie retorted. "Come and sit down."

As Helena obeyed, Billie walked across to the stereo and turned on a Beethoven violin and piano sonata. The music came softly across the room as she came back and sat down on the sofa. They sat silent for a few minutes.

Then Billie said, "Perhaps it was just as well that Rachel did not dress you for your first interview with Daniel. I'm sure that then you looked competent and modern and quite unremarkable. He was reassured. He would not have felt quite so reassured if you had come in looking the way you do now." She was smiling as she spoke. "It took me quite a while to talk Daniel into hiring a woman as manager. He was quite uncertain about how firm and businesslike and able to confront crises in the business a woman would be."

"Really? And how about his grandmother?"

"Oh, you can't compare any woman with Old Leah, to Daniel! I'm afraid you will find that most of the older members of the family are the same way. You cannot win an argument by reminding them that Old Leah was a mortal woman and that what she could do another woman might also do. She is larger than life, even in memory."

"Rachel was telling me that Daniel sometimes is difficult to deal with — as for instance if he thinks the new fashions are too provocative."

Billie nodded. "Daniel's ideas about women's clothes antedate Schiaparelli. Poor Rachel. Since Old Leah died she has had some awkward moments with Daniel. Of course, some of the older Rosensteins thought she might leave Rosenstein's at that time and take her reputation and her experience and skill somewhere else. That frightens everybody very much. Of course, I know that Rachel never will. As long as Rosenstein's is Rosenstein's she will stay. She knows there's no duplicate, no substitute for Rosenstein's anywhere. But she does get some very tempting offers."

Helena did not reply and they sat for a while listening to the music. The piano's earnest voice asked questions and the strings answered. Then the piano became talkative and the strings murmured responses.

Billie suddenly asked, "Do you see a lot of Esther?"

"No, not a lot. I meet her sometimes in the elevator or in the corridor."

"She doesn't come to visit you?"

"Not since that first time. She and Rachel don't like each other, do they?"

Billie smiled. "So you have noticed that already. No, they don't. In fact, they detest each other. Esther thinks Rachel is no better than she should be, and Rachel — well, Rachel thinks Esther is a blot on the landscape of Rosenstein's. Of course, they've both been at Rosenstein's forever and they're both invulnerable, so it's a fair fight. I think you know that Rachel was a protegee of Old Leah's and a great favorite of hers. Esther —" Billie paused. "Esther is a Rosenstein, a cousin. Her father was never successful as a businessman. He was somebody who always had to be looked after by his relatives. When they were children, she was a playmate of my mother's. She is still very close to my mother."

Helena said impulsively, "I always feel that I should be careful when I talk to Esther. But she is always very friendly."

"Yes, of course she is friendly. But you should be careful." Her tone was short but she did not explain.

86

Helena said, "There is someone else who makes me uneasy. James Barton."

Billie's gaze, which had wandered off across the room, returned to her at once. "You've not mentioned him to me before."

"He came to see me just after the board meeting, when I was introduced to the directors and officers. He was out of town at the time and said he wanted to meet me. In fact, he said that had he known that I was actually going to be hired, he would have postponed his trip."

Billie was listening closely to what she said. "He told you everything that is wrong with Rosenstein's, didn't he? He told you that we should cut the staff, weed out the older people, trim the quality while keeping the appearance of it. But in the end we'll have to sell out to a conglomerate. Otherwise the store is doomed."

"Yes, in general that is what he said or implied."

"And what did you tell him?"

"I said that I had not been hired to reorganize the store, but to modernize the management of the Company, increase its profitability."

"He said something else to you, didn't he? Shall I tell you what he said? That there is a division of opinion among the Rosensteins, that you should join him with those who favor this way to go, that you don't want to stick with those who think Rosenstein's should be preserved the way it is."

Helena noticed that Billie's face had become pink with the strength of her feeling. "Yes, he indicated that. In fact, he got annoyed when I didn't agree with him at once. He went away from my office in a huff. I was glad that he left me alone, though I admit that I worry sometimes about this. After all, he is a vice-president and I understand he is a particular friend of a cousin of yours."

"Moishe." Billie shrugged.

"But yesterday I met him in the corridor and he wanted to have lunch with me."

"It must have been Rachel's clothes," Billie quipped. "Did you?"

"No."

"You don't like him."

"I don't trust him."

Billie looked at her inquiringly. "There was something else that he talked to you about."

"Yes. He said in so many words that he is staying with Rosenstein's because the Company can provide an avenue to the Rosenstein Enterprises. He suggested that I should view the matter in the same light. He has no interest in the store."

"He despises us and he thinks we don't know it."

Helena realized that Billie was angry. "Billie, nevertheless, I must tell you that there is a lot of substance in what he says about the store. In the past the store could produce big profits in spite of all the drains on it. It was able not only to maintain itself in splendor but it provided funds for the other enterprises. But that day is past. There is a lot that can be done to modernize the business through better management. But there is only so much that can be done. It can't go on indefinitely funding all these special events, carrying an enormous staff, paying all these generous employee benefits — no other store does what Rosenstein's still does."

Billie listened to her without interruption. When

she had finished, she said, "You've learned your lesson well."

Helena flushed, "I'm not echoing Barton. But I would be failing my responsibility if I did not point out to you that this is the situation."

Billie shot her an angry glance. "Do you think I don't know all this?"

Helena sank back in her chair. "But then why did you persuade Daniel to invite me in?"

"Because I don't agree with Barton — and Moishe."

Helena was aware that she had reached a stone wall. She sat silent, waiting for Billie to speak again.

"Barton must have thought he could make an ally of you — because you're a newcomer, inexperienced, and a woman, therefore easily influenced."

Helena was stung. "I don't intend to be anyone's cat's-paw."

Billie's smile was faint. "I'm sure you don't. I must admit, knowing the situation here, that I had some doubts after I got Daniel to agree to hire you. I had no idea what you would be like. I had only your resumé to go by and from that you could be any woman a few years out of business administration school with excellent academic ratings and a little experience in manufacturing."

"Daniel seems to have known more. From what Barton says, he knew that I wasn't sexually promiscuous and had a limited social life."

Billie laughed at her obvious chagrin. "Of course. You must have learned by now that the men always have their own grapevine, especially when a woman is involved. Daniel is not comfortable with modern young women. But never mind. He likes you. He is beginning to trust you. He has admitted that I was right — that if we are going to have a manager, we should have a woman."

"I gather from what you say, that Daniel thinks the way you do: that Rosenstein's can survive as it is."

For a moment she thought Billie was going to answer. But then she seemed to decide against this and closed her half-open lips. Presently she got up and walked across the room and through the bedroom door, whistling a soft accompaniment to the muted music.

Helena sat pondering, stirred up by having said so much that she had been keeping to herself for so long. She still did not understand Billie, what Billie's real role was in the running of Rosenstein's. What had Esther said? That she was lazy. She knew now that Billie could not be pushed.

Billie came back into the room and stood beside her chair. In her fingers hung a gold chain — the one she had been examining in the store? Or the real thing? It hung like a faintly glittering web of tiny loops in her delicate, rosy-tipped fingers. Billie's fingers always captured her attention whenever she was with her. Pulling her eyes away she looked up at Billie, to meet her eyes smiling down at her.

Billie said, "You liked that little chain you saw in the store, didn't you? Well, this is much nicer." She reached down and clasped the necklace round Helena's neck. "Your costume is not quite complete without an ornament like this. You have a lovely neck to show it off." She brought the tips of her fingers forward along the ridge of Helena's jawbones, finishing up by tipping her chin up so as to look at her more squarely.

A tremor went through Helena at her touch. Though it was as light as thistledown, it acted like an electrical current, a lick of fire that did not scorch but instead roused an exquisite sensation of pleasure so great it left her unable to move.

Billie took her fingers away. Still smiling she said, looking at her, "That's the way I thought it would look."

Helena roused herself to protest. "Oh, you can't give me that!"

Billie opened her eyes wider. "I can't? Of course I can!" She stepped back, her smile fading. She gazed down at Helena soberly, as if waiting for a response. When Helena, tongue-tied, stayed silent, she walked away and stood at the window, her back turned.

Helena, miserable at her own inability to speak, sat quiet, struggling with the turmoil within herself. Presently, Billie turned around and said in a matter-of-fact voice, "I want to take you to visit a cousin of mine — my cousin Michelle. It's not very far. We can walk there." She waited for Helena to respond.

Helena said, with difficultly, "Why, if you want to."

Billie said in her usual mild voice, "Let's go, then."

As they walked along the street, empty and quiet in the Saturday afternoon, Billie said, "I'd better tell you. Michelle has a live-in lover."

Helena, surprised, said, "Well, that's usual enough."

"Yes, but this one's a girl."

Billie was looking at her out of the corner of her eye. She's not really my height, Helena was thinking, remembering that Billie wore heels higher than her own. They were strolling because the weather was mild and this seemed the pace Billie wanted. She seemed in no hurry to arrive at her cousin's.

Helena said, "That's not entirely new to me, either."

"The family pretends that Michelle does not exist — at least they try to. But she is a shareholder in the Company and has inherited quite a lot of stock in the Rosenstein Enterprises. Also she contributes to all the pet Rosenstein charities and she is a trustee of the scholarship her grandfather established at Brandeis. So they really can't ignore her altogether."

"They've cut her off because she is a lesbian?"

"Yes."

"Does it bother her?"

"Yes, of course. How could it not, since she is a Rosenstein? On the other hand, she is pleased that she does not have to pretend to do all the things the family would expect her to do. She has rejected her religious inheritance; her parents are more observant than the rest of us. But we pay some attention to the outward form of things — the holidays, for instance — simply because we are Jews and we don't want to deny that."

Helena said, soberly, "A lot of us, not just Jews, have lost an active interest in religion."

"But with Michelle this is a deliberate rejection. So she is happy that she does not have to go through the motions. Daniel feels badly about this. She is banished, as far as he is concerned. Daniel is Orthodox and continues to live in his old family

92

house because he is near enough to the synagogue to walk there on the Sabbath. He will not live in an apartment house because he might have to use the elevator on the Sabbath. Most of us don't want to do as he does, but we respect the prohibitions he lays down — like not speaking to Michelle."

"But obviously you don't ignore Michelle."

"Ah, but that's a different matter. But my mother does not know that Michelle and I are good friends." Billie suddenly stopped walking and as Helena stood still, turned to face her. "And don't say anything to Esther about Michelle. As far as Esther is concerned, you know nothing about Michelle, even if Esther mentions her." Realizing that her tone had become peremptory, Billie spoke more gently. "You see, there is no way you could have heard about Michelle — beyond the fact that you might have seen her name in a list of shareholders of Rosenstein's — except through me. And that would be disastrous."

She began to stroll on and Helena fell into step. Billie went on talking. "You know, Old Leah was not a submissive woman. She had strong political opinions which she voiced. She was a socialist. She wanted votes for women and she was an active supporter of the big garment workers' strike in 1913. The family — especially Daniel and some of the older women — try to cover that up as much as they can. They praise Old Leah for being such a good Jewish wife and they say she went to work simply because she had to in order to support her husband and children. That is nonsense. She was an ambitious woman and she knew she had the gifts necessary to deal with the world and succeed. She enjoyed her life, she enjoyed fighting her way to the top in a competitive world. It is an insult to her to say that she was simply a pawn of circumstance."

She fell silent and they walked along without any further conversation until Billie stopped in front of a tall red-brick house sandwiched in, with one or two others like it, between high-rise apartment houses. It was a survivor, Helena supposed, of the days when the whole neighborhood was one of private residences.

"We're here," Billie said and climbed the short flight of shallow steps that led to the front door. In the entry she pressed a button and they waited for a buzz. Billie said into the mouthpiece above the button, "It's me, Billie. I've got someone with me." Helena heard the sound of the lock of the door releasing.

Inside, the vestibule was lit by a tall lamp in the form of a bronze woman, standing in the corner. The bright day did not penetrate through the narrow chased glass windows on each side of the front door. Billie pressed the button at the side of the door in the rear wall and it slid back noiselessly to reveal the brightly lit interior of a small elevator. She motioned for Helena to get in ahead of her and then pressed the button that said five. The lift rose immediately and swiftly and came to an abrupt halt, the door opening simultaneously. They stepped out into a big room — it must take up the whole length and breadth of the house, thought Helena. At the front and back in the center were several lamps to dispel the gloom that would otherwise have prevailed.

A woman came across the room to them. She was middle-aged, shorter than Billie and thin, wearing her brown hair smoothly drawn back from her face and gathered into a chignon at the back of her neck. Large earrings hung almost to her shoulders.

She said, "Hello, Billie. Nice to see you." As she spoke, her greenish eyes were fixed on Helena.

Billie said, "Hello, Michelle. This is Helena."

Michelle said, "Hello, Helena. Come and meet people."

She gestured towards the other women who sat or stood around the big room but she made no effort to introduce them. Instead she stood close to Billie and fell into a murmured conversation with her. Helena strolled over towards the windows at the front of the house. The room was divided up into groups of big sofas and low coffee tables. Around the walls were grotesque figures in ebony and other dark woods — African art, she realized as she examined them. There was low music in the background, Oriental music, not loud enough to predominate over the chatter of voices. At one end of the room, near the front windows, there was a group of girls. One of them, with her hair caught back in an Indian bandeau and wearing a body suit and shorts and heavy socks and running shoes, was jogging in one spot. Talking to her was an Asian woman wearing a sari and obviously striving hard to understand what the jogger was saying.

A young dark-skinned black woman whose hair was fastened on top of her head with large, exotic combs and wearing a multicolored robe and many bangles and necklaces, came up to Helena.

"I'm Arlette," she said. "Billie brought you, didn't she?"

Helena nodded.

Arlette's large eyes were fixed attentively on her. "This is the first time you've been here."

Again Helena nodded. There was lively curiosity in Arlette's eyes as she continued to examine her appearance. Suddenly she reached out and touched the necklace around Helena's neck, murmuring, "That's beautiful."

Surprised, Helena said, "Yes, it is, isn't it?"

Arlette's dark eyes were raised to hers, while her fingers still lightly felt the links of the necklace. "It is not usual — and it is very expensive."

Before Helena could reply, she looked beyond her and smiled. Billie's voice said, behind Helena, "Hello, Arlette, how are you?" As she spoke Billie put her arm through Helena's and said, "Come downstairs with me."

Arlette persisted. "But the poetry reading —"

Billie said in her usual equable manner, exerting mild pressure on Helena's arm, "We'll be back."

In the lift Billie pressed the button for the floor beneath the one where they had been. The room they stepped into occupied only the center of the house and was dark except for lamps hanging over a long table on which a buffet was spread. Two or three women were standing at one end, talking and munching. One of them paused long enough to say, "Hello, Billie," but though their talk continued, their scrutiny of Helena was prolonged and intense.

Billie ignored them except for a brief nod and walked down to the far end of the table, where there was a bar, equipped with many bottles and glasses. "No ice," she said, as if to herself, and pressed a button in the wall and spoke into the mouthpiece above it. "We need ice, Marie." She picked up two

96

glasses and poured scotch into them, dropping in the ice which came up on the dumbwaiter with extraordinary and silent speed. She handed a glass to Helena. Helena took it and held it, looking at Billie over it.

Billie tapped her arm. "Don't worry. It's the first one today."

Helena dropped her eyes. "Sorry, Billie, I didn't mean —"

But Billie cut her short. "Oh, yes, you did." She stepped back to the table and, surveying the dishes arranged there, speared a small crusty ball out of a casserole. She lifted it to Helena's mouth. "Try this. Marie makes lovely appetizers."

Helena, feeling the veiled scrutiny of the women at the other end of the table, stood silent. Billie paid no attention to their audience, choosing tidbits from the various dishes. She had set her glass down close to Helena and did not touch it after the first sip. At last, picking it up again, she said, "Come and sit," and led the way to a settee placed against the wall.

Helena said, "Tell me about Michelle."

"Her grandfather was Old Leah's third son, Jacob, who founded the Rosenstein Pharmaceutical Company. His son, her father, is still the chief executive officer; the company is now public and listed on the New York Stock Exchange. Michelle's brothers are professional men. They have nothing to do with business."

"I wish you had a genealogical chart I could consult."

Billie laughed her throaty little laugh. "Michelle inherited this house from an aunt on her mother's side. She has lived here since she came of age."

"What does she do?"

"She teaches design in an art school and also gives courses free at several neighborhood centers — to teach ghetto children. She is quite well known as a designer."

"And Arlette?"

"Ah, you guessed that Arlette is her live-in? Arlette is learning design. She has a gift for it. Right now she makes a living designing costume jewelry. She wants to work with real jewels eventually."

"Ah," said Helena."

"Michelle found her in one of the classes she teaches at a community center. She moved in with Michelle a few months ago. Michelle does not like permanent partners. And she prefers young ones."

The lift was coming and going often now, bringing women from the studio upstairs. A crowd had gathered around the table. What Billie was saying could not be overheard above the babble.

Helena said, "Billie, isn't it dangerous for you to come here? Someone might recognize you."

"Yes," said Billie and smiled. "They might suspect that you are with Rosenstein's, too."

Helena glanced around at the women filling the room. When her working days had not been so hectic she had often gone to feminist meetings, political rallies, protest demonstrations, places where some of these women might also have gone. But she saw no one she recognized.

"I've been given the once-over by several women," she said.

"That is because you are with me. I'm an object of curiosity to Michelle's friends." Billie stood up. "Let's go. Come back to my place. I'll have to find

Michelle." She took their empty glasses and placed them on the corner of the table as they passed.

In the studio upstairs there were only a few women left, including, Helena guessed, the poet, who was surrounded by a small group. Michelle sat on a sofa, her legs crossed and her arm resting on the back. She smiled as she saw them come out of the lift. Billie sat down beside her.

Michelle looked up at Helena and said, "I'm sorry we've not had a chance to talk." Her eyes, boldly outlined in mascara, gazed into Helena's. She was not a handsome woman. She was thin to the point of gauntness and her nose and cheekbones stood out in her narrow face. But there was an air of authority about her, of hardness, of a woman used to dominating wherever she was, of asserting exactly what she would do and with whom she would do it.

"You have quite a crowd here," said Helena.

"Yes, there usually is on Saturdays. Billie must bring you again, at a less busy time." She glanced at Billie. Billie nodded and stood up. They had been dismissed, Helena guessed.

They walked along the street together in silence. There were more people about now in the early evening and somehow their world did not seem as private as it had been when they had come that way before. They arrived in Billie's apartment before Billie said, taking off her jacket, "Stay here with me."

Helena, troubled by the softness in her voice and still under the influence of the sense of commotion in Michelle's house, did not answer. When her silence had lasted for a while Billie came back to stand in front of her and take hold of her arms. "Won't you?"

"Yes," said Helena.

Billie dropped her head and leaned her forehead against Helena's shoulder, her hands still clinging to her. Helena put her arms around her gently. "Billie, what is the matter? Why are you so unhappy?"

Billie straightened up and caught Helena's head in her hands. "I am not unhappy now, with you. Now I have you here. I can feel you, kiss you." She paused and kissed Helena on the lips. "You don't know how miserable I am sometimes, when I see you across a room, down a corridor, in a crowd of people. It's as if you're a mirage that will disappear when I try to reach you." She dropped her hands to clasp Helena's, as if to reassure herself of Helena's substantiality.

Helena still held her in her arms, trying to understand her own feelings. Billie was no longer the woman she had met as a stranger. There was a coming together of their spirits, as if they had known each other for a long time.

There was a pinker than usual flush in Billie's face, a brighter than usual sparkle in her blue eyes. Without saying anything she took hold of Helena's wrist and drew her after her as she walked to the bedroom. Helena went with her, unresisting. In the bedroom, Billie let go of her and began to undo her suit jacket. Helena stopped her by taking hold of her hands.

"I can do that myself," she said.

Billie nodded and turned away.

Methodically Helena took off her clothes, while Billie watched. She wondered at herself, for she was not used to nakedness before another pair of eyes, at least since she had shared rooms with other girls in school and at camp. But now she seemed to be in a dream-state, acutely aware of herself, of the cool air

100

on her body, of Billie's scrutiny, and yet remote from herself, as if she observed the scene in a looking glass. When she had tossed away her last garment she walked across to the wide, satin-covered bed and lay down, pushing the pillow up to raise her head so that she could watch Billie.

Billie's soft pink body emerged from her clothes. She stood now only in her bra and bikini — black lace that accentuated the plumpness of her breasts, her thighs, her stomach. She is delicious, thought Helena. She looked to see whether there were any fine little red-gold tendrils showing around the edges of the bikini, wondering if Billie shaved herself there. But then Billie pulled off the bikini and she saw the neat triangle of red-gold curls between her thighs.

Suddenly aware that the avidity in her own eyes must show, Helena dropped her gaze. Billie, without a word, cast herself on the bed so that her face came to rest on Helena's thatch of crisp brown pubic hair. She rolled her head from side to side, to rub her cheeks against it.

Helena reached down and pulled her up so that they lay embraced, breasts pressed together, stomachs, thighs, feet entwined. At this point Helena lost the sense of being an other, watching their love act from the outside. She was aware only of Billie and Billie's invasion of her senses, of the warmth of Billie's body, of the fire in her own veins when Billie's desire overwhelmed her. Later she could not remember the mechanics of that physical act, only the overpowering sensations that it created. This was due, she realized then, to the deftness of Billie's fingers, the artistry of Billie's fondling, the profound knowledge that Billie brought to rousing her. Never before had she experienced this abandon. There had always been restraint in her response to love-making, for deep within herself she disliked being handled. Billie had completely dissolved that dislike.

When the heat of the passage beyond herself subsided a feeling of tranquility spread through her. She felt Billie's lips moving delicately over her face. Then Billie was still and raised her head to look down into her eyes. Billie was smiling, a soft, sweet smile. All Helena could find to say was, "Billie."

Billie answered, "You've held yourself back for a long time, haven't you?"

Helena waited for the regret that would follow such a complete abandonment. But instead she felt a pervading sense of happiness. The warmth and softness of Billie's body, lying so naturally in her embrace, kept awake the joy of being there with her. Billie lay absolutely quiet, as if drifting in her own cloud of contentment.

When they finally got up it was dark and Billie turned on the indirect lighting. She sat on the edge of the bed and said, "It's pretty late. Shall we get something to eat?"

"I am hungry."

"There is nothing here to eat. I could call the caterer."

"Just as you like."

"There's a Chinese place a couple of blocks away."

"Then let's go there."

It was a small restaurant, at that hour not crowded. They sat in a booth toward the back which Billie sought out, as if she ate there often. "The drinks are good here," she said, and ordered a couple of scotches.

Helena, feeling the outer world invading their close privacy, welcomed their semi-dark corner. Even if anyone came in who would recognize Billie or herself, they would not be noticed. They were seated side by side on a leather-covered bench against the wall, which gave them a view of the rest of the restaurant, through the branches of a plant in a tub.

Billie said, "This is a free weekend for me. That is why I asked you come to me."

"What do you mean by a free weekend?"

"Nobody is watching me."

Helena looked at her inquiringly.

Billie smiled. "I live in a goldfish bowl. Do you know why I don't have a regular maid? It's odd, isn't it? Because I don't like spies."

"But, Billie, who would spy on you?"

"My mother. She would love to have someone right there, in the midst of my daily life, seeing everything I do, knowing everybody who came to see me."

"Billie, that sounds —"

"Paranoid. Not as much as you think. My mother wants me to have a maid, someone she would pick out. I say I won't have one. So she compromises. Every few days she sends Elise over to look after my clothes. She says I don't know how to take care of my things. Perhaps that's so. I am careless. Elise is her own maid. She has been with my mother since I was a baby. Do you wonder why my apartment looks the way it does — like an expensive hotel suite? My mother furnished it. I can't have anything there that would give me away. I am very careful not to have anyone stay with me. Did you think you were one of many?"

"I didn't think about that at all."

"Well, you are not one of many. In fact, you're unique."

The waiter rolled his trolley close to their table and they sat silent while he dished up the meal. They ate a few mouthfuls before Billie said, "In Rosenstein's, it's Esther. Esther keeps an eye on me there."

Helena said, disbelieving, "Does your mother really suspect you?"

Billie did not answer at once. "No. I'm being unfair to her. No. She doesn't suspect and that is why I am so careful. I don't want her to suspect. She thinks I'm just —" Billie didn't finish her sentence and Helena waited. "I'm her child, her only child. She has always babied me."

After a moment Helena said, "Rachel is your friend, isn't she? She seems very fond of you."

"Yes. Rachel is my friend. She has always been, since I was a child. She would never give me away."

"Then she knows all about you."

"Oh, yes. She has always known."

Helena looked her question.

Billie answered it. "No, Rachel has never been my lover. She always treats me like — a special creation that can't be touched by human hands."

"Then it was Michelle you learned from."

Billie was silent, as if disconcerted by the directness of her question. Then she said, "Yes."

They ate for a while and then Helena asked,

"Your mother, of course, knows that Michelle is a lesbian."

"Of course. All the Rosensteins know about Michelle. Michelle saw to that. She simply defied them. After Old Leah died, she came out in the open and told them that she was going to live the way she wanted to and no one could stop her. Her parents and her brothers were outraged. They've never spoken to her since. She is the shame of the Rosenstein's, their worst scandal. There is nothing they can do about it. After all, she is a Rosenstein, with her share of the Rosenstein wealth. My mother and Daniel are especially upset by her, for different reasons."

"So why is this weekend free?"

"My mother is on a cruise. She likes to go on long cruises. This one was to China and she has been gone since August. She gets back in a couple of weeks' time."

Billie finished her dinner and leaned back in her seat. "You know, I was astonished the first time I saw you. People told me a lot of things about you. I wondered what I would find when I met you myself. You seemed too good to be true. And then, when I did see you, I knew I had to be careful."

"Careful?"

"Careful not to be seen too much with you. You'd be surprised how much gossip circulates around at Rosenstein's about you. You're an exotic creature there. I can't get near you."

"Then it's true. You do avoid me in the store."

"You've noticed? I wondered if you did."

"But you really have no enemies."

Billie's smile was bleak. "You mean, everybody is

105

Billie's friend? Well, that's not true. There are some who would like to be rid of my influence in Rosenstein's."

"Barton, for instance?"

"Yes. And there are always jealousies and resentments to be dealt with, you know. There is one woman, for instance, who dislikes me because she thinks I prevented her from being made the supervisor on the sixth floor — the Teen Shop and Sportswear — when Mrs. Gifford retired. I knew that Melba should have that promotion. Melba had been there longer and was a better manager. Melba is black and I pointed out to Daniel that if she was not promoted, we could have a discrimination suit on our hands. Not that Melba would have sued us. She is too loyal to Rosenstein's. But I did not tell him that."

Helena broke her fortune cookie's shell to draw out the slip of paper. "Esther is not your enemy. She seems fond of you."

"Oh, no. Esther is not my enemy. She is just my mother's eyes and ears in Rosenstein's. My mother, you know, has the reputation of having no interest in business. Rosenstein's just exists, because Old Leah founded it and it must therefore go on forever. But Esther thinks she must be informed about everything and my mother just lets her talk on and on. I don't think she listens, really. But if Esther says something about me, she will pay attention at once. Esther's real loyalty is to my mother. Rachel knows all about this and she protects me if she thinks I'm in danger."

Helena unfurled the little slip of paper in her

fingers. "It says here that I must seize opportunity when it presents."

Billie laughed. "Mine says that I should value friendship."

The meal over, they walked back to Billie's apartment. It was not until they were inside with the door shut and Billie had caught her in her arms that it occurred to Helena that she had not given a moment's thought to going anywhere but Billie's place. Billie turned the stereo on and they sat together contentedly. After a while they went to bed, making love in the warmth and softness of each other's arms and at last falling asleep, to wake still content in the comfort and pleasure of each other's body. It was a sunny day and in the middle of the morning they went out to a delicatessen for bagels and Danish pastries. They spent the day reading the Sunday papers and talking, intimate, uncalculated talk, exploring the ranges of their lives. In the sunny afternoon they went for a walk in Central Park and afterwards to an evening meal in a quiet little French restaurant that Billie knew about. As they returned to Billie's apartment, for the first time Helena felt a prompting of conscience, aware that she had for the last night and day not given a thought to the professional problems and worries that had ridden her ceaselessly since she had joined Rosenstein's.

"I'm going to pieces, Billie," she said, but Billie kissed her and they went to bed for another night of calm, peaceful, love-making.

It was Billie who roused first in the morning and helped her dress quickly so that she could return to her own apartment and prepare for the business day. As she dressed she found it difficult to recapture the sense of herself as the woman who was Rosenstein's new manager. It was as if she were awakening from a dream in which she was the real, essential Helena, someone she had lost touch with since the far-off days of her little girlhood.

She left with the taste of Billie's last kiss still in her mouth.

II
Helena

When Helena arrived at Rosenstein's somewhat later than usual, she walked through the early Monday morning bustle with a strange sensation that she had been far away for a long time. As she passed through the ground floor showroom she was greeted by the saleswomen setting up their counters for the day's business. She realized that they had not failed to note her late arrival and that they would probably speculate on the sort of weekend she must have spent to account for it. This idea made her a little self-conscious when she greeted Sherry, already busy at her desk. Sherry, whose social life was an active one, often told her about her own weekends, about the men she went with, the places they had been, her maneuvers in balancing the demands made on her, since she was a very popular girl. She lived in the suburbs and her parents, she said, worried about the hectic pace of her after-hours activities.

Now she gave Helena an arch look when she came in. "Oh, oh. Where did you go? I'll bet you had a big weekend."

Helena smiled. "What makes you think so?"

"You've never been as late as this before. In fact, nobody gets here before you do."

"Well," said Helena cheerfully, "things are different sometimes."

She went into her office and the habits of years asserted themselves as she stepped back into the quick-march that characterized her business day. But underneath she knew there was a well of psychic vigor that she had not been aware of before, an awakening in her emotional life that bubbled beneath her workaday activities.

In the course of the morning she found herself waiting for the elevator with Esther. Esther as usual had a great deal to say, much of which she scarcely heard. She became preoccupied by a great disquiet, as if Esther must surely know that she had spent the weekend with Billie and had gone to Michelle's house. This was ridiculous, of course, she told herself. It came from a sense of guilt, which was unaccountable. Was this paranoia, she wondered, and had it rubbed off on her from Billie?

110

Esther was saying, "Mrs. Alfred will be getting back in ten days. She's Billie's mother, you know. She's been on a trip to China, through the Panama Canal. She invited me to go with her but of course I can't leave my job here." Helena wondered if this was so or if Esther simply did not like to be away from the hub of things for so long. "I can't wait for her to be back. She'll have so much to tell."

Esther's voice pattered on. There was not much going on in this week before Thanksgiving, she said, as far as the directors were concerned. The press of holiday business was not felt up on the twelfth floor. Lionel had gone to his ranch in Arizona, as he always did at this time of year, and the other directors were otherwise busy.

"Billie is the only one who sticks around. She's always here — unless she's abroad. You'd think she had to earn her living. That's what her mother says. She thinks Billie ought to pay more attention to her social life. She'll never give up trying to make Billie into a social butterfly." Esther paused and her bright eyes fixed briefly on Helena's. "Billie isn't as young as she used to be, you know, and her mother wants her to get married. I think she'd like to have a grandchild. She thinks she's a failure, otherwise."

"Who? Billie?"

"Oh, no! Herself. She thinks she ought to be a matriarch by now, you know, but she can't be unless Billie has a family." Esther glanced at Helena again and laughed. "Now, you and I don't feel that way. We're working women. At least, I'm speaking for myself. Of course, you're young enough to make a change in your life, though it must be pretty difficult to combine a career like yours and a husband and

111

children. Some women do, though. I don't believe you've given much thought to that, have you? Or am I wrong?"

Helena recognized Esther's technique now: the apparently artless flow of talk that provided a net with which she sometimes caught the information she was fishing for. Helena said sharply, "No, I haven't. As you say, it is a difficult role, playing superwoman. I don't really have time for that sort of speculation."

Esther smiled, as if pleased at having drawn her out even so far. "Well, of course, Billie doesn't have that problem. Getting married and having children wouldn't get in the way of what she does here at Rosenstein's. That's just traditional for her, what her people have always done, looking after the business. So her mother gets pretty frustrated about her refusing to marry."

"Does she refuse to? It seems to me she might just not have met the man she wants to marry."

"Mr. Right? Now that's such an old-fashioned idea in this day and time, and a foolish one, too. Most women, if they decide they want to marry, have to make some compromises, don't they? There are plenty of men Billie can choose from — if she would even look at them. That's what her mother complains of. Billie doesn't pay attention to anybody. She's such a sweet, dear girl. She would never quarrel with her mother about anything. There's Moishe, for instance. He's her cousin. He's a little younger than she is but that doesn't matter. I think Mrs. Alfred would like it if Billie married him. He's such a nice boy and very clever. In fact, he's the family genius."

"She doesn't like him?"

"Oh, Billie likes him very much! They're like

favorite brother and sister. Of course, they don't agree about what's to be done about the store. I'm sure you've heard all about the dispute over whether Rosenstein's should stay the way it is or be swallowed up by a conglomerate. Well, Moishe is all for that and Billie doesn't like the idea at all."

"He doesn't have any connection with the store, does he? I know he is not in the Company."

"Oh, no. He's his father's right hand man in the banking company, even if he is only twenty-seven years old. He's Daniel's nephew and he likes to argue with him about Rosenstein's."

"He seems very young to be Lionel's son."

Esther giggled. "It's as if he would be his grandson, doesn't it? He was an afterthought, I suppose you'd say. He's much younger than his brothers."

The elevator finally came and they parted company. Helena thought, So this was the Moishe that Barton had said was his close friend.

Her euphoria lasted most of the day. It was only when she returned to her apartment in the evening that she felt a reaction. Billie had not been in the store that day. She had not expected her to be and yet she felt deprived, hungry for Billie's presence. As the evening hours wore on her happiness ebbed. When they had parted Billie had said nothing about when they would meet alone again. She tried to distract her thoughts by going over the day's problems but without success.

The phone rang about nine o'clock and her heart leapt. But it was her mother, calling from Texas. Her mother called frequently but no special day. She guessed that she called when she knew Helena's

113

business day was over and also — and importantly — when her stepfather was certain not to be present. Her parents had been divorced when she was eight years old and at first she had felt no particular unhappiness, because she had never seen much of her father, who resented the fact that she was not a son and largely ignored her. Alone with her mother she did not feel any emotional deprivation. But her mother could not reconcile herself to the idea that she had been rejected by her husband and suffered considerably until she succeeded in finding another. Helena knew she herself was not welcomed by her stepfather. He knew and disliked her father and was not pleased when her mother was granted sole custody of her. Her mother, apologetic for the situation in which she had placed her child, sought to assuage her feelings of rejection and abandonment by sending her to expensive boarding schools and summer camps. This solution only made Helena more resentful than ever so that when on occasion she and her mother were alone together it was impossible for them to recapture the easy closeness that had once existed between them. As she grew older she realized that however much her mother loved her, she would systematically put the wishes of her stepfather first.

Her mother had not liked it when she went to college and decided to make the business world her career and had gone on to do graduate work in business administration school. This was not the proper thing to do, her mother said. She was a girl of good family, with a better than average economic background. She would never have to work for a living. She should be following the route preferred by other girls like herself — a social whirl followed by a

114

suitable marriage. It was what she herself had done. She expected Helena to do likewise. Helena, with the cruelty begotten of her years of resentment, said bluntly that her mother could not really argue that way. Look at her own situation: divorced by one man and the insecure wife of another. She knew she had wounded her mother very deeply and would not have been surprised if this had caused a complete breach between them. But her mother, after a period of silence, again started to call her, ignoring the past. Since she herself had felt guilty and unhappy over the strain between them, she had been softer thereafter when they talked.

But her mother did not give up her attempts to persuade Helena to change some of her ways. She suspected that Helena, in college and afterwards, had experimented with sexual liaisons which she did not admit to, like all the other girls of her acquaintance. She worried because there was so little opportunity for her to monitor what Helena did. What troubled her most was Helena's rejection of the idea of marriage. Sometime in the future, Helena had said, insincerely, I might get married. But I've got more important things to do now. She despised women who were unable to separate their emotional lives from the world of business and professional demands — her friends who gave up careers to become wives and mothers. That was something men always cited as evidence that women were basically unreliable, unable to stick to the rigors of the competitive commercial world and therefore no better than dilettantes. Her mother despaired when she turned a deaf ear to all her protests — her emotional life would atrophy, she would find herself a disappointed, embittered woman with none of the family ties that made life worthwhile.

As usual, when Helena lifted the receiver and heard her mother's voice, she felt the familiar annoyance that always got in the way of their intimacy. The conversations had become false, she telling less than the truth of any situation, her mother vainly seeking to reach the reality of her life and thoughts, both of them aware that there lay a vast field of feelings, opinions, desires that neither of them could express.

Her mother's voice on the telephone said now, "Where have you been all weekend, Helena? I've tried and tried to reach you without success. I even called the phone company to see if anything was wrong."

"No, there's nothing the matter. I was with a friend over the weekend." She knew her mother wanted to know who the friend was, was he a suitable prospect as a husband, but she refused to satisfy that unspoken curiosity.

"Well, as long as you are all right. You've not been home every time I've called lately, so naturally I was alarmed."

"You needn't be. There's not likely to be anything wrong."

As usual, their conversation was desultory and, yes, pointless, thought Helena, except that they heard each other's voice and in that way kept in touch. There was nothing she could tell her mother about her working day, since her mother had no interest in and little understanding of how a business was run. And on the other hand she did not know any of her mother's friends and therefore could not ask about them. They never spoke about her stepfather unless her mother mentioned that he was away on business.

There was a further impediment to their conversations now: her mother did not understand why she had chosen to leave the company she had been with and go to Rosenstein's. She had tried to explain: I think it is time for me to make a change. I can't go ahead where I am. But her mother had countered: Aren't they Jewish people? And she had answered: Of course. They are a wealthy and well-established family here in New York. Her mother had said then: Well, won't you be rather a fish out of water? Impatiently she had answered: They've made me a very good offer. It is a challenge I want to meet; and she had refrained from any further discussion, since she was irritated by what she recognized as her mother's voicing of her stepfather's prejudices.

The next morning she went to see Daniel, with the figures, the charts, the forecasts that he expected her to bring to him. These meetings, which took place once or twice a week, had quickly become an important part of her routine at Rosenstein's. She had soon learned that he had no intention of really examining her conduct of the Company's business nor of questioning her in detail about what she presented to him. She came to value this evidence of his trust in her, for it was based on his shrewdness in sizing up her capability. She was also reminded of one of the basic tenets governing the life of a rising young executive: to be seen to be in the confidence of people with power in the organization added luster to her own status. She realized that Daniel's approval in hiring her and then in visibly relying on her was producing an effect on everyone in Rosenstein's. It was known that she had been invited to dinner — a kosher meal — at Daniel's house, and that Mrs. Daniel had invited her to a social function held by one of her charities. Helena supposed it was Esther who spread this information. Even Barton, when she came across him by accident, no longer patronized her but treated her with a careful outward respect.

As she was leaving Daniel's office she met a young man who stood aside to let her pass and then sprang forward to open the door of the outer office. He followed her through it and said, "You're Helena, aren't you?"

She turned to look at him and saw that he was about her height, probably her own age, and that he was very handsome. He wore a thin line of beard of glossy dark-brown hair, closely trimmed along his jawbone, contrasting with the clear, rose-flushed sallowness of his skin. At once she thought, "He's a Rosenstein, surprising herself with the quickness of her ability now to recognize the often indefinable quality that set off members of the family. His dark eyes were fixed on her boldly. Before she could reply, he said, "I'm Moishe Rosenstein. Sorry I wasn't here when you first came. I've just got back from Japan."

She noticed that he skipped what he considered nonessentials, that he knew her name and who she was and that he assumed that she would recognize him. He went on talking. "Daniel keeps you pretty busy, doesn't he? He's enjoying himself now. For the last two years he's been complaining about being worked to death." All the while he talked, his bright, inquisitive eyes were on her. She knew he had taken

118

in her appearance, her clothes, her manner, the way she carried her briefcase, in a lightning glance as he followed her out of Daniel's outer office.

The thought crossed her mind that perhaps he had known she would be in Daniel's office and had waited for her to come out. She remembered what Barton had said, that the Rosensteins had a highly efficient grapevine that carried news among them. Esther, no doubt, had told him all he wanted to know about her.

It was now past noon — she had been with Daniel for two hours — and he said, "How about having lunch with me? I'd like to catch up with the latest about what poor old Rosenstein's is doing."

She did not want to go to lunch with him. Her head was filled with the discussion she had had with Daniel and she longed to get back to her office and sort it all out. But she realized that that would not be the best thing to do. So she compromised by saying, "I have to get back to my office right away. I've been gone for quite a while."

But he said smoothly, "How about an hour from now? I'll come for you in your office." He raised his wrist to look at his watch. "We can eat in the Elysian Room. That will not take much time."

Reluctantly she agreed. The hour vanished. She became aware that he was in her outer office, chatting with Sherry. She sighed and decided that she could make up the loss by putting in another hour at the end of the day.

The Elysian Room was almost empty when they entered. Monique came over to them immediately and exclaimed, "Why, Moishe! You're back!"

He spoke with careless good nature. "Oh, I'm just

back. I've got the Japanese under control. Decided I'd better come back and see what's being done to bring old Rosenstein's into the modern age."

Monique laughed and led them to a table.

Moishe had plenty to say, ranging over a wide variety of topics, and Helena thankfully left the conversation to him. At first he talked about Japan, explaining that his father had sent him there to see if they should set up a branch office or join with a Japanese firm. He talked about the Japanese and how they differed from Americans and how he liked some of their social customs, their feeling for the aesthetics of existence. He means Japanese women, thought Helena. She learned that he was a fitness buff, a skiing enthusiast, that he liked to jog in Central Park when he was in Manhattan, that he liked travelling, that he had spent several years of his adolescence in a Swiss school. Then he asked if she skied and when she said No, asked her what sports she liked. When she said tennis, he asked whether she had played in intercollegiate sports.

"No," said Helena. "I never seemed to have the time for consistent training. I only play now for exercise. I don't have time for anything else."

"Rosenstein's keeps your nose to the grindstone. Well, you ought to take a stand about that. You have to put a value on yourself, on your own time, you know." He went on talking in a fatherly tone that made her smile inwardly, as if he wanted to pass on to her his own wealth of experience. It made him seem even younger in her eyes than he actually was.

Then, finishing the last bite of steak on his plate, he said, "You ought to get Billie to play tennis with you."

The sound of Billie's name disconcerted her. He took her reaction for surprise and said quickly, "Billie's gone to seed now, but she was an intercollegiate champion when she was at Smith. You'd be doing her a favor if you made her play. She needs to lose weight. She's lazy."

He's the second person to tell me that Billie is lazy, she thought. "I'm not in the same class with her, then."

"She's too out of shape to give you much challenge. She's getting to look like a matron — a Rosenstein matron, like her mother. Maybe you can do something about that."

Helena laughed this time. "Why should I? She probably wouldn't appreciate it."

He let the subject drop and asked suddenly, "What college did you go to?"

Ah ha, thought Helena; unlike Billic, he has not read my resumé. She told him and answered some more rapid-fire questions about her decision to follow a business career, why had she decided to be a manager, what led her to Rosenstein's, what did she think of the present state of the Company, how she liked working with Daniel, did she find any difficulty dealing with the older employees. She fended off his questions as best she could, and presently he left this subject and started to talk about himself, why he preferred banking — it wasn't just because he was Lionel's son, he said — it was where the excitement lay in the modern business world, what were the hazards of dealing with older men who were not altogether ready for change. There were a lot of Rosensteins, he said, in the professions and in the arts and scientific fields. But that sort of thing

121

wasn't for him. Only the financial market interested him.

"I had my own consulting service when I was fourteen," he said matter-of-factly. "My grandfather was still alive then. He let me try out in his office just to see how good I could be. He was satisfied."

He was quick-witted, with a sharply humorous tongue, and he made her laugh till she had to drop her head in her hand to recover. She was aware of the intense interest their tête-à-tête aroused in Monique, in the waitresses standing idly along one wall of the almost deserted dining room. Recovering a little, she glanced up to see the delighted expression on his handsome, mobile face, realizing instantly that he was pleased at having made her laugh and at the attention they were getting. Moishe, she decided, would never be unaware of the impression he was making on an audience, especially an audience of women.

He leaned over towards her. "How about a night out with me sometime? We can go anywhere you like."

He watched her closely as she sought quickly for the right excuse. He was a charming companion and besides that, he was Lionel's son and she did not want to risk ill-feeling of any sort with any of the Rosensteins. Finally she said Yes, warning herself to be wary.

When she got home that evening, her first impulse was to call Billie. But then she checked herself. She really could not seek advice from Billie about dealing with Moishe. She had only a vague idea of what the relationship between them really was.

She spent the evening hoping Billie would call. But the phone did not ring.

When he came to get her the following evening his swift glance, as it had the first time he saw her, took in her dress and accessories. He obviously had the Rosenstein sensitivity to a woman's appearance. Bless Rachel again, thought Helena, confident that there could be nothing lacking in the impression she made. They went to a nightclub she had never been to before and then to the loft-studio of another Rosenstein cousin, a woman sculptor. Moishe was driving his own car, a Porsche. Evidently the expense of operating a car in Manhattan did not concern him. The loft party was noisy and crowded and she began to wonder how much of the night she would have left to recover in for the next day's work. Even when she was younger she had not enjoyed all-night parties, since she had never acquired a taste for drinking or experimenting with drugs. At last, Moishe, who like herself drank very little, asked, Would she like to leave?

He drove up through Manhattan and then turned south again along the express highway and Riverside Drive — a very roundabout way to her apartment, and the significance of the maneuver was not lost on her. Rapidly she reviewed the options open to her, the things she could say, could do to extricate herself from what she foresaw. It was some time since she had found herself in such a situation. Then she had been younger, less fixed upon the way she wanted to go. Now there was a great deal more weighing in the balance. She had a reputation to maintain which would not be enhanced by rumors that she was having an affair with the youngest and most eligible of the Rosenstein heirs.

She did not need to talk. Moishe did that. Adeline, he said, only gave such parties now and then. She was really a hardworking woman. She used these bashes to keep up her end of her social life. Then he grew silent. Though it was almost December, the night was mild. They drove through the nearly deserted streets, the street lamps occasionally illuminating a human figure — some homeless derelict, she supposed. It must be getting close to daybreak. She guessed that Moishe's unusual quietness had a purpose: to create a sense of intimacy between them in the muted darkness.

When they finally reached her apartment house he parked his car in the only available space, in front of the door. Obviously he was not concerned that it was illegal. He got out of the car and determinedly followed close behind her when she got out her key and punched out the combination on the board that released the inner door. When she entered the downstairs lobby he stepped in with her and followed her into the elevator, without saying a word, and down the corridor to the door of her own apartment. Desperate, she stood squarely in the doorway and said, "Not tonight, Moishe," and closed the door on his disbelieving face.

When she got into bed she surprised herself by falling asleep almost at once, a deep sleep that lasted beyond her usual time for getting up, so that she had to scramble to reach her office within an hour of her usual routine. Sherry greeted her with a number of reminders of things to be done, watching her covertly out of the corner of her eye. It bothered her that she had become the object of special admiration and concern to Sherry. It meant that any deviation in her usual schedule focussed Sherry's attention on her. Sherry confided in her the details of her own affairs. No live-in boyfriend for her, Sherry said firmly; there were too many traps in that situation. What if she tired of one man and wanted to try out another? When she talked about these things she watched Helena closely, eager for any indication of a similar wish to confide. This morning, since it was the second time Helena had been late arriving, Sherry lingered for a moment as if to elicit an explanation, but Helena, aware of her intent, ignored her.

But in the afternoon she was surprised to hear Rachel's voice speaking to Sherry and then to see Rachel walk into her office. Rachel never waited for Sherry to announce her.

Helena sat back in her chair and asked, "How was the trip?"

"Oh, the usual sort of thing. Everybody wanted to hear the latest gossip from Europe in the fashion world. They held the show in the newest luxury motel in town — you know the sort of thing. They were impressed with our clothes." She looked down at herself in satisfaction.

Helena nodded, knowing the allure that Rachel's social acquaintance and sophisticated mode of life had for many women who knew her only by reputation. She also knew that no one was less bemused than Rachel herself with the glitter of the high fashion world she represented.

Rachel, noticing the expression on Helena's face, said, "Now, just bear in mind that gossip is the life-blood of the social world. Where would we all be

125

— yes, even Rosenstein's itself — without it? It is a natural force. You have to take it into account. Old Leah understood that very well. She taught me how it should be used."

She gazed at Helena for a moment and then said, "Talking about gossip — I've come back to a buzzing hive — all about you." She broke off and stepped quietly across the room and gently closed the door. When she came back she sat down in the chair opposite.

"It seems Moishe is about to make a conquest of you. The women can't talk about anything else."

Helena answered defensively, "I only met him three days ago."

"Moishe is noted for being a very fast worker. You had lunch with him in the Elysian Room within minutes of meeting him for the first time."

"It was his suggestion."

"Well, naturally. He wanted everybody to see. And then you had dinner with him and went to Adeline's party. My God, Helena!"

"Is that so extraordinary?"

Rachel gave her a long look. "Do I have to tell you what this means — Moishe Rosenstein and the new woman manager of Rosenstein's! If the significance has escaped you, it hasn't anybody else."

"It has no significance at all, so far as I am concerned."

"Well, perhaps not." Rachel looked at her again closely.

"Rachel, I'm truly not interested in having an affair with anyone, including Moishe." As she spoke she thought of Billie. But Billie was not the subject of an affair.

Rachel was still gazing at her with a certain skepticism. "I suppose I can believe you. But Esther is in a lather of excitement. She's got you married to Moishe already and Mrs. Alfred in a nervous breakdown. I pointed out to her that Moishe isn't thinking of marrying. Moishe just likes to sleep with women — lots of women."

"Mrs. Alfred? Is she back? And why should she be so upset?"

"No, she's not back yet. But in a few days. Moishe is her fair-haired boy. She'd have a fit if he married a shikseh. Excuse me. That was not nice. That's what she'd call you. It means a woman who is not Jewish. Mrs. Alfred lives in terror of the idea that Moishe will be captured by a Gentile."

"He's not her son. Why should she be so concerned?"

"No, he's not her son, but he's her ideal boy, the one she would have liked to have had. She'd like him to marry Billie. The fact that he is younger doesn't make any difference. He's always been a prodigy — years ahead of the average bright boy in school. He can think circles around men twice his age and they admit it."

Dismayed, Helena was silent. Rachel watched her for a moment. She seemed to guess her feelings. She said sympathetically, "He's hard to deal with because he can be very seductive,. He's used to having his own way. He's convinced that any woman will be only too delighted to give in to him. He'd sleep with me if I let him — something new, sleeping with a woman old enough to be his mother." She laughed her rough-edged, ribald laugh. "You didn't let him in?"

127

"No, I did not."

"Well, it's Daniel you'll have to be careful about. Remember, he's narrow minded. He won't like any suggestion that you could give in to Moishe."

"What about Esther? Will Esther talk to Daniel about these stories?"

"Oh, Daniel doesn't pay any attention to Esther. He always rejects anything she says. But Mrs. Alfred is something else. She'll be back in about a week. The trouble is that Mrs. Alfred thinks Moishe is irresistible. And she'll be ready to believe that you are playing around with Moishe because you think this will forward your advancement at Rosenstein's. No, don't get angry with me. I don't believe that. But Mrs. Alfred would not believe that any woman, no matter who, would refuse to use sexual allure as a means of getting what she wants. She herself is a virtuous woman but she knows how to tantalize men."

"Well, what am I to do about it, then?"

"Nothing, right now. Perhaps Billie can take care of the situation, as far as her mother is concerned."

When Rachel left, Helena tried to bury the turmoil in her own feelings by concentrating on the detail of her work. She was relieved when she paid her next visit to Daniel to notice no difference in his manner towards her. Whatever was being circulated through the store had not filtered in to him.

Through that day and the next she heard nothing from Moishe and she began to wonder whether his feeling of resentment had grown to the point of preventing him from approaching her again. Friday evening, when she sat in her apartment in a cloud of depression, unwilling even to think of getting herself

128

something to eat, the phone rang. She looked at it for a moment, fearful that it was Moishe. But when she picked up the receiver it was Billie's voice that she heard. Hearing it she felt a sudden lifting of the unhappiness that weighed on her, as if in a moment the world, her world, had come out of shadow into sunshine.

"Billie, where have you been?"

"Nowhere in particular," Billie's voice was tranquil.

"I've called you several times."

"Have you?"

"You've not been in Rosenstein's."

"That's true."

"But why haven't you called me?"

There was a pause before Billie said, "This is only Friday."

"It seems much longer than that."

"Yes, it does, doesn't it?" Then, after another pause, Billie said, "Come to me tomorrow afternoon. Come when you're through at the store."

Saturday afternoon, when Helena arrived at her door, Billie pulled her into the apartment and kissed her. Helena saw that she was dressed in a blue silk tunic and a pair of white satin trousers gathered in above her ankles, clothes that undoubtedly came from the After Hours boutique at Rosenstein's. As they embraced Helena breathed in the fresh seductive scent of Billie's soft pink flesh. She marvelled at how abruptly her own dark mood could change so rapidly under the influence of Billie's presence.

Releasing her Billie said, "Come and have a drink. It will relax you."

Helena looked at her anxiously. Billie was paler

than usual and more languid in her movements, but there was no smell of liquor on her breath.

A small smile appeared on Billie's face. "No, I'm not on a binge now. It's quite safe for me to have a drink, since you are here."

"I would not want to start you off," said Helena, candidly.

Billie reached up to take her head in her hands and kiss her again. "I drank too much for two days. But it seemed pointless. I stopped."

Helena watched as she went to the liquor cabinet and got out glasses and a bottle of scotch. She placed them on the coffee table in front of the sofa.

"Shall I get the ice?"

Billie nodded and sat down on the sofa.

In the kitchen Helena took the ice from the ice-maker and put it in the ice bucket. She felt at sea in a confusion of emotions. It amazed her how she had felt at first this surge of happiness and reviving self-confidence, being here with Billie. The strain, the uncertainty, the foreboding that had ridden her for the last two days seemed suddenly set aside, and yet these feelings were still there, lurking under the euphoria. She glanced through the doorway into the living room. Billie sat quietly, as if lost in thought.

She looked up as Helena approached with the ice bucket. She said, "I did call you Wednesday evening but you did not answer."

"I was out, with your cousin Moishe."

Billie did not look surprised. "Moishe got back from Japan on Sunday. He came to see me Monday."

Helena demanded sharply, "Did you know that he made a date to take me out Wednesday night?"

"No, I didn't. But when you didn't answer I

thought that was what he had probably done. He took you to Adeline's, didn't he?" And then he went home with you."

"He stopped at my apartment door."

Billie laughed, her soft little laugh. Her eyes sparkled and for the first time since Helena had arrived she seemed the normal Billie. "So. That much for Moishe's blitz-kreig. Usually his attack is more successful. But that's only a temporary setback. He's good at getting around obstacles — such as a stubborn woman."

She was looking at Helena through lowered eyelashes, her head tipped back. Helena said angrily, "Don't talk to me that way."

But Billie continued to gaze at her. "When he came here on Monday he wouldn't talk about anything but you. He'd been hearing things from his friends in the banking business about the new lady manager at Rosenstein's. Usually he is bored by news about Rosenstein's. Nothing could interest him about such a backward place except the announcement that we're going to sell out. But — I think it must have been Esther who wrote and told him about you. She whetted his appetite. You know, Esther has a knack for stirring things up."

"Why should he be asking you about me?"

Billie smiled her small smile. "I *am* a director of Rosenstein's."

"He could have asked Daniel. Or his father, Lionel."

Billie went on smiling. "Moishe is a very bright boy. Also, he and I have always had a special understanding. He knows very well he would find out more from me — especially about things that really

131

interest him. And he wouldn't want to rouse suspicions. He likes to carry on his affairs outside the family limelight."

"Billie, why do you assume he wants an affair with me?"

"He gives every indication of it, doesn't he?"

Exasperated, Helena said, "Billie, this is a serious situation for me. I don't want an affair with anyone, especially someone connected with my business life."

"You mean, you don't want people saying you're going to the top at Rosenstein's by sleeping with Moishe."

Angry, Helena pulled away from her. "Moishe can do me a lot of harm. He can make it impossible for me to stay at Rosenstein's."

"And now you want to stay."

"Of course. To leave would do serious damage to my business future."

"Moishe doesn't think about that aspect. Most men don't care about how their actions will affect a woman's future. He's only interested in testing himself out. I think he is looking for a woman who can outdo him, but he's sure that she doesn't exist. He just wants to try you out."

"Buy why should he pick on me?"

"You don't know why?" Billie smiled again. "Of course you know why. In the first place, you're a woman doing something that's not been done before — managing Rosenstein's. Moishe thinks he despises Rosenstein's but he's just as much affected by the mystique as any of us. He heard all about your business competence but what did he find when he saw you? Honey, you're a stunner and you know it.

That's probably part of your problem in getting people to take you seriously, isn't it?"

"Billie, I haven't time for these games. How can I get rid of him?"

Billie was thoughtful. "Moishe is a nuisance. He can make himself a bigger nuisance. But he is not all that important. Daniel does not approve of Moishe. Moishe makes fun of Daniel behind his back, but it is Daniel who controls Rosenstein's and will, at least as long as Rosenstein's stays the way it is. The main thing is that Daniel must not get the idea that you're running around with Moishe, for whatever reason. He must believe the truth, that Moishe is chasing you and that you're not encouraging him. It's always hard to make any man believe that a woman does not want to be chased, that she would rather be doing something else.

Helena said bitterly, "That there must be something the matter with her, that she's not normal."

Billie murmured, "The biological pattern, or so they say. But Daniel believes in virtue, in chastity. You've got to see as much of Daniel as possible. The more he sees you, the more he will believe in you. Your honesty shows through, honey."

"But what about your mother? Rachel says she dotes on Moishe and will always believe what he tells her."

Billie's eyebrows went up. "Rachel?"

"She is back. She came to my office today. She came to tell me all the rumors she had heard about me and Moishe."

"Yes, I know she is back. She called me today.

What she says is true. Mamma thinks Moishe is irresistible to any woman. But she wouldn't want him marrying you."

"Marrying me? I don't intend to marry! Billie, you can't take that seriously!"

Billie did not answer. She drained the last of her glass and then said, "We'd better go and fetch some other clothes for you. You're staying here with me tonight, aren't you? Tomorrow we're going to dinner with Michelle. She invited me and I said Yes for you."

The distance to Helena's apartment was not great and they strolled along Madison Avenue looking in the windows of small shops at antiques, china, leather goods, even men's accessories, with preoccupied inattention. Helena's thoughts were on Billie. The more she saw of Billie, the more time she spent in her company, the stronger became her feeling of complete harmony with her, and at the same time, she was aware that there was a great deal in Billie that she did not understand. What went on in Billie preoccupied her as she had never been preoccupied by anyone else.

When they reached her apartment and she was gathering together the garments she wanted to take with her, she came upon her tennis rackets and shoes and set them out of the way so as to reach a small suitcase.

Billie picked up a racket and swung it. Inspired, Helena said, "Shall we go and play? We can get a court at my club. I need the exercise."

Billie did not answer at once but stood balancing the racket in her hands.

Helena persisted. "I know you play. Moishe told me so."

"He also told you that I should play now so as to lose weight."

"Yes, he did. But I'm not suggesting it now for that reason. I just want to play."

Billie put the racket down. "Don't be so touchy, honey. Yes, let's go and play."

Billie, it turned out, still had her own rackets. So they went back to her place to fetch them and then to the health club. At first Billie played badly, uncoordinated in her swing and sluggish in reaching for balls. But presently she seemed to regain her skill and Helena shortly became aware that she was playing with someone quite beyond herself in ability and experience. At the end of an hour she was badly beaten and out of sorts.

As they sat down for a breather she said, "You might have told me that I'm not in your league, that you could beat the pants off me with one hand, even now."

Billie looked at her in surprise and said nothing.

"Oh, Billie, I'm sorry, but it's very humiliating. I thought I was pretty good."

"Well, you are. It's not important, honey. It's just a game." Billie reached out and covered her hand with her own. "It's just that you always have to try to be the best, isn't it?"

Feeling childish, Helena answered, "Yes. I suppose that's true."

"Well, then, let's try again," said Billie equably.

But though they played for another hour, Billie won every set easily. Tired, they spoke very little on the way back to Billie's apartment. When they were inside Billie took her in her arms. She murmured, "You don't have to fight against me in anything, honey. You don't have to prove anything to me."

Helena answered with a little sigh into her neck.

The afternoon had waned while they were at the health club. They showered and changed their clothes. Then Billie said, "You fix us a drink. I'll get dinner. I have things ready. Come into the kitchen with me."

Helena followed her and saw her take prepared dishes out of the refrigerator and set them on the counter while the oven heated. She began to prepare a salad. Helena watched her in astonishment. It had not occurred to her that Billie could cook.

Billie said, pointing, "You can set the table. The dishes and silverware are there."

Helena obeyed, carrying the things into the living room and preparing the small table where they had sat to eat the first time she had come to Billie's apartment. When she returned to the kitchen, Billie had set the condiments and the napkins on a tray for her to take in. A tantalizing aroma was filling the kitchen.

Billie stopped what she was doing to hug her again and kiss her.

Helena said, "I am very confused, Billie. This is so different from anything that has ever happened to me before. I don't really know you and yet —" She could not find the words to say what was in her heart.

Billie put her arms around her neck. "My honey. I feel as if I have known you all my life and yet as if you're not real. How can you be? How can anything that is so wonderful really be?"

The oven bell sounded behind them and they

parted, to fetch the dinner to the table. They ate at first in silence. After a while, Billie said, "Daniel adores my mother. Anything within reason she wants he tries to give her. He thinks of her as someone to be protected and pampered. But she rarely says anything to him about business. He doesn't expect her to, because he doesn't think it is a proper sphere for women. His grandmother, Old Leah, was a special case, outside the normal. Now that she is safely dead he can forget the things that shocked him while she was alive — that she was not a devout Jew, that she had radical sympathies in social reform and politics, that she could always get the better of men when she was pitted against them. She was his grandmother, she created Rosenstein's, and that is all that needs to be remembered."

Helena said, sopping up the last of the sauce on her plate, "Billie, this is delicious. People have said to me, though, that Daniel always listens to you."

"Yes, I've trained him to. It's become a habit now. He thinks I take after my grandfather Moses and Old Leah, that I have the right ideas for Rosenstein's in my blood. My mother thinks that, too."

"Then why have you never tried to run Rosenstein's yourself?"

Billie did not answer right away. "Because I've never done anything systematically in my life."

"And why not, Billie?"

Billie put her elbows on the table and propped her head on her hands. After a long moment she said, "Perhaps you'll be able to tell me sometime."

"If it doesn't get too late. Something must be done soon if Rosenstein's is to be kept as it is."

"That's what Moishe keeps saying." He is an

investment banker and he thinks he has the answer
to everything. He has always been led to believe that
he is the greatest in everything, you know."

"So I gather from what he says himself. But why
don't you act, Billie?"

Billie merely shook her head and got up and
began to gather up their empty plates. Together they
cleared the table and filled the dishwasher. When
they returned to the living room they sat together on
the sofa for a while before going to bed. When they
lay in bed, Helena suddenly asked the question that
came belatedly into her head, "What if Moishe comes
to see you?"

Billie answered calmly, "I'm not answering the
intercom. They won't let him come upstairs if I don't.
He'll think I've had too much to drink. He won't try
to check that out. He hates that sort of thing. He
always stays away when he thinks I'm drinking."

"What if something should happen to you
sometime?"

"It would be my mother who would come to find
out."

Sunday morning was cloudy and cold, with the
threat of snow, and they stayed indoors as they had
the first time they had spent the weekend together.
Again Helena felt the habit of being always keyed up,
always striving to make every moment count,
dissolving in the blissful peace of Billie's company.
Late in the afternoon they walked to Michelle's
house, briskly because of the cold.

Michelle awaited them in the drawing room
furnished with massive dark furniture brightened by
the glow of an electric fire in the fireplace. She came
across the big room to greet them. She wore a long

138

robe of quilted silk with sleeves that hung down to her fingertips, the nails of which flashed a fiery red — more brilliant than Rachel's, Helena thought. She gave Billie a swift kiss and reached out her hand to Helena and then led them to the ring of sofa and chairs around the fireplace. Marie appeared with a tray and Helena accepted the drink offered her.

Michelle was a rapid talker, used to an audience, ready to dwell at length on her own interests and activities. But suddenly she said, "So you are going to revive Rosenstein's. Do you like the challenge?"

"It is more of one that I knew at the beginning."

"Well, you have a formidable job — to recreate something that was unique when it first came into being — and which some people say is now an anachronism."

Helena merely nodded.

"You know, I take very little interest in business. I am content to leave that to Billie. However, I see this as an artistic enterprise — the revival of an art form, if you will. Old Leah would probably appreciate that point of view."

"You remember your great grandmother, don't you?"

"Oh, yes. I was twenty-five when she died. She lived to be almost ninety, you know, and her mind was never clouded. I will tell you an anecdote about her. I was unhappy in college, yet my father insisted that I must have a formal education, like my brothers. But I felt I was wasting my time. I wanted to go to art school. So I went to see Old Leah and told her how unhappy I was. She said that I must have the opportunity to do what I felt I was meant to do. Of course, when she spoke everyone had to

139

agree. My father was overruled. I spent my four years in art school. I cannot thank her enough, even now. If I was religiously inclined, I'd say prayers for her every night. That would have amused her. But she did understand the yearnings of one's heart."

"Rachel has told me quite a lot about her."

"Ah, Rachel." Michelle did not look at Billie, who was sitting beside her on the sofa, but Helena had the feeling that some understanding flowed between them. "I've wondered what Rachel would have been if she had not become a Rosenstein apprentice in her teens. She's an artist at heart. What extraordinary things she can do with clothes and women's love of fashion! She is a true disciple of Old Leah's."

"Esther told me how Old Leah came to establish her business. She must have had great determination."

"Oh, she did! It is a romantic story, isn't it? Such enormous changes have taken place in the retailing of women's clothes since the beginning of this century. That, of course, is the whole problem with Rosenstein's. Can it survive under modern circumstances?"

"I believe it can, if certain things are done."

"And you think you can bring this about? I shall be interested to watch you. Then Esther has been friendly?"

"Oh, yes." Under the strong pull of Michelle's personality, Helena felt a little desperate. Michelle's luminous green eyes were fixed on her.

Then, as if to change the subject, Michelle took a ring off her finger, a wide band encrusted with tiny jewels — rubies, diamonds, amethysts, sapphires. "Do you like this?" She held it out to Helena.

"Why, it is lovely. Is it Italian?"

"That is a good guess. No, it isn't Italian. It is Arlette's work. I think she is getting better all the time. I am proud of Arlette. You met her the first time Billie brought you. She is a discovery of mine. I teach classes in design, you know, and the applied arts. Arlette was one of my pupils. I think she has unusual gifts — great creativity, so I encouraged her. She has quite a growing reputation now as a designer. In fact, she cannot be with us today because she has an exhibit at a small gallery."

"That must be very gratifying to her."

"Yes. Soon Rosenstein's will be offering some of her work." Michelle slipped the ring back on her finger.

Helena did not reply and Michelle went on talking.

"Has Rachel ever shown you the design books created by Old Leah? No? They belong to me. My great grandmother gave them to me because of my interest in design — all kinds of design — clothes, house decoration, jewelry. Of course, the appreciation of design was the essence of her success and she knew it. These books show it — the little sketches she made for babies' things and wedding dresses when she first went into business, the other sketches she made when she used to go to Paris to see the new creations of the great couturieres. But then she had many gifts — an instinctive knowledge of how to present something so that the viewer was seduced, how to manage people so that they could function at their maximum. Her business shrewdness was only a part of the whole. And she knew how to rein in her own impatience with other people's slowness, vanity,

141

arrogance, stupidity. She could always foresee how someone would react to a situation and how she should act to forestall them, if she wanted to. People became superstitious about her power. So she gave me the design books while she was still living. She did not leave them to me in her will because she knew that my grandfather and his brothers, her sons, would have caused trouble. They were angry enough as it was when they learned she had given them to me. My grandfather thought they ought to go to a museum. Well, they will eventually. They are wonderful to study. Old Leah had kept the designs she had used from the very beginning — little sketches, some of them, on odd scraps of paper. Sometime later she had them bound into covers, so that they are a kind of history of her maturing thought."

Helena looked at Billie, but Billie gazed steadily into the flickering light of the electric fire. It was as if Billie had brought her here into Michelle's presence and abandoned her. She made an effort to assert herself and said, "What would she think of the present situation?"

Michelle was thoughtful, turning her long, narrow face away from her. "When I remember her best she was in her eighties and had given up the real management of the store, leaving it in the hands of Moses, Billie's grandfather. But then he died, just a year before she did, and she took over again, but with Daniel, her grandson, to help her. He was the only one who had a dedication to the store. Given the present situation, she might well agree to selling the store. She was a very practical woman and she felt the loss of Moses. Without him she probably felt that

142

the reason for keeping it going was considerably diminished. Billie was just a child then and she could not have known that Billie would have her feeling for it."

"Then she would agree with Moishe."

Michelle suddenly frowned. "Moishe?"

"Moishe is eager to sell Rosenstein's to a conglomerate."

"Billie has mentioned that to me. Are you in favor of that?"

Cautiously, Helena responded, "I can't really say at this point. I do think that his plan would result in a greater income for all the shareholders."

"I haven't seen Moishe since he was a child. But I understand he is considered in the family to be a financial genius. Do you think he will succeed in bringing this about?"

"I believe he would need your cooperation to bring this about. You are a shareholder, aren't you?"

There was a flash in Michelle's eyes. "Yes. He won't get it unless Billie agrees."

So that's that, thought Helena. Her brief glance at Billie brought no response. She decided she had better go no further in that direction and waited for Michelle.

Michelle said, "You know, Billie takes after Old Leah in other ways, too. Old Leah was very well known in our community for the work she did for charitable and educational causes. Billie does that, too, especially for the kind of organization that is made up of people with more goodwill and kind intentions than a sense of business. You can imagine how useful she is to them. She hasn't told you that, has she?"

"No, she hasn't," said Helena.

"And she never would. Well, I think we shall go to dinner."

All through the dinner and the rest of the evening Michelle said nothing more about Rosenstein's or her family. She talked ably about a great many things, and Helena found herself sinking into a state of wonder, bemused by the woman herself, the faintly perfumed air of her house, the seduction of her voice. She was relieved when Billie said it was time to leave.

Back in Billie's apartment, Helena was aware that they had returned from Michelle's with a heightened sense of each other. It was a feeling, Helena mused as they began to undress, engendered by the sensuousness of Michelle's house, as if its luxuriousness awakened the stirrings of bodily pleasure beyond mere warmth and comfort. There was something about Michelle herself that aided in this. She was not a handsome woman; she could never have been, even in youth. But Michelle's angular body gave off some sort of aura that in an insidious and not immediately realized way aroused sexual desire. And she does this, thought Helena, deliberately. She intends to invite you, to stir your senses, lead you in the first steps of seduction. The invitation was there when she turned her long face, framed by the dangling earrings that glittered in the lamplight, toward you; an invitation difficult to resist, partly because you were only slowly aware that the invitation was there.

Helena raised her eyes to find Billie looking at her with a faint smile on her face. She realized then that for several moments she had paused while taking off her panties, that she had been standing there with the garment in her hands, prevented from completing her action by the force of her recollection of Michelle.

Billie said lightly, "Michelle is dangerous, isn't she?"

Helena blushed. "How did you know what I was thinking?"

Billie laughed at her. "Because I know Michelle. Because I know you. Because I knew what Michelle wanted to find out about you, and because she did."

Hotly Helena answered, "She asked me very little about myself. I didn't tell her anything about myself."

Billie, still in her bra and bikini, came over to her and took her head in her hands. "Honey, there is nothing you could have told her that would have told her what she wanted to find out. She had to find out by seeing you, testing you in a way you would not be conscious of. You're transparent, you know. At least, to someone who wants to know about what you are inside — not in your business self. And Michelle always wants to know about someone who is important to me. She doesn't trust my judgment in picking friends."

"That's why you took me there this afternoon."

"Of course."

She moved away from Helena, and Helena, dropping her last garment on a nearby chair, stretched out on the bed. The touch of Billie's hands had driven all other considerations out of her mind. The afternoon with Michelle faded away. She watched as Billie came toward her in the muted light of the bedside lamp. She reached out to draw Billie closer. She was intoxicated by the sensation of her fingers touching that fragrant pink glowing flesh. There was immense pleasure in the feeling that she was rightfully where she was, that she was to Billie what no one else could be. How had this intimacy come about? This destruction of physical and mental barriers between them? The first time she had gone to bed with Billie their act of love had happened so naturally that she had not even been aware of thought, had not even stopped to fear frustrated desire. That fear had been part of the reason she had shunned intimacy. Her attempts at it had been hollow, unfulfilling, repelling.

But Billie's loving, insistent fingers moving gently over her breasts, her stomach, the small of her back, the insides of her thighs, aroused her to a demand she could not deny. When Billie pressed against her the tickle of Billie's crisp red-gold curls drove her further, beyond any more reflection.

It was only later, when she was up and dressed, ready to go back to her own apartment to change her clothes before going to her office — it was after all Monday morning and the return to the working world loomed before her — that she thought about herself and Billie. She sat in the armchair and watched Billie, naked, pad back and forth from the bathroom to pick out a pair of panties from a drawer and put them on. She felt at ease here, as she had never really felt at ease anywhere else since she had been a little girl with her mother, her nerves relaxed, her mind at rest, with none of the vague forebodings and anxieties that usually lay beneath her dealings with other people, the feelings of inadequacy that underlay the driving ambition she had carefully cultivated to disguise this uncertainty.

146

Billie put on a pair of dark blue slacks. She glanced at Helena and smiled.

Helena said impulsively, "Billie, I feel wonderful, as if I can take anything that comes without worrying about it."

Billie continued to smile. "They say, don't they, that having sex is a real calmer of nerves, destroyer of inhibitions."

Offended, Helena shot back, "Is that what you think — just sex — with anybody?"

Billie reached over to touch her. "No, of course not. That would mean nothing to me. It would have the opposite effect — make me unhappy, frustrated, certain that nothing meant anything. If sex isn't the fulfillment of intimacy with somebody you love, it must be a great annihilator of one's value for one's self. It would be a triviality, like most things we do in life."

Helena got up from her chair as Billie continued to dress, pulling a white satin blouse over her head. Her movements were unhurried but decisive. When she had clasped a couple of bracelets around her wrists and glanced into the mirror at her hair, she came over to Helena and put her arms around her. She said, "You may not hear from me for a little while. My mother gets back Wednesday. I've got to get ready for her."

"This puts an end to your freedom."

Billie said equably, ignoring the accusation in her voice, "Not altogether. It simply means I must plan things a little differently." She kept her arms linked loosely around Helena's neck. "You've never told your mother that the reason you don't want to get married is that you prefer women."

"No, of course not."

"Well, neither have I. Has your mother ever guessed?"

"No, I don't think she would ever think of it. Beyond that, she has not known that much about my private life since I was a child. You could say I left home when she remarried."

Billie nodded and kissed her as she released her.

Helena noticed that before they walked out of the apartment, Billie moved slowly around, surveying the bedroom, the bathroom, the living room with calmly vigilant eyes. At last she gave a little nod. "Everything of yours is in your overnight case. There isn't anything left about."

Suddenly uneasy, Helena said, "How about the people at the reception desk — the security guards? Is it likely that your mother might find out from them that you had someone staying here with you overnight?"

Billie considered and then answered, "I've wondered. This has never happened before, you know. You're the one and only visitor I've had to stay overnight. And I don't think my mother would go to the lengths of questioning them. And Elise wouldn't think of talking to strangers. Esther never comes here. So we're safe, at least for now."

An hour or so later, walking into her office, Helena's preoccupation was so great that she was slow in answering Sherry's greeting. Just as they parted Billie had said casually, "Be careful with Moishe when you see him again." She was uneasy, both at the idea that Billie took it for granted that she would see Moishe again and at the admonition. Careful? Careful, she supposed, not to betray any of

148

her new knowledge — about the details of the Rosenstein family affairs, about Michelle, about Billie herself. It was a new burden, this new knowledge which in itself could create pitfalls for her in her dealings not only with Moishe but also with Daniel, with Esther.

She jumped when Sherry, laying on the desk in front of her the most important letters that had come in the morning mail, said, "Mr. Barton called first thing this morning. He wants to see you as soon as possible."

She was annoyed and said sharply, "Well, he'll have to wait till I've seen what is in the mail." She was aware that Sherry was watching her eagerly and had observed that she frowned. "If he calls again, tell him I'll come and see him at ten."

Sherry's glance was full of admiration as she went smiling out of the room.'

At five minutes to ten, Helena stood waiting at the elevator, having been downstairs in the credit department. It seemed inevitable that Esther should appear at her side.

"Wasn't it a nasty weekend?" Esther asked. "All that wind and rain. I'm afraid Mrs. Alfred isn't going to like this weather, coming back from her cruise. She's been in so many nice places with warm weather. I tell her that she should always arrange to get back in the spring or the autumn, not in the middle of winter. It's so depressing, all this grey cold weather and they're talking about snow. But of course so many of the organizations she is concerned with have their busy season now. And this is the peak season for the store. I don't have to tell you that. Everybody likes to come to Rosenstein's for

149

special Christmas presents or just to look at our Christmas decorations. They are putting up a big tree in the first floor lobby. I expect you saw that when you arrived this morning."

Helena, who had not given even a passing glance at the activity on the first floor as she walked by, nodded vaguely.

Esther rattled on. "Daniel always insists on having some things on display for Hanukkah. That's a new idea — I mean, it's something that's been done the last few years. Christmas has always been the great thing at Rosenstein's. It was Old Leah's idea, of course. She knew that would please the greatest portion of her patrons."

The elevator door opened. Helena made a slight gesture toward the empty compartment, but Esther said, smiling brightly, "Oh, no. I'm going down," and waved amiably as the door closed on Helena.

Helena dropped her from her mind at once. It was Barton that she must think about. Barton's secretary ushered her into his office at once. She noted this fact, having half expected that he would keep her waiting for a few minutes in retaliation for her delay in coming to see him.

He was jovial, getting up from his chair to greet her. "Sit down, sit down, Helena," he ordered, returning to his own chair. "I haven't seen much of you lately. How are you coping with Rosenstein's?"

Deciding to match his arrogance she replied, "Very well."

He cocked an eye at her. "You think you are on top of the job, eh? Well, I haven't heard anything that would contradict that opinion. Daniel seems to think so, too."

She was amused by this attempt to establish his position as being privy to Daniel's private thoughts, as offering her the reassurance of someone able to speak as Daniel's confidant. She had learned in the course of the preceding weeks that Daniel held Barton carefully at arm's length and that if there was anyone who could claim some knowledge of Daniel's closely held opinions, it was herself. She said, "Daniel doesn't hesitate to let me know when he thinks I'm on the wrong track about something."

She saw that he was aware that she was putting up a defense against him. "I'm sure he must be learning to place great trust in you. But you remember what I told you about the Rosensteins: they're very clannish and you can't be too careful in dealing with them. They're not likely to let you know when they disagree with you unless they see an advantage to doing so."

She merely nodded, annoyed by his manner of assuming some solidarity between them as adversaries of the Rosensteins.

He went on. "There is one of them I find much easier to deal with. Unfortunately he doesn't have anything to do with the Company. He's not even a director, though he has a few shares. I believe you know him. I mean young Moishe Rosenstein." He paused as if to see what response she would make.

How quickly the news circulated, she thought, remembering vividly the lunch with Moishe in the Elysian Room and the avidity with which they had been watched by the Rosenstein employees. As noncommittally as possible she replied, "Yes. I've met Moishe. He is with his father's banking firm, isn't he?"

"Yes. He is a financial genius, really. That's not just a notion of his relatives'. He has a great future ahead of him. He's worth cultivating, you know."

"He's very young." There was a note of condescension in Helena's voice.

"That's what makes him so extraordinary. He can think circles around men with a great deal more experience. Even his father, Lionel, respects his verdicts." When Helena said nothing, Barton went on. "It's wise to listen when he comes up with new ideas, even though they have not been proven. Don't overlook what he has to say."

"I've not heard him talk about business matters."

Barton gave her a knowing smile. "Ah, he talked about personal matters?"

Disgustedly Helena said, "I've met him only once or twice, socially."

Barton laughed. "I'll bet. He has an eye for good-looking, intelligent women. Ask any of the girls around here."

Furious, Helena did not respond. But for some reason not apparent to her, Barton's good humor increased.

"What I am saying is, that Moishe has some sound ideas about what to do about the Rosenstein store. We've discussed his ideas, he and I. I asked you to come here because I think it is essential for you to listen to what he has to say."

"Have you invited him to come here now?" Helena demanded.

"Oh, no. I don't think the moment is appropriate. I think you should arrange an opportunity for him to talk to you on your own. You have an advantage in being a woman. It will be easy enough for you to provide the occasion!"

Helena's patience ran out. "Mr. Barton —"

"James, surely."

"James, then. I don't mix business and personal affairs. I think I made that plain to you when we first met. If Moishe wants to talk to me as manager of the Rosenstein Company, I'll be quite ready to listen to him, in my office. He surely is capable of making his own arrangements for such a conference. It's my responsibility to safeguard the Company's welfare, to see what can be done to improve its profitability. Therefore, I would not refuse to listen to any reasonable recommendations from someone who has a sound basis for offering them, though I must tell you that Moishe can have no standing with me on the subject of the Company's future except as a member of the Rosenstein family. Really, if he has ideas he wants to put forward, he should make them known to the directors. They can require me to consider them."

She knew she was on solid ground and that he recognized the fact. She was pleased to see him back away. He said, "Oh, yes, yes. You're quite right. But, my dear, you should use what natural advantages you have in a situation like this. Don't be so doctrinaire. That's a mistake you women so often make in dealing with situations where the elements are not clear cut. My only thought was to give you a hint about how things are going. I'll be frank. Moishe thinks that the only future for the Rosenstein Company is to sell the store to a conglomerate, preserving its unique character and at the same time modernizing its methods."

153

"Has he discussed this with any of the members of the board?"

"I suppose he has probably discussed it with Lionel. Lionel would be sympathetic to the idea." Barton paused. "You realize that is what we're up against. The Rosensteins discuss things like this among themselves and we never know what they decide until they're ready to tell us."

After all, thought Helena, they own the Company. "Does Moishe intend to have his father present this idea formally to the board?"

"Ah, now that's something you could find out, isn't it?"

"He hasn't told you?"

Barton answered smoothly, "We haven't got to quite that stage of discussion about it, between the two of us."

"I don't quite see how you think I would find out — unless Daniel tells me."

A look of disgusted annoyance crossed Barton's face. But he was determined to be diplomatic. "I should think that there are ways that would occur to you. I'll assume that if you do find out, you'll let me know."

"I don't think you had better count on me. Speculation about the future of Rosenstein's doesn't come within the scope of my responsibilities. I think I had better wait until I'm informed through the usual channels."

She saw that he was angry at her rejection of his suggestion. He said, "Well, I can understand that you must be preoccupied with the daily details of running the Company. I don't envy you that job. However, I think you had better consider seriously this matter of the future of the Company. It is one that concerns you and me and any other officer who is looking forward to greater rewards in business success. And you should be aware of the good fortune of having the benefit of Moishe's interest. He is the only Rosenstein who has a really progressive attitude, a really modern approach. He is our only hope in persuading his relatives that there must be a radical change if Rosenstein's is to become profitable again — by expanding with the market."

Keeping her tone as bland as possible, Helena said, "I'm aware of the problem. It is part of my job to look for the best solutions for the question of profitability and growth."

"Well, then, you should make every effort to consult Moishe. Show him you agree with him and would like his help in seeking a way —"

"I'm not sure that I do agree with him — or you."

"I don't see how you could disagree. It is stupid to continue in the same old track, which is leading to nothing but lower income and eventual stagnation. Certainly you must agree with him and with me."

"Nevertheless, I am withholding judgment until I've had a chance to discuss this with Daniel. I know that you think Moishe's ideas are the same as yours, but I must have an opportunity to hear from him directly and also from others."

He glowered at her in silence for a few moments. She could see that he now wished the interview at an end, that he was sorry he had called her in. Before he could dismiss her, she stood up and said that she had to get back to her office. On the way there she thought about the probable results of their confrontation. She knew that any goodwill he might have felt toward her was gone. She wondered whether he would complain to his fellow officers and to the members of the board he had access to. She could hear the pitch of his complaints: Women never recognized the difference between broad ideas and the minutiae of their jobs.

There was something more that the interview had told her by implication: a decision about Rosenstein's future was inevitable. When she had first joined the Company she had given only passing attention to the rumors of a possible sale of Rosenstein's. It had seemed to her to be a decision that must be made by the Rosensteins. Since then the question had gradually become less nebulous, more pressing, never openly discussed but apparently looming in the minds of many people. Perhaps Moishe's return had increased this pressure. As she had become more and more acquainted with the history, the past glories, the present fading of the store, she realized that it was she and only she who had the overall, compelling knowledge of what the Company's true financial situation was. None of them — the officers, the members of the board, even Daniel himself — could see as she did what the daily evolution of the store's business could mean to its future.

She found that the outlines of the situation were much clearer in her mind. Perhaps that was so because the store had proved to be a much stronger personality as she became more intimately associated with its functioning; it was an entity, almost a living creature, no doubt projecting the force of its founder's character. She remembered the vivid impression it had made on her the first time she had seen it, empty and lit up, awaiting the day's activities. Once she had mentioned this to Rachel. Rachel had said that this was no doubt the presence of Old Leah's ghost, still hovering over her creation. Rachel had also said that some of the old-timers still felt the impress of Old Leah, still accepted the traditional store practices, because these had been established by the founder. It was just this attitude that was bringing about the crisis now looming concerning the future of the store. Was a compromise possible in reconciling the old with the new?

She took the problem home with her in the evenings, to mull it over without interruption, except for an occasional telephone call from friends anxious to break up what they considered the monastic seclusion into which her dedication to her job had driven her. She thought of Billie, trying to separate in her mind the Billie she knew so intimately and the Billie she knew so little about. That other Billie — where would she stand in dealing with her on the question of Rosenstein's? The thought of Moishe pushed itself in. She had not seen or heard from him since the evening at Adeline's. She would have supposed that he had lost interest in her, except that Billie had said that he would not give up. She wondered whether he was as closely allied with Barton as Barton wanted her to believe. There was also the possibility that consideration of the sale and transformation of Rosenstein's had gone much further ahead among the members of the Rosenstein family than she was aware of. Daniel, whom she now saw almost every day, had never made the slightest, vaguest reference to the fact that some change in Rosenstein's might be looming in the near or far future.

Moishe, Rachel told her, liked to come and strut around the store as the handsome young heir to the business. "He likes to think of himself as Old Leah's favorite young scion. He was much too young to know anything about her from his own recollections but he's heard enough from his elders to imagine himself in the center of the picture. He's certain that he is just what Old Leah would imagine as her true successor."

During the day she did not have much time for brooding. As Esther had said, the store was moving into the peak period of the store year, the Christmas season, and though the day-by-day operation of the store itself was not in her hands, the impact on her daily work load was great. Sherry reported to her that several times Moishe had come to find her but had gone away because she was engaged with other people. Finally, he called and left a message that he would come to her office the next afternoon at the end of the day unless he heard from her to the contrary.

That evening, at home, tired from the accumulating pressure, she sat and pondered what she should do, how arm herself against whatever scheme Moishe might have in mind involving herself or Rosenstein's. Several times, in the last few evenings, she had been prompted to call Billie. Once she had even crossed the room and picked up the phone but put it down without dialing. But now with a sense of despair engendered by fatigue, she rang Billie's number. Billie answered the first ring.

"Billie," she said, "can you talk to me?"

"Yes. Is something the matter?"

"I haven't heard from you —"

"I haven't had much chance to call. Once or twice I rang your number but you were still at the store. Rosenstein's must really be hopping."

"You haven't been in the store."

"No. Mamma has been too busy catching up with her social calendar."

"Does that involve you?"

"I have to trail along with her. I take care of her charities when she is away and she likes to be brought up to date with me present. She likes to hear people say that she has such a faithful little helper when she isn't able to be here herself. They say things like, 'Oh, Mrs. Rosenstein, Billie does such a good job for you! We adore having her. Just the same, we're so glad you're back!' " Billie's voice changed to a higher register when she mimicked her mother's friends. "Mamma wants me to be aware of the fact that I have responsibilities and that I'm accountable to her for them."

"That must be a nuisance. I've wanted very much to talk to you."

"There's something wrong, isn't there?"

"Perhaps not wrong. I'm simply not — I simply don't know how to handle it." Helena took a deep breath before she asked, "Billie, how far has this idea of selling Rosenstein's gone?"

There was a long silence on the other end of the wire. Would Billie tell her? Or would the traditional Rosenstein reticence about the family business assert itself?

Finally Billie said, "I don't know how far it's

159

gone. I very much wish I did. Why are you asking me this now?"

"Barton called me in for a talk. He insisted —"

"Oh, Barton!" Billie's voice held contempt.

"He insisted on talking to me about this. It's really annoying because I have so little time to spare. But he said that this possibility — he talked as if it were an inevitability — is something I should be considering. He spoke as if there was a lot going on that I don't know about. He especially mentioned Moishe —"

Billie's voice was sharp. "Have you seen Moishe?"

"No. That's really why I called you. He's been trying to see me. Now he's coming to my office tomorrow. I haven't the foggiest idea what he's going to talk about. This is terribly distracting."

"I see." Billie's voice was suddenly cautious.

"Barton gave me the impression that he and Moishe are working together to bring this about — the sale of Rosenstein's. Can this be true? Are they so closely allied?"

"I doubt it." Billie's tone dismissed the idea. "I don't think that's what is motivating Moishe right now. If Moishe wants to promote the idea of selling Rosenstein's, he has other people he'd be working on."

"You mean Daniel?"

"For one."

Helena waited for her to go on but Billie said nothing further. "Then why is he so anxious to see me?"

"Because you are hard to get." Billie's voice was sweetness itself.

160

"Damn it! Billie, I'm not interested in him. Something like this is a nuisance when I am so busy."

"You mean it wouldn't be at another time?" There was laughter in Billie's voice. "No, no. Don't get upset. I'm just teasing. Don't you see? Moishe likes to chase women when he thinks they're pretending not to be interested. But it's beginning to dawn on him that you're not pretending. That's a new experience for him."

"Has he been to see you?"

"Yes, of course. And he asked a lot of questions about you, some of them personal. I told him I was not an authority on you."

They were both silent for a while and then Helena asked, "Well, what should I expect tomorrow?"

"A new pitch. I don't know what it will be."

"I haven't time for chatting during office hours."

This time Billie laughed out. "You can be as short-tempered as you like. You'll only stoke the fire."

"Oh, Billie!"

"You can always change the subject to Rosenstein's."

"Rosenstein's problems are not a subject for chit-chat as far as I am concerned."

Billie's tone was cool. "That's nice to know."

"I wish I knew more about this situation as far as your relatives are concerned. As it is, I'm working in the dark. There are very good arguments for doing what Moishe advocates, you know."

Billie did not answer at once and Helena waited

anxiously, aware that she was treading on delicate
ground yet trying once more to get past Billie's wall
of noncommunication.

Finally Billie said, a slight hardness in her voice,
"Rosenstein's will not be sold if I can prevent it."

"But you realize that as manager I must
recommend what is best financially for the Company."

"What you believe to be the best," Billie corrected
her.

"So you and Moishe are at odds on this — really
at odds?"

"Yes."

"Why is he so involved in this? He is only a
shareholder."

"And a minor one. It's his instinct for making a
success in business: the store is old-fashioned, it is
losing money, it can't really be modernized, etc. etc.
The whole family thinks a lot of Moishe's business
acumen. But there are other reasons. One is that this
has become an obsession with him, simply because he
has been thwarted so far. Another is that he, the boy
wonder, wants to demonstrate in a spectacular way
that he can control the family the way his great
grandmother did — that in spite of his youth he's
her real successor. Moishe has to go on proving that
he is a prodigy, that there has never been anyone
like him, at least among the Rosensteins."

"I see. Do you think he can win, that he can
convince your relatives?"

"He won't win if I can prevent it, regardless of
what anybody says."

"Perhaps he should win, Billie. You can't run a
business on sentimental motives. Rosenstein's was an

innovation when Old Leah created it. She saw what could be done and did it in the context of the time. What was valid then may not be valid now."

"What is needed is new ideas. I have them. Doing what Moishe wants to do is throwing in the sponge, giving up. He's dazzled by doing something new. Rosenstein's can stay the way it is, a unique store, like no other. But it must be adapted to modern circumstances. To do that I need a free hand. I don't have it now. All I can do is persuade Daniel to accept my suggestions. That wastes time. Moishe won't listen to anything that can't be done instantly. If it's not instant, it's no good."

"Well, that is the principle of modern business, Billie. Things have to be instant, to be competitive — the faster, the better. He is right there."

"Not in the way I see it. Rosenstein's is a special case. It can survive because it doesn't have real competition. There is nothing else like it. That's what Moishe does not understand. I won't give in — to him or to anyone else." Helena heard the note of iron determination in her throaty voice.

It was the first time she had encountered it and she was alarmed. She said hesitantly, in the pause that followed Billie's statement, "Billie?"

Billie's voice softened at once in response to her anxiety. "This has nothing to do with you and me, honey. I'll call you in a couple of days." And she hung up.

The next afternoon, the end of the working day came before Helena was aware of it. She felt the gradual slackening of the pace only subconsciously as her mind became freer from interruptions and she was able to concentrate more fully on the problems at hand. She was startled when she looked up to see Moishe standing in the doorway, watching her.

She said sharply, "Isn't Sherry there?"

He grinned. "She's gone. So has everybody else."

Vaguely she remembered Sherry saying Goodnight, after inquiring whether she wanted her to stay.

Moishe went on. "You didn't call me, so I decided I'd just come along. You forgot, huh?"

"I'm sorry. The time just went by so fast. "Won't you sit down?"

He made a gesture intended, she supposed, to mean, in a minute, and walked over to the window to look down on the crowds in the street below, brilliantly lit by the big shop windows decorated for Christmas.

He turned back to her. "There was some good skiing in Vermont this past weekend. How about joining me this Saturday? It's getting better all the time, with this weather."

"I'm not free for weekends right now. Besides, I don't ski."

"You can always learn. I'm a pretty good instructor."

"Nice of you, but not now. There's too much pressure here in the store at this season. You know that."

"But you don't run the store. You've got people to do that. I'm sure you know how to delegate authority."

There's been to much of that already, she thought. She said, "This is my first Christmas with the Company. I think I should be here — if for no other reason, for the experience."

She saw the annoyance pass over his face, but he covered it up. "Well, how about having dinner with me? You have to relax sometime. It's not good for business if you don't."

She knew he was mocking her. She remembered another of the admonitions for women executives: The image of the industrious ant was not the one that gained the greatest admiration from male colleagues. If you had to be one, you tried to hide the fact. Besides, she could not avoid Moishe indefinitely, unless she was prepared to drive him away entirely and that was not a sensible thing to do.

So she agreed. They went to a small restaurant nearby, a quieter place than the one he had chosen the first time. There were other differences from their previous date. Moishe's banter was less obvious. There were sometimes moments of silence, which he made no special effort to fill. She was uneasy since this very awkwardness seemed to signal a growing intimacy, or at least, a wish on his part for a growing intimacy, which she was reluctant to accept. That first evening Moishe had been the hunter out for a conquest he thought would be easy, enjoyable and transient, leading to the sort of liaison he liked, in which he felt a minimum of responsibility. But now he was appearing in the guise of a serious suitor who looked beyond the pleasure of the moment. He did not seem as anxious to portray himself as the ultimate playboy, the dazzler.

Halfway through the dinner he asked suddenly, "Why did you come to Rosenstein's?"

Helena took a deep breath. "Rosenstein's said they wanted a professional manager. I decided to accept their offer."

He nodded. After a pause he said, "I think you have probably found that there are some special handicaps here."

Suspicious of what he had in mind, she replied, "There are always hidden problems in every situation which you don't see ahead of time."

"But there is a serious flaw in this set-up which was hidden from you when you were offered the job: the fact that the store is going down the drain unless there are major changes made. Has it occurred to you that this fact was purposely hidden from you?"

She had finished her meal and she sat silent for a moment. Finally she said, "No. I haven't thought about that. Are you talking about Daniel? Do you want me to believe that he purposely did not give me a true picture of the store's financial situation? Why should he have done that? There is nothing on paper that gives a bad view of the Rosenstein Company. There hasn't been any real growth in the last ten years or so. But that could have been the result of poor management — or inadequate management."

Moishe made an impatient sound. "No, I suppose I don't really accuse Daniel of trying to deceive you. Or anyone. I think it's worse. I don't think he understands what the true situation is. The point is that you have to know more about an operation like Rosenstein's than what shows up on the balance sheet at the end of the year. There is the question of potential. Daniel really thinks that Rosenstein's is eternal, that it can go on forever just as it is. He doesn't have a modern perspective. But how are you going to deal with that? You realize that he's wrong. Rosenstein's is slowing down. Soon it will just stagnate and that means the end."

"I don't know that it's up to me to deal with that. All I can do is show Daniel what the store can do, is doing. Profitability is up already, you know."

Moishe shrugged. "That's peanuts. The handwriting is on the wall for Rosenstein's. It needs a rescue operation. It seems to me that what you need to do is demonstrate what the rescue operation should be."

"In your opinion, that the Company should be sold to a conglomerate —"

"With adequate safeguards for the Rosenstein family interests."

"And become a specialty outlet, in the guise of the old store. It would not be Rosenstein's any more, you realize."

"You've got it. Most people wouldn't realize that it isn't the same store any more. You can have the best of both worlds — a modern clothing outlet, with modern methods of competition and the prestige of old Rosenstein's."

"I think," Helena said slowly, "you are underestimating the value of what Rosenstein's is now and has been in the past. It would lose its character very quickly. You have only to look at the other famous stores that have been swallowed up to see that. Also I think that perhaps some of your relatives would not like that transformation."

"They're behind the times. I don't think they're that much concerned, really. Except for Daniel and my father, they don't have anything to do with the store."

She wanted to ask, "What about Billie?" but she did not.

He went on, enthusiastically. "Daniel is the main

167

obstacle. The others don't really care. Rosenstein's has always existed and has always been profitable — enough to satisfy them. Take my father, for instance. He sits in the chair at directors meetings thinking about something else. But of course he's like my grandfather. He's a banker and never did have much to do with the store. In fact, nobody in my branch of the family ever gave a thought to Rosenstein's except to see it as a sort of ancestral monument."

"So why do you now?"

He seemed to find the question interesting and stopped eating his dessert. "Well, I suppose I had an idle moment or two and I began thinking about what could be done to bring Rosenstein's into the modern world. You know, I have been out in Japan. We've been thinking of expanding our operations in the Far East. The old man has given me a free hand. Now that's a field for real growth. When I came back home I was suffering from a letdown and it seemed to me that Rosenstein's needed a little reorganization. I think in the end I can convince Daniel that we've got to make a change." He ate another bite and then looked across the shaded lamp at her. "You know, you'll have a real future if we transform Rosenstein's. You can bet on it that Rosenstein Enterprises would have a controlling voice in any arrangement to sell the store."

"So, then, if you convince Daniel, he'll convince the rest."

His eyes were on his plate. "It's not as simple as that. There's Billie, of course. Billie is hard to handle."

"She doesn't agree with you?"

He looked up at her again. "She has told you,

hasn't she, that she doesn't want to sell Rosenstein's. She has talked to you about this, hasn't she?"

Not wanting to lie outright, Helena said, "She's indicated that she thinks Rosenstein's can be modernized without selling out."

"You'll have to disabuse her of that notion."

"I? I should think that would be up to you and Daniel."

"She is not going to listen to me. She and I have a big row every time I see her. But Rosalie is back now. That'll make a difference?"

"Rosalie?"

"Mrs. Alfred — Billie's mother."

"I've been told that Mrs. Alfred is not interested in the business."

He laughed. "Rosalie doesn't waste her time thinking about how to make money. She's always had more than she needs. But if you pin her down, you'll find she's got the Rosenstein instincts for managing it properly. I can talk to her."

"And you think she will agree with you?"

He shot an indignant glance over at her. "Why not? Haven't I just demonstrated to you that Rosenstein's is on its last legs unless we do something drastic? It's a fact that's got to be faced." He paused as if another idea had occurred to him. "You don't have to be so cautious with me. You don't have to walk a tightrope because you think I'll go and report what you say to my relatives. This discussion is between you and me."

She did not answer and he seemed to mull over what he had said. All at once he asked, "Has Barton been talking to you?"

In spite of what he had said she was careful. "He

has talked about the possibility of selling Rosenstein's."

She saw a flash in Moishe's dark eyes. "I thought so. Of course you realize what he is interested in. He wants to transfer to another Rosenstein company. He thinks that'll have more prestige. He gets that from talking to some of the other officers. Retailing may make money but it is not as prestigious as some other lines of business. Haven't you noticed that?" His glance was genuinely curious. "That is one reason why my grandfather decided to go into investment banking. Oh, yes, he wanted to get away from his mother. She underwrote him, of course. She didn't care what any of her sons did as long as they realized their potential. She gave him the money to get started because she knew he wasn't going to be happy staying with the store like his brother Moses. She did the same for her other two sons. So now we wind up with Daniel and Billie. They think Rosenstein's is sacred. Daniel is worshipping Baal and doesn't know it." He saw that Helena was uncertain about his allusion. "Did you know that Daniel wanted me to be a rabbi? Can you imagine me a rabbi?"

Helena shook her head noncommittally.

They had finished their meal and declined the waiter's offer of coffee and liqueurs. I suppose, thought Helena, the natural thing would be for me to invite him to come and have coffee at my place. Her antagonism towards him had faded and in its place she felt a certain mellow friendliness. Moishe evidently had a heavy beard and the late evening blueness showed under the rosy flush of his healthy skin, from his cheekbones to the narrow band of silky brown hair along his jawbone.

As they walked out of the restaurant, he said, "To get back to you. So you didn't come to Rosenstein's as a stepping stone to some other Rosenstein company."

"No. I would not have made such an important decision at this stage of my business life on that sort of a basis."

He smiled at her earnestness. "I'd say that your business instincts are a lot sounder than Barton's. What's he been telling you exactly?"

He was peering at her in the light that came out onto the street from the restaurant. Cautious again, Helena said, "He is impatient to move things along toward a decision about the store's future. He said that he was glad that you're back because he thinks you share his views." I shouldn't, she told herself, let him know that Barton talks as if they are buddy-buddy.

Moishe did not seem to be paying much attention. He said off-handedly, "He wants out of Rosenstein's into something else more modern, more prestigious. But I don't think he knows just what's involved. He knows how to put up a good front. That's an asset in any business."

As they talked they walked along toward her apartment. In spite of the cold wind she said she would rather walk than take a cab. He fell in step with her. He was not quite as tall as she — in fact, he is the same height as Billie, she thought.

He asked, "Didn't you ever want to learn to ski?"

171

"I never thought about it. It takes up so much time, which I've never had to spare. I was in college on scholarships."

"That's too bad. You ought to change that. That's the mistake Billie makes — doesn't keep in good physical condition. You ought to talk her into playing tennis with you on a regular basis."

"I'm afraid I don't have that much influence with Billie." She was wary of the assumption that there was a close friendship between herself and Billie. "At the moment I don't even have time for my regular workout at my health club."

She was startled when he reached out and took her hand. By an effort of will she refrained from drawing it away but left it in his warm, strong clasp.

"I'm glad you came and had dinner with me, Helena." He was looking at her sideways with candid friendliness. Again she felt an impulse of comradeship. It was, she supposed, a normal female response to his aggressive maleness. But she took warning. Moishe must be very adept at seizing on any softening towards him and ready to use it for his own advantage. She said nothing about coffee at her place.

Moishe was saying, "When you're not so busy, maybe we can arrange a weekend."

For something to say, she asked, "You're staying in Manhattan?"

"Oh, yes. Until Rosenstein's future is settled."

"You think that is going to happen soon?"

"It had better. If this goes on too long, the Company is doomed. I won't be interested in it then. It'll just have to sink by itself."

Stunned by the casual certainty with which he spoke, she did not reply. They reached her apartment house. Helena stopped on the pavement in front of the door and started to say Goodnight. Instantly Moishe's good humor disappeared and in the light of the street lamp she saw the flash of anger cross his face. But he swallowed it and, making no move to follow her up the shallow steps, he said cheerfully, "At least, we can have dinner again soon."

"Of course. It was nice of you, Moishe. I enjoyed it."

He covered his real feelings enough to say, "The worst thing you can do, my old dad says, is eat by yourself. Goodnight, Helena." And he turned and walked away rapidly down the street.

She was surprised on Sunday morning to hear the buzzer on the house phone. She never had a visitor on Sunday mornings. She had convinced her friends that she needed that time to recover from the stress of the preceding week. As Christmas drew near Rosenstein's shopping hours grew longer and her own stretched accordingly. She was still in bed, only half-awake, and she looked at the phone for a long moment before picking up the receiver. The voice of the receptionist said, "Miss Rosenstein to see you."

Her grogginess cleared. Billie. What on earth brought Billie to see her at this hour? She got out of bed and put on a robe — a flowing, diaphanous garment that Rachel had picked out. When she opened the door Billie walked in and said, "I woke you up."

When she put her arms around her, Helena felt the damp chill of the winter morning in the fur coat she was wearing.

"Not exactly. Let me get us some coffee."

Billie took off her coat and hat and followed her

into the small kitchen. Still clumsy from sleep, Helena filled the coffee maker and reached down the cups from the shelf. When she had done so she became aware that Billie was gazing round in curiosity. Suddenly she saw her apartment as it really was, not as it appeared to her as she lived in it. Shorn of its familiarity it was a nondescript dwelling place with commonplace furniture and little decoration. She had never expected to entertain here and she owned very little in the way of pictures, mementoes, family objects. It provided comfort and efficient mechanical devices and she had not given as much thought to it as she had to her office at Rosenstein's, which was furnished in keeping with her status in the Company.

Billie looked at her with a twinkle in her eyes, having caught the bemused expression on her face. "You didn't expect me to turn up here, did you?"

"No. It didn't occur to me."

Billie nodded. "This is the only way I can see you."

Helena said, "I can't come to your place and you can't see me at Rosenstein's."

Again Billie nodded. "Perhaps some time in the future. Mamma has to get used to the idea that you exist. She mustn't think of you right off as my friend. That comes later."

She sat down at the small table by the window. Helena brought the coffee and started to fill the cups. Annoyed, she realized that her hand was shaking. Calmly Billie took the pot out of her hand and filled the cups.

"You've been working too many hours. Or is there something else?"

174

Helena blushed under Billie's direct gaze. She shook her head, not sure what Billie meant. It dawned on her that Billie was dressed in a fashionable costume, a gold wool dress with long sleeves and a high neck, and that she was wearing a necklace of several strands and bracelets. Surely she would not have dressed this way simply to come and see me, she thought. Billie, seeing her bemused scrutiny, said, "I'm on my way to Temple. Mamma expects me to meet her there."

"On Sunday?"

"Yes. We're Reform Jews."

Half-enlightened, Helena said, "I see. What do we do?"

Billie looked at her quizzically. "Do? Well, nothing, I suppose. Oh, honey, I did want to get a glimpse of you!" She got up and came around to put her arms around Helena, pressing her head against her breasts.

Helena leaned against her passively. "I feel cut off from you, Billie."

Billie looked down at her in concern. "You're worried, besides being tired. What is it?"

"It's difficult to deal with company problems when you're kept in the dark about essential facts."

Billie let go of her and returned to her chair. "Company problems?"

"What is going to happen to Rosenstein's? If I had a better idea of that, I could project future plans better."

"Who has been talking to you? Moishe?"

"He insisted on having dinner with me Friday evening. He did tell me a few things I did not know before — or at least he confirmed my suspicions. But he's very sure he's going to have things his own way."

"Moishe is always sure he is going to have things his own way. He's been doing that all his life. Especially with my mother."

"He said —" Helena began and stopped, uncertain how to go on.

"He said?" Billie's voice allowed no retreat.

"He said that now that your mother is back, things will be easier — or words to that effect."

"Easier for him to persuade Daniel to do what he wants. Daniel is very vulnerable to my mother."

"He did not mention you except to say that you're hard to handle."

"That's typical Moishe."

"What do you mean?"

"He knows by instinct where to find the weak spot in any person or situation. It is a gift to him, to have a woman in your position. I should have thought of that."

Aroused now from her lethargy, Helena demanded, "What are you talking about?"

"You're a woman. He expects you to side with him automatically. And you're in a strategic position to help him achieve what he wants."

"You mean, he's after me so that he can get me to play his game."

Billie nodded.

"That's not very flattering to me," said Helena, indignantly.

Billie laughed. "Oh, now, now. Moishe wouldn't do it unless he found you attractive in the first place. He'd zero in on any pot of honey, whether it was profitable to him or not. And that's what you are on both counts." Billie suddenly reached over and touched her cheek.

But Helena was outraged. "You make me out a pretty silly fool! Billie, don't you realize that I have my own ideas about Rosenstein's future and they've nothing to do with what Moishe wants?"

"Except that they are close enough so that he can exploit your cooperation. The trouble is —" Billie paused, gazing pensively into space — "he has a trump card in my mother."

The way in which she said this made Helena suddenly aware that Billie had come to her because she was unhappy. Helena fell silent, her indignation at once dissipated. She longed to reach out, to hold Billie in her arms, to comfort her for this sorrow which she only dimly understood. She had never felt before that Billie needed comforting, protecting. Finally she said, "I'm sorry, Billie. I don't really know what to say. If I knew more about how your family feels about this situation, I would be in a much better position to see what can be done. All I've got to go on are the profitability figures, the accounting projections —"

Billie cut her short. "I didn't come here to talk about Rosenstein's. I just couldn't stand not seeing you, honey, and this was the only way I could do it." She dropped her head in her hands, leaning her elbows on the table.

Devastated by the sight of her discouragement, Helena got up and went around to her. "Come on, Billie. Let's go into the other room."

Billie responded to her touch, getting up and as she did so reaching under her robe to touch her skin. They stood for a long moment embraced. Finally they

177

went into the living room and sat down together on the sofa. Billie put her head on Helena's shoulder. She said, "I can't even get drunk, now that my mother's back and watching me every second. I can't let her walk in and find me out for the count."

"Does she know that you drink too much sometimes?"

"Of course. You can't fool her. I'm always afraid I'll give something away when she calls me on the phone. She knows instantly when I'm tiddled, though she does not acknowledge it, and then she just listens while I babble on. And I can't remember afterwards what I said to her."

"Billie, you shouldn't do it — drink too much. It doesn't help, you know."

"It fills a void."

"Does it?"

"Well, there's less of a void now." Billie reached up to pull her head down to kiss her.

"What is it you are afraid you'll tell her?"

"What do you think? I'm afraid I'll say something about Michelle, about Rachel, something that will damn me. And now there's you."

"Billie, do you really think she hasn't guessed about you? Doesn't she ask you why don't you get married, why don't you have boyfriends?"

"Is that what happens with your mother?"

"Yes — it used to. But she's reconciled now to the idea that I'm not going to get married — at least, not any time soon."

Billie did not answer. Helena felt her breath against her cheek, felt the weight of Billie's soft body against her own. The now familiar feeling of a

178

loosening in her own tenseness began to creep into her.

"In five minutes," said Billie gently in her ear, "I'm going to have to leave. Mamma is probably tapping her foot right now, wondering where I am."

When Billie left Helena felt a letdown. It was always like this now, when she had been with Billie — a sort of yearning for the comfort of Billie's presence, as if a gap was made in her private world. And this time she did not know when they would be together again. Her only solace was the demands placed on her by Rosenstein's busy season. She welcomed the constant interruptions, the cries for help from the people who ran the store.

She was surprised on Monday evening to have a call from Billie. Tomorrow night, said Billie. Would she come over tomorrow night?

"Yes, of course," said Helena eagerly.

"My mother is coming over to have dinner with me. She wants to meet you and she wants to meet you here, not in the store."

Billie's voice was quiet, too quiet, thought Helena. "Is there a special reason?" she asked, uneasy.

"She has heard a lot of talk about you — from Esther, from Moishe, and I suppose, Daniel. She has to see for herself. You must come, honey. And wear the dark red ensemble."

When she arrived at Billie's door Billie kissed her and when she saw her surprise, kissed her again. Billie was smiling, but there was a nervous look in her eyes, as if she sought to give and receive reassurance. Helena noticed that Billie wore an evening pantsuit in pale green silk.

"Mamma is not here yet," Billie said, leading her into the living room to the big sofa.

But Billie sat beside her only for a moment, getting up to go and check something in the kitchen. She watched Billie's restless movements. Billie asked a question about Rosenstein's and the Christmas rush. Helena answered her and then a silence followed. She knew that Billie had not been listening.

When the intercom from the reception desk buzzed, Billie jumped to answer it. Its sound, usually so muted, seemed to shout. Billie stood still and waited for several minutes before she went to the door to open it and wait there. Helena could not see into the vestibule from where she sat.

Then a voice, like Billie's but higher pitched and louder, rang out, "My doll baby! Really, that woman downstairs ought to know me by now." There was the sound of kisses and then the voice went on, "She always keeps me waiting. I'm going to walk by her one of these days."

Billie's quieter voice said, "She has to do that, mamma. She'd lose her job if she didn't."

They came into the room together. So this is Mrs. Alfred, thought Helena, getting up to greet her. She was a couple of inches shorter than Billie and where Billie was fifteen pounds heavier than she should be, Mrs. Alfred was thirty. She had the same fresh, clear, pink skin. Her hair, instead of being Billie's red gold, was a reddish brown — helped out, no doubt, by Rosenstein's hairdresser. She was wearing what was obviously a Rosenstein creation and her arms and hands were laden with bracelets and rings; the Rosenstein's were partial to diamonds, Helena had

180

noticed. When she came across the room, Helena saw that her eyes were the same blue as Billie's but instead of Billie's mild gaze, they were sharp, intent, appraising. She paid no attention to what Billie was saying but said to Helena, "Ah, you're our new manager."

She looked Helena up and down, assessing her clothes. Bless Rachel again, thought Helena, feeling awkward under her scrutiny. "I've heard a great deal about you. In fact, it seems you're a nine days' wonder. I suppose you've got used to that."

She had taken off her hat and let Billie take it and her coat. Then she sat down and looked around the room as if making sure that there were no changes since she had been there before.

Obeying Billie's gesture, Helena sat down where she had been. Billie went to the liquor cabinet and took out glasses and bottles.

Mrs. Alfred, watching Billie, went on. "Before I left on the cruise Daniel told me that he was hiring a woman as manager for the Company. I had my doubts about that. But it seems you are doing very well. Do you like it? I understand you do not have a background in the retail apparel business. Or fashion."

As she spoke her eyes continued to rove over Helena's face and clothes. Through some chemistry that she did not fully comprehend, Helena found herself relaxing under this intensive examination. Obviously Mrs. Alfred did not approve of beating about the bush. There was an invitation in the directness of her gaze and manner, an invitation for a talk between equals.

"I do like it, Mrs. Rosenstein, though it is true that I have no background in this sort of business. I find it a stimulating experience."

"Well, I'm not a businesswoman but I understand that there is a new theory that, if you're qualified, you can manage anything. At least, that's what I'm told. That's what Daniel said when I questioned what he had in mind. Daniel seems very well satisfied with his experiment."

Billie came back to where they sat and put the tray of drinks on the coffee table. She handed her mother a tall clear drink — vodka, Helena assumed. Mrs. Alfred's attention went at once to the glass of scotch Billie took for herself. Would she have said something, Helena wondered, if I wasn't here? Helena took her own drink from the tray.

Billie said mildly, "Daniel thinks Rosenstein's is very lucky to have her."

Mrs. Alfred glanced at her but said to Helena, "Why did you decide to come with Rosenstein's?"

Helena was prepared for this question, which she had had to answer many times. "Because I had come to a place where I needed to make a change, if I was to go ahead. There seemed to me no real chance, where I was, for a woman to win promotion."

Mrs. Alfred nodded, as if this answer was self-evident. "But didn't somebody tell you that Rosenstein's is not a growth industry — isn't that what they call it? People talk about Rosenstein's as if it is a dinosaur."

"No, nobody actually said that to me. But it is a challenge to try and revive its old glory."

Phrasing it this way seemed to please Mrs. Alfred. She settled back in her chair more comfortably.

182

"Well, I don't understand the problems. Daniel has explained them to me but I suppose I don't pay enough attention to what he says."

She was obviously dropping the subject. Instead she began to ask Helena about herself. Who were her parents? As she answered, Helena was aware, from some subtle change in Mrs. Alfred's expression, that divorce was not well thought of among the older generation of Rosensteins. Did her mother, asked Mrs. Alfred then, approve of her business career? And why was she intent on making a successful business career instead of getting married?

"You're not married, are you? Well, I suppose you're young enough to wait a while longer. But not too long, if you want children."

Through the rest of the evening Mrs. Alfred talked about her cruise, about China, about politics, about her opinions generally. As they sat down to dinner she turned her attention to the food. It was obvious that Billie had gone to a great deal of trouble in preparing this meal for her mother. Mrs. Alfred was admittedly a gourmet cook herself and she gave her mind to the details of Billie's menu. She seemed gratified by Billie's efforts to please her and discriminatingly indulgent in her comments.

"I didn't think you paid that much attention to what I taught you, doll baby," she said. "This is very good." She leaned over to kiss Billie and pat her hand.

At a decent interval after the meal, Helena, feeling the strain under which Billie suffered, left. Mrs. Alfred was cordial but did not suggest that she stay longer. Billie, who had been almost silent through the evening, took her to the door. They stood for a

moment without speaking. Helena looked at Billie.
Billie's head was turned as if she listened for sounds
from the living room. Going home Helena felt
relieved, as if she had escaped from danger. Billie's
murmured "Goodnight, honey," whispered in her ear
till she fell asleep.

In the following days she found herself constantly
in the store, often taking Daniel's place, as she had
come to do on Saturdays. Rachel, who dropped in to
see her frequently, was quick to sense the tension
under which she was and tried to ease it with humor.
Daniel, she told Helena, was very happy that she was
on hand to take his place, so that he did not need to
suffer conflict between his religious duties and his
business responsibilities.

"You know what the Rosensteins call you —
Daniel's shabbes goy," said Rachel.

Helena, too exhausted to pay more than half a
mind to her, asked, "What is that?"

"Well, in the past, some strict Jews used to hire
Christians to do things for them on the Sabbath
which the law forbade. Daniel is strict, you know.
You're a real joy to him there." Rachel, trying to
lighten her mood, laughed, not succeeding.

The holiday rush at Rosenstein's came to a climax
on Christmas eve. The store's tradition was to remain
open till midnight, with special attention given to
those customers who had postponed their gift
shopping purposely to enjoy this last frenzy in the
splendor of Rosenstein's festive setting. There were
those, Helena was told, who looked forward each year
to the excitement of these hectic moments as a part
of Christmas joyfulness. It was often past midnight
when Rosenstein's closed its doors and the still

clamorous crowd went out into the street from the brilliance of the chandeliers, the scent of the evergreens festooning the pillars, the air of happy expectancy of Christmas morning.

It was the day after New Year's that Helena, when she got up to go to work, found that the extreme grogginess of her night's uneasy sleep refused to leave her. For several days she had felt the onset of what she supposed was the flu, but she remembered the admonition of her training — an executive woman did not admit to illness except under the most extreme circumstances. She forced herself to bathe and dress, conscious with every movement that heavy weights seemed to be attached to her arms and legs. She reached her office, eager to feel the sense of security, of readiness for the day's events, that came to her whenever she sat down at her desk. But this morning she sank into her chair, unable to summon up any feeling beyond that of despair. She struggled through a couple of hours and then, aware that Sherry was looking at her with alarm in her face, decided that she had better go to the store's emergency room and consult the nurse. She succeeded in getting that far but from then on she had no clear idea of what happened to her. Later she had a confused memory of being handled by strangers, of things being done to her body, of herself being present and yet aloof from what was happening. There was a sense of Billie, of Billie being near her, of the sound of Billie's voice, of the touch of Billie's hands. When she awoke to reality she was in a private room in a hospital.

She gazed about her at the pale-tinted walls, at the flowers on a table across the room. This stillness

185

both soothed and troubled her. She was grateful for the quiet, for the tranquility. Yet at the same time she was uneasy with a sense of time passing over which she had no control. This was only a glimpse of consciousness before sleep claimed her again.

When she woke the next time she opened her eyes to see Billie's face hovering over her, to hear Billie's voice murmuring "Are you awake, honey? Your mother is here." And then Billie vanished and her mother's anxious face filled the same space.

Later, when she was stronger, she was able to piece together what had happened. Sherry, arriving with a fresh bouquet of flowers — these from Rosenstein's board of directors — told her that she had collapsed in the nurse's office, that she had been brought to the hospital unconscious, that the flu she had ignored had turned into pneumonia, that Billie had sent for her mother — Billie seemed to be the only person who knew she had a mother who lived in Texas — and that Rosenstein's directors were eager for her to know their concern and their ardent wish that she would soon be well and back at her job.

She had cards and messages from her friends but her mother was her only visitor in the first days. She was aware that her mother had established an immediate understanding with the nurses. They exclaimed over the close physical resemblance between them — "We knew right away you were her mother," they said. Her mother was pleased at this, though Helena knew that at the same time she was dismayed at the fact that her age was emphasized as the mother of a daughter almost thirty years old. "You don't look it," said the nurses in genuine admiration.

Sherry came each morning bringing messages from

186

Daniel, from Rachel, from Esther speaking for Lionel and the others, and one morning with an immense armful of roses from Moishe. These visits of Sherry's were brief — permitted, she understood, to allay any anxiety about her abandoned job. Her mother observed all this with obvious curiosity. There was no sign of Billie and in a half-foggy way she was unhappy about this. She had been delirious — Sherry reported this — and she wondered whether in that delirium she had said things, had talked about Billie, had betrayed some of her most private feelings.

Her mother had arrived when her condition had worsened. Now that she seemed out of immediate danger she sat beside her bed, patiently reading a book while Helena slept, ready for brief conversation when she awakened.

Growing stronger, she was able to sit up against the pillows and eat from the tray the nurse's aide brought, while her mother watched. Her mother said, "I'm staying in your apartment, of course. I'm learning my way around New York again. There are so many changes since I used to visit." After a pause she added as a conscious afterthought, "I'm here by myself, of course. You know how Floyd is. But I call him every night and he always sends his love."

Helena did not reply. Her mother always made these semi-apologies for her stepfather, trying vainly to foster the idea that there was between her daughter and her husband some measure of ordinary family affection. Helena dismissed her mother's words and wondered with a twinge of anxiety whether she had left anything lying about her apartment that might speak of Billie's presence. She remembered the care with which Billie always surveyed her own place

187

after they had been together in it. She had never entertained in her apartment and since her mother had not been East for several years, she had grown careless.

But there was nothing in her mother's manner to show that she was distressed by anything she had noticed. Her mother said, "Miss Rosenstein is very attractive and very kind. She was the one who let me know that you were so desperately ill. Do you know her well?"

Helena put down her fork. "Billie?" she asked weakly.

"Is that her name? She is making every effort to reassure me. She has taken me to dinner several times and to meet her parents. Mrs. Rosenstein is a lively little woman, isn't she? She always asks after you."

"I've only met her once," said Helena, picking up her fork.

"Oh? Well, I must say that these people you are associated with are all most cordial. That young man — I believe he is the cousin of Miss Rosenstein's — he sent those roses over there. The nurse says he sends fresh flowers or fruit or something every day."

"You mean Moishe?"

"It's a curious name, isn't it? He's very handsome and most charming. Is he wealthy?"

"He's a Rosenstein."

"They all are, is that it?" Her mother hesitated and then said delicately, "Is he interested in you?"

Helena pushed the tray aside. "I've been out with him a couple of times."

Her mother was silent for a moment, obviously

188

seeking a way to continue her inquiry. "He has taken me to dinner. The first time I met him he was with Miss Rosenstein. Then he invited me out. We went to a show and a nightclub. He's an excellent host. And he often comes here to the hospital to inquire after you. Now he has invited me to dinner at his parents' house. He says his whole family are very concerned about you — that they value what you are doing for their company. I don't think he was trying to flatter me. There's no reason why he should."

"Moishe is a nice fellow," said Helena.

"All this is why I asked whether he is interested in you," said her mother, tenaciously.

"You mean, does he want me to marry him?"

"Well, I have wondered."

"Moishe is not interested in marrying anyone. Neither am I."

Her mother signed resignedly and then said anxiously, "Don't get upset, Helena. You mustn't get tired or anxious about anything."

"There's no reason for me to get upset about Moishe. I like him but that's as far as it goes." She knew her mother would understand by this that she was not sexually involved with Moishe. That was a question her mother would never directly ask, had never asked about any of the men who in the past had figured in her life or who her mother believed she had been involved with.

She had spoken sharply and she knew that her sharpness had wounded her mother. She said lamely, "Mother, I do wish you would accept the fact that my business career comes first. I cannot give thought to anything else."

189

"But surely, dear, there is always the possibility that you will find someone who will mean so much to you that you will have to give him priority."

"At the moment I don't believe that will ever happen. I'm sorry, but that's the way it is." She lay back against the pillow and closed her eyes. She knew her mother was gazing at her sadly and somewhat anxiously. She had often wondered, when they had these disguised sparring matches, why her mother, whose two ventures into marriage had not been satisfactory, still clung to the idea that a suitable husband was the real goal of any woman's life. It did upset her that her mother would not accept her denials, because of the distress it caused both of them. Why, she wondered, was it so impossible for them to speak frankly to each other when to both of them the other's real thoughts and feelings were so apparent.

Presently she was aware that her mother had quietly left the room, thinking that she had fallen asleep. But first she had gently removed the tray from the bed and had bent over her for a moment in a loving gesture.

In fact, she did doze off and after a while awoke again, conscious of the disturbing images that had filled her sleep. The most vivid was the feeling of what it was like to be in Billie's bed — an almost palpable sense of the white, downy bed and Billie's soft warm body. But she opened her eyes on the austere hospital room, aware that she was filled with longing for even a moment of Billie's presence.

The peaceful remoteness created by illness was beginning to erode under the pressure of returning strength. The nurse said that she would be having

190

more visitors — various of the friends who had been sending messages wanted to come to see her. "Your mother," the nurse said, "thinks it will be good for you to see other people."

Did that mean, Helena wondered, that her mother was getting uneasy at outstaying her husband's patience in putting up with her absence. But when she asked her if she was getting ready to return to Texas, her mother said, "Oh, no! I'm staying till you are out of the woods. I'll be here to look after you for a while when you leave the hospital. You won't be able to fend for yourself right away. Right now I'm going to leave and go shopping. Then someone else can come and see you." She got up and kissed Helena briefly. "You've been terribly ill, my darling. You must be careful when you get up so as not to bring on a relapse."

The afternoon, which Helena could see out of the window, was brilliant, a Manhattan winter day of vast blue sky and sparkling air. Some of its brightness came into her room and lit the figure of her mother, about to leave, and that of Billie, standing aside in the doorway to let her pass.

"Why, Miss Rosenstein —"

"Billie," said Billie, smiling.

"Oh, Billie, how nice to see you!"

"Yes. We must arrange for you to come and visit Rosenstein's."

Helena was speechless when finally Billy walked into the room, calmly closing the door behind her, and leaned over her.

"The nurse has gone away for a few minutes," said Billie softly. "I asked her to."

Helena looked up into Billie's face, framed by the mass of red-gold hair. "Billie," she said faintly.

Billie sat down on the edge of the high hospital bed and leaned across her so that they were closely face to face. "It's so hard for me to see you, honey. I'm glad your mother likes me. She won't make it difficult for me to come."

Helena, too full of longing, of psychical and physical yearning to speak, swallowed tears of weakness. Billie, noticing, kissed her. "I've not been far away, ever. It has been a terrifying time, honey. But never mind. You're getting better now. You can go home in a week or so."

Helena's voice was a croak. "My mother is going to stay with me for a while."

Billie was silent for a moment and then said, "You couldn't be alone right away. I can't be with you. You'd have to have a nurse, if your mother didn't stay. It's not so bad, honey. I can always spell your mother so that she can get out every so often." Billie was thoughtful again. "I expect she will be anxious to get home, won't she? Evidently she worries about her husband. He's pretty demanding, isn't he?"

"Yes. She's always nervous about what he'll think or do about things, especially if I'm involved."

Billie nodded, dismissing the subject. She put her finger on Helena's nose, tracing its length. Helena sank into a delicious languor permeated by the sense of Billie's nearness. She did not really know what Billie was saying. It was simply the sweet savor of Billie, of the loving, soothing touch of Billie's hands stroking her skin, of Billie's warmth close to her, that drugged her senses.

192

When she woke Billie was not there.

The next day, when her mother had gone out to lunch, Esther came to visit her. She came carrying a large hothouse plant and a basket of grapes tied up in ribbons. Daniel, said Esther, had asked her especially to come and bring these and to inquire for him how she was doing.

Esther's bright, inquisitive eyes took in her appearance, the obvious effort it took for her to talk. She said, "Daniel said to tell you that he certainly has missed you. He said you must take good care of yourself when you come back. You know —" Esther paused to give her a close look — "I think he feels a little guilty, because he left everything to you during the holidays and you worked yourself to death. He's very sensitive to his responsibilities for that sort of thing."

Distressed, Helena tried to stop her flow of words. "He mustn't feel that way. I picked up a virus — there are plenty of them around. There were such crowds of people and I am not used to dealing with that sort of situation."

"That's just it. He's always stayed away from the store in the holiday season. He doesn't like to deal with it. He has depended on some of his old employees and let me tell you, it's been hard on them. Now you are here and he did not have to worry so much. So he feels guilty. Now don't get upset. He wouldn't want me to tell you this. But you know the way men are. They want you to know how much they appreciate what you do but they don't want to be blamed if anything goes wrong."

Helena made a slight gesture of protest, the most that she could do. Esther, busy arranging a place to

193

set the potted plant, said over her shoulder, "Oh, and Mrs. Alfred wanted me to tell you how glad she is that you're getting on so much better. She'll probably come to see you herself soon."

Helena said, "Please thank her for me."

"Oh, of course. She told Billie that she should arrange for you to go on a little cruise when you leave the hospital, before you go back to work. You'll need some sunshine and warm weather. Won't that be lovely?"

Helena did not pay much attention to this statement. Esther made her nervous. She was determined to get back to her job as soon as possible and in her own mind brushed aside any obstacle that would prevent her. She was relieved when Esther left.

She left the hospital a few days later, eager to escape more visitors. Her mother, with the nurses' help, gathered up her belongings and took her to her apartment in a cab. Helena reproached herself for feeling impatient and ungrateful for her mother's care. But she had come to feel that her mother's presence was a barrier to visits from Billie and this feeling overrode the gratitude she should have felt.

She and her mother had fallen back into the pattern their relationship had always had — a pattern of unspoken but well-understood knowledge of each other's feelings and thoughts, a careful sidestepping of any real expression of intimacy in words which nevertheless was based on the most profound intimacy of all: an unfailing grasp of each other's nature. Throughout her childhood Helena had constantly been offended and frustrated by her mother's ambivalence in sacrificing the expression of her love for her daughter to her need to placate her husband. She had not forgiven her this, though as she grew older she realized that her mother, under the carefully maintained surface cheerfulness, was unhappy because of this constant tension.

Now, together in the apartment, it was obvious that her mother had many questions to ask her but did not. Instead, she commented on the various members of the Rosenstein family she had met. Moishe's father and mother had been gracious hosts at the dinner party Moishe had arranged.

She explained, "He's their youngest child — much younger than his brothers — in fact, his father seems quite elderly. He's a banker, isn't he?"

"Yes."

"Do you like them, Helena?"

"Moishe's parents? Yes. They've been very friendly to me. His father is president of the Company and chairman of the board of directors."

"Do you mingle much with them socially?"

Helena took a deep breath. "Mother, I don't have time for a social life. Besides, I don't think it is a good thing for me to see too much of the Rosensteins outside of business. In the first place, I don't think they would want that."

She could see that her mother found this strange, but she shrank from the task of trying to explain herself. She said in a conciliatory tone, "I've only been with Rosenstein's six months. I'm still feeling my way. I don't want to make any missteps through ignorance."

"I see. Well, they speak of you in a very friendly manner. Of course, they know I'm your mother and perhaps politeness enters into it." She paused and then added, "I've never known many Jewish people.

There was a girl in college with me that I liked and her family was friendly to me. But my parents were not anxious for me to have too much to do with them. Oh, I realize that was pretty narrow-minded. But you remember your grandmother. She had very definite ideas about what was proper."

Yes, thought Helena, I do remember her and I remember she rode you pretty hard because you had to get a divorce. Aloud, she said, "The fact that the Rosensteins are Jewish is not a problem for me. It is simply that I have undertaken a job that is completely new to me and that I have to learn the ropes. Rosenstein's is a family-owned business. That is something I must bear in mind."

Tactfully her mother dropped the subject.

The next afternoon, in the midst of a long silence between them, the intercom from the reception desk announced "Miss Rosenstein" and within a few minutes Billie was in the apartment. She came into the room without haste, throwing Helena a smile as she spoke first to her mother.

"Mrs. Sherwood," she said, "I thought perhaps you would like a chance to see some of the spring fashion collections, including Rosenstein's. Would you like that?"

Taken by surprise, Mrs. Sherwood said, "Why, I hadn't thought of it —"

Billie smoothly went on. "Our head buyer, Rachel, will be delighted to take you with her. She's making the rounds. Would you like to go with her? She's waiting downstairs."

Helena saw that her mother was intrigued. She had heard of Rachel and her place in the fashion world. "Why, that would be lovely —"

"I can stay here with Helena while you're gone, so you need not feel concerned."

Five minutes later Mrs. Sherwood left the apartment. Billie, waiting for the sound of the closing door, came over to Helena. She was smiling.

"You had it all arranged," said Helena.

Billie went on smiling as she bent over to hug and kiss her. "The idea is not to give time for second thoughts. Besides, I'm sure your mother is going to enjoy the next two hours with Rachel."

"Oh, Billie!" Helena reached up to put her arms around Billie. "It seems such a long time that I've been laid up."

"You gave me a terrible scare, honey. Sadie, the store nurse, called me while they were waiting for the ambulance. She thought you might be having a heart attack. Naturally, she thought of calling me first, before Daniel. Daniel would have been dreadfully upset and Mrs. Nathan would have been at a loss at what to do. I went with you to the hospital and when they told me how ill you were I thought your mother ought to know. She wouldn't have forgiven us, would she, if she'd not been told."

Helena did not answer at once. Then she said, "At one time, before this happened, I'd have said it wouldn't really have mattered. But now I think she would really not have forgiven you. Up till now I would have said that she had put me so firmly into second place in her life that she would have said she couldn't come. But I was mistaken."

"But didn't she used to call you all the time?"

"I always thought that was for appearances' sake, or because of guilt feelings. I used to think that perhaps she was doing it just in case."

197

"Just in case of what?"

"Just in case she might need me sometime. She's been divorced once, deserted, really. My father walked out on her. I suppose, in the back of her mind, she thinks it might happen again. I think my stepfather is a very selfish man."

Billie gazed at her for a moment. "She is not a very secure woman, is she?"

Helena did not answer. Instead, she moved closer to Billie seated beside her. Billie put her arms around her and said into her ear, "Don't frighten me like that again, honey. I don't think I could stand it. Come on, now, you mustn't get too tired."

She got up and went into the bedroom and came back with a pillow which she gently pushed behind Helena's head so that she could lie full length on the sofa. Then she sat down beside her.

Billie said, going back to what she had said earlier, "At first somebody from Rosenstein's had to look after you and it looked all right for me to be the one. The only other choice was Esther and Esther is too busy with her own little games — not that she isn't kind-hearted enough. But after your mother got here I've had to take a back seat. Esther, by the way, has been telling my mother all about Moishe — how he's brooding over you. My mother is getting alarmed."

"Alarmed?"

"She's very upset at the idea that Moishe might marry a shikseh — a woman who is not Jewish." Billie leaned over and kissed her.

"But, Billie, you know that Moishe isn't interested in getting married to anyone."

"Ah, that's what everybody thought. But mamma believes in the power of a woman to get anything she wants from a man. She thinks a determined woman could make even Moishe want to get married. She doesn't think any man capable of withstanding that. And she sees you as a determined woman, who naturally would think Moishe is a prize. When Moishe gets ready to marry — and that's inevitable — it's his duty to — she wants to pick his wife."

"This is very involved, Billie."

"No, it isn't. It's very simple. She wants Moishe to remain under her influence. She has always treated him as if he was her son. She says his own mother is too old to be a proper mother to him. If he has a wife, she wants to be sure she is someone who'll bow to her prior claims." Billie laughed at the baffled expression on Helena's face. "You've never been in this situation before, have you?"

"Billie, this is ridiculous. I don't want to marry Moishe."

Billie teased, "Are you sure?"

But Helena said angrily, "It's not a joke. I don't want to marry Moishe or have an affair with him, and that's what he really has in mind."

Billie leaned over and stroked her head. "I'm not so sure about that. Up till now Moishe hasn't wanted a wife. But I think he wants you. Moishe is very possessive. Up till now he has never met a woman he wanted to own for more than a few weeks. But I think you've changed that. He wants you and if he has to marry you to get you, he will."

"But I don't want him."

Billie contemplated her for a while without saying

anything. Annoyed, Helena sat up and raised her hand to smooth her hair. "Do we have to talk about Moishe the only time we have here alone together?"

But Billie was not ruffled. "I just wanted to warn you. You'll be hearing from Moishe and from my mother. She's probably deciding that things have gone far enough. She won't rely on Esther any more for her information. In the meantime she's playing for a little time to assess the situation. I've brought you a present from Rosenstein's board of directors."

Billie got up and walked across the room to her handbag — a large, many-pocketed one she favored — and came back with a colorful jacket folder in her hand which she held out to Helena.

Helena looked at it in dismay. It was the sort of elaborate glossy envelope that travel agencies used to hold tickets and other documents. Billie laughed softly. "It won't bite. These are tickets for a four-day cruise in the Caribbean for you and your mother. It's just the thing, mamma says, to put you back on your feet — sea air, sunshine, warm weather, beyond the reach of the office."

Helena reluctantly took the folder from her. "This is impossible! I've been away from my office too long now. I can't waste any more time. I've got to get back. I left everything up in the air. Surely you can understand that I can't do this."

There was a quirk to the corner of Billie's mouth but she said reasonably, "Of course I know how you feel, honey. But it's true you can't go back to the office in the shape you are in now. You'd be back in the hospital at the end of the first day. The Caribbean is a much better place in which to recover

200

quickly." She glanced out of the window at the grey windy day. "We haven't got rid of the slush from the last snow storm."

"If I'm here, at home, Sherry can bring me things from the office. She can work here with me. There's a lot I can do to catch up."

"That's all the more reason for you to go to the Caribbean — away from such temptations."

Helena stared at her in distress. "Don't you care if I'm several hundred miles away? I'd never see you." In spite of herself her voice broke.

Billie's eyes widened in alarm and she came back to sit close to her and take her in her arms. "Honey, I'm not talking about what I want. It would be lovely if we could go away together. You've got to give yourself time to recover. But that's impossible." She placed little kisses on Helena's tear-wet cheeks and murmured softly as Helena collapsed in her arms. "Honey, honey, my little sweet. If you knew what it means to have you here in my arms!"

After a while, under Billie's soothing, Helena quieted and presently was able to sit back against the sofa. Billie stopped speaking and watched her closely, her arm along the sofa-back behind Helena's head.

Helena asked, "This is your mother's idea?"

"She's made up her mind that you're to go to the Caribbean. So she talked to Daniel and told him that the only right and proper thing for Rosenstein's to do was to send you there to recuperate, with your mother along to look after you. She can persuade Daniel to do anything and besides, he is still feeling guilty about you. Now he's enthusiastic. It solves everything. You can't get out of it."

"Daniel had nothing to do with it. The same thing would have happened even if he had been in the store every day."

Billie shrugged. "You can't change his mind — nor my mother's. So you'll just have to go. Rosenstein's board of directors will never forgive you if you turn down their present. They'll feel very annoyed."

"But why does your mother want this?"

"You'll be out of Moishe's reach for another week, which will give her time to figure out how to deal with him."

"Billie!" Helena started to get up, enraged.

Billie pushed her back down. "It doesn't help to get overwrought. Do as I say. Go on the cruise with your mother and try to be calm so that you can benefit physically. You're really not in very good shape."

But Helena sat up again and seized hold of Billie in a desperate grasp. She pulled her to her, thrust herself into Billie's arms, so that they were locked in a tight embrace. She felt a surge of erotic power. It welled up in her like a quenchless spring, driving her body against Billie's soft, generous breasts, yielding stomach. This fiery urge seemed to flow from her into Billie's body and she could not hold back. The sexual drive enveloped her, becoming a violent need to engulf Billie in herself. Billie, holding back in alarmed prudence, gave way and Helena was conscious of her response. Billie was here, there, everywhere, Billie held her captive as she finished in an overwhelming orgasm that left her spent and trembling, limp in Billie's arms, her inner self quaking.

Billie, breathing fast, held her quietly for several

minutes, finally pushing her gently onto the pillow. They sat motionless for a while, Helena helpless in weakness. Billie said softly into her ear, "You mustn't do that again for a while. You can't stand it yet."

Helena raised her head to look at her. "I didn't know I wanted you that much."

Billie caressed her gently. "You don't know what you mean to me, honey."

For a long time they sat quietly wrapped in a mute communion. The buzz of the intercom from the reception desk roused them and for a moment they stared at each other bewildered. Then Billie said, sitting up and smoothing her hair, "That's your mother. I'll answer."

She did so and then went into the bedroom and brought a throw from the bed which she tucked around Helena. "Just lie quiet. Your mother won't notice anything."

Mrs. Sherwood came into the room talking vivaciously. Her usually sedate manner was for the time being eclipsed by the stimulation she had enjoyed during the last two hours.

"I've never experienced anything like it!" she exclaimed. She stopped abruptly when she saw Helena lying on the sofa covered by the throw. "Oh, darling! Were you asleep? I hope I didn't wake you."

Billie said, "Oh, no. She's waking up now. So Rachel gave you a good time. I thought you would enjoy it."

"Indeed I did enjoy it. I've never really paid a great deal of attention to high fashion, though of course I know the value of dressing well. It is certainly a different world. And Miss Leventhal is so knowledgeable! She took me to half-a-dozen fashion shows and explained all the details to me. I never realized before what goes into creating new styles. I must admit I found some of it bizarre. I cannot imagine myself or any of my friends wearing some of the clothes I saw being modelled. And the models themselves!"

"As you say," said Billie amiably, "it's a different world."

Mrs. Sherwood grew more like herself. "I can see that Helena would have difficulty explaining all this to me." She paused and looked at her daughter. Helena had sat up. "I still wonder —" She did not finish her sentence, as if she suddenly doubted the advisability of what she was about to say.

Helena said to Billie, "Mother does not understand why I should go into the women's apparel business. Well, I've just found a new way of applying my training."

Her mother, with a quick glance at Billie, said, "Now, of course, Helena, I understand that this is a career opportunity for you. You've explained that." Then, as if to divert the talk into less controversial lines, she asked Billie, "Your great grandmother founded the store, didn't she? Miss Leventhal was telling me something about her. She must have been a remarkable woman."

Billie nodded.

"It was quite unusual for a woman to found such a business in those days, wasn't it? Miss Leventhal told me that she was so successful that she was able to help all her sons establish themselves in business. She must have been quite gifted. Are you active in the business also?"

Billie shook her head. "No. We have Helena now instead."

Mrs. Sherwood looked startled. "Why, that is very flattering, Helena."

Helena looked at the floor and did not answer. Billie, aware that Mrs. Sherwood was now looking at her closely, said she must be going.

"But before I go," she said, "I want to tell you that Rosenstein's board of directors wants Helena to go for a little cruise in the Caribbean to recuperate before she goes back to work. We're hoping you will be able to go with her — all expenses paid, of course."

Mrs. Sherwood stared at her in surprise. "Why, that is nice of them!" She looked back at Helena. "Dear, this is really a godsend. You should have a break before you go back to work."

"Yes," said Helena, wearily.

The next day her mother packed for both of them, exclaiming at Helena's Rosenstein wardrobe. "Really, dear. These things are exquisite. You know, I bought a few things for myself yesterday. Miss Leventhal picked them out for me. I would never have had the courage to buy them on my own, but now that I have them I realize they are just my style of thing."

"Rachel has wonderful taste," said Helena.

They went by cab to the airport on a grey, chill morning. Her mother, looking out of the window, said, "It will certainly be nice to see some warm bright sunshine, won't it, dear?" and Helena agreed. They were to join the cruise ship in Florida.

The four days of the cruise passed more quickly than Helena had anticipated. She tried not to be broody, to spoil her mother's pleasure. But she longed for Billie. The awareness that Billie was far beyond her physical reach cast a pall over her spirits. The whole setting — the tropical luxuriance of the ports they stopped in, the pampered ease of their lives — seemed only to heighten her depression, as if her senses were being titillated by promises with no hope of satisfaction.

Her mother was overwhelmed. She was used to a degree of physical luxury but not this complete exemption from responsibility. "Helena, this is too much! It must be costing a fortune!"

Helena roused enough to reply, "Well, I suppose it is. But Rosenstein's is paying for it."

They were sitting at breakfast in the sitting room of their suite, gazing out at the tropical scene beyond their window. The brilliant light was blinding on the white house walls, sparkled in the vivid blue-green of the harbor water, shone on the leaves of the tropical plants that broke the harshness of the sunlight. Helena knew that her mother was watching her closely. She supposed that her moodiness was apparent. Presently her mother said, "The Rosensteins certainly seem to place a high value on you."

"Why do you think so? Because they are spending money on me?" Helena knew that her tone was ill-natured. "After all, Floyd's company certainly keeps him and you in considerable luxury. This sort of thing isn't new to you."

She saw the pain register in her mother's face. Her mother said, "Of course. That's true. But after all he is a very valuable man to his company. The company knows that it must provide him with the best if they want to keep him."

"Well, don't you think that Rosenstein's might be interested in keeping me?" Helena challenged her.

"Why, yes, of course. It just doesn't seem to be the same thing."

"Because I'm a woman — and especially because I'm your daughter."

Her mother hurried to be soothing. "Now, dear, don't get upset. Of course you must be important to them. I quite understand. But you must remember that I still think of you as my child —"

"Not as somebody else's business manager. Oh, all right! Let's drop it."

She made an effort to be less hasty, more amiable. She realized that the real spur to her ill-temper was not in her mother's automatic discounting of her career success. She was used to this dismissal of any proof that she was an independent woman who did not need a man to define herself. No, her impatience, her snappishness was really caused by something entirely different — the fact that she was far from Billie. Billie had disrupted the life she had so carefully planned for herself, and yet nameless and faceless dangers menaced her relationship with Billie, dangers she was powerless to oppose.

It was near the end of their cruise that her mother first mentioned Moishe. She introduced his name into their conversation with obvious care. Helena realized then that her mother had charitably assumed that her moodiness and bad temper was the result of her illness and had been patient and forbearing. But now she said, when Helena made no attempt to disguise her eagerness to get back to New York, "It's such a paradise here. New York is going to be very disagreeable after this warm weather and lovely scenery. But I suppose nowhere is paradise when one's hankering for something or someone else. Really, dear, you do act as if there is someone you want to be with."

The remark so exactly touched her real feelings that Helena stared at her in dismay. But her mother could have no idea what Billie meant to her. Then she heard her mother probe delicately: Was she anxious to see Moishe? He had been so attentive, so concerned about her. Helena's relief at this misconception made her answer good-humoredly, Oh, no. She was not thinking about Moishe. Though she realized that it was impossible to explain adequately to her mother what the problem was with the future of the Rosenstein store, she seized on this subject as something to talk about. She noticed that, while listening to her attentively, her mother looked at her every so often as if speculating about whether this was a cover-up for something else that troubled her. Her mother would never believe that business concerns would take the first place in any woman's mind. There must be some more personal, more intimate affair, something that engaged her heart — therefore, a man.

Her mother finally interrupted. "Well, I'm sure you're very clever at all this, Helena. But I do think you're apt to forget that there are other relationships in life that you should not ignore. It's all very fine to think while you're young that these impersonal things are sufficient but when you are older and find yourself alone you will regret that you did not establish some sort of private life when you had the opportunity."

Helena did not answer, deciding that silence was the best way to avoid further probing.

But when they arrived back at the airport in New York she was dismayed to see that Moishe was waiting for them at the gate. He grinned at her, his eyes glinting, before he greeted her mother. He had brought a bouquet of roses and talked volubly all the while. The tropical brilliance of the Caribbean sky had given way to the cool blue of a bright Manhattan morning. He found them a cab and joined them in it for the ride to Helena's apartment. When they got there he lingered on the doorstep until her mother, quick to recognize and acquiesce in a man's demands, suggested that perhaps he would like to come and visit that evening, after they had had a chance to unpack.

When he had gone and they were alone in the apartment her mother looked at her nervously, as if waiting for some protest. But Helena said nothing. She was tired and she realized that after all her mother would be leaving for Texas within a day or two. The thought sustained her through the dinner and the show that Moishe insisted on taking them to in the evening. She was annoyed by the fact that his attention was fastened on her while all the time he was talking to her mother. Her mother was obviously fully aware of his intent and responded as he expected her to.

Her mother said, as they were getting ready for bed, "Helena, he is really in love with you. It is perfectly plain. What are you going to do?"

"Do? Nothing. Why should I do anything?"

"Well, you can't keep him dangling like this. He's not the sort to be put off."

Helena flung her robe over a chair, ready to get into bed. "Oh, Mother, I'm tired! I can't talk about Moishe now!"

For a while her mother said nothing further, as she put on the face cream she used at night, eyeing herself in the mirror of the vanity. There were twin beds in Helena's bedroom. At last, getting into bed herself she paused before turning out the light and said, "Dear, there is something I must really speak about. I do like Moishe. He's so charming and so agreeable. If you really like him, I will not make any protest. But I must warn you that there will be a real problem if you marry him. I'm afraid Floyd will not accept the idea of his daughter marrying a Jew —"

Helena exploded. "Floyd is not my father! How many times do I have to point that out to you! His prejudices mean nothing to me. What I do with my life is none of his business."

Her mother said angrily, "Your own father won't be any different."

"Then what I say goes for him too. He's never paid any attention to me. Why should I be concerned about his opinions? As for Floyd, you can tell him for me that what he thinks means less than nothing to me. I despise him, always have —" She was stopped in the midst of her outburst by the stricken look on her mother's face. Of course, if she made a breach between herself and her stepfather, it would be her mother who would be caught in the middle. Before this illness she would have dismissed the idea that her mother would be much affected by such an event. Now she realized that she held a greater value for

210

her mother than she had thought. Neither one of them could cast the other off.

Her mother persisted. "But, seriously, Helena, do you think you might be —"

"I'm much more likely to have an affair with him than to marry him. Does that make you feel any better? I'm not thinking of marrying anyone." To cover her own distress she was purposely and unavoidably cruel.

"But, Helena, he seems very serious about you."

Helena took a deep breath to control her impatience. "I've told you, Moishe is not ready to marry. He's playing the field. What he wants right now is for me to go to bed with him."

"I hope you don't have any intention of doing that."

"Well, as a matter of fact, I don't. It would be a serious mistake for me to do that, as far as my position in Rosenstein's is concerned."

Her mother was silent for a while but made no move to turn out the light. Presently she said, "Helena, the real reason is that you are not interested in men, are you?"

Shocked, Helena did not answer.

"I've always thought — I've always told myself — that you have simply not met a man you really liked. Darling, I've always hoped that you would not make the kind of mistakes I've made. I've always hoped that you would be luckier — or more astute — than I have been, and would find real happiness in a good marriage. But you don't really want that, do you?"

Helena, pierced by the humble tone of her words, said, "Oh, mother! I'm sorry I'm so impatient sometimes —"

Her mother ignored her response. "You've tried to tell me, before this, haven't you?"

"Yes," said Helena, eagerly. "Yes, I have. I don't want the intrusion of a man in my life. I had given up thinking you could understand that."

"But, Helena, I am very unhappy at the idea that you will never have a real intimacy in your life. That is dreadful."

The silence that followed between them was filled with a rush of unspoken thoughts. Helena found herself unable to say anything further and her mother seemed to have withdrawn into herself. Finally, Helena said, "Let me go to sleep now. I'm really tired."

Her mother sighed and turned out the light. Grateful for the dark, Helena tried to quiet her own inner turmoil. The truth had come so near the surface. Now it had sunk back into the mass of unacknowledged understanding that always lay between them.

Her mother left the following day. She was anxiously affectionate as they drove to the airport, reminding her that she must not return to the strenuous schedule of work that had led to her collapse. At the airport, as they waited for the plane's departure to be called, her mother gazed at her for a while, as if trying still to understand what she really felt. Helena, embarrassed under her earnest eyes, looked down. They were both aware that they had been closer in spirit during the last few days than at any time in their joint lives, certainly since Helena's childhood. When the plane's departure was announced, her mother suddenly took her in her arms.

"Darling, you know that I'm always ready to come to you if you ever need me. It doesn't matter what you do. I'll try to understand. Don't let anything come between us so that you can't confide in me."

Helena lifted her eyes to meet her mother's gaze, guiltily conscious of what she could not acknowledge, for the first time regretting that she could not speak of Billie, of what Billie meant to her. Her mother went on, "I do mean under any circumstances. I have come to realize that you have a life that does not match mine — that you have preferences of your own. Do understand that I will never act to estrange you from me."

The second announcement of departure sounded and they kissed hastily and Helena watched as her mother hurried through the departure gate. For a while she stood unheeding the throng of people passing to and fro around her, amazed by what her mother had said, amazed and bewildered. Had her mother after all guessed that it was not Moishe who absorbed her but Billie? Was the link between herself and her mother, which she had thought to have faded in the last few years, proved still strong enough to convey the truth of her emotional life? A feeling, which grew stronger as she pondered, told her that this was the fact.

Returning to her apartment she was glad to be alone, to study this new phase of her dealings with her mother. Slowly she came to terms with it. Her mother indeed knew now what she was, what Billie meant to her. They would never discuss this openly; it was not in her mother's nature nor her own to do so, to say in so many words what they both accepted. But the bond between them had suddenly become

213

stronger, no longer falsified by the doubts that had shadowed their relationship. From now on there was an underpinning of truth to their dealings with one another. Her skittish, nervous mother had bravely followed her heart in speaking as she had.

When Monday morning came and Helena walked into Rosenstein's at her normal early hour, she was aware that she was returning to her real life. It was as if she had been away from the normal events and circumstances of her daily activities for a space of years rather than weeks. There was a silent welcome in the appearance of the store, in the usual promise of the coming bustle and hubbub that would fill the presently empty aisles. It was true, as she had felt all the time she had been laid up, that Rosenstein's had become her world. It was the world in which she knew how to act, to think, to plan for the day's activities. She tried to retrieve the memory of what she had been doing the day she had collapsed. The life of the store had gone on. It certainly had not been suspended during her absence. Esther, in her visits to the hospital, had told her that Daniel had taken up the daily problems, unwillingly. Probably there were things postponed that would greet her when she reached her desk. This idea actually reassured her. It meant that she would quickly once more be in charge.

That first day back passed in a blur of activity, from Sherry's delighted greeting when she arrived to the security guard's Goodnight when she left the deserted store long after dark. The following days melted away under the press of accumulated business, till she arrived home exhausted on Saturday afternoon. Even Moishe had not tried to interrupt

214

her, apparently realizing that she had no time to give
to any personal concern. She had not heard from
Billie. Sitting in her armchair passively, grateful for
the quiet, she was startled when the phone rang,
scattering her thoughts. Billie's throaty voice said into
her ear, "Put some things in your overnight case and
be downstairs at the curb. I'll pick you up in ten
minutes." Just before she hung up she added, "Bring
some boots."

Helena put the phone down and stared at it for a
moment. Then rousing herself, she packed her
overnight case. Down on the street she watched
anxiously for a few minutes until a small, ten-year-old
cadillac sedan pulled up to the curb. She had never
thought about the fact that Billie might have a car or
what sort it might be. The difficulties of owning a
car in Manhattan made the question academic for
most of her friends. But now Billie reached across the
front seat to open the door and beckon her in. She
jumped in and tossed her case and a pair of boots
into the back seat.

Billie said nothing. Her attention was fixed on the
Saturday afternoon traffic, into which she moved
expertly. They drove in silence up the island,
obviously headed out of town to the north. Helena
was surprised at the smooth, effortless skill with
which Billie handled the car. She had not associated
Billie with any sort of mechanical deftness. As the
traffic grew less and they moved out onto the
interstate she wondered where they were going. There
had been a snowstorm while she was away on the
cruise and there were still patches of frozen snow on
the hillsides in many spots. The air was coldly damp
and she saw that Billie wore a fur jacket and hat and

leather gloves, and knee-high boots. In the heated car she felt comfortable but suddenly wondered if she had brought enough protection from the wintry weather outside.

As if in answer to her thoughts Billie said, "Don't worry. I've got some warm things for you to wear."

"I didn't think about the weather."

"I didn't warn you that we were going out of town. I didn't have time. Or I didn't want to take it." Billie's tone was crisper than usual.

"Where are we going, then?"

"Up the Hudson." Billie did not say anything more. They drove on for another hour or so and then she turned off the interstate onto a secondary road that wound among hills and through small towns. Presently she turned off again into a narrow road that ran along by a stream with steep banks and across a wooden bridge. The declining sun shone without warmth on the leafless trees and snow patches. Eventually they entered a long drive leading to a large colonial house surrounded by huge old shrubs. A signboard said the name of the inn. Billie, getting out of the car, merely said, "I come here sometimes when I get a chance. They stay open all year."

The man carrying their bags — Billie had a couple of suitcases — led them up several steps from the reception hall down a long narrow corridor to a corner suite that looked out on the wooded hillside behind the house. When he had gone Billie took off her hat and jacket and stood for a moment gazing out of the window. She said quietly, "Nobody is going to find us here." She came over to Helena and put her arms around her. "Honey."

216

Helena buried her face in Billie's shoulder. Billie said into her ear, "I had to take the chance. Mamma has gone out of town for the weekend. I was afraid that Moishe would come to get you. I know he was just waiting for your mother to leave."

"He has not bothered me this week. He knows I don't have any free time. But he might come looking for me this weekend. If he does not find me, will he come looking for you?"

Billie smiled. "There's nobody to tell him where I am. Only Michelle and Rachel know I come up here sometimes."

They both fell silent then. Billie, restless, paced about the room. Presently she said, "Put on your slacks and boots. I want to go out."

Obediently Helena did so, aware that Billie's inner turmoil demanded motion. They went out of another door of the inn that led onto a terrace and then onto a path that climbed the wooded hillside. Billie knew her way and Helena followed her up to a knoll from which they could catch a glimpse of water among the trees. The sun, already low in the west, was veiled by light clouds. A damp evening chill had taken possession. In spite of the fleece-lined jacket Billie had provided, Helena shivered. Billie asked sharply, "Is it too cold for you?"

"No. I think it's more psychological."

Billie nodded in abstraction. "I had to be with you. I had to get away. Honey, it's as if I was in jail, looking through the bars at you."

Helena heard the note of desperation in her voice. All at once she realized that, uncharacteristically, Billie was out of control. She gazed at her anxiously and was pierced by the stricken, grieving look on her

217

face. "Billie, don't be so upset! We can find a way out of this. Surely you can find a way to deal with your mother. She can't dominate you forever!"

Billie looked at her mutely and turned away to stare at the stretch of river visible below them. The wintry quiet of the woodland settled over them. Helena put her arm around Billie's waist under her jacket and they stood for a few minutes without speaking. Then Billie said, "At least your mother is two thousand miles away."

Helena heard the attempt at humor, but answered seriously, "Before I got sick I would have agreed with you — that she's far away and out of my life. I'm not sure about that any more."

"You mean, she's changed her attitude?"

"No. I just didn't understand how she felt. I've always been sure that she was afraid that I'd do something — marry the wrong kind of man — disgrace her somehow — so that she would have to disown me to please my stepfather."

Billie's smile was ironic. "She could make the other choice."

"No, she couldn't. Her whole life has been lived on the principle that women like her are only acceptable in society if they have the right kind of husband. Otherwise, they're lost — have no status."

Billie studied her for a moment. "So now you think she's ready to accept you as you are. Do you think she has guessed that you prefer women?"

"I think so. I think —" Helena paused to look at Billie. "I think she knows what you mean to me. But I'll never be able to talk to her about it."

Billie did not answer but continued to look at the

river, a lighter patch of grey in the dull grey evening light.

Helena asked anxiously, "What would your mother do if she knew about you?"

"I suppose, disown me."

"Well, if it came to a showdown, wouldn't it be worth getting rid of this schizophrenia, this pretending all the time?"

"You mean, do what Michelle did."

"Yes."

"I could never do that. Michelle's mother isn't like mine. Michelle's mother is a self-centered woman. I don't think she has ever felt a strong emotion for anyone, not her husband, not her children. Michelle didn't have any real closeness with her, and now she rejects the idea of filial obedience, of blood being thicker than water. But she's bound by it just the same. Michelle can't escape from the feeling that after all she is a Rosenstein." Billie paused for a moment and then asked, "Would you be able to cut yourself off altogether from your mother?"

Helena answered slowly, "I suppose, not in my heart, even if I went through the motions — I don't know."

Billie eyed her quizzically. "If it all came out in the open, you'd probably be more worried about the effect on your career, wouldn't you? The world isn't ready to accept openly lesbian corporate executives, is it?"

There was no disapproval in Billie's voice but Helena was vexed. "That's putting it pretty boldly."

"It all comes down to what's most important to you."

Helena, still smarting, snapped, "And what's most important to you?"

Billie did not reply but turned away from the overlook and started back along the trail. Helena hesitated for a while and then followed her. The evening was darkening among the trees and, hurrying to catch up with Billie, she tripped and fell when her foot caught in a tree root. Billie was beside her instantly.

"Have you hurt yourself?"

Annoyed, Helena scrambled to her feet. "No, of course not."

But Billie stood beside her till she got her breath. They went more carefully down the rest of the path. By the time they reached the terrace night was gathering. In their room they stopped as soon as the door was closed and sought each other in a tight embrace.

Helena felt Billie's hands searching over her body, down her back, over her legs. She pressed herself against Billie's soft breasts, her fingers kneading the little roll of extra flesh around Billie's waist. Without words they undressed and sought the bed, Billie flinging the covers back impatiently. The pent-up eagerness created by their absence from each other burst its bounds and neither of them felt any constraint. Billie covered her with her more ample body, kissing her ears, her breasts, exploring the soft spots of her body, searching for the expectant center of her desire. Time lost its definition. They were aware of each other only in the heat of their conjoined bodies, each other's quick breathing, the energy that flowed between them. When Billie sank back on the pillow, Helena leaned over to look into her eyes. The love she saw there overwhelmed her and she pressed her face into Billie's breasts. Billie clasped her to her with a frantic grip.

After a long spell of quiet, lying close together to enjoy the feel of each other's body, returning slowly to the rational world, Billie said, "There's nothing more important than this, being here together."

Roused from the luxurious abandon of the last hour Helena raised herself on her elbow. "Well, then, what are you going to do about it?"

Billie brought her gaze back from the ceiling. "There is nothing I can do."

"There must be some way we can solve this! We can't go on like this."

Billie reached up to brush her hair away from her face as it hung above her. "There's such a thing as reality. I have mine. You have yours. You're not willing to risk your career. I can't face my mother. She's my mother and she loves me and I love her. How can I tell her the worst thing she could imagine — that her only child has put herself beyond the pale of society as she knows it?"

Helena sank back into the pillow. Billie went on. "We're not teenagers. You're well on your way in the life you are creating for yourself. You know you have to manage your personal affairs so that they don't interfere with that."

Helena snapped, "And how about you? You're not doing anything with your life."

Billie reached over to stroke her cheek as if to banish the bitter taunt. "I know that. I've never been able to make up my mind what I should do and now, since you're here, I'm totally at sea."

Helena, ashamed of her own sharpness, rolled over

221

closer to her. "Billie, Billie, what are we going to do?"

For a long time Billie did not answer and they returned to kissing and fondling one another. At last Billie said, "We'd better go and have some dinner. They serve till ten o'clock."

The inn dining room was almost empty. Two couples sat at widely spaced tables and one or two single people sat near the windows. Billie led the way to a table in the corner, as if this was a preferred spot.

"You've been here a lot?" Helena asked.

"Yes, by myself. I found it once when I was late coming back from college. I liked it because it is a rustic kind of place — and no skiing."

"In other words, Moishe wouldn't be coming here."

"Right. He's always wanting me to ski — or play tennis — or golf. He says I'm going to seed. He has told you that."

"Yes, he says I should encourage you."

"Moishe always wants to run everything and everybody. He was in prep school when I first went to college. He caught up very fast. He was in college in his middle teens. He wasn't very far away from where I was and he liked to be my date. He got a big kick out of going to weekend bashes with me — everybody else was five or six years older."

"And you agreed to that?"

"Why not?" Billie looked at her with a mischievous smile. "I didn't care if everybody thought I was naive. And it was a lot more convenient for me than having somebody my own age who wanted sex along the way."

222

"You mean, he didn't?"

Billie's eyes opened wide. "Oh, no! Moishe is very strict about that sort of thing. He's not a practicing Jew but he believes in all the prohibitions, especially for me. I have to be the proper Jewish girl."

Helena looked thoughtfully down at the soup that had been placed before her. "Billie, did you know you wanted only women?"

"I didn't analyze myself. I just accepted the fact that I didn't want to go to bed with men."

"But what about Michelle?"

Billie was silent for a while. "Michelle was in a special place with me."

There was another silence before Helena asked, "Did your mother approve of your going around with a kid?"

"Oh, she has a blind side where Moishe is concerned. She thought it was cute of him to want to be my date. She thought he was too young to be dangerous. Besides, she was afraid I would get involved with somebody who was not Jewish. Most of the men I knew were not."

"Is she really so prejudiced?"

Again Billie smiled at her. "It's a qualified sort of prejudice. It's a little hard to explain to you. She doesn't dislike people because they are not Jewish. Since she isn't observant, she doesn't care much about religious differences. She wouldn't mind if I married a Jew who didn't keep kosher or the Sabbath. But she doesn't trust non-Jews. She has a sort of nervous fear of getting too close to them. It's a deep-rooted thing. She wouldn't want a non-Jew for a son-in-law. He wouldn't understand about how Jews feel about family matters. She feels he probably

223

wouldn't be prepared to acknowledge what being a Rosenstein means and what her rights and privileges are."

Helena looked at her curiously. "Does she like me?"

"You're still under probation."

"As manager of Rosenstein's?"

"Well, no. She accepts you there because of Daniel. She is very shrewd about men and about Daniel in particular. She understands that he has come to rely on you and that there isn't a sexual basis for his fondness for you. Oh, yes, Daniel has become very fond of you, but he doesn't think of you as an object of sexual desire. My mother knows he approved of you in the first place because you're serious-minded and clever and ambitious — that you don't intend to make your way in business by exercising your woman's wiles in the workplace. Not that she would rely on a man's judgment about that."

"So she just tolerates me because of Daniel?"

"Now don't get your back up. No, she is prepared to like you — she does, in fact, like you now. But she is suspicious of women who demonstrate an ability to dominate other people. That's why I am careful not to let her think that you're important to me. She would begin to suspect you right away." Billie paused and then added with a trace of bitterness. "Nobody is to breach the invisible net she has over me. Remember, Esther is right there to report everything to her."

"But, Billie, why does she treat you like this?"

"Because she does not think I have sense enough to come in out of the rain." Billie's voice was tart.

They spent a long and blissful night. In the quiet of the old house they lost themselves in their own private world. Billie's warm, soft flesh was seductive, comforting. Helena felt herself drowning happily in the sea of erotic emotion that Billie's gentle yet purposeful, insistent hands, Billie's enveloping body, created. She herself felt an unavoidable urge to have Billie, to thrust her own violent desire on Billie, to evoke from Billie the same complete abnegation of separate identity. She wanted Billie, every inch of Billie, and she wanted Billie to accept the whole of herself. In their mutual success the night passed in quietness broken only by their murmurs and eventually the light rhythm of their sleeping breaths.

When they woke to daylight it was with a feeling of completion, of having reached a new place in their lives. Billie got out of bed and walked naked to the window, shivering a little. The sun lit her body, arousing in Helena an irresistible desire to get up and go to her, to press her own body against Billie's. They stood kissing for a few moments before going to shower and dress.

A light snow had fallen during the night and the hillside behind the inn sparkled as the sun's rays reached in amongst the leafless trees. They would go for a walk there, after breakfast, said Billie.

The drive back to Manhattan that afternoon was as silent as the one that had brought them there up the valley, but this time it was a silence filled with contentment. It was only when they reached the Sunday emptiness of the Manhattan streets that their anxieties returned. Billie stopped in front of Helena's apartment building and they said a brief goodbye, conscious now of the surveillance they were returning

225

to, of the distance they must keep between their bodies while in view of others.

Monday morning, when Helena reached her office, eager to take up her interrupted work, she felt unaccountably hampered and impeded by the cordiality of the people with whom she worked. It was as if she begrudged the few seconds it took to respond. Her energy must be returning, she thought, nourished by the hours with Billie. In midmorning Sherry brought Mrs. Nathan into her office. Helena had not seen Daniel during her few days back. Now, said Mrs. Nathan, he was in the store and ready to see her.

Daniel sat behind his big, bare desk, the bright window behind him. His office was very large and furnished in a manner to emphasize the impression of luxury and power. Helena had decided that this was the work of the people hired to decorate the store's offices, because Daniel himself was mild-mannered, reserved, a man who did not try to impose his authority by means of any outward show. Now when he saw her come in he got up and came to meet her halfway across the deep-piled carpet.

"My dear, how glad I am to see you back! You're quite well?" He was wringing her hand with both of his, the diamond on his finger winking brilliantly.

"Oh, yes. That's all past. I'm ashamed to have taken so long."

"It was hardly your choice. Well, come and sit down so that I can bring you up to date."

Helena sat down across the desk from him and put her bulging attaché case down on the floor at her feet. She felt a sense of relief. With Daniel she knew where she stood. Whatever he told her would be straightforward, without equivocation — no half-truths, little traps to catch her unwary feet. Daniel had been a long time testing her out when she first came to Rosenstein's but when he had satisfied himself of her ability and trustworthiness, he had given her his complete confidence.

First he went quickly over the main events of the store's life while she was gone — minutiae which, she knew, he was glad to turn over to her again. Then, as the pace of their conversation slowed down, he seemed to ponder, paying only partial attention to what she was saying. Eventually, when she finished her report of the previous week, there was a few minutes' silence. She knew something was coming and she braced herself for it.

At last he said, "Helena, while you've been gone there's been a lot of discussion about the future of the Company, whether Rosenstein's should be sold to a conglomerate. I know this idea is not new to you. Barton says he has discussed it with you."

"Yes, he has talked to me about this. He has indicated that there is a difference of opinion among the directors about it."

Daniel nodded his neat grey head. "What do you think about it?"

Helena hesitated and then plunged in. "I don't really have any views in the sense you mean. I don't feel that comes within my province. My only concern is the health of the Rosenstein Company as an ongoing business. It is true that the store has not been living up to its potential in the last ten years, perhaps more. We have to find answers to the problems that have caused this decline and for that we must first identify the problems."

227

Daniel was nodding his head in agreement. "Barton thinks he knows what the problems are and so does my nephew Moishe." He sent a glance in her direction as if to see whether she recognized Moishe. "They both think that these problems are obvious and incurable unless Rosenstein's sells out. They think that the store is behind the times, that it can't really be brought into today's competitive market, that we can't go on running a store like this. We have to adapt to modern times and Rosenstein's can't be adapted."

"That depends on what you want to achieve. If you want to make Rosenstein's a big money-maker in a mass production market, you'll have to sacrifice the store's character — make it like any other of the older retail stores that have been consolidated into chains."

Daniel scanned her face shrewdly. "You don't like that solution."

"It's not a matter of what I like. I know the history of Rosenstein's. In its heyday — in your grandmother's time — it was such a big money-maker that it could afford to subsidize enterprises that are now much larger than it is. Is that what you wish to achieve now — regain that capacity for financial spin-off?"

Daniel did not answer but waited. She went on, "If you want simply to revive the store, I think it can be restored to real profitability. That does not mean that it will become a chip to be used in creating a new financial empire, but it will be the pre-eminent retailing outlet it once was."

Daniel turned in his chair halfway away from her to look out of the window behind him. When he

228

turned back he said, "You know, Helena, I'm the voting fiduciary on the board of directors for several members of the family."

Helena nodded. Mrs. Alfred, she knew, was one of them. Michelle must be another.

Daniel went on. "Therefore, I have to consider a number of things. There's the matter of income. The source of income my beneficiaries depend upon, in part, at least. I must bear in mind that I must seek the greatest financial benefit for them compatible with prudence. They know nothing of business and depend on me to safeguard their interests. Another matter is how they, as Rosensteins, view the question of preserving the store's traditions. I realize that some of the younger ones are not as concerned about this as those of my generation. But none of them can be entirely immune to some feeling on that subject."

Helena thought of Moishe. She did not want to contradict Daniel, but she was painfully aware that what he said was more what he wanted to believe than what actually was the truth. She debated whether to speak of Moishe or to wait to see what further Daniel had to say. She ended by replying, "I think the alternatives I've mentioned cover that point: either you must concentrate on reviving the store as it is; or you must embark on a ruthless dismemberment so that it can be incorporated into a conglomerate. If you choose the latter, you must make sure that you retain a majority interest in any merger. I don't have to tell you that there will be a difference in the amount of control you will have if it becomes a public company."

He gave her such a long mournful look that she became uncomfortable. He said, with gentle reproach, emphasizing the "we," "We must do one or the other. We must decide. Otherwise Rosenstein's will die of stagnation. You're part of Rosenstein's now, Helena. I would not be discussing this with you in this way if you were not."

Astonished, Helena said hastily, "That's extremely kind of you. I do feel I'm a part of Rosenstein's."

He went on immediately, his voice changing to a more decisive tone, "However, as you have said, there is a difference of opinion among the directors and officers. Barton is the most vocal on the side of transforming Rosenstein's. He wants the greater scope that would provide for himself. He finds a ready ally in Moishe. Moishe can see nothing but the glories of financial manipulation. Rosenstein's is a prize piece for juggling in the financial market." He looked over again at her and smiled. "Moishe thinks in superlatives. He's a very clever boy. We're all proud of him. But he lacks seasoning. He wants to forget the past. One of these days he'll come to value what Rosenstein's represents. Just now he thinks of it only as a chip to gamble with, as you say. He has the lucky touch. He'll succeed at anything he undertakes."

After a silence Helena asked, "Has anything happened while I was out?"

"Nothing decisive. What I wanted to warn you about is that the question is to come up in the next board meeting. I told Lionel that we could not possibly discuss this matter until you were back. Moishe is very impatient. So is Barton. They're pushing for a quick decision."

Helena, frustrated by the thought that she would

be excluded from this meeting, left hanging about the door unable to observe the process going on in the board room, said in anguish, "When will this meeting take place? What should I do —?"

Daniel cut in. "It is scheduled for a week from today. Now, Helena, I want you to be there. I'll tell you what I have in mind. I want you to prepare a presentation to show what you think can be done to revive Rosenstein's — keeping the store as it is but modernizing it, just what you have been saying to me, with the necessary details. I want a visual argument, you understand, something dramatic that the others can grasp easily, something to hold their attention to the problem. I know you can do that."

Speechless with relief, Helena nodded.

"You'll be present as my assistant — not to give an argument, you understand, just to illustrate what I'll be saying. The board meetings are always closed, of course. Esther is the only person present who is not a member. She takes the minutes. However, this is an unusual occasion and I'll need your help."

"In that case, I should not only prepare a presentation in favor of preserving the store but also a presentation in favor of the opposite, the advantages and disadvantages of going public and selling out to a conglomerate."

Daniel seemed to hesitate at this suggestion, but after a thoughtful moment he replied, "Yes, I think you are right. We should do that."

Helena asked anxiously, "Moishe will not be present?"

"Oh, no. He is not a director. His father is his voting fiduciary, as he has always been since Moishe

231

inherited his shares in the Company. That's never been changed. I think he'll certainly want to change it after this." Daniel was smiling to himself.

"And Lionel, of course, will vote his own shares."

"Yes, but he has only a small interest in the Company now. He has given most of his shares to Moishe. Even so, Moishe's interest is comparatively small. The others, with the exception of Mrs. Alfred, have altogether among them twenty percent of the stock. They will be guided by what Lionel and I do. The largest shareholder, of course, is Mrs. Alfred. Nothing can be decided without her concurrence."

"You are prepared to vote against the sale of Rosenstein's?"

Daniel's face took on a stubborn look. "I can't say that. Like you, I have to think beyond my own inclinations. I cannot ignore the wishes of those whose interests I represent. I can only persuade them of what I think should prevail. Lionel especially won't be convinced. Moishe has great influence with him. No, remember when you make your presentation you must balance it against the advantages of going public and selling out."

Helena went back to her office in a bemused state. There was no clear-cut position she could take. In the back of her mind hovered the thought of Billie. Daniel had made no reference to Billie. Billie would vote her own shares but these represented a minor interest in the Company. But she must not let her knowledge of Billie's passionate attachment to Rosenstein's preservation get in the way. What she must do was to concentrate on the preparation of the presentation to the board meeting.

Combined with the heavy work scheduled,

resulting from her absence, this new commitment kept her at her desk far into the evening of each day. She was glad this was so. She knew she could not expect to hear from Billie and these long hours saved her from having to agree to meet Moishe in the evenings. She knew he was vexed. He took out his vexation by ridiculing her devotion to her job. She did not answer him. At the end of the normal business day she sent Sherry home, amused at Sherry's dismay at this threatened invasion of her social life.

Absorbed as she was in the work she was doing, Helena nevertheless felt the loneliness of the empty, deserted building which she shared for several hours only with the security guards. She tried to dismiss this feeling, which had never visited her before. The solitude, the silence was what she welcomed after the constant activity and interruptions of the day. But there was also this sense of mysterious life beyond her office. Was it in fact, she asked herself half-humorously, the spirit of the store, of Old Leah?

But the next evening, after Sherry had left, she was surprised when she went into the outer office to consult a file, to see that a middle-aged woman sat at Sherry's desk. She stared at her.

The woman smiled back at her. "I'm sorry, Miss Worrall. You were so absorbed in what you were doing when I came in that I did not disturb you. Is there anything I can do for you?"

"Why —" Helena began and stopped.

"They didn't tell you that I was assigned here for the evening as long as you need someone? My name is Marcia Stillman. I'm new at Rosenstein's. I'm a floater." She was a pleasant-faced woman and her smile was friendly. As an after-thought she added,

233

"Miss Billie asked me if I'd like to work for you in the evenings."

Collecting her wits, Helena said, "Why, that's fine. No, I wasn't informed. Yes, there are things you can do for me."

The uneasiness she had felt was dispelled by the woman's presence. How, Helena wondered, had Billie divined what her feelings might be? And what particular notion had prompted her to arrange this?

That question was answered the next evening when Marcia was briefly absent from her desk. Startled by a sound from the outer office Helena looked up to see Moishe come through the door.

"Hi," he said. "Burning the midnight oil again. That's silly."

He came over and sat down on the corner of her desk. "Is all this zeal necessary?"

"I wouldn't be here if it wasn't," Helena retorted.

"The capable executive — the executive who is on top of things — doesn't have to slug it out like a junior apprentice."

She knew he wanted to enrage her and she struggled to hide the fact that he had succeeded. She was not certain whether he knew that it was the preparation of her presentation to the board of directors that was causing her extra hours. She did not know, to begin with, whether he had found out that there was to be such a presentation. She supposed he did, for Daniel must have told Lionel.

He peered now sideways at the papers spread out on her desk and then glanced at her. She said as calmly as she could, "We're not all geniuses."

She had been goaded into piquing him and the

234

reference to his family reputation did sting him. He had begun to resent this family admiration which seemed to project him as still a boy prodigy. He stood up and walked away to the window with his hands in his pockets. When he turned back he said, "Daniel's been talking to you."

"He does — several times a week."

He made a rude noise. "I don't mean that. You know it. He's told you that the board is going to vote on selling Rosenstein's."

Very carefully she replied, "The board wants a presentation of the facts about the store's possible future projections. I'm preparing that."

"You mean, Daniel wants it."

Her patience wearing thin, Helena said, "Moishe, I have a job to do. Would you mind leaving, unless there's something positive you want to ask me."

She was daring him but he did not take up that dare. Instead, he walked out of her office without replying.

He left her with a sense of uneasiness that continued to underlie the rest of the evening, in spite of the attention she concentrated on her work. She hoped she had discouraged his interest, but she was dismayed to see him come into her office again the following evening. This time he was not facetious.

"Come on, Helena. You can stop for a while and have dinner with me."

"No, I can't. I cannot spare the time. Besides, I'm not in the mood. I've got too much on my mind."

"Well, we could talk shop," he coaxed.

She laughed. "Not with you, Moishe!"

"Why not with me?"

"I'm not taking sides."

"What's that got to do with it? You can hear what I have to say about it."

"I've heard that several times. What I'm concerned with is what is best for Rosenstein's."

"Do you tell Billie that?"

She was always shocked when he brought Billie's name into their talk. "Billie knows how I stand on this."

Nervously she had got up from her chair and they were now standing close together. She was not prepared for his sudden movement to put his arms around her. He held her against his strong, eager body, reached his lips to hers and thrust his tongue into her mouth before she could turn her face away. When she was able to push him away a little she gasped, "Moishe, let go of me!"

His arms relaxed but he did not let her go. "I've been wanting to do that for quite a while. How about it, Helena? Come on and spend the night with me. Haven't you heard that some good sex makes the mind work better?"

She tried to free herself but found she was firmly imprisoned in his arms. She realized that her struggle to break free only spurred him on to hold her tighter. She relaxed, keeping her head away from him. "Will you back off? I don't like cavemen."

He grinned and let her go. "I thought you might try karate."

She moved away from him just in time. Barton's voice sounded in the outer office, saying something to Marcia, who had returned to her desk. He put his head in at the door and a look of astonishment appeared on his face as he saw Moishe. He glanced at

236

Helena with a dawning grin. "Well, well, am I interrupting something?"

"Not really," said Helena, as casually as she could. "You want to talk to me?"

"Well, yes," he replied, noticing the scowl on Moishe's face. "Maybe about the same thing he's here for." He nodded his head toward Moishe.

"And what is that?" asked Helena, sitting down at her desk.

"Why, I just wanted to talk about the next board meeting. There're a lot of rumors going around about the directors getting ready to sell Rosenstein's. I guess Moishe knows more about that than I do." He looked at Moishe as if to say, It's your turn.

Helena glanced at Moishe, who had said nothing. He had moved away and now stood half-turned away with his hands in his pockets. She noticed the haughty expression on his narrow, tanned face. It told her that at this moment he did not like Barton.

Moishe said coldly, "All I know is that the subject of Rosenstein's disposal is coming up for discussion at the next board meeting."

"Well," said Barton heartily, "that's a big step forward, isn't it?"

Moishe shrugged.

Barton looked from one to the other of them. "I guess I had better run along now. I'd like to talk about it with you, Helena."

"How about during business hours," said Helena. "I've a lot of work to do just now. I need this time, free from interruptions."

Barton gave a brief glance at Moishe, as if in comment. "Oh, yes, of course. So long," he said and left the room.

Moishe was silent for a while and then asked, "Does he come in here a lot?"

Surprised, Helena answered, "He drops in sometimes during the day. He's never bothered me in the evening like this before."

"Bothered you?" Moishe's tone was suspicious. "Well, I'm glad to hear that." He came over and stood near her, looking down at her with brooding eyes. Suddenly he turned away to go out of the room, saying over his shoulder, "Maybe you'll change your mind."

The tension suddenly lifted, she dropped her head in her hands, covering her ears in an attempt to stop the jangling in her nerves. It was useless, she knew, to try to return to her concentration on the problem before her. Moishe did not arouse a real erotic response in her, but there was a teasing in his embrace. She knew what it was: he was like an echo of Billie, without the powerful magnetism that Billie held for her. The thought caused a shudder to go through her, an upheaval in her nerves, the most intense and immediate longing for Billie, for Billie's quiet presence, Billie's soft warm body, for the feel of Billie's hands.

It was some time before she could deal with the papers on her desk, piling them up neatly preparatory to leaving. Then she remembered the woman in the outer office. How much had she overheard? But Marcia was her usual placid, unobtrusive self as they said Goodbye.

The next evening again she stayed in her office, striving to keep her attention on her work, distracted by a sense of apprehension. But neither Moishe nor

238

Barton came in. She knew these conflicts within herself were making her testy in her dealings with others. She needed someone in whom to confide, someone to whom she could unburden herself. She thought of Rachel, but Rachel had gone abroad again for one of her buying trips, preparing for the spring fashion shows.

She heard the phone ring. Who on earth — surely Billie. But she stayed her hand halfway to the phone, remembering Marcia in the outer office. Marcia appeared in the doorway and said, "I know you don't want to take phone calls, but Miss Rosenstein wants to talk to you."

Her heart in her throat, Helena nodded and reached for the phone. But it was not Billie who spoke at the other end. Michelle said, "You're never at home, are you? Do you spend twenty-four hours a day at Rosenstein's?"

"Not quite," said Helena, swallowing her disappointment.

"Well, can you shake free Friday evening — that's tomorrow — and come and have dinner with me?"

Taken aback, Helena said Yes. An inner voice told her that she could not turn down this invitation. What, she wondered during the intervening hours, was it that Michelle had in mind?

Michelle welcomed her in the drawing room of her house. She was alone. Arlette, she explained, went on Fridays to Columbia University where she taught a class in ceramic design. No one else joined them at dinner, which was served by Marie in the formal dining room. During the dinner Michelle talked about the theater, about ballet, about arts and crafts, and

239

Helena began to think that there was no special purpose in this invitation beyond a wish to know her better.

Back in the drawing room, seated in a small enclave of chairs and sofas before the fireplace, with a tray of coffee cups and liqueur glasses before them, Michelle said Goodnight to Marie. Then lighting a cigarette in a long holder, she said, "I understand that you are working night and day because Rosenstein's is to be put up for sale."

This is it, Helena thought. Now what do I say?"

But Michelle, after glancing at her, went on. "Of course, I know perfectly well that you can't discuss the ins and outs with me. I'm just a minor shareholder."

"The decision is not yet made. The directors are to consider the matter in the next board meeting, this coming week."

Michelle nodded, her long dangling earrings swinging gently. She blew out smoke. "I suppose you know that it is Daniel who votes for me, and Daniel and I don't talk to each other. All I can do is to write him a formal letter saying that I want my shares voted such and such a way. I've never done that. When I get notices of actions to be taken I simply send him my proxy. I know he is thoroughly reliable and that what he decides will be much better for me than any choice I could make."

"You don't really need to worry, Michelle. Whichever way the decision goes, your rights will be protected. As far as your income is concerned, there may very well be an advantage to selling. In the long run a decision to sell may mean a greater income.

That is the purpose of the proposed sale — to maximize the Company's profits."

"But Rosenstein's would be destroyed."

Helena hesitated. "Undoubtedly, if Rosenstein's is sold to a conglomerate, it will no longer be what it has traditionally been, even though your family would continue to hold a majority interest. It will cease to be a single, unique store, even if the outward appearance is preserved. That would be impossible. But its profitability would be much greater."

Again Michelle nodded, as if she understood this and it did not much interest her. "You're probably wondering why I wanted to talk to you about this. I must confess that I've never been overwhelmed by the mystique of Rosenstein's. It's a very useful source of income, of course, and I am thankful that Old Leah was such a clever woman that she could create a business that has made all her descendants wealthy. But I have reservations about that, too. I've always been too spineless to act on them, too self-indulgent to consider giving up my privileges for abstract principle. Nevertheless, I've never worshipped Rosenstein's and I think the premise on which it is built is frivolous — the adornment of women for the gratification of men."

"Perhaps there is more to it than that. However, does that mean that you'd just as soon see the store sold and the Company merged with a conglomerate?"

Michelle smoked in silence for a moment. "For myself, Yes. Because of Billie, my answer is No."

"Billie wants to keep Rosenstein's as it is."

Michelle stopped in the act of putting the cigarette holder back in her moth. "Yes, of course.

Rosenstein's means a great deal to Billie. On her account I shall do everything I can to block the sale. And I want to tell you something else. If Rosenstein's remains what it is and if in some way Billie could be in charge of it, I believe you would be surprised how it would revive — how its profitability, as you call it, would increase. Billie has a feeling for the store. In the family she has always been credited with having a strong inheritance from Old Leah, with having an instinctive grasp of Old Leah's way of thinking, of Old Leah's gift, if you like."

"I see. Perhaps it takes more than such a feeling to bring the store back. Perhaps the change in the times would work against it, especially if you look at Rosenstein's as an enterprise that has outlived its day. I agree that, in the hands of the right person, the store could flourish, for a while in any case, because it is unique and that uniqueness could be capitalized by someone in sympathy with it. But why do you think it is important to Billie? It seems the only thing she feels deeply about."

"The only thing?" Michelle smoked for a moment. Then she said seriously, "I know. Billie seems passive. In fact, she is, most of the time. She has always accepted what's expected of her — she's Rosalie's little doll baby, not able to call her soul her own, going through the motions of living. Do you wonder why that is? Do you wonder why she sometimes drinks herself stupid?"

Helena nodded.

Michelle answered her own questions. "Billie is made of finer substance than most of us. She can't be what she knows she should be because doing so would hurt others, especially her mother, so she drifts in the shallows of life. You know, I'm twelve years older than Billie, so I've known her from babyhood. I'm the only one in the family who realized that, when she reached adolescence, Billie is a lesbian. When she realized it herself, what it meant was that she had to hide the fact from her mother. It has been a hard job for her. All her natural instincts — her outgoingness, her initiative, her mental quickness — was sacrificed to hiding what she really is. I had given up on Billie before you came along. I thought she'd never find the woman who would really rouse her, for whom she would feel a strong enough love that she would break through the barriers that held her prisoner. It turns out that you're the one. You're the only person who has ever sparked Billie into action. She adores you. Because of you, Billie's inner fire is bursting forth. If you fail her, she'll be doomed forever."

Overwhelmed, Helena turned away. When she recovered herself she asked, in a voice that did not sound even to herself like her own, "But I've not done anything. It's Billie who has captured me."

Michelle smiled ironically. "You can't look it in the face, can you? You're too used to hiding your feelings behind practical considerations."

Helena could not answer and they sat in silence for a while. Eventually Helena said, "Yes, I suppose I do. My feelings are more manageable that way. I know where I am with practical considerations. I know where I am when I think about Rosenstein's problems. I am at a loss when it comes to dealing with Billie."

"And Billie's emotional involvement with the future of Rosenstein's. It is her inheritance from Old

243

Leah. To Old Leah Rosenstein's became more than a store. It was an artistic and spiritual triumph, besides being a financial success. She was very well aware that it was based on the concept of women as men's playthings. But that was the world she grew up in, the world she lived in. She saw it as a means of empowering women — women who were caught up in the society she knew. Women could exercise power over men — as some still do — if they were able to dominate men through their senses. That's something that goes back to Biblical times. And Old Leah could provide them with the weapons for this — if they could afford them or could cajole their men into providing them."

"You waited, didn't you, till your great grandmother died before you cut yourself off from your family?"

"Yes, I suppose I did wait, without really deciding to. I suppose I felt in my bones that I shouldn't cause a breach in the family while she lived. I didn't care about my other relatives. In fact, I rather enjoyed thumbing my nose at them — especially my parents. They had never been sympathetic to any of the things I wanted to do. But I knew that to Old Leah her sons and their children were a fortress that she had defended all her life. She had a shrewd knowledge of their individual weaknesses, but together, as her family, they were to be defended." Michelle paused and looked at Helena closely. "Perhaps you find it a little difficult to understand this. It is very Jewish."

"Billie has explained it to me."

"I don't know how she would view this plan to sell the store. She was not sentimental. I've often

244

wondered what she would have said if I had told her that I was a lesbian. I've often also wondered if she guessed. She was a complicated person. You could never really foresee just how she would look at things. She was deep. What she knew and what she let you know she knew were two very different things. As far as the store was concerned, it was very important to her because she had created it and it was the symbol of her success in life, of her triumph in overcoming the odds life had presented her with. But on the other hand, she was an astute businesswoman and there was nothing soft about her approach to business dealings."

"So you don't know whether she would side with Billie."

"That is impossible to say. Rosalie and Rosalie's daughter were special to her. She never played favorites otherwise."

"But if she was alive now, would she possibly favor Moishe?"

Michelle laughed. "This is a guessing game, isn't it? I don't know who would win in a tug-of-war."

"Do you think this is a tug-of-war between Billie and Moishe, with Rosenstein's as the prize?"

"Perhaps it is. Billie and Moishe have always been rivals, in a way. Because he has always been so precocious the age difference between them has never seemed as much as it is. Moishe is very competitive. He's never interested in anything that does not arouse his competitiveness. He's always competed with Billie because she is the closest to him in intelligence — in fact, she can sometimes outthink him, though he does not admit it. Now she has really challenged him and he knows that the arena is Rosalie's favor."

"If Moishe wins this tug-of-war and Billie loses Rosenstein's, would her mother loosen her control — be more interested in Moishe?"

"Oh, no! Rosalie never gives up anything that belongs to her and Billie belongs to her. She is not going to let anyone else have her. She might let Billie marry, but her son-in-law would have to acknowledge the fact that Rosalie comes first with Billie. But I think Rosalie has given up the idea that Billie will marry. So she has Billie for life."

"Does Moishe know anything about Billie's private life?"

"Good God! No! He doesn't even know about me. I understand I'm not mentioned in the family, especially to the younger ones. If he found out, he'd rage around and tell Billie that she mustn't come here, that she should pretend I don't exist, like the rest of the family. Moishe is great at laying down the law for other people, especially Billie."

"Well, surely she wouldn't pay any attention to him."

"Billie is very loyal and she's not easily intimidated. But it would be agony for her. Don't you see? He would threaten her by saying he was going to tell Rosalie and you can imagine what Rosalie would do to Billie. Well, if you can't, I can tell you. She would make Billie's life a hell — what kind of an ungrateful daughter are you? Do you want to drive me to my grave? Do you want to be a pariah like that woman? Somebody that nobody — none of your relatives — would speak to?"

Helena asked weakly, "Is Moishe really that bad? He must have known some gay people."

"He has nothing but contempt for them. He has

met some gay men and he thinks they're an offense to mankind. I don't think he's ever been aware that he has met a lesbian."

Helena was silent in dismay. Michelle smoked for a while. Then Helena said, "There doesn't seem to be a way out."

"For you and Billie? No, I don't see one now." She paused and added in a sympathetic tone, "I expect what you had better do is concentrate on your job. You'll have to make your decisions on Rosenstein's future purely on business considerations."

"I intend to. I do not have the power to determine the Company's future. I can only present the facts that support the alternatives."

Aware of the emotional tension underlying her statement, Michelle said grimly, "But Billie has no intention of giving up the store. She is immoveable there."

"But what will she do if the directors vote against her?"

"I really don't know. But you'll have to stand by Billie."

It was almost midnight when Helena got home, turmoil in her heart and mind. Vainly she tried to sleep, but she could not escape Michelle's remembered words — "she adores you — you can't fail her — her mother owns her and will not give her up."

Throughout the rest of the weekend she strove desperately to keep Billie out of her mind, to concentrate on the problems of the presentation. The board meeting had been set for Wednesday. She realized that in her nervousness, as the days went by, she was doing the work twice over, shaking and worrying at it in search for every possible flaw, like a terrier with a rat. There was no sign from Billie. She drove Moishe away with blunt statements: You must leave me alone. This is no game. It is not ethical for me to discuss this matter with you. I'm not playing sides. I will not go out with you. Don't come to my apartment. I won't let you in. Eventually he was convinced that she meant what she said and reluctantly let her alone.

Barton also came to see her, in her office. Apparently he remembered the evening when he had found Moishe with her, and was more circumspect when he approached her. He talked chiefly about the impending sale of Rosenstein's. He seemed to emphasize this possibility, treating it as inevitable, watching her face to see how she took his remarks, as a threat or an opportunity to talk. When she did not react, he became more personal. There would naturally be, he said, changes in the personnel set-up of the store. There were bound to be some unhappy people who would find themselves dismissed, even some who had been with Rosenstein's for years. Things like that were an inevitable consequence of corporate moves of this sort, as she well knew. But the human factor could not be allowed to stand in the way of what was in the best financial interests of the Company, of the need to increase its profitability. Of course she knew that. But the newer people, the more wide awake ones, had no reason to fear such consequences. He made it plain that he was referring to himself and to her.

She tried to be noncommittal. Yes, she understood the toll that would be taken in the destinies of individuals. She understood even better that what he was trying to probe, with more than a trace of malice, was her probable fearfulness, for her own future. Finally she instructed Sherry to tell him, whenever he came seeking her, to say that she was unable to talk to him without an appointment.

She thought of Billie constantly, in that part of her mind that underlay the rational process of preparing her presentation. How ironical, she thought, to find herself in this situation. Prior to this she had congratulated herself on being safe from the one great pitfall that lay in the path of women seeking advancement in business or the professions: seduction by male attention, men's promises, men's threats. She was immune to the allurement of sexual intimacy with men. She could turn down such invitations from men who could be dangerous to her career. She had escaped the worst in the sexual harassment that often dogged women in her position. She had never supposed that she would find herself in such a situation with another woman; probably because she knew that few women held power that could be used to thwart her ambition. She had seen that dealing with women held another set of problems. She wanted to treat other ambitious women as equals, not rivals, not to suspect them of intrigue and manipulation, yet she was aware that such openness was a potential danger, that the tactics of deceit and betrayal in which women had been trained through centuries could not be erased in one generation.

But where was she with Billie in all this? Billie did not fit into the situation in which she found herself. Billie had become a part of her she could not excise. Billie was inextricably involved in her working life, yet Billie was outside it altogether. Billie would exist for her if Rosenstein's ceased to be; even if the whole fabric of her life collapsed, Billie would be there. She tried to stop thinking at that point, for beyond it there seemed to be only an abyss.

The morning of Wednesday she arrived at her office even earlier than usual, nervous and striving to build up within herself a fund of stable feeling on which she could draw when the time came for her to present the material she had prepared. She wondered briefly how she would know that she was wanted in the board room. That question was answered by the appearance of Esther, who came smiling into her office to say that Daniel would like her to come to the twelfth floor. Sherry, who had been aware of her nervous preoccupation throughout the morning, sprang up from her desk to hand her her attaché case full of papers and give her a silent look of sympathetic encouragement.

Fortunately Esther talked easily and without pause during their trip up in the elevator and across the deeply carpeted vestibule to the tall mahogany doors of the board room. At this point she had no attention left for trivial conversation.

Esther pushed one half of the door open and they stood for a moment surveying the room. The long table was surrounded by tall-backed chairs, most of them occupied. Helena immediately saw Lionel, at the nearer end, lolling as if at ease in his own house. He was white-haired and spare but otherwise did not give the impression of his true age, having preserved the good looks he had passed on to Moishe. Daniel sat near him, leaning on his elbow. They both looked up at her as she crossed the room, and Lionel gestured to an empty chair beside him. He said to the other men, "As you know, we've asked Miss Worrall to join us at this time to present some facts that Daniel thinks we should all consider concerning the future of Rosenstein's. Please sit down, Helena."

He had an urbanity that Daniel lacked but she realized that with this went a greater detachment from the fortunes of the Company. He was here as chairman of the board because he was the ranking member of the Rosenstein family, but his interests primarily were with his own banking firm. She gave a brief glance around. She had been aware from the first moment of entering the room that Billie was at the other end of the table, half-hidden behind another director and apparently indifferent to her entrance. Resolutely she barred Billie from her mind.

Once launched on her presentation she lost nervousness in her absorption in her job. There was general agreement, she began, that the Rosenstein Company faced a crisis and that its future prosperity depended on the right choice of actions to be taken to remedy the drop in profitability. She had two alternatives to suggest and she would proceed to outline them.

At first, taken up entirely with the task of presentation, she was oblivious to the reactions of the others in the room. But as she gained confidence she became aware that she had captured their undivided attention. This told her that she had succeeded, that the hard work of the last week or so was paying off. She had graphs ready to display on a tripod Daniel had provided and everyone craned their necks to examine these with curiosity. When she came to a pause she looked up to meet a broad, congratulatory smile on Daniel's face.

When she finished she spent another hour answering questions. Many were probing questions, but some, she recognized, were inspired more by the interest in herself that had been aroused in the men asking them. They all knew who she was and had in fact met her in the course of business, but this was the first occasion they had to focus on her as a person as well as manager of the Rosenstein Company. On leaving the board room she had no idea what the result of the meeting would be. She had not expected any real indication. She felt only relief. Lionel stood up to bow to her as she left the room, congratulating her on her presentation. Her work at least had been properly done.

In the following days she longed to be in touch with Billie yet instinctively held back from calling her. She did not see Moishe. He had gone again to London, she heard, on business for his father. She supposed that his canny sense of strategy had overcome his desire for her. She had fallen into the habit of lingering in her office well beyond the normal close of business, though there was now little there to hold her. Sherry left at the usual hour and was not replaced by Marcia, so that she spent these hours solitary, in brooding thought, finding that she remembered with extraordinary clarity most of what Michelle had said. How difficult it was to estimate her situation with Billie — Billie who was so close within the gates of herself and yet still so much a stranger.

Then one evening as she was absentmindedly putting her things together she was startled by a sound from the outer office. Half-alarmed she gazed at the doorway and was astonished to see Billie standing there in her hat and coat.

Billie said, "Come on, honey. Let's get out of here."

She obeyed, following Billie's quick steps down the corridor to the elevator and out into the lingering light of the lengthening spring day which filtered down into the canyon bottom of the street. She expected Billie to hail a cab but instead they set out at a brisk pace through the thinning crowd. They reached Central Park and Billie struck out across it. Obviously she was not headed for her own apartment. The evening light here was brighter, away from the overtopping buildings. The air was mild but a brisk breeze had come up as the day waned. It fluttered flags on the hotel marquees and flapped awnings.

They arrived on the west side and presently Billie led them down a side street that still kept the grandeur that had once characterized this neighborhood, still uninvaded by new immigrants. Helena recognized it as having once been the fashionable precinct of well-to-do Jews, in the earlier part of the century. Daniel still lived nearby. The old apartment buildings had the ornate facades of the last years of the nineteenth century, some of them still maintained with a not-quite-shabby elegance. When they reached one large building with many windows overlooking the Park, Billie stopped and rang the bell for the security guard, who greeted her as a well-known visitor. They went up in the large, iron-grilled elevator to the top floor and walked down a discreetly lit deep-carpeted corridor to the door at the end, which Billie opened with a key.

The vestibule was dark when they stepped into it and so was the big drawing room beyond, because the tall windows were covered by heavy drapes. When Billie switched on the lights, Helena saw that the room was filled with heavy dark opulent furniture and that every small table and every other surface was crowded with china figurines, photographs set in ornate frames, bibelots of every description. This was a museum, she thought, noticing the long fringes on the curtains and on the runners that covered the tables and the big piano looming in a corner. A prosperous family had lived here in the days before the first world war, accumulating things that had never been discarded or rearranged.

Billie, who had already taken off her hat and coat, noticed her bemused expression. She smiled. "This is Rachel's home. All these things came to her from the Rosensteins — most of them from Old Leah. This place belonged to Old Leah at one time. She left it to Rachel. You'd never guess she would hoard such things, would you? But Old Leah lived here once. These things were hers. So Rachel keeps them. It is sacred to her memory." Billie sat down on an overstuffed chair that rested on claw-feet and added mildly, "You might as well take off your coat. We'll be here for a while."

Helena obeyed. Glancing again at Billie, she realized that Billie was not ready to go on with the explanation. All through their walk they had been silent because she had learned that questioning Billie when she was in this mood was useless.

After a while Billie said, "I've brought you here because we're safe in this place. If we went to yours, Moishe might turn up. He got back from London this

254

afternoon. If we went to mine, my mother might come in. Rachel is away. She's in Italy with the Countess."

Helena, still circling around the big room to look at the bibelots, stopped and said, "The Countess?"

"The Countess Pietri. She has been Rachel's beloved for twenty years. She belongs to one of the oldest Milanese families but she is also a top house decorator. She was at the fashion show last October but you would not have known her. Did you happen to notice a spectacularly dressed woman wearing a lot of jewelry talking very fast to several people at once? She is not easy to forget. She makes Rachel look as demure as a missionary."

"No, I don't remember. Everything was too new and strange then. Nobody has said anything to me about her."

"Nobody would. She and Rachel are very discreet — about each other, that is, not other people. The Countess is a great gossip — that is why she is so popular. She always has scandal to relate. She can be outrageous. But she knows that anything to do with Rosenstein's is out of bounds, for Rachel's sake." Billie got up and walked across the room. "Let's have a drink. No, I'm not going to get drunk."

She opened the ornate doors of a lowboy placed along the wall. Inside were bottles, decanters, glasses and a small refrigerator. Billie explained: "Rachel leaves it on when she's away because she knows I come here sometimes, as a refuge."

While Billie set out two glasses and a bottle of scotch, Helena looked around the room again — at the Victorian symbols of prosperity and respectability, at the golden menorah standing in solitary splendor on a sideboard. In spite of the incongruity between these furnishings and Rachel's personality, she recognized the link. Loyalty and devotion were obviously important traits in Rachel's character. Gazing about Helena saw among the many framed photographs the face of Old Leah, sometimes as an aged matriarch, sometimes as a vigorous matron, never as a young woman. Rachel, as an apprentice of fifteen, must first have known her when she was already a grandmother. The apartment was indeed a memorial to her.

Billie turned around. "Remarkable, isn't it?"

Helena agreed silently. Billie said, "Here. Let's drink to a few hours of freedom."

She thrust a glass into Helena's hand. "Come over here," said Billie, taking hold of her arm and pulling her down onto the big sofa. She sat close to her, with her arm along the back of the sofa behind Helena's head, which she gently stroked. "It's not me that my mother thinks is in danger from you. It's Moishe. She's so frightened at the idea that you will capture him that it hasn't occurred to her that you might have designs on me."

Helena was indignant. "Has she been talking to you about Moishe and me?"

"Oh, yes. She can't stand the idea that Moishe might marry a shikseh — a Gentile. It's become an obsession. Moishe is rather enjoying this. He's a little sadistic. She is so obviously upset."

"But it's so silly! Besides, she is not religious. Why should this worry her?"

Billie said thoughtfully, "No, she is not religious. None of us are, except Daniel. But we are Jews and there is this fear that intermarriage means that there will be fewer of us. Once assimilation into the world around us here in America was the great thing for people like us. But a lot of terrible things have happened in the last fifty years. My mother is very conscious of being a Jew and protecting her heritage."

"I can understand that, Billie. But this is such a silly fear — that I would marry Moishe — or he me, for that matter."

"Perhaps it is a mistake to assume that."

"Doesn't your mother know that Moishe plays around with a lot of women? He has no intention of marrying anyone."

"You don't know Moishe the way I do, though I admit that I am surprised at the change in him lately. Yes, I know that he doesn't want responsibilities, especially where women are concerned. Where the bee sucks, there suck I, is his philosophy. But, honey, you have caught him, whether you like the idea or not. And all at once he's become much more narrow-minded than he used to be. He's worse than Daniel now. He certainly is not going to marry a woman who sleeps around and he knows you don't. Oh, yes, Moishe has suddenly got serious. In a way I always knew that when he got ready to do his duty as a good Jewish boy and settle down with a family, he would not marry a girl who wasn't one that Daniel would approve of. I'm just surprised at how quickly and how thoroughly he's changed. As for my mother, she's very sensitive to anything that concerns Moishe and I know she has picked up all these signals just as I have. After all, nobody admires Moishe's good looks and charm more than she does."

Helena cut in, "I just can't believe all this, Billie!

It's as if you're talking about somebody else, not me. Even if you think that Moishe wants to marry me, you know I don't want to marry him."

"I hope not. But the more you run away from him, the hotter will be his pursuit. Besides — honey, listen to me. Moishe has fallen hard for you. It's more than just contrariness. I think he's surprised at himself. He wants you and he's ready to go to all lengths to get you."

Overwhelmed by vexation Helena got up and walked across the room. Billie's insistent voice followed her: "There's a very important reason why I am telling you this. My mother does not know what I really am. Moishe doesn't know it, either. But his whole attention is concentrated on you. He watches you every chance he gets. Sometimes you don't know that he is watching you. He's very jealous of everybody who is a friend of yours. Why do you suppose I've been so careful to keep a distance between us in public? Partly because of my mother, of course. But Moishe has become the greater danger. He mustn't have his suspicions aroused. If he learns the truth about us — or suspects it — he will tell my mother."

Helena switched around and said in despair, "But what can I do about it? I've tried to discourage him in every possible way."

Billie's voice was calm. "As long as my mother thinks you are trying to entrap Moishe, she will not suspect that I love you. As long as Moishe thinks you're free of emotional entanglements, he'll think he can make progress with you. He won't think of me."

"Good God, Billie! What do you mean?"

"I mean that under the circumstances, Moishe

258

gives us a kind of protection. It's fragile but it's there. You must try not to destroy it."

"What do you want me to do — go to bed with him?"

In her exasperation she was surprised when Billie did not answer right away. Billie said, "That would spoil it. He won't want you, then."

Helena opened her mouth to upbraid her but then she saw that Billie's calmly rational manner was crumbling.

"Billie, I'm sorry. What are we going to do?" Standing over her she looked down on Billie's drooping head. She had never seen Billie so close to tears. Horrified, she dropped down beside her and put her arms around her. She felt the defeat in Billie's body. "Billie, Billie," she crooned.

With a shiver Billie answered her embrace. Shakily she said, "I don't know what we can do, honey. You're more to me than anyone or anything has ever been. How can I give you up — to Moishe, to anyone else? It would kill me."

Helena said firmly, "It is not a question of giving me up. You can't give me up. There's part of me that will always be yours, no matter what happens — the most important part."

Billie tried to gather herself together. "Let's stop talking about it. We have this moment together."

Later, in bed together — in Rachel's big ornate bed — their love-making had a sober quality, lacking the exuberance that had marked their first discovery of their passion. Before now they had both revelled in an unfettered feeling of joy, able to thrust aside all thoughts of intrusion and fears of interference. Now they were aware of their unity in the face of grave danger. Their outer circumstances — of difference in heritage, family ties, upbringing — which had before seemed only a foil to the strength of their attraction to each other, now fell away from them. When Helena's hands sought Billie's soft, warm body to reaffirm this, without hesitation Billie gripped her. In the morning, when they got up and dressed and left the apartment together, they found little to say. They both realized that words could not capture what lay between them, that they could not reduce to speech their awareness that what lay ahead might not be within their power to resolve.

Helena said, as Billie tried the door of the apartment to make sure that it was locked, "Rachel will know we've been here, won't she?"

Billie nodded. "I think she is coming back today."

That afternoon, Helena found herself alone in the elevator when it stopped before reaching her floor and Rachel stepped in. Rachel's eyes opened wide on seeing her and she exclaimed, "Ah, I was coming to see you! But this is better." She reached over and pressed the button for the board room floor. In answer to the question in Helena's face she said, "There's no one there — not even Esther. We'll be really private."

The elevator came to a gentle stop and the door opened. Stepping out Rachel caught Helena's arm and walked her toward the window at the end of the wide lobby. She said, "I hope you were quite cozy last night. I'd like to have been there to play hostess. But that's not what you wanted, is it?"

Embarrassed Helena murmured, "Billie says she often goes to your place when you're away."

Rachel's dark eyes sparkled. "But never with a companion. Yes, Billie has come to me for comfort ever since she was a little girl. And now as a woman she comes there to try to restore her sense of herself. Billie should rebel. She must — soon — or it will be too late. Perhaps you will be the one who will bring this about."

Helena did not answer, the weight of last night's confrontation with Billie still too great.

Rachel, noting her silence, went on, "Well, let's not talk about that. You've been very successful with the Rosensteins. They all like you. So what are you going to do with the store? I hear all kinds of rumors."

They had reached the window at the end of the lobby. Here, Helena realized, they would not be interrupted by anyone they could not see coming towards them.

They stood facing each other. "Rachel, I'm not going to do anything with the store. I haven't the power nor the inclination to pretend that I do. All I have done is present the arguments for and against selling it to a conglomerate. It is up to the board of directors to decide." As she spoke she considered the fact that that decision was of vital importance to Rachel. "I'm sorry I can't give you any assurances. I am as much in the dark right now about what will be decided as you are. Of course you know that Billie is dead set against such a sale. But she has powerful opposition. You know all this better than I do."

Rachel nodded. "Moishe. He's behind this talk of selling Rosenstein's. He doesn't think about Old Leah and remember that what he is now and what he has achieved is all due to her. He just wants to prove what a brilliant young fellow he is."

Hearing the anger in Rachel's voice, Helena said quietly, "Yes, I think that's part of it. Without him the others would be content to let things go along as they have been going. But, Rachel, you must realize that the store cannot go on declining financially this way indefinitely. Something must be done to bring it back. Moishe is not sentimental about it and perhaps he is without feeling for what his great grandmother achieved. But he does understand how to make money."

Rachel listened to her attentively. "Tell me: do you like Moishe?"

Helena showed her surprise. "Why, yes. I find him attractive."

"Is that all? The handsome young scion of the Rosensteins who isn't making any attempt to hide the fact that he wants you? All the women in the store are agog. They can't talk about anything else."

Helena flushed with anger. "Rachel, I'm not interested in Moishe in a romantic way. Nor am I anxious to use his interest to get ahead in the Company. Surely you believe that?"

The thought of Billie stood between them and they were both aware of this. Rachel dropped her eyes. Of course, thought Helena, remembering Rachel's background, she naturally would think that someone like me couldn't resist such a temptation, couldn't refrain from playing both sides.

"Rachel, do you think I could pretend to Billie? Do you think I would use Billie?"

Rachel's dark brows drew down in resentment. Watching her, Helena understood the struggle that

262

was going on in her — whether to persist in her suspicions of her or to accept her because of Billie's preference. Finally Rachel said, "I know how Billie feels about you. I don't know you very well. I can only hope —" She broke off and turned half away from Helena, as if uncertain. After a moment she said reluctantly, "Well, I should warn you. Moishe is dangerous. If he finds out that you and Billie love each other, he'll hate you and he'll revenge himself — on both of you. He'll begin by telling Rosalie."

Her manner struck cold to Helena. "Do you have any reason to think that he will find out?"

"If you mean, am I going to tell him, no, of course not." Rachel was angry now. "Do you think I don't love Billie as much as you do? Oh, I don't go to bed with her! But there is only one person in the world I love better." She paused and let her anger cool. "There is one thing you must remember: there is a spotlight on you. I don't know how these things get to be known, but everyone has heard how much the directors liked your presentation, how pleased Daniel is with you. For a while, you know, the gossip was that Daniel was infatuated with you — yes, Daniel! The speculation now is mainly about Rosalie. How is Rosalie going to take it if Moishe decides to marry you. At least they're not talking about you and Billie — not yet."

"What do you mean, not yet? I don't even see Billie in the store."

"Yes, I know. The two of you stay out of sight of each other. Billie sees to that. Which makes some of them think maybe Billie doesn't like you, and they're on her side. But I've an uneasy feeling that Moishe is on the lookout. You know, he has never paid any attention to his female relatives, except Rosalie and Billie. Lately somebody told him about Michelle — that is, he has focused on the fact that he has a cousin named Michelle and why she is ostracized by the family. I suppose he has heard about lesbians, probably as women who perform in pornographic movies for the stimulation of men. I'm told the very idea disgusts him. I understand he's deeply shocked about Michelle — someone like that in the family!"

"Who would have told him?"

"Esther, perhaps, or one of his male cousins. Probably he heard that Daniel voted her shares in the board meetings. The danger is that he may find out that Billie goes to see Michelle. Moishe is brooding a lot these days. Everybody says it's because you're playing hard to get and he feels frustrated."

"Aren't you carrying this speculation too far?"

Realizing that she spoke out of shock, Rachel softened and put her hand on Helena's arm in a comforting gesture. "Yes, maybe so. I'm upset. I'm looking for disaster. It's all tied in, you know — Moishe and the decision about the store."

Helena sighed. "Rachel, I know how this must worry you — about Rosenstein's. I don't know how much influence Moishe does have with his relatives. You're probably a better judge of that than I am."

Rachel's expressive face grew dark. "He has a lot of influence with Rosalie and she's the one that counts. I'm sure he is pressing her to agree to its sale. If he finds out about you and Billie, there's no question that he'll use that to clinch the matter. In that case, it's a foregone conclusion that the store will be sold and that your career with the

264

Rosensteins will be at an end. So will mine, for that matter."

Helena saw that there were tears in Rachel's eyes. Rachel was twice her age, with a life-long commitment to Rosenstein's, with memories and emotional ties that could not be cut away. Rachel's own reputation, in her career as a priestess of high fashion, could not be destroyed. But the personal toll for her in the liquidation of Rosenstein's would be devastating.

She said, seeking words to express her sympathy, "That's not true. Whoever buys Rosenstein's would be insane not to try to persuade you to stay with them. Your reputation is supreme."

"I'll never stay with the store if they sell it — if it becomes — a — bargain basement — an outlet of a chain! If they sell the store, it's gone — it will be dead, as dead as Old Leah herself. I'll not do it — make money for a bunch of money-grabbing machines!" Rachel's voice was passionate and her dark face flamed in anger.

Again Helena sighed. Unreasonable as it might be, she knew that in Rachel's shoes she would have done the same. She herself, she knew, could survive. There were other opportunities she could find in the corporate managerial sphere. But she was filled with dismay at the idea of the rumors and sly gossip she would have to surmount while looking for a new business connection.

In the silence that followed Rachel's outburst she finally asked, "What will happen to Billie?"

"You mean, what will Rosalie do to her?" There was a savage tone in Rachel's voice. "She will treat her as if she has a loathsome disease — but she won't turn her loose. She'd kill Billie rather than that. And maybe one of these days she will kill Billie. I've seen Billie often enough after her mother has given her a working over about something she doesn't like. And that wouldn't compare to this." Rachel's voice dropped to a fervent mutter. "I could kill that little bitch for what she does to Billie."

"But Billie doesn't feel that way."

"And Rosalie knows it. Rosalie knows that she can control Billie through Billie's love for her. She knows Billie is absolutely loyal to anyone she loves. And I suppose it is hard to hate your mother and Billie is not good at hating anybody."

"It's not inevitable that Moishe will find out about Billie and me."

"No, it's not inevitable. But if he does — well, you'd better be prepared to defend yourself against Rosalie. She'll have your skin."

Rachel broke off abruptly. A soft sound had registered in Helena's mind in spite of her absorption in their conversation and now she realized that it was the murmur of the elevator arriving at their floor and its doors opening. Rachel muttered hurriedly, "Now we have Esther with us."

Even across half the width of the building and in the muted light Helena recognized Esther at once by the mincing step and peering glance. Esther paused for a second before coming towards them.

"Why, it's you, Helena! Were you waiting for me? Hello, Rachel. How are you? I couldn't imagine who was up here when I got off the elevator. It is such a quiet spot for a private chat, isn't it? I didn't know you were back, Rachel."

How like Esther, thought Helena, to put her finger immediately on someone's motivation and not fail to speak of it.

"I got back this morning." Rachel's manner was short.

"Well," said Esther, casually rattling along, "a lot has been happening while you were away. I'm sure Helena is the best one to fill you in." She beamed a smile at Helena.

Helena, vexed, tried not to show it. "I think Rachel has heard all about it already."

"But you're the one who can give her the details."

"All I can add is that I have made a presentation to the directors, who now have to make their decision. I assume they will make an announcement in due course — to the management first, I should think."

She meant herself but did not say so. She knew from Barton that there was a great deal of argument going on among the Rosensteins. He tried to convey the impression that he was abreast of the day-to-day situation, but she was certain that he was as much excluded from these intrafamily discussions as she was. She did not think that Moishe would make him as much a confidant as he had in the past. It amused her that Barton, like several of the other officers, treated her with a greater respect and caution than they had before it became apparent that she had the approval of the directors. She wondered how much of all this Esther knew about.

Rachel said, "I'm late for an appointment. You seem to be in good shape, Esther. I'll see you another time."

Helena went with her across the lobby as Esther went to the tall board room doors and unlocked them, looking over her shoulder to watch them get into the elevator.

She and Rachel said nothing to each other except Goodbye as the elevator reached Helena's floor. She found great difficulty the rest of the day in concentrating on her work. Moishe dominated her thoughts. It was true that she had not seen him for a number of days. He had not visited her office. He had not called her in the evenings. Now this sudden absence created a sense of foreboding in her, which she could not shake off.

That evening the phone rang as she stepped into her apartment. She was astonished when she heard Billie's voice and more surprised still when Billie said, Would she come over to her place? She went immediately, a thousand questions filling her mind. She looked anxiously at Billie when she opened the door to let her in.

But Billie seemed as calm as usual. She did not explain why she had called her. She walked across the room in front of her and sat down on the sofa. Helena sat tensely beside her, waiting. Finally she asked, "Billie, what is the matter? Why did you send for me?"

Billie smiled. "Can't I ask you to come over without giving a reason?"

"Yes, of course. But something is wrong. You haven't wanted me to come over here for quite a long time."

Billie put her arm around her shoulders and kissed her, a lingering kiss, the sort that always transmuted the warm softness of Billie's love.

"I just decided," said Billie, leaning back, "that I couldn't get through another evening without you. My mother is going to a charity benefit performance tonight. Moishe is going with her."

"Has anything happened?"

"Anything?" Billie was thoughtful for a moment. "I don't know. In any case, let's have a drink."

She got up and went to the cabinet to get out the glasses and the bottle of scotch. The ice bucket was full, Helena noticed. Billie brought her a glass and one for herself and sat down again.

"Rachel is back," she said.

"Yes, I know. I saw her this afternoon. Billie, she knows all about us, doesn't she?"

"Of course. I've never hidden anything from Rachel."

"She's worried about the decision about the store."

"It would affect her more than anyone."

"More than you?"

Billie did not answer.

After a long moment, Helena said, "Billie, your mother has the key to this solution. Do you have any idea what she will do?"

Billie, who had been looking down at the floor, raised her eyes to look at her. "My mother," she said, in a tone that matched the sardonic defiance in her eyes, "has the key to more than Rosenstein's survival. No. I don't know what she will do."

"Rachel is upset because she thinks Moishe will find out about us and tell her. That, she says, will be the end of everything."

"The end of everything," said Billie softly. "That depends on you and me, doesn't it?"

They looked at each other. Helena said, "No, it can't be."

Billie nodded. Helena was suddenly struck by the air of authority that Billie had all at once assumed. Occasionally, in the past, she had noticed a brief gleam of this side of Billie — the gentle, malleable Billie, the sympathizer with others' troubles, suddenly transformed in a subtle way into someone not to be questioned.

Before they could talk further the buzzer from the reception desk sounded. Billie sat for a moment looking at the phone before she got up to answer. When she put the instrument down she stood still for another moment before turning to Helena. She said with enormous calm, "It is my mother. We shall have our answer now. We can't dodge any longer."

They waited in the silence until the doorbell sounded and Billie walked across the room into the vestibule, gesturing to Helena to stay where she was. Helena heard the door open and a sudden burst of Mrs. Alfred's voice, high-pitched in anger.

"Is she here? You've got her here!"

Helena heard the sharp sound of a slap.

Billie's murmur was barely audible. The next moment Mrs. Alfred burst into the room. Rage made her blue eyes blaze and reddened her cheeks. She wore a fur hat and a fur coat, since the weather had turned cold again. Making no effort to take either of them off, she ran across the room towards Helena, who in instinctive alarm, jumped up from her seat and backed away behind the sofa.

"You bitch, you pervert, you dirty thing!" Mrs. Alfred screamed. "How dare you come here! You've fooled everybody else, I know what you are now! It wasn't enough for you to try to ruin Moishe! He saw through you in time. Now you get away from Billie. I'll see you get what you deserve! You thought you could worm your way into my family — that I wouldn't find out what you are doing. I'll make you see how mistaken you are, you vile creature —"

At first, receiving the full force of her attack, Helena was stunned, frightened by what she said, alarmed for Billie. But almost at once her own anger rose. To her own surprise she instinctively controlled her own impulse to respond physically to the woman who was striving to reach her with doubled fists.

She interrupted the stream of words. "You've no right to talk to me that way. You'll apologize for what you've said —"

Her words seemed to madden Mrs. Alfred even more. They now stood so close that they almost touched. The blue eyes, so like Billie's and yet so unlike, blazed up at her. "Apologize! You're a filthy thing! You get out of here, right now! I'll not let you stay here another minute. Get out! Get out!"

Helena expected her to strike her and braced for the blow, but Billie's imploring voice intervened. "Mamma, mamma, please don't do this! It's not Helena's fault. Please don't say these things —"

Mrs. Alfred whirled around to face her. "You and your damned shikseh! You're no better than she is. How did I ever come to have such a daughter? But she's not going to get away with it. And you'll see what I'm going to do to you, you little — Everybody's going to know what she is!"

She glared again at Helena, meeting her eyes in fury. But Helena did not quail and she moved away and began to walk about the room, showering them both with an endless stream of invective. Helena, seething in silence, was startled by Billie's hand on her arm.

Billie murmured, "You'll have to go, honey. I'm dreadfully sorry. I didn't think — I didn't want to think this would happen."

Furiously Helena said, "I'm not going away and leave you alone here with her. She can't treat you this way. I don't care if she attacks me. I'm not frightened of her."

Billie made a little sound of despair. "She can't hurt me, honey. She's been like this before. Come on, please, honey, please go."

She drew Helena unwillingly out of the room and into the vestibule, waiting for her to pick up her hat and coat and pushing her gently toward the door. Just as she closed the door on her she said, "You must wait till I call you, honey. I don't know what is going to happen. But don't give up on me, please don't give up on me."

Helena went away, haunted by the sight of Billie's white face in the crack of the door.

III
Billie

Billie opened her eyes. The sunlight came beaming in through the windows because the curtains were not drawn. Of course she had been in no state to draw them the night before. She was lying on the sofa in the living room.

The telephone rang. Yes, that was what had wakened her. She lay and looked at it and presently it stopped ringing. She groped through the mists in her mind, seeking clues to what day it was, what had happened the night before. Helena. It had something to do with Helena. But then every time she waked from sleep she thought first of Helena. My honey. And then remembrance came flooding back. Her mother. And she had had to send Helena away and she wanted her now — needed her — more than she had ever wanted her before. And she couldn't have her.

After a while she sat up and put her feet on the floor. She still wore the clothes she had had on the evening before. When she came back into the living room from seeing Helena out of the door her mother had raged on, saying terrible things about her, about Helena, and finally had stormed out of the apartment flinging threats over her shoulder, prophesying disgrace, revenge, destruction physical and moral. And she herself had sat on and drunk scotch till oblivion overtook her.

If only that oblivion could last. A wave of nausea swept over her as she sat swaying. She had made a mistake. She should not have called Helena ΄to come to her. She had known at the time that she should not do that. Had she really thought that her mother was safely occupied elsewhere? Doubts of that had lurked in the back of her mind but she had deliberately ignored them. Yes, it had been a deliberate decision; she recognized that now. She had, without at the time acknowledging it, deliberately set the stage for what had happened last night.

Why had she done it? Because — she admitted it now — she had come to the end of her tether. She could no longer dodge and hide and lie about this most inner element of her being; could no longer live through these distortions of her real nature. She had no interest in proclaiming herself to the world; it was not the world's business. But she wanted to bring things out into the open in the most intimate relationship she had ever had — with her mother. She wanted to challenge the tenuous and powerful forces that had always kept her in thrall. She had to break out of her prison or she would no longer continue to be a person, she would become a nothing, a living and breathing shell of a woman. In no other way could she ever win Helena. Last night was only the first step. She was astonished that she did not — even now, with a hangover — shrink from what she knew was coming.

Her head seemed to clear as the idea of a confrontation grew stronger — a confrontation with the reality of her situation, a confrontation with the need to establish the direction of her life — yes, that was what confrontation with her mother must mean.

She would have to begin there, with her mother. Helena was right: her mother held the key to everything — to her own future, to the future of Rosenstein's, to what her life would be henceforth. Or, really, could the key be in her own hands? Hadn't it always lain there in her own passive hands, whose fingers had been too nerveless to make use of it? As she thought this the image, the spirit-presence of Helena, came strongly into her consciousness — her honey, her darling, and she felt herself softening, as she had so often in the past, reaching once again for compromise. But this time she tried to put even the idea aside. Even Helena must not get in the way, must not turn her away from what she must do.

She must begin with her mother. The thought brought back to her her first clear remembrance of herself. It was an image set in a familiar frame: her mother's boudoir. Her mother had always spoken of that room as her boudoir and it was furnished accordingly. The soft colors of the rugs, the wall-coverings, the furniture draped in satin frills, the pervading scent of cosmetics created this sense of being lapped in her mother's special place. When she was very little she had loved being in this perfumed nest. It seemed an extension of her mother. At that time there was no conflict between them. She knew she was her mother's darling, special, valued beyond any other of her mother's possessions.

But that sense of boundless security and happiness had vanished when during her teens she awakened to the fact that she and her mother were indeed separate beings, that there was a discrepancy between her mother's nature and her own. When she was very little she had accepted herself as being unique because she was Rosalie's child and Rosalie was obviously considered by everyone — everyone in her world, her father, Old Leah, Daniel, her other relatives — to be of special creation. When she got older she realized that this must be because Rosalie was Old Leah's only granddaughter — Old Leah, that enormous, potent presence that loomed over the whole family, who had no daughter of her own and therefore lavished affection and indulgence on this grandchild as she had not done with any of her sons or their sons. From her very earliest days Billie had been aware of the vast power that resided in the almost silent, formidable old woman whom she saw only when she was with Rosalie. Rosalie did not seem to suffer from any such fearfulness, and Billie, when the black, hooded eyes had occasionally dwelt on her, sought refuge behind this undaunted mother. Rosalie herself treated her grandmother in a carefree way, obviously confidant that she could not outrun Old Leah's affection. Rosalie's own parents chided her for this behavior, but a twinkle awakened in Old Leah's eyes as if she enjoyed this irreverence.

The trouble for Billie came when she was thirteen, shortly before Old Leah died. Old Leah, who had never been known to be seriously ill, had had a bout of pneumonia and after that had begun to fail — because, the family said, her son Moses had died. She seemed to withdraw into her shell, indifferent to her family, heedless even of the store, which up till then she had visited every day. Billie remembered how this weakening of her grip had unsettled her sons and grandsons. After all, they had never been without her active presence in their lives. In the pall that hung over everyone Billie's private anguish developed. Rosalie, wrapped up in the grief brought by her own father's death and her grandmother's failing and in the consequences of Old Leah's death — Rosalie was assumed to be her natural heir in all the causes and charities Old Leah had supported and in some cases founded — did not notice what was happening to Billie, did not notice that Billie lost her appetite, looked pale, had no interest in her schoolwork. If she gave it a thought, she doubtless considered it a natural result of puberty.

The one who did notice was Rachel. Rachel was part of her world from the very beginning. Rachel chose her clothes as a baby, tried out on her the latest fashions for small girls, for seven-year-olds. At that time Rachel was in her thirties, just beginning to establish the reputation in the world of high

277

fashion and design that Old Leah had planned for her. Now Rachel no longer designed clothes for children. She had graduated into the world of glamorous women in high society, women at the top of the entertainment world. Billie had always supposed that that was when Rachel first met the Countess. In any case, Rachel's sharp eyes had seen the signs of Billie's malaise, had noted Rosalie's inattention.

Rachel had several years before moved into the big westside apartment that had been Old Leah's and which Old Leah had given her. She lived there with her parents, elderly people who had come years before from the Old World and who spoke English with strong accents and preferred to speak Yiddish. Billie remembered her first visit to Rachel. It stayed in her memory for several reasons. In the first place, it was the first time she had visited alone someone who was not a relative, though Rachel was so much a member of Old Leah's household as almost to be one. Rosalie was always vigilant even when Billie went to visit cousins, and her coming and going was closely monitored. But this afternoon Rosalie, mourning for her father Moses and for Old Leah's steadily worsening state, absentmindedly consented when Rachel suggested that Billie should come with her while Rosalie took her own mother to visit Old Leah.

The apartment house sat in all its 1890s elegance in the warm sunshine of a spring afternoon. There were benches in the narrow strip of garden that separated it from the street. These, sheltered from the wind, were a favorite spot for the elderly residents to gather for an hour's sociability, the old men on one long bench and the women on another. She remembered how they greeted Rachel, with friendliness tinged with a trace of deference. In the apartment Rachel's mother greeted her with astonished exclamations, asking Rachel in rapid Yiddish what this meant.

Rachel took her into her own bedroom, dominated by the huge ornate bed that had once been Old Leah's, chattering all the while. After a few minutes, she had paused and looking closely at Billie, asked, "What is the matter, Billie? You're so unhappy." Billie did not answer but tears overflowed her eyes. Rachel had not persisted in questioning her but started to show her photographs of places she had visited abroad, to talk to her about the fashion shows she had been to, had brought out portfolios of fashion models and designs. Even in her withdrawn misery Billie realized that Rachel wanted to cheer her, to draw her out into a happier mood. Her dark eyes as she looked at Billie shone with kindness instead of their usual sharp inquiry. Billie, who did not understand fully her own despair, could not keep the tears from welling up and spilling out. Noticing, Rachel said, "It's something you can't tell your mother, isn't it?" And Billie, terrified at hearing this suppressed fact spoken, sobbed.

Rachel gave her a handkerchief and said soothingly, "Here, go ahead and cry. You'll feel better." She sat by her then silently until Billie's sense of hopelessness subsided.

Billie said apologetically, "It isn't anything."

But Rachel shook her head. "You don't want your mother to see you cry. So what is it, Billie? Is it because of your great grandmother? She is a very old lady. We all know she is dying and that is terrible for all of us. Your mother is probably as upset as you are. So can't you talk to her?"

Sniffling, Billie wiped her nose. Looking back on this memory now from a later perspective, she realized that Rachel herself must have felt even more sorrow, more despair, at the idea of Old Leah's coming death than most of the relatives. Feeling obliged to respond to Rachel's kindness, Billie said timidly, "It's not just that. I'm sorry Nana is dying and I'm sorry mamma is unhappy. But it's more than that."

A certain wariness came back into Rachel's eyes. "Has something happened to you, Billie? Has someone done something bad to you?" Even as she asked she seemed to doubt that anything could happen to Billie, so closely guarded by her mother.

Billie shook her head and said hesitantly, "Oh, no. I just don't like things — I just don't want to do things — the things I'm supposed to do —" Her voice trailed off as the hopelessness of putting her feelings in words assailed her. She had always liked Rachel, had felt at ease with her as someone she had known all her life and who was always friendly. But to explain even to Rachel seemed an impossible task. "It's just the way I feel."

A possible explanation occurred to Rachel. "It's just your age, Billie. Most girls go through feelings like this. It's because you're getting to be a woman. You know something about that? Your mother has told you?" Rachel trod delicately, fearful of broaching a subject Rosalie might object to.

But Billie said simply, "I know about having my periods. Mamma has told me all about that. I began a couple of months ago."

280

"Well, you know, sometimes it may make you feel sad. That's nothing unusual."

Billie nodded. She understood what Rachel was thinking. "It's just that I don't seem to want to be what everybody says I'm going to be."

"What you're going to be?"

"What mamma is — that I'm going to grow up and get married and have children. That frightens me."

She looked anxiously at Rachel to see whether this feeble explanation conveyed anything to her. Rachel's black eyes looked into hers for a while before looking away. "I wouldn't worry about that, Billie. Your mother wouldn't want you to be unhappy. She wouldn't want you to do something that would make you unhappy. She wouldn't let anybody else make you unhappy. Come on, cheer up. I think my mother has made some cookies for you."

Sitting now in her own apartment in a present-day haze of misery and looking back, she realized that at the time it seemed an unresolved situation, but in fact this visit with Rachel established a bond between them that grew gradually stronger as she grew older. Each time her mother took her to Rosenstein's for Rachel to plan new wardrobes for both of them, she was aware of a special feeling between Rachel and herself, an understanding that was not based on what they said to each other. Sometimes Rachel took her to her own apartment, something her mother now tacitly accepted. Rachel's mother, a fair, softly plump woman from Hungary, treated her as if she were the daughter of very important people to whom she owed allegiance. Rachel herself was always circumspect,

281

aware that she had to account to Rosalie for every moment Billie spent in her care. Billie knew that her mother's attitude towards Rachel was ambivalent. Rachel held a special place among the Rosensteins because she had been Old Leah's favorite apprentice and therefore Rosalie reluctantly agreed to this first adult friendship of Billie's. To Billie Rachel's company was enchanting. Rachel was always coming and going from exotic places, dealing with exalted people, creating the most alluring clothes. She introduced Billie to all sorts of ideas strange to her sheltered childhood, talked about the world beyond that of the Rosensteins. Rachel was not a bookish person, but she went often to the theater, knew many artists and actors and musicians, not only well-known people whom Rosalie also knew, but often struggling people still reaching for success.

Chiefly Rachel treated her as a contemporary. At least, her manner was that and it deceived Billie, who did not realize till much later that Rachel was always acutely aware that she was an adolescent girl. Then there came an afternoon, a golden early autumn afternoon when she was visiting Rachel in her apartment and it was time to go home and her feelings overwhelmed her — the wayward, impulsive, unpredictable feelings of a fourteen-year-old. She and Rachel stood in one of the big bow windows of the living room looking out on the sunlit Park. Rachel's mother was not there. Suddenly, overtaken by a rush of loving fervor she put her arms around Rachel. She had grown in the last months till she was as tall as Rachel, who was thin and nervous, and she was strong from the active sports she played in school.

She seized Rachel and said fervently, "I love you."

282

For a moment Rachel stood perfectly still, whether from surprise she did not know. She remembered looking eagerly into Rachel's eyes. Then Rachel, instead of drawing away, put her arms around her and said in a steady voice, "I love you too, Billie. Now quiet down a bit." She continued to stand with Billie in her arms, as if receiving into her own body the throbbing pulse of Billie's inchoate desire. Billie put her head down on Rachel's shoulder and gradually the fire that had blazed up in her died down. She did not remember that they talked for the rest of the short time before Rachel took her home. The next time they met Rosalie was present but even so the little episode had deepened the bond between them.

Thinking about it at night in bed Billie wondered, half in embarrassment, what Rachel thought. It had been a violent momentary impulse to take hold of Rachel that way, to force upon Rachel the strength of her feeling. She had sometimes felt a much weaker version of the same impulse with her mother. She was used, since she was a baby, to get into her mother's bed and enjoy the soft, warm, perfumed feel of her mother's body. This closeness seemed to arouse a longing she could not define. It had overflowed with Rachel. Now she felt obscurely that it was not safe to seek an explanation of this from her mother. But Rachel was different. She thought Rachel understood without explanation.

Thereafter whenever Rachel took her for a visit to the apartment they were always as they had been, easy and companionable, Rachel the good-natured fount of all sorts of bits and pieces of knowledge, the raconteuse of lively stories about people in the world of fashion, art and music, stories that echoed with the faint laughter of the scandalous, which she never mentioned explicitly. It was a wonderful relief to Billie's spirits to be with Rachel. She forgot the dark pits of self-doubt, self-distrust, horror of the world she only half-knew that threatened to engulf her. She realized that Rachel watched her with sharp eyes but Rachel never asked her probing questions.

Rachel, when she told stories about people, very often pointed out their likenesses in the many framed photographs that stood about on tables in the apartment. One face appeared everywhere — a dramatic woman in a variety of costumes. Rachel never referred to her. When Billie asked who she was, Rachel seemed to hesitate and then said in a casual tone that she was the Countess Pietri, an old friend who had made a success as an interior decorator. Her family, said Rachel, had suffered badly in the second World War and had no money, though they were of ancient lineage. She said nothing beyond this and it was only later that Billie learned that the Countess spent long periods with Rachel whenever she came to the United States to see prospective clients.

It was also Rachel who explained to her the sudden and complete disappearance of her cousin Michelle from all family gatherings. Once or twice she had mentioned Michelle to her mother but Rosalie either ignored what she said or made some excuse for Michelle's absence. Finally one day when her mother was planning a party for her fifteenth birthday she asked bluntly why they were not inviting Michelle. For a moment her mother was silent and then declared, as if making up her mind to a disagreeable duty, "We won't talk about Michelle. She isn't coming to your party." When Billie asked why, Rosalie said, "Well, she'd done something she can't be forgiven for and besides, she's shameless. I don't want you to have anything to do with her. Nobody in the family has anything to do with her."

The unusual hardness in her mother's tone of voice bothered Billie. Her mother was not often censorious. Billie was not rebellious and had always accepted without question her mother's restrictions on her freedom. But something in this situation nagged at her. The idea that Michelle was purposely excluded from family gatherings was distressing to her. Her usually soft-hearted mother seemed suddenly so adamant that a chill went through her. Rachel, noting her brooding, persisted in gentle questioning till she confessed what the trouble was.

"But, why, Rachel, why should mamma and all the others act that way to Michelle?"

Rachel's answer was careful. Her expressive dark eyes widened when Billie mentioned Michelle. "Well, Michelle wants to live her own life. Her parents don't like her living by herself. They think she should get married and have a family. She says she doesn't want to get married. You know she inherited that house from one of her mother's sisters. She says she is going to live there alone and invite just the sort of people she likes to come and see her. Her parents don't like the sort of people she makes friends with and she has defied them."

Billie digested this information. What a dreadful thing, she thought, it would be to be disowned by your mother. Finally she said, "She shouldn't make her parents unhappy. But they shouldn't cut her off that way. You don't think they should, do you, Rachel?"

Rachel shrugged nervously. "I think they're both wrong. Michelle is just as obstinate as her parents. She says it's unreasonable for them to say she has to live the way they approve of and they say she is not a good daughter."

Billie pondered for a moment. She had never been close friends with her cousin. Michelle was so much older than she, a grown woman, in fact. But she had always found Michelle interesting. Michelle did not talk or act the way her other relatives did. Billie asked, "You like Michelle, don't you, Rachel?"

"Oh, yes. We've always been good friends."

"Do you go to see her now?"

"Yes, when she invites me. But don't tell your mother."

"Well, I'd like to see her sometimes. Will you take me with you when you go to her house?"

Rachel looked aghast. Then she collected herself to say calmly, "But, Billie, your mother does not want you to have anything to do with Michelle. I can't ignore that."

"But I'm the one who wants to see her. We don't have to tell my mother."

Rachel stared at her for a few moments. Billie saw that she recognized this statement as a first sign of rebellion. "You don't realize what would happen — to you, to me — if your mother found out."

Billie was not frightened by her manner. "Nothing would happen to me. Mamma would be very angry for a while. That's all. I'm sorry about you, Rachel. But you could tell Michelle that I'd like to go and see her

286

and I can arrange it with Michelle. It needn't involve you."

Rachel made a sound like a groan. "Billie, it doesn't matter how you arrange it. Your mother would know I was involved somehow. She would know that I would have to be the go-between. That would be the end of me with your family."

Billie answered her gaze steadily. "I don't think so. Nana has been dead two years but nobody is going to do anything she wouldn't like. She wouldn't like anything to happen to you."

In the end Rachel agreed to let Michelle know that Billie wanted to see her. Whatever else she told Michelle Billie did not know. Neither Rachel nor Michelle ever told her. The next step was to find some way to visit Michelle. It occurred to her that she could sometimes stop off at Michelle's house on her way home from school. Rosalie sent her to a girls' school that was not far from her home and was also quite close to Michelle's house. There was a real advantage, she thought, to having acquired a reputation for docility and studiousness. On fair afternoons she went with a bunch of girls in her class to some nearby tennis courts for an hour or so of exercise. Her mother believed that she always walked home with another girl or two who lived nearby. But she could linger, she decided, until the others went on ahead and then slip down another street alone.

She was fascinated with Michelle's house, which had once belonged to Michelle's aunt. She had found Michelle interesting when she herself was a little girl. Now she found her, a woman almost Rachel's contemporary, exotic and exciting. At first Michelle was grudging in her welcome, partly amused, partly annoyed. She dropped these attitudes after Billie's first visit. Michelle seemed to divine immediately what the situation was and made things easy. At first Billie was anxious to let Michelle know that she was a friend, that she did not share her relatives' censure. But Michelle smiled at her earnestness and did not hesitate to show that she was amused. Then realizing that Billie's feelings were easily hurt, she grew more serious.

Once when Billie apologized for the fact that she had not been invited to a family wedding, she said, "Billie, I don't want to be invited to these family parties. They bore me to tears."

Billie answered, "But, Michelle, you must be unhappy because you can't see your father and mother."

Michelle's pale green eyes suddenly sparked. "You probably won't believe this, but I'm not in the least unhappy about that. They don't understand me. They never have and they have never wanted to hear what I had to say. They're narrow-minded and bigoted and I don't think they have any real love for me."

"But why are they so angry with you?"

"Because I was honest about myself and told them I'd never fit into the kind of life they expected me to lead."

"What kind of life?"

Confronted with Billie's candid, puzzled blue eyes, Michelle hesitated. "Billie, I don't want to get married and have children and be a good Jewish matron, like my mother. My parents can't conceive of any daughter of theirs not conforming to that ideal. Now, look, Billie, I think you'd just better skip all this. You don't want to make your mother unhappy. She means a lot more to you than mine does to me. You shouldn't be coming here to see me. She'd be furious if she knew you were disobeying her."

"You don't want me to come?"

"Oh, Billie, yes, I want you to come. I'm not rejecting you. I like you, not because you're trying to be a peacemaker between me and the rest of the Rosensteins. I like you because you are such a nice person. But it won't do."

The whole memory was still so vivid. Looking back Billie wondered why at that age she had so determinedly undertaken this rebellion against her mother, with no feeling of guilt. Was it because she had felt then that what she was doing was the right and only thing to do and that eventually she would confess to her mother and convince her that this was so? Perhaps that was the answer. But the situation had not remained that simple. When she asked Rachel again what was the trouble about Michelle, Rachel temporized and then said flatly that she could not tell her. "You'll have to find out from somebody else. You probably will. But watch out for Esther. If she gets the least suspicion that you're seeing Michelle, she'll tell your mother. Don't ask her any questions about Michelle."

Billie, who knew there was no love lost between Rachel and Esther, did not answer. Rachel was right about Esther. She would not try to find out from Esther. She took to listening carefully whenever Esther talked privately with her mother about family affairs. Esther often spoke in mysterious terms, sometimes nodding in her direction, if she was with them both in her mother's boudoir, which was often

289

the case. Rosalie's responses to Esther's ramblings were brief and noncommittal, as if her attention was really fixed on filing her nails or spreading cream on her face. But Billie knew her mother's multilayered mind, how she seemed to be able to pursue several lines of thought at one time.

Occasionally Esther mentioned Michelle's parents and perhaps there was some hidden meaning in what she said that referred to Michelle herself, some meaning that was clear to Rosalie. Michelle's brothers got married and had children. Billie encountered them at the wedding parties and other family gatherings. They were staid, unimaginative people, not at all like Michelle.

As she grew older Michelle fascinated her even more. She was a highly intelligent woman with a sardonic outlook on life. Rachel told her that Michelle's house was the gathering place for all sorts of people with unusual talents or occupations. But Billie never encountered them. The only ones she did meet sometimes, in her brief afternoon visits, were always women, some of them like Michelle, others quite different and all of them with some indefinable quality that Billie was at a loss to explain. They were not like the women in her mother's circle of friends. They were not married. They did not have children. Or if they had been married and had had children, this was a phase of their lives that was not important now. Also, as time went on, she became aware that they were always a little guarded when they talked to her and often glanced at Michelle, as if taking a cue from her. In spite of these unresolved questions she felt happier in Michelle's house than in those of her other relatives — not as happy as she was with Rachel, who was so much warmer in nature. But she did not feel as strained as she did with the matrons and coming-out belles who were her mother's friends.

She was sixteen when she learned definitely about lesbians, that there were girls and women who preferred to be with other girls and women. This to her was still a half-understood thing, in spite of the teaching she had had from her mother and from her teachers. She read a book she found in Michelle's house — reading it in snatches whenever she had the opportunity — about a girl who seemed to feel much the same way she felt but who was less sheltered and more knowledgeable, a girl who went to bed with women and enjoyed the pleasure she found there. She was suddenly enlightened and wondered why she had been so slow to realize what her own impulse towards Rachel had meant, why Rachel called out in her those intense feelings which Rachel was careful to restrain.

At first this enlightenment brought a kind of joy and then the reality of her situation overwhelmed her. Her first impulse, as was always the case with anything that touched her deeply, was to share it with her mother, to seek her mother's affirmation, to receive sympathy from her warm, cosseting mother. Then a warning sounded in her innermost being: her mother would not accept what she would say. For the first time she felt a check on the absolute trust she placed in her, for the first time she felt alone with a problem she did not know how to handle. Anxiously she watched and listened to the other Rosenstein women who came to see her mother or whom her mother took her to visit. She saw that an enormous gulf divided her from them and their world of suitors, husbands, engagements, marriages, children, grandchildren. At last she understood what their ostracism of Michelle meant.

The next time she was alone with Rachel she asked her the question again: Why was Michelle ostracized by her relatives? And when Rachel began to temporize she cut her short.

"It's because she's a lesbian, isn't it? And those women who are friends of hers, they are, too, aren't they?"

Disconcerted, Rachel said reluctantly, "Yes. But, Billie, who told you? Has your mother found out that you go to visit Michelle?"

Billie shook her head. "No, I just woke up to this. I've been pretty stupid, haven't I?"

"No, no, Billie! Why should you think of it? Oh, I suppose you're getting older and are bound to realize. Have you said anything to your mother?"

"No. I can't. She wouldn't like it. She would be very angry if I told her that I go to see Michelle."

"Are you going to stop going there, then?"

Billie thought for a moment. The idea had not occurred to her. "No. I like Michelle. Besides, Michelle can explain things to me."

Rachel almost groaned. Billie noted the fact and said nothing further. But it was true that she could ask Michelle questions, with a firm belief that Michelle would give her truthful answers. She did talk to Michelle about her new awareness. She said to her that she now understood why Michelle had nothing to do with the rest of the family.

Michelle's pale green intense eyes looked at her sidewise as she said this. "So, little Billie, you've waked up to the big world, have you? Did some of my dearly beloved kin enlighten you? No? So you've arrived at this knowledge all by yourself? Well, what are you going to do about it?"

The bitter undertone of Michelle's voice grated on her. She learned that there was an underside of harshness to Michelle's invariable cold composure, something she had never found in Rachel. "Oh, Michelle, I'm not going to do anything! I think it is terrible that people are so narrow-minded!"

Michelle interrupted her savagely. "Even your mother?"

Billie was silent. Of course even her mother was no more tolerant than any of the other Rosenstein women when it came to this.

But Michelle's anger was soon buried again. The next time Billie visited her Michelle was smiling, friendly, with the usual satirical brightness in her eyes. What worried Billie now was that she began to hope on each visit that Michelle would be alone and miraculously this began to happen. The fascination that Michelle held for her grew still more and Michelle seemed now to be much more aware of her, or at least, more ready to acknowledge that there was something new and unusual in her visits, in Billie herself. Michelle kissed her now when she arrived and Michelle's arms stayed around her for a long moment before she withdrew them.

Looking back, Billie knew that this was a seduction, deliberate on Michelle's part. At the time she did not realize this. She did not question what Michelle did, why her welcome had become so much warmer. She simply wished Michelle to hold her closer, to fondle her in this new exciting way. All the chaste feelings that had been semi-aroused but never

293

fulfilled when she was alone with Rachel blossomed with Michelle until sometimes she was in a state of bubbling excitement which she tried to subdue as she walked the rest of the way home.

Michelle of course knew the effect she had on her. Remembering her sixteen-year-old self, Billie saw it all now very clearly. An afternoon came soon when, with a brief, impatient sound, she had led Billie up to her bedroom and taken her to bed. Billie shivered as Michelle deftly removed her clothes, passing her long-fingered hands lightly over Billie's burgeoning adolescent body. Billie, her pent-up, never-realized desire released by Michelle's expert, adept touch, lost all sense of herself, her surroundings, and was astonished, when Michelle brought her gently back to earth, to find that so little time had passed.

Even now, with the jaded feelings of her present dilemma, she could remember the feel of Michelle's fingers in her soft, warm, moist cleft, the deliciously tantalizing little strokes and touchings that brought her to her first climax. So vivid was her recollection that she got up from the sofa and walked about the room to dispel the remembered ecstacy.

She went back to her memories. Fortunately that afternoon her mother had not been home when she reached there. She did not think that it would have been possible for her to hide from her the keyed-up state of her nerves. Rosalie was an avid card player and an active organizer of bridge tournaments to raise funds for Jewish causes. At that time she was especially involved in efforts to promote the finding and punishment of war criminals responsible for the horrors of the Holocaust. Typically, she had thrown all her energies into these efforts, as usual never stinting her time or her considerable organizational skill.

So Billie returned home to a house empty except for the servants; her father was always preoccupied with his own business, the discovery and identification of ancient scholarly manuscripts. Esther, always at her mother's elbow, had accompanied Rosalie to the fund-raising. Billie had a chance, therefore, to gather herself together, to put on the outward show of demure docility that her mother expected. Even then she realized that it had, with that afternoon in Michelle's arms, become just that — an outward show.

Michelle had created an irreversible inner turmoil in her. She spent more and more time with Michelle, inventing reasons for staying late at school, in the library, at tennis. It was Michelle who had to detach her clinging arms, remind her that her mother would be waiting, send her home in time so that Rosalie would not become suspicious. Billie's infatuation made her reckless, but Rosalie was too absorbed in the indignation aroused by the effort to vindicate the victims of the Holocaust. By the time Rosalie's fervor had subsided into more sustained, rational support for her cause, Billie had learned to sit quietly in her mother's boudoir, listening to her mother's angry diatribes against the persecution that Jews had suffered through the ages. If her mother — or more often Esther — noticed that she was absentminded, not fully attentive to what was being said, it was assumed to be adolescent daydreaming.

After a while her absorption in Michelle grew less intense. Thinking about it now, she supposed that Michelle had begun to grow somewhat tired of the game, as it was to Michelle. Probably at first Michelle had been motivated by a wish for revenge in seducing Old Leah's most valued little great granddaughter, a means of flouting the power of the family. But then a bond of real affection, real kinship had grown up between them, so that when Michelle's ardent pursuit had flagged there was a comfortable residue of fondness left. At the time she had really loved Michelle with all her heart — the gentle, kind initiator into sacred rites, not the witch, the pariah that Michelle was called by her other relatives. But there was another thread in this web of learning. She had learned also to be deceitful, wary, untruthful. It created a barrier between herself and her mother, a barrier her mother did not know about and this fact alone produced a pain she could not assuage.

The only outlet she had for relieving her own pent-up misgiving was as always Rachel, who had watched with anxiety the transformation in her. Rachel was often away on business but whenever she returned to New York she stepped back into the role of comforter, confidante. Somehow she managed never to introduce Billie to the Countess. Fear of the consequences if Rosalie should hear about it was the probable reason, thought Billie. She supposed that Rosalie must not approve of the Countess.

It was a relief when she went to college. With her usual docility she had not tried to persuade her mother to send her away to college and she had expected to go to Barnard. She never knew why Rosalie decided against this. She asked Rachel if she knew why her mother was sending her away to college. Rachel said that probably Rosalie had been under pressure from some of the older Rosenstein women to find a suitable husband for Billie. After all, was college really necessary for a Rosenstein girl who had everything she wanted? And Rosalie, annoyed, had flared up and said that Billie was going to college as an intelligent girl should. A reason behind this, Rachel guessed, was that Rosalie feared marriage for Billie, except under circumstances she could control — that is, marriage to a man Rosalie would pick out who would be amenable to her own dictates. College was a safe haven for a few years, especially one of the few remaining all-women colleges. Billie, Rosalie had been heard to state defiantly, would never marry a goy, and most of the men she would meet during those years would be Gentiles.

"Of course," Rachel concluded, "you're not going to marry a man anyway, are you?"

"No," said Billie, knowing that Rachel had for some time realized what her relationship with Michelle was.

The first two years while she passed leisurely through her college courses — she had the knack of learning things easily with neither the need nor the desire to study earnestly — she was able to avoid any real involvement in social activities off campus. On campus she found no one who compared with Michelle. Her mother seemed very satisfied with this state of things.

When she reached her junior year and the pressure from her peers was stronger for involvement with boys from other nearby campuses, she was rescued by Moishe — Moishe the indulged, the admired, five years younger than she, who was suddenly available as an escort. Goodnaturedly she wondered why he was so anxious to be her escort and thought that probably he needed a good screen against the curiosity of his fellows five or six years older than he. Yes, Moishe had been a godsend, though she was teased and laughed at. So young, they said, and already robbing the cradle. But knowing this to be the lesser evil, she laughed with them. Her mother, she was glad to see, found it humorous also, but was complacent about it. Obviously there was no danger of a Gentile son-in-law while this game went on.

When she came home from college she asked for an apartment of her own. Rosalie asked Why? Well, she wanted a little more independence. And because she did not press for it vehemently but with an air of casual wishfulness, she got it. But what was going to happen now, Rosalie asked suspiciously. You're going to run around with men? Of course not, said Billie, and with the inspiration of the moment, added, I'm going to learn the business. Rosenstein's? Rosalie demanded. Of course, said Billie, and Rosalie, delighted at the safety thus offered, said, I'm delighted darling. Everybody knows you're just like Nana. By everybody, Billie knew, she meant all the Rosensteins.

That was when this life of subterfuge and drinking began. There were only Rachel and Michelle to take refuge with. She often went abroad with Rachel — and met the Countess, who, whatever her reputation for cynicism and social backbiting, was kind to her, for Rachel's sake. With Michelle she was more ambivalent. Occasionally when she had come home from college for visits, they went to bed together, but their relationship had gradually retreated into a platonic friendship. Michelle, she knew, had never seen her as anything but a seductive little girl. Now she respected her as a mature woman with other interests.

Moishe remained what he had always been, her favorite and only real playmate. They had grown apart after she finished college and especially when she became involved in the problems of Rosenstein's. He scoffed at the idea that she had any real understanding of business. To him this was proved by her preoccupation with the store. Rosenstein's was an anachronism, he said, good only as an asset to be used in creating a new enterprise. She sat quietly while he chided, was scornful, and ended in exasperation. Don't you intend to take my advice? he demanded. She had smiled and said No, and he flung off in a huff, to come back later in his usual high spirits to talk about something else.

She had not expected him to suddenly grow serious over Helena. It was normal for him immediately to become alert when he heard that the new manager of Rosenstein's was a good-looking woman, smartly dressed, able to hold her own when the talk was about business and the world of money-making. But then he became moody, irascible, wrapped in a sulky silence whenever he came to see her. When he demanded information about Helena she had been careful to deny that she knew much about her. Instinct told her that he did not believe her, and she felt a sort of dread that eventually he would learn what Helena meant to her.

As time went on he got more and more captious. Couldn't she ask Helena questions about herself and tell him the answers? I can't do that, she objected. Why don't you ask her yourself? Because she won't answer me, he said morosely. At the same time that Moishe was badgering her, she was aware that her mother's alarm over his interest in Helena was growing. She considered mentioning this to him and decided not to. Moishe would scorn the idea that his actions could be governed by what any woman had to say, even Rosalie.

As her recollection reached these recent events, Billie came back to the present, to her apartment as the scene of last night's battle, to her own disheveled, disoriented self. As she stood in the middle of the room, uncertain what to do, the phone rang again. Reluctantly she crossed over to answer it. Rosalie's peremptory voice said, "I expect you over here for dinner tonight. Be in my room at five-thirty," and the phone clicked off. Billie stood for a while longer staring at the instrument before returning it to its cradle. Slowly and clumsily she showered and dressed as carefully as she could. Her stomach still heaved at the thought of what confronted her. Helena was life to her, but Helena was out-of-bounds until she could come to the ultimate understanding with her mother. Rosalie must accept what she was, that she could not change, that she did not want to change, that Helena meant far more to her than anything or anyone, including Rosalie herself.

As she dressed she suffered a chilling sense of despair and terror at the thought of what all this would mean to Helena. She had brought this catastrophe on Helena and she wondered bleakly whether Helena's awareness of this would alienate her from her. For a long moment she stood still seeking a way to begin the task of finding an answer to the situation. Could she, by thinking hard, place a finger on the moment when Moishe's suspicions had become certainty? The memory came to her of an evening when she and Helena had by accident emerged from Rosenstein's together and had stood waiting for a cab in front of the big lighted door. It was the only occasion when this had happened and Moishe had materialized out of the crowd on the street to approach them. There must have been a brief moment when their gaze at each other had been unguarded and he had seen it. She remembered now more clearly than she had noted at the time that his stare, at first suspicious and then indignant, had gone from one to the other of them. He had obviously been on his way to catch Helena in her office and was annoyed and disgruntled that he had missed his opportunity. At the time she had thought it was only that, but now she seemed to see in the encounter something more significant. He had given them another piercing glance and then said Goodbye in a very stiff voice.

Why had he come to suspect them — to suspect Helena? Because of herself. His attraction to Helena had heightened his awareness of everything and everyone who had close dealings with her — the jealous suspicions of a lover. For after all it came down to jealousy. For the first time in his life he had learned to be jealous, because for the first time a woman had aroused in him more than a wish for conquest. Poor Moishe.

And in the spirit of revenge, driven probably by an urge he could not resist, he had gone to her mother. That would be the perfect revenge — to tell

Rosalie that she need not fear that he would be marrying a Gentile but that her darling Billie was a lesbian who had found a Gentile lover.

Billie finished dressing. Carefully she put on a pair of fine wool pants and a silk blouse with a collar that tied under her chin. She must present her best appearance, minimize the evidence of a hangover. Sitting down in the armchair in front of the silent television set, she concentrated on remembering what her mother had said after Helena left. First her mother had raved, accused her of every sort of promiscuous behavior, threatened her with social ostracism, not only by the Rosensteins — "Look at Michelle!"

And at that point Rosalie had suddenly stopped, glaring at her with a renewed anger. She demanded, "Did you learn this from Michelle? Has she corrupted you? Have you been going to her behind my back? How long has this been going on?"

Billie did not answer. She had said nothing since Helena had left.

Her silence infuriated Rosalie more. "How did you meet Michelle? Nobody speaks to her. She doesn't exist as far as we are concerned. Did she entice you into her house? How long have you been carrying on behind my back?"

Billie still did not answer. She could not say, I'm not a child. I'm a woman thirty years old. You can't dictate to me what I should do. No, she could not say that because she had never resisted her mother's control.

Rosalie railed on. "You can stand there like a mute and not answer me, but let me tell you, I'm going to get to the bottom of this. You know who

302

told me about you and that worthless shikseh? It was Moishe and she has broken his heart. He's not having anything more to do with her. He says you've ruined her. I say she has ruined you. He can thank his lucky stars that he found out about her before he got any more involved with her. He won't touch her now with a ten-foot pole. She's not fit to be called a woman. And he won't have anything more to do with you, either. He says you've been a shameful thing for a long time. How does he know that? When did he find out?"

Rosalie suddenly stopped. Billie saw that instinct told her that she had overstepped a forbidden line, that she had undermined her whole attack upon her by mentioning Moishe, by bringing Moishe into their private dealings. She had lost her advantage and she was silent, breathing heavily, for several moments. Then she began again to castigate her but now she seemed acutely aware of her misstep and in a little while she had flung out of the apartment.

So, thought Billie, where do I stand? Her mother's command to come to dinner could not be avoided. A sudden determination went through her. Whatever her life was to be after this would be fixed by how she acted now. This was not another defeat that she must absorb. This meant that she must fight and she had never fought before. She had to make her calculations in the dark. How much did Moishe really know? How much of what he had said to her mother as fact was really only the imaginings spawned by his angry jealousy? Was he likely to voice his suspicions among his male relatives? He had always been her playmate. They had always sided with each other against the tyranny of older members of the family. But that was a childhood thing. She had never at any time enlightened him about her own private worries and concerns. He knew nothing of what Michelle and Rachel meant to her, nothing of the subterfuges she had used to keep her mother in the dark about herself. She supposed Moishe had had his own private problems which he had never spoken of to her. Now he was obviously entirely concerned with his own place in the family's world, the defense of his own preeminence in his own eyes. He would be extremely sensitive to anything that threatened that. It would make him jealous of anyone who competed with him. He would never give away any information that would in any way show him in a poor light. The only way in which she could discover what Moishe really knew was through her mother.

Slowly she prepared to leave. She looked at the little clock. It said five o'clock. When she arrived at her mother's apartment she looked at Elise, her mother's maid, whom she had known all her life. But Elise greeted her with the slightly condescending air she always used towards her. Elise was devoted to her mother but Billie knew that she thought Rosalie's daughter to be somewhat wanting, a spinster in her thirties.

"How is my mother?"

"I'm sorry to say she isn't feeling well. She called Mrs. Solomon to take her place at the Hadassah meeting this afternoon."

Alarmed in spite of herself, Billie asked, "Why, what is the matter?" Rosalie always boasted that she was as strong and healthy as a peasant.

Elise shrugged and did not answer, walking towards Rosalie's boudoir. At the door she paused as usual and announced, "Miss Billie is here, madame," and walked away.

Billie stepped into the room. Her mother was lying on the chaise longe. She wore a negligee that was a froth of white lace, something, Billie felt sure, Rachel had brought her from her last trip to Paris.

Before she could speak, Rosalie said sharply, "I'm sorry, Esther, I don't feel like dealing with that today. Daniel will have to wait."

Billie was instantly aware that her mother was warning her of Esther's presence. Esther sat in the satin-covered armchair, not at once visible from the doorway. She said now, in her usual bright cheery voice, "Oh, Billie, how are you?" her eyes eagerly searching Billie's face.

Her nerves tuned up to a brittle pitch, Billie sought for some clue to Esther's possible knowledge of what had happened between herself and her mother. All her life she had been used to Esther's presence as her mother's bosom companion. But she could see in Esther's eyes only the usual avid curiosity. She murmured a response and turned away. She was surprised to hear her mother's voice saying crisply, "Esther, I'd appreciate it if you'd go and call Daniel and tell him that I can't see him tomorrow. I'll let him know when I can talk to him."

Esther, from long habit sensitive to every nuance of Rosalie's moods, understood at once that her presence was not wanted and got up to leave. "I do hope you feel better soon, Rosalie. If not, you'd better see the doctor."

Rosalie dismissed her with an impatient wave of her hand and Esther went out of the room with a lingering glance at both of them.

305

Then the silence in the room was unbroken for several minutes. Outwardly quiet, Billie inwardly fretted. She knew she must not start talking into this vacuum, because then she would give away the strength of her resolve. Her will to confront her mother would ebb away like water into sand.

Finally Rosalie said, staring at her angrily, "You spent the night drinking, didn't you? Of course I knew that you sit there guzzling whiskey by yourself, if you can't get anybody else to join you. Do you think I'm stupid? I didn't know why before but I do now." Rosalie swung her legs off the chaise-longe and sat up, gathering her thick glossy hair with both hands and fastening it on the back of her head. There was tremendous energy in this gesture and no sign of real or pretended weakness. Billie knew that her mother despised women who used physical weakness as an emotional weapon to gain their own way. She made fun of some of her older female relatives — Michelle's mother was one of them — who sought to control husbands and children through this device.

Ignoring her silence, Rosalie went on, "You've been very clever all these years, being my good little daughter, just as docile as can be." Her voice dripped sarcasm.

How can I tell her, Billie thought, that I always wanted her to know?

Her mother's voice rose in volume and harshness of tone. "What I want to know is when all this began. Was it that —?" She seemed to choke on the thought. "Was it Michelle who taught you this filthiness? Was it Michelle who made you what you

306

are? Did she do it for revenge against me? And how old were you? She's going to pay for this."

Billie was bemused. What sort of divination gave her mother so accurate a guess? Was it some sort of affinity that led her at once to suspect Michelle? A warning bell rang in Billie's consciousness. In some way she would have to divert her mother's attention away from Michelle and prevent her suspicions from straying to Rachel. She had never known how much her mother knew or suspected of Rachel's liaison with the Countess. These two must not suffer from her mother's rage.

She said nothing aloud and her mother rounded on her. "You needn't think you're going to get away with keeping your mouth shut. That's a trick you've played on me before. I'm getting to the bottom of this, with or without your help. You needn't think Michelle is going to go scot free —"

Billie was at last goaded into speaking. "Mamma, you can't blame Michelle. She was not to blame."

The quietness of her statement brought Rosalie up short. "What do you mean? If it wasn't Michelle, who was it? Some stranger —"

Ah, thought Billie, then Michelle is not a stranger; she's still a Rosenstein. She said aloud, "It was nobody. Mamma, I'm just me."

Rosalie's face became red with rage. "What are you? I always thought you were my daughter, a decent Jewish girl. If you've been to bed with women, some woman must have taught you. Who was it? And when?" Her blazing eyes held Billie's. "So that's why you wanted your own apartment, instead of staying here with me. You must have been doing this when you were in college. Is that where you learned this?"

307

Billie shook her head, again speechless under the torrent of her mother's words. At least her mother seemed to know that women could go to bed with each other and that they experienced some sort of pleasure. It was implicit in Rosalie's manner that she was well acquainted with what women might do with each other.

Rosalie said, "You're lying to me. I thought you never lied to me. I've always told everybody: Billie is perfectly truthful. I can rely on her. Now I know I've been a fool. And how many other people know about this? Come on, tell me. Michelle. Who else?"

"I've never told anybody —"

"You haven't told them. They know, that kind, when you're dying to go to bed with them. How many others are there besides this shikseh? I tell you, she's not going to last another week at Rosenstein's —"

"Mamma!"

"Ah, I've got you there! Don't mamma me. Do you think I'd let her stay there and poison the air —"

Billie's voice was suddenly strong and demanding. Her question, "Are you going to tell Daniel?" broke into the flow of Rosalie's words and for a moment Rosalie was silent, breathing heavily. Then she said, "Tell him? Tell him what? That I've got a crazy woman for a daughter? That there's an uncleanness right here in the midst of my life —?"

Billie interrupted her again. "I'm not crazy and there is nothing unclean about me. These are ideas from the past. You're not that ignorant. You —"

Rosalie jumped to her feet and came to stand in front of her. Billie realized that she had never spoken to her mother in that tone of voice. "You shameful, impudent little —" Rosalie choked. "Calling me ignorant. Have you lost all decency and respect? I'm your mother. I won't tolerate this."

Billie relapsed into silence. At least she had not been disowned. This was a familiar pattern in Rosalie's outbursts of temper, something she could remember back to her earliest childhood, when occasionally she had provoked her mother's anger by something she had done or said. But while she stood and listened to Rosalie wearing out her rage, she felt a great heaviness of spirit. It was reassuring — she felt an odd joy in realizing it — that her mother had no intention of disowning her. That had been a great fear that had underlain her flight into drunkenness the night before. But there seemed no way in which she could reach her mother, impress the truth upon her. The spate of words left no opening for what she wanted to say. Even if she were able to speak, she realized that her mother would not hear what she said, could not possibly absorb the meaning of what she said. A sense of hopelessness — a familiar feeling — overcame her and left her silent.

Her silence infuriated Rosalie anew. She came closer to her and spoke into her face, looking up, for there was just enough difference in height between them to make this necessary.

"How can you shame me this way? Even if you don't feel your own disgrace — your own depravity — you might think of me, what you are doing to me. My own child, who has had every advantage I could give you, every ounce of my love —"

Overwhelmed, Billie put out her hands to touch her, but Rosalie struck them away, screaming, "Don't touch me! I'm not one of your filthy women! To think that my little girl has been in the hands of such creatures —" Rosalie suddenly turned away and began to sob.

Appalled, Billie stood frozen. The only other time she had seen her mother weep so was when Old Leah died. Rosalie's volatile temperament very often brought her to a few tears, of sympathy, joy, unhappiness. But these sobs came from her heart and shook her body. Billie's impulse was to take her in her arms to try to soothe her, but she was paralyzed by this new, strange distancing.

After a while Rosalie straightened up and wiped away her tears. She looked at Billie as if to see how she was reacting. Billie dropped her eyes. Her mother said, with a note of triumph in her voice, "So you are ashamed."

Billie looked up to meet her eyes again. "No, I am not. I am sorry that I've made you so unhappy. But, mamma, I'm not ashamed, and you shouldn't be ashamed of me. Mamma, I love you so much. I'm me, as I have always been. I've wanted to tell you about this ever since I realized it myself. I've never wanted to deceive you. I've never willingly done that. And nobody is to be blamed for me. Nobody has done anything to me that I didn't want. Don't you understand that?"

Rosalie's rage surged back. "What do you mean? That I've given birth to a monster?" She seemed to realize the moment she said this that she had lost her ascendancy in the struggle between them.

Billie said quietly, "Am I a monster?"

Rosalie turned away. After a moment she said petulantly, "I don't know what you mean. I don't

310

understand how you can act the way you do. I've never been harsh with you. I've given you everything you ever wanted —"

"So why can't I stay your little girl, your obedient little daughter? Mamma, I'm a woman. I've been a woman for quite a while. I have to have a life of my own. If I had wanted to marry a man, you would have taken that for granted —"

"Because that's normal. And I could have had something to say about the man you would marry. But this! You've put yourself outside decent society. How could I ever explain to your father, to the rest of our relatives? What would Nana have thought of this? Thank God, she's dead. Even Michelle had the decency to wait till she was dead before cutting herself off from us."

What would Nana have thought of this, of her, of Michelle? Billie conjured up the memory of the very old woman, somber, uncommunicative, that she remembered from her childhood. Nana had always seemed impervious to emotional crises, to the volatile opinions of her descendants.

Rosalie had gone on talking. "You've made it perfectly clear that you didn't want to marry. And have I pushed you, have I told you you had to, so that your father and I could have grandchildren? I've accepted you. I've respected your feelings —"

"And now you know the reason, so why can't you accept that, too?"

Rosalie's eyes blazed with a mixture of surprise, anger, chagrin. "Why can't I? You know the answer to that. I'd rather you were a cripple, an idiot —"

"Would you really?"

Rosalie stopped short, staring at her, looking her

311

up and down, as if weighing what she saw. Billie knew that her mother had always been proud that she had such a pretty daughter, such a bright daughter. Rosalie did not answer and for a while the room was silent, containing the sum of their unspoken feelings.

All at once Rosalie roused. A new thought seemed to have occurred to her. Billie recognized this abrupt change in her. Rosalie seldom was unaware of her surroundings, of the people who might be within sight and sound. Of course, thought Billie. She had sent Esther away, but where was Elise?

Rosalie walked quickly across the room to look through the door into her bedroom. She seemed relieved as she came back.

Billie heard her mother's sigh of relief. Then Rosalie said, "I've got to get dressed for dinner." She touched a little bell on her dressing table and they both waited till Elise appeared. Rosalie pointed to a chair. "You wait here for me," she ordered. And Billie sat and watched while her mother dressed, as she had many times throughout her life.

At dinner there was nothing in outward appearances to indicate that anything unusual was taking place. Her father accepted her presence as he always accepted her presence or her absence, with equanimity. Esther, who usually had dinner with her parents, seemed to watch constantly for something, but then, thought Billie, she always does that. When dinner was over her mother dismissed her, saying, out of earshot of the others, "I expect you here for dinner tomorrow. Mind you, leave the whiskey alone."

Billie walked slowly back to her own apartment,

automatically crossing streets at the proper places, pausing to gaze without seeing at the shop windows, the tears in her eyes blinding her. It was the first time in her life that she had taken leave of her mother without a kiss.

Back in her own place she stood for a long time in the middle of the living room, her mind going round and round in search of explanations, guidance. Her mother did not intend to turn her loose, did not intend to deny her as her daughter. But what did she intend? The relief she felt was offset by a sense of foreboding.

In the days and evenings that followed Billie found herself engaged in a battle she could not avoid. She went obediently whenever her mother summoned her, which was every day — went and sat alone with her while she repeated what she had said at first. But each time there was an enlargement of the field of combat. Rosalie now not only berated Helena, called her vile, underhanded, venal, but also she probed. Why had Billie become infatuated with her? Why did she find Helena so fascinating? Didn't she see that she was just a dupe in the hands of an astute woman who was using her to gain a position of power among the Rosensteins? Didn't she see that the tactics Helena had used to bemuse Daniel were now being used on her?

Billie sat silent most of the time while her mother drew these pictures of depravity. At first she was simply relieved. Obviously her mother had said nothing to Daniel about Helena, had made no move to have Helena dismissed as she had threatened. But as each session came to an end she rebelled.

"Mamma," she cried at last, "this isn't so. You don't want to believe what I tell you. I love Helena. I love her in a way I cannot love anybody else."

Her mother broke in angrily, interrupted her with denials that any such thing could possibly be so. Finally Rosalie broke off the session, saying she could not tolerate the ravings of someone who was not in her right mind. Billie must learn to see things in their true light.

Each day she was required to go with her mother to whatever social or charitable gathering was on Rosalie's calendar. Certainly this seemed to reenforce the idea that Billie was still her darling daughter, the inheritor of her position in such affairs, as she herself had been Old Leah's. Each evening Billie was required to come to her mother's apartment and, after a session in her mother's boudoir, sit down to dinner with her parents. If her father wondered about this — it was a departure from the routine he was used to — he did not indicate it. These dinners would have been silent meals without the constant stream of small talk provided by Esther, chiefly about the day to day affairs of other members of the Rosenstein family. When Rosalie dismissed her it was always with a warning not to go home and drink.

Her mother was holding her captive. This much Billie understood. Elise came to her apartment more frequently. Billie had always accepted the sharp-eyed, dour-faced Frenchwoman, knowing that she was her mother's eyes and ears. Elise's visits now, she supposed, were to see if there was evidence that she was drinking or that she had Helena in to visit her. It was remarkable, she thought, how Rosalie could inspire the most devoted loyalty in the women who worked for her. She was naturally a charming, gracious woman. That image did not wear away in the close quarters of daily contact.

Rosalie did not mention Moishe but Billie felt sure that he still came to see her, if not always willingly, then because she summoned him. What did she say to him? And what did he say to her? How frank were they with each other?

At last, in mild rebellion, she told her mother that henceforth she could not always be available to go with her to her daytime engagements. She was going to spend part of her time at Rosenstein's. At first Rosalie was ready to refuse. But then she said shrewdly, "Well, it's about time you settled down to some serious work. If you had done that long ago, you wouldn't be in this mess now and we wouldn't be having this uproar about what to do with the store. But you keep away from that woman."

Billie sat very still hearing her say this. It was the first time that Rosalie had mentioned to her the conflict over the store's future. She supposed Daniel had discussed with her the alternatives being considered and certainly Moishe must have bombarded her with his own wishes. She had given up hope that Rosenstein's could survive, that Helena would continue as the Company's manager. Now her mother's words seemed to hold out a precarious hope. It was true that you could never predict just what Rosalie would think or do. The fact that she listened, with apparent good humor and sympathy, receptive to whatever might be said to her, did not mean that she accepted it. A shrewd brain lay behind this amiable facade. She remained uninfluenced, uncommitted until she had reached her own conclusions. Rosalie was not an obedient, subservient woman. Nor was she entirely swayed by the sort of emotional, sexual blandishments that Moishe liked to lavish on her. She had become angry at his undisguised pursuit of Helena. She would not forget that anger now.

Billie was brought back to the present by a sudden awareness that her mother was still staring at her. What penalty, what punishment would she have to accept to heal this breach? Obviously Rosalie had not acted on her threat to have Helena's connection with Rosenstein's brought to an abrupt end.

When she walked into Rosenstein's for the first time since her mother's explosion, Billie stepped cautiously, testing with her eyes, her ears, the atmosphere about her as she crossed the ground floor showroom. But the women behind the counters seemed as always delighted to see her. She noticed no cold stares, no hostile looks, no curious side-glances. So there could be no rumors circulating. The bad moment came when, while chatting with the woman in charge of the sportswear department, she saw Helena across the floor, on the way to the elevators. She saw her suddenly stop and stand irresolute, at sight of her. As casually as she could Billie waved and deliberately turned away, but not before she caught a glimpse of the dismay on Helena's face. If she'll just believe in me, know that I'm locked in battle with mamma, that I intend to win, for both of us, that I'm not going to give up Rosenstein's. She found herself trembling. The sight of Helena brought back to her the utter void in her life without Helena. She strove to overcome the passionate longing to rush across the space between them and to maintain her usual calm manner while she took leave of the saleswoman, whose quick glance had followed hers across the floor.

She forced herself to walk leisurely down the aisles, pausing briefly to answer greetings from the saleswomen, making sure that Helena was no longer in sight before she took the elevator to the twelfth floor. The office she had always used was tidy. Taking off her hat and coat she sat down at the big, bare desk and rang the personnel office for someone to help her. She could detect nothing but surprised and friendly greeting from the other end of the line. The woman who came up was Marcia, who had worked for Helena during the Christmas rush overtime. She seemed delighted to see her.

"Oh, Miss Billie!" she exclaimed. "You haven't been in the store for so long we thought you had gone away."

Billie smiled back at her. "You will be seeing a lot more of me now."

She sent for files and computer printouts. Her first job was to scan carefully the text of the presentations Helena had made to the board of directors, which were confidential and which she had to obtain from Esther. As the days went by she resumed her habit of wandering about the store, talking to the saleswomen, watching the customers. This method of observing and measuring the rhythm of business in the store, she realized, was a far cry from the evaluations based solely on statistics, which the management had relied upon. Beyond a doubt the faith of these new people in charge — men like Barton, eager to use their skill and their jobs as stepping stones to more spectacular business success — in the new techniques was correct for the kind of store Rosenstein's would become if it was sold to a conglomerate, to be simply another retail outlet for a chain. But it was the reason that Rosenstein's was not now flourishing. Rosenstein's had been created on another model altogether: Old Leah's unique vision. What she must do, as Old Leah's successor, became clearer to her day by day.

She did not see Helena again in these perambulations around the store, and though she was relieved that this was so, she wondered uneasily why. Did it mean that Helena had given up on her? Back in her own apartment at night she stared at the telephone, itching to lift the receiver and press the buttons of Helena's number. She did not, afraid.

It did not surprise her that Esther dropped in frequently to chat. She was quite sure that her mother had said nothing to Esther about the true state of affairs between them. Yet Esther must have sensed that there was some sort of tug-of-war going on between them and that as Rosalie's faithful ally she must keep an eye on Billie. Perhaps she was uneasy because Rosalie obviously was not confiding in her. Billie thought, in spite of years of the closest association, Esther had not learned to fathom the springs of Rosalie's thoughts and feelings.

"What's going to be done with the store, Billie?" she asked.

"I don't know."

"Oh, you must have some idea! I know you don't like the idea that Rosenstein's is going to be sold. How your great grandmother would have hated that!"

"That's true. I don't like it."

"But what's going to happen?"

"You'll have to ask Daniel."

318

"Oh, there's no use asking him!"

"Then ask mamma."

"She won't say a word about it. I'm sure she won't like it if the store disappears."

"I don't think it will disappear whether it is sold or not."

"Oh, you know what I mean! Of course, Moishe says it will bring in a lot more money that way. Do you think that's true?"

"If Moishe says so, it must be true."

"I wonder what Helena thinks about it. She just won't discuss it. She says it's out of her hands now."

Billie did not answer.

Esther persisted. "I wonder what the other shareholders think. Michelle, for instance. I sent her a copy of the minutes of the last directors' meeting. I'm supposed to do that as secretary."

"Then I expect she will get in touch with Daniel, if she hasn't already." Billie gave no sign of the surprise she felt. Esther had never spoken to her of Michelle before.

Esther, having failed in one direction, tried another. "You know about Lionel, of course."

Billie raised her eyebrows at the question.

"Well, of course, this is very confidential. I thought your mother would have told you. He's thinking of resigning."

"Resigning? He's not sick, is he?"

"Oh, I don't mean he's retiring, not from the banking firm! I expect they'll have to carry him out of there feet first, even with Moishe as a junior partner. They say he listens to him more than to any of the older men. No, I mean, resigning from being chairman of Rosenstein's board. He says he needs more time to give to his own affairs. I suppose you could say this means he assumes that Rosenstein's is going to be sold and he's no longer interested."

Billie said nothing and after a while Esther left. But each time she came in to chat she brought another nugget of gossip, ever anxious to prompt a response from Billie. She mentioned Helena. There was a great deal of speculation, she said, about Helena's future.

"Some people seem to take it for granted that she will leave if the store is sold. Naturally she wouldn't be manager of the Company any longer. If Rosenstein's becomes part of a conglomerate, there'd be an entirely different set-up, wouldn't there? At least, James Barton says so. He seems to think there'd be much greater opportunity for himself."

"Perhaps."

"But it's funny about Moishe. Nobody has seen him for days. He never comes to the store any more. He must be really busy. He's been to see your mother several times. But you probably know that. He is trying to persuade her to support him, isn't he?"

Billie merely nodded.

These days in the store helped to strengthen her for the evening sessions with her mother. At least her mind was filled for several hours with something besides the continual consideration of what would happen to her.

Rosalie hammered away at the main thrust of her assault. Why had she chosen this path in life? Who had led her into it? How long had this been going on?

For the most part Billie kept silent. She realized that her silence goaded her mother into more and more violent accusations. She did not want to do this. She knew she could never reach her mother by antagonizing her and yet as long as Rosalie demanded her presence there was a bridge between them. Her only hope was through appealing to Rosalie's love, her sense of justice. But Rosalie's tirades left her speechless, unable to formulate sensible replies. She was terrified also at the idea of giving something away, of providing Rosalie with more ammunition, through some incautious statement. It was this reserve of hers, she saw, that most infuriated Rosalie. Did she really, Billie wondered, suspect Michelle? And how far away from her mind was Rachel?

Tonight Rosalie stopped abruptly in mid-sentence. Her tone of voice changed from anger to supplication. "Billie, why don't you answer me? You have always been my little girl. You've never acted like this before. I don't understand it. You're hiding something from me. You never used to do that."

Billie tried to pull herself together. "Mamma, I don't want to hide anything from you. I never told you about what I felt — how I saw things —"

"Why?" Rosalie demanded, impatient at her hesitation.

"Because I was afraid to, because I knew you would not want to hear about it. I longed — I really did long — to tell you. Can't you understand that?"

Some of Rosalie's anger came back. "Certainly I wouldn't want to hear of such wickedness. But if I'd known, I would have prevented it. Or stopped it. I could have saved you. I wouldn't have allowed anybody to steal you from me."

Sadly Billie shook her head. "You couldn't have done anything about it. Nobody has stolen me from you. I love you as I always have. You're my mother. I've known about myself — I've known I don't like men — I mean, I don't like the idea of being intimate with a man. I've known that since I was in my teens."

"What do you mean?" Rosalie's eyes were fiery. "Of course I've known that you don't want a man, that you've not wanted to marry. Have I ever reproached you about that? But that's one thing. Chasing after women — going to bed with women — that's terrible. That is disgusting —"

"Not to me, not to a lot of women." Billie's tone was firm. "Mamma, those are the ideas of men. Those are the words men use. They want to keep women submissive. You're a woman, like me. There cannot be anything disgusting about loving a woman. Don't you realize: these are men's thoughts, what most men want women to believe. Men are afraid of women's bodies. That is why they beat us, rape us, kill us. That is why they invent these religious taboos about our bodies. Tell me, did you really feel unclean when you gave birth to me? Did you really think you had to be purified in a man-invented ritual so that you would not contaminate papa?"

Rosalie's face flamed. She burst out. "No, of course not! That's nothing but superstition! You know that we do not believe that sort of thing any more."

"Well —!"

They stared at each other for several moments. Then Rosalie turned away, striking her hands together in frustration.

But she came back at once to the attack. "So

what you are telling me is that you don't intend to change, you don't intend to stop going with women."

"That's not what I've been doing. There's just one woman in my life."

"Don't quibble!" Rosalie took a deep breath and held it as if she would burst with rage. Billie expected her to let loose another stream of invective — she was always surprised at the store of bad language her mother owned but seldom used. but instead Rosalie seemed to quiet down and presently said in a normal voice, "You realize what the consequences will be, don't you?"

"What they might be, yes."

"You'll be another Michelle. Nobody will have anything to do with you. You'll certainly not have anything to do with Rosenstein's. And what do you suppose that creature you're enamored of will do then? She won't be interested in you, if you're not important any more. Why do you suppose these women suck up to you? Because you've got money, because you're a Rosenstein, because you've got family and position."

She went on, speaking in an even, deadly serious tone, chipping away at Billie's self-confidence. Billie listened, half-objectively, aware that in the past she had heard her mother do this with other people, people whom she intended to dominate, to continue to dominate. Billie had never been the victim of such an attack because she had never resisted her mother's power. Nothing and nobody had seemed important enough to make her endure it. Until Helena.

Rosalie finally stopped. She seemed to wait, as if to see whether her threats had taken effect. Billie, in the midst of a painful recollection of all that had happened between herself and Helena, knew that the sound of her voice had ceased but made no response. Rosalie made a sound of disgust.

"You think you can get away with this by pretending you don't hear me. You'll learn. Other people won't be so easy with you."

Billie lifted her head. "They won't know anything about it unless you tell them."

She knew, by the expression on Rosalie's face, that she had reached her on a sore spot. Why was it? she wondered, that Rosalie had kept this struggle between the two of them, unless because she thought she could persuade her to capitulate and then they could bury the memory of it so deep that it could be forgotten. Poor mamma.

Rosalie was goaded into fury again. "You want to go on living a lie — pretending you're just a nice girl who just doesn't want to marry. Pretending —"

"I don't have to pretend. Michelle does not pretend."

"If you dare to do what she's done, I'll disown you! You'll not be my daughter any longer! Do you hear me? Do you understand what that could mean? You'd never see me again. You'd be out in the cold, among strangers. You'd find out soon enough what you've thrown away —"

Billie did not answer but let her wear herself out. After that evening, which left them both exhausted with no more conclusive an end than any that preceded it, their sessions together were more acrimonious, Rosalie's attacks more bitter. Billie was aware that time was running against her. Some sort of solution to the impasse must be reached and it began to seem as if only defeat for her could be the end.

In the daytime, at Rosenstein's, she sensed a growing tension, also. The long delay in any announcement of some decision about the store's future was obviously causing murmurs and short tempers. She saw items in the business and trade journals commenting on the mysterious lack of action by the directors of the Rosenstein Company. Even James Barton, who usually avoided her — because of the embarrassment, she thought, he felt in dealing with her in the anomalous yet powerful position she seemed to hold in Rosenstein's affairs — found an opportunity to fall into conversation with her.

"We're seeing a lot of you, Miss Billie," he remarked heartily as they met in the aisles of the men's accessories, where he was picking out neckties.

Billie nodded.

"We're all waiting for some really exciting news," he continued.

Billie thought, Stupid of you to talk about it out here in public, but you're afraid to come and see me in my office. She said aloud, "You think so?"

"Well, you know how it is when there's no official announcement. Everybody speculates. Of course, it can have a really bad effect on people who have personal decisions to make."

"Yes, I can see that," said Billie, with genuine kindliness. "Why don't you talk to Daniel? Or to Moishe?"

"Daniel says he hasn't any information to impart yet. Moishe won't talk. I think he's lost interest in Rosenstein's."

"I'm sorry, but I can't help. Perhaps things will clear up soon."

She walked away, her attention caught by his remark about Moishe. Could it be true?

That evening she was aware, as soon as she stepped into her mother's boudoir, that Rosalie was on the warpath. Rosalie's back was turned as she came in and she did not at once turn around.

Billie said apprehensively, "Mamma, how are you?"

Rosalie switched around. Her face was flushed and her eyes glittered. "How do you suppose I am? Do you think I have a second's peace, a moment's relaxation?"

Billie waited while she launched into a bitter review of the unhappiness that Billie had brought upon her, how faithless Billie had been all the while she had showered her only child, her little daughter, with every gift of love and cherishing. Billie knew that her mother really did feel the acute unhappiness she was voicing, but also that she intended to inflict as much pain as she herself received. Finally, after wiping away a few tears, she lapsed into morose silence.

Billie, feeling helpless to improve the situation, made no attempt to comfort her. After a while Rosalie said, in a more matter-of-fact voice, "You're going to have to do something. Moishe says people are beginning to notice."

Moishe. So that was it, thought Billie. Moishe has been here today. He has really upset her. She said aloud, "Notice what?"

"Notice that nothing is being done about

Rosenstein's, of course. What else? The business is going to the dogs."

Billie said boldly, "That is not up to me, mamma. It's up to you."

Rosalie gave her a brooding look. "You know perfectly well that he wants the Company to be sold. He says it will double and triple in value, if that's done. He says the way things are it will just dwindle away. He says it is ridiculous to let it slip away from us like this, for sentimental reasons or because we're too apathetic to do anything about it."

"Do you agree with him, mamma?"

Rosalie's mouth worked before she answered. "He's partly right. The store isn't what it used to be when Nana was alive. But what's the matter with it now is that it doesn't have anyone looking after it the way she did."

"I know that, mamma. I know the store needs somebody who has a feel for what it should be. The best I could do was persuade Daniel to hire a woman manager for the Company. The men who have been running it all think like Moishe: use Rosenstein's to build up a retail outlet business. They think of bigger profits, bigger jobs, bigger salaries for the people at the top. They forget that the Company is nothing unless the store survives. It is only Daniel who doesn't think that way and he can't stop the tide by himself. You know that Nana was generous to everybody. Look where Lionel and Moishe are now because she was. But she kept Rosenstein's for herself. She knew it was the source. Without it there would be nothing. Perhaps there is nothing now, that all we've got is the husk of what it used to be."

At first Rosalie was impatient listening to her but as Billie talked she grew attentive. Presently she turned away without saying anything and Billie's urge to explain faded. After a while, when she turned back she said, "It's what you should be doing. We don't need strangers in Rosenstein's."

"I can look after the store. I can't manage the Company. Things have changed since Nana died. We do need modern management there."

Rosalie did not dispute her but seemed to take thought about what she had said. It was remarkable, thought Billie, how Rosalie's shrewdness came to the surface at such times.

There was a long silence and Billie thought that this particular session had come to an end, like all the others, without a solution. But then Rosalie, who had walked away from her, suddenly came back to face her closely.

"If I had the daughter I thought I had, I wouldn't think twice about telling Moishe that I don't like his plan. I wouldn't think twice about risking Rosenstein's. Why should I care now about any of this?"

Billie said in anguish, "Mamma, I'm not different from what I've always been! I'll always be your daughter, whatever you say."

At first Rosalie's stare became a glare and then gradually her expression dissolved into misery. She dropped her face into her hands.

"Oh, why, oh, why does this have to happen to me? I've got only you, Billie. I've never wanted another child. I won't lose you!"

Impulsively Billie put out her hands and took hold of her mother's arms. This time Rosalie did not push her away. "You're not going to, mamma — unless you drive me away. And I'll always be here when you want me."

Rosalie did not respond for a moment and did not look at her. Her voice had hardened when she did speak. "I won't have that woman in my house! I won't have any of your women near me!"

Billie hesitated. Somehow Rosalie seemed to have moved several steps closer to her in imagination. Why should she speak as if Billie had threatened her with Helena's bodily presence? "Helena will not come near you unless she is invited. You can't have me without her. She is my only love. Can't you understand that I love her with all my heart and soul?" As she spoke her anger rose till she was aware that she was shaking.

Rosalie started to speak but then, feeling her emotion in the grip of her hands, stopped. Up till now, in their interchanges she had been the one to rage, to storm, to accuse. She had never seen such violent emotion in Billie's face and she stared in consternation.

Billie's low voice went on. "I've listened to you for days now, while you accused me of being the lowest of the low, the vilest thing on earth, and my dearest love only a fit companion for such as I. I'm nothing of what you've been saying, nor is Helena. If you cannot accept that fact, if you can't accept the fact that I'm the daughter you've always had, then we shall have to part, forever. I will not have a mother. You will not have a daughter. We'll live truncated lives — at your choice."

When she stopped speaking Rosalie sat down in stunned silence. Billie, exhausted, sat down with her

329

head resting in her hand. She was aware that after a while Rosalie moved about the room, finishing her dressing with automatic movements.

Then Rosalie said, in a tentative voice, "You haven't any more to say?"

Billie lifted her head. "There isn't anything more to say."

Rosalie looked at her with unusual calm. "No, I don't suppose there is." She hesitated and then asked, "How long have you been doing this?"

Billie's smile was weary. "I've not been 'doing' anything. I learned when I was fifteen that I didn't want boys, that I preferred to be with women. But I haven't been 'doing' anything. You should know. You've kept me under your eye. You've had Esther and Elise spying on me —"

Stung, Rosalie flared up. "That was because of your drinking. Besides, you're too much of a woman to live like a nun."

"So first you thought I was running around with men."

"I didn't think anything of the sort!" Rosalie defended herself. She paused and then plunged ahead. "I just couldn't believe it when Moishe said you and that woman were — lovers." The word dripped with scorn from her mouth.

"Is that what he told you? Did he say that?" Billie's demand fixed her like an arrow.

Rosalie faltered and turned away. "No. He just hinted."

"Hinted what?"

"He said he'd decided that you must be like Michelle."

Billie looked at her indignantly. "Moishe has

never known anything about Michelle till the other day, when somebody told him. Nobody in the family ever talks about her. How could he have known?"

Rosalie looked at her shrewdly. "How did you find out about Michelle? Oh, I know. Little pitchers have big ears. You heard me say something — or somebody said something to me. That wasn't the way Moishe found out. He wanted to know who were the shareholders in Rosenstein's. He found Michelle's name in the list and he naturally wanted to know why all the mystery about her and asked around. Perhaps Daniel told him. He thought it was funny at first — women going with women are a joke to him. Until this business with that woman came up."

"She has a name, mamma," said Billy softly. "It's Helena."

Rosalie paused as if she was biting back a sharp reply. "He said he was intrigued when he heard about her, while he was still in Japan. When he got back he was tantalized — I'll admit she's a stunning looking woman. But she wouldn't go to bed with him." Rosalie broke off into an aside. "You know that Moishe likes to tell me all about the women he chases or who chase him. His own mother's no good for that sort of thing. She's really too old, always has been." Rosalie paused again. "Then he says he fell in love with her. He thought if she knew he was serious she would soften up. Moishe marry a shikseh! I told him what I thought of that!"

"So then?" Billie prompted her.

"He said at first he couldn't understand why she wouldn't have anything to do with him. You wouldn't help. He thought you were jealous of her. Then he began to notice things about you, you didn't have any boyfriends and so on. Before he knew about Michelle he hadn't thought about you that way. You've always been like his sister. But then he saw you with that — with Helena and it struck him like a lightning flash. He was so disgusted that he couldn't bear to see either of you again." Rosalie broke off to stare at Billie. She said in a horrified voice, "Billie, he hates you now! He thinks you ruined her!"

"And you think she has ruined me."

Rosalie was shaken. She said helplessly, "Billie, what is the meaning of all this? It's like a nightmare."

Her resolution hardening, Billie answered, "The meaning is right in front of you, mamma. Neither Helena nor I are monsters. We love each other. She is the only person I've ever loved in this way. It is a natural thing to us — and it won't change. Look at me, mamma. I'll still be Billie and you will love me. I know you will."

Rosalie's eyes lingered on her for a long moment and then she looked away.

Suddenly Billie realized that their positions were reversed, that she had the upper hand. She demanded, "When Moishe was telling you what he thought of me, what did you say?"

Rosalie looked up at her again. "I told him that if I ever heard him talk about you like that again, to me or to anybody else, I'd tell everybody that he was a liar, a nasty-minded little nothing. I said in that case he could never come to see me again — that he would be dead to me and that I'd see to it that his parents knew just what kind of a son they'd produced. If he spread stories about you, I'd see that everybody and especially his mother would know what a low-minded, worthless sort of creature he was, without a shred of loyalty or family feeling, not fit to be anybody's husband —"

Billie listened, at first incredulous and then realizing that Moishe had badly miscalculated his place with Rosalie. Nobody — Rachel had often told her this — could trespass in any way on any possession of Rosalie's — and Rosalie's prize possession was herself. For this first time she was sorry for Moishe. He had felt so secure as the favorite. She knew that he, in spite of all his sophistication, put more dependence on Rosalie's affection and good opinion than on anyone else's.

She became aware that Rosalie had stopped talking. She looked up to see that Rosalie was holding her head in her hands and wiping away tears. Again she reached out to touch her. Rosalie did not draw away but she made no answering move. After a few moments Rosalie roused and glanced at the little clock chiming softly on her dressing table.

By the time they arrived at the dinner table it was well beyond the usual time. Billie saw her father's inquiring glance, and that the maid standing waiting by the serving table looked anxious. But her mother gave no explanation. When Esther exclaimed how late they were, she did not answer. She was almost completely silent through the meal, as if oblivious of the increasingly worried glances from her husband. Usually the conversation at dinner was a running counterpoint between Rosalie and Esther. Now there would have been utter silence if it had not been for Esther's nervous attempts to keep talking. Finally as they were leaving the table Billie heard her father ask anxiously in a low voice, "Are you all right, Rosie? Is anything the matter?" and Rosalie snap back in irritation, "No, why should there be?" Esther's astonishment was obvious in her face.

The next morning Billie was conscious of lassitude from a sleepless, doubt-filled night, spent rehearsing the long session with her mother, fruitlessly trying to arrive at some idea of what her mother intended to do next. Now, entering Rosenstein's, returning the greetings of those she met, her mind reverted to another worry.

While she was contending with her mother, her mind had been completely absorbed by the need to hold her own in their struggle. She had given no thought at all to whether Helena was wavering in her feelings towards her, whether Helena really understood what she was going through, whether Helena continued to be willing to wait patiently while she tried to resolve their situation. Now a cruel doubt assailed her. She had not seen Helena, except for that brief glimpse across the showroom, since her mother had stormed in upon them. Helena must be completely in the dark about what had happened since. She could only have faith that their relationship remained firm. How strong was Helena's faith? How much right, thought Billie miserably, do I have to depend so much on Helena's blind loyalty?

As she sat in her office before a desk piled high with papers that were at the moment meaningless to her, she sank into a new slough of despond. She scarcely heard the light tap on her door and was only aware that someone had come in when she heard Rachel's voice.

"I suppose I can take a chance on interrupting the new mastermind at Rosenstein's without a previous appointment," she said, coming over and leaning down to give Billie a quick kiss. "A lot seems to have been going on while I've been gone." She stopped abruptly and Billie saw her black, probing eyes suddenly widen. "Billie! What's the matter? You're as pale as a ghost."

"Nothing," said Billie.

Rachel continued to look at her. Billie interpreted the look: she thinks I've been hitting the bottle.

Rachel said, "You've been having trouble with your mother. What is it, Billie?"

Billie was unable to answer. Rachel went on, "It's about Helena, isn't it? She looks worse than you do. Come on, Billie. Tell me."

Billie found her voice. "What did Helena say to you?"

"Nothing about you. Billie, has your mother found out about you and Helena?"

Billie nodded.

"How did she find out?"

"Moishe told her."

"Moishe told her! What does he know about it?"

"Just his suspicions. You know he was in love with Helena. When he couldn't make an impression on her, he got suspicious. I thought we were careful. But he did see us together. He had got to the point of being jealous of everybody who had anything to do with her. I suppose that sparked the thought in his mind. He unburdened himself to mamma."

"And she believed him. Dear little Moishe. Always her pet."

Troubled by the sarcasm in Rachel's voice, Billie protested. "She believed him but she gave him hell."

Rachel's dark face lit up. "She did? Well, good for her! So now where do you stand?"

"I wish I knew."

"She hasn't disowned you?"

"Not quite. Oh, Rachel, if only I could have talked to her about this years ago. I hate all this deception. That's what upsets her most now. She thinks I've been hiding from her all this time, letting her think I was her good little girl while all the time I was this monster —"

"Monster? What's all this nonsense, Billie?"

"I can't convince her that I'm just what I always have been."

"Nobody can convince Rosalie of anything unless she wants to be." Rachel paused for a thoughtful moment. "This must have been a pretty big shock for her — her little doll baby. I think you'll have to give her some time to digest it. But she hasn't disowned you? No, I don't suppose she would turn you loose. You're still hers." Rachel paused again and then asked delicately, "Has she said anything about me?"

"No. She thinks it was Michelle — which it was."

Relief showed in Rachel's face. "She would, of course."

Billie said, melancholy overcoming her, "I've had a bad time while you've been gone, Rachel. Mamma has insisted that I have dinner with her and papa every evening and we always have a battle beforehand, just the two of us."

"She hasn't brought your father into this?"

"No, and nobody else."

"You've told her just how it is with you and Helena?"

Billie nodded.

"And she accepts that?"

"No, of course she doesn't. She keeps telling me that I am deluded, that Helena is a dreadful creature, just out for what she can use me for. And I keep telling her that that is not true, that I love Helena, that I won't give her up —" Billie's voice faltered and Rachel put her arm around her.

"Billie, you must not let her wear you down."

Billie rested her head against Rachel. "I can't. Nobody, not even mamma, can make me give Helena up. But —"

Rachel looked down at her. "But what, Billie?"

"I haven't seen Helena for more than a glimpse since mamma came into my apartment and drove her away. It seems like years. I'm afraid to see her, as long as there is a chance that mamma will give in or at least compromise. But now I'm beginning to doubt —"

She stopped and Rachel squeezed her shoulder. "You doubt what?"

"I wonder whether I'm taking too much for granted. I think of Helena as being just as firm as I am. But she does not know what has been going on between mamma and me. I've been assuming that she understands what I am trying to do. But will she wait indefinitely —?"

"You needn't worry about Helena. She is being eaten alive by worry over you."

"Yes, yes, but —"

"Well, of course, she's not clairvoyant and probably she is wondering whether you're throwing her to the wolves. I've talked to her only very briefly, of course. There hasn't been time for more since I got back. I think you ought to talk to her. You can come to my place."

"No, no, Rachel! No, no!"

"Why not?"

"I've done everything I could to keep you from being involved. And mamma has spies."

"Well, yes, I see your point. But, Billie, you'll have to do something."

Billie was silent for a long while and Rachel waited. Finally Billie said, "Perhaps I shouldn't draw her into my life. I don't know what the future is going to be for me. And, Rachel, Helena and I are strangers to each other's worlds. She is not as much aware of this as I am."

"Naturally," said Rachel, understanding her unspoken explanation. "But, Billie, it is possible to overcome all kinds of barriers, if you want to badly enough and if it means enough to you — religion, race, upbringing." She tried to bring a lighter note into her voice. "Look at me and the Countess. Is there anything more unlikely than us?"

Billie managed a wan smile. "Rachel, you're a darling. But I must solve this myself."

Through the rest of the day she debated with herself how she should approach Helena. Not on the telephone. They had to be face to face. When the end of the business day came and she got ready to go to her parents' apartment, she remembered what in her misery she had forgotten: that her parents were going out to a dinner party and for the first time she was not expected to face her mother beforehand. Her mother had said that she could not go through another session with her and then go out for a social affair with her nerves jangled. But she expected Billie to eat dinner at her parents' place. Esther would be there.

Putting on her hat and coat Billie stood for a while and pondered. In the end she decided, yes, she would go and have dinner with Esther. That was the safest thing to do. But afterwards —

She endured Esther's ceaseless talk, aware of the subtle questioning imbedded in the flow of trivial words. She felt certain that her mother had disclosed nothing at all to Esther and so she made only the vaguest responses. Finally, giving no indication of the eagerness with which she wanted to escape, she said goodbye to Esther and left the apartment.

There was only one thought in her mind: go to Helena. Her heart was beating fast while she waited at the reception desk to be announced. What if after all Helena was not home? Or would refuse to see her? But the receptionist said, "You may go up," and she almost ran to the elevator.

Helena stood in the open door of her apartment when she walked quickly down the corridor. The door closed behind them and they stood in silence facing one another.

How thin she is, thought Billie. The elegant lines of Helena's figure had lost their rounded sleekness. She was uncomfortable under the intense gaze of the shadowed grey eyes. She turned away abruptly and walked into the living room. Helena followed after her and helped her off with her coat silently.

Billie said humbly, "Honey, I couldn't come before this."

Helena sighed, as if she had been holding her breath.

"You do know that I would have come sooner if I could?" Billie asked anxiously.

Helena said dully, "I don't know anything."

"Honey!" There was anguish in Billie's voice. "I can't stand it if you doubt me. Do you?"

Helena's eyes were downcast. "I haven't seen you — I haven't heard from you since your mother drove me out of your place." Then her voice grew angry and she began, as if reciting the resentful thoughts that had filled her mind for the intervening time, "I'm not the sort of creature your mother called me. Because I love you — because I love you with my body as well as my soul — doesn't mean that I'm a despicable kind of person, that I'm perverted. I'm not somebody who is corrupting you for the sake of money or influence in the Rosenstein Company. Everything you've meant to me has been tainted by what she said."

Billie, hearing the heartache and bewilderment that had built up during their separation and that still seethed in Helena, caught hold of her. "No, no! Don't let what she said hurt you so! Of course it is not true! She doesn't understand — she doesn't want to believe that I love you, that you love me. She thinks there must be another explanation. Don't you see? She is fighting against the idea that we're together now, that I am joined to you in a way that makes it impossible to separate us. That is what I have been trying to do — make her understand that she must accept you, that she cannot drive you away from me. If she does, she must know that she will make her own life desolate and mine also. Oh, honey, do you see why I haven't been able to talk to you?"

Helena gazed at her, listening to her pleading.

340

"All I know is that apparently you cannot free yourself from your mother. I've begun to wonder whether I've been a big fool — whether when it comes to the pinch you will abandon me rather than quarrel with her, whether in fact you've already done so."

Under her gaze Billie wilted and sat down on the sofa. "I will never give you up. You must believe that. There is no meaning to my life without you in it. Yes, I do love my mother and I know she loves me. But I must teach her that now you come first — that you are so precious to me that —" Billie faltered and stopped speaking. How, she thought desperately, can I make you understand that I cannot abandon my mother, that I cannot allow her to drive me away from her, that I cannot allow her to destroy the bond between us. I must make her see that, in spite of her feeling for her family, her faith, her heritage, I am too much a part of her for her to deny me the most vital, the most fortunate gift that has ever been given me — your love? How can I explain to you that, if I do not succeed, if I have to cut myself off from her, I destroy so much more than my own happiness?

Looking across the gulf that seemed to stretch between them, Billie felt despair at the thought of explaining the weight of ages, the mass of tradition that had created it. She looked up at Helena standing with her arms crossed, gazing down at her. Presently Helena came and sat down beside her.

Helena said, "I was in an absolute desert before Rachel got back. Everybody else seemed to be watching me. Have you any idea what it is like to be surrounded by people you suspect know something

341

about you that you cannot acknowledge? Daniel seemed to be the only person who treated me as if he trusted me as he always has. And yet I know that was so because he did not know what was happening. It made me feel guilty, as if I were deceiving him, betraying that trust."

Billie roused to anger. "That is not so! You give Daniel more devoted support than he has ever had from anyone! What is between you and me is none of his affair. If he ever learns the truth, he must accept it, accept me and you."

"Did your mother say anything to him?"

"No, she has said nothing to anyone. This is something that must be resolved between her and me. She knows that, as I know it. Nobody suspects you of anything. What people are wondering about is what you will do if Rosenstein's is sold. Or perhaps they are speculating about you and Moishe. They think Moishe wants you to marry him but you won't. They wonder why."

"I haven't seen Moishe at all. He won't have anything to do with me because he knows now that I love you. Isn't that so? I assumed that he would spread the news everywhere, to get his revenge."

"He would have, except for my mother. She has warned him that, if he talks about us, she will tell everyone that he has invented this as revenge because you have turned him down. He would hate the very idea of that. And he is afraid of my mother. He has never seen her like this before."

"Why should she protect me?"

"Not you. Me. She wouldn't care what he said about you but she won't let him talk about you if I'm involved. So I must teach her that she must stop saying you are someone strange and evil. Otherwise she will be his ally, not mine."

"I don't know that I want to be accepted by her on those terms."

"Then you would give me up?"

Helena shook her head but did not speak. There was a long silence, fraught with the unbroken battle of their emotions. Then Billie reached out and gripped Helena's arm.

"You must give me a little more time to deal with my mother. You're a stranger to her — someone who comes from outside her world. She knows now that, if she will not accept you, I will walk out of her life. I don't know whether you can understand what a terrible thing that would be for her, what a burden of guilt it will be for me."

Helena did not answer. After a while Billie said quietly, "If she will not accept the reality of what we are, we shall both be living in a very different world. Can you face what it will mean for both of us? It is a sacrifice I should not ask of you."

Helena turned her head to look at her. "There's no going back now and I would not do so in any case. No, it is impossible for me to realize what it will be, except in the abstract. I don't know what I shall be able to do if I have to leave Rosenstein's in the midst of a personal scandal. I'll manage somehow. But I do see that you will be isolated, Billie — isolated from everything that has been important to you up till now."

There was another silence and then Billie asked, "What would happen, in that case, between you and your mother?"

She saw the startled look on Helena's face. Helena

said, "I haven't thought of her." She pondered for a while. "When she was here she tried to tell me that she understood at last why I never responded to her when she urged me to create a private life for myself. It was when I saw her off at the airport. She said that she would never cut herself off from me, under any circumstances." Helena paused again and then said slowly, "She would accept you. She likes you very much. I think she would be happy that I have found someone to love. After all, she has never had real love from anyone except me."

"Oh," said Billie.

Helena went on. "But I would never confront her with the fact of our situation — I mean, I would not describe it to her, tell her that I love you with all my heart and soul, that you are much more my lover than any man could ever be. She and I can't talk about that sort of thing. It's too — embarrassing. To put something like that in words falsifies it, somehow. But she would understand. In fact, I think she is already aware of what you mean to me. I think she guessed it the day you stayed with me when Rachel took her to see the fashion shows."

"I see." Her matter-of-factness seemed to Billie to make their future more stark. She said lamely, "At least, we would not have to quarrel with her."

Helena's composure collapsed. "Oh, Billie! What am I to do? I love you, Billie. You'll never leave me, even if I never see you again." She reached out and caught Billie in her arms.

Billie pulled her head down and kissed her, her lips moving over Helena's face. "There's never any question that I'd leave you, honey." For a long moment they sat pressed together, feeling the beating of each other's heart, feeling the tide of their desire flowing between them.

Billie finally stirred and gently straightened up. How much time, she wondered, had passed since she had arrived at Helena's apartment?

Helena, responding immediately to her anxiety, asked, "What is it?"

"I've got to get back to my place."

"Can't you stay here with me?"

"No, honey." Into Billie's mind flashed the vision of her own apartment and the phone ringing. "I've got to get back before my mother calls."

"Oh, Billie! What does it matter?"

"It matters a great deal. Until I've settled with her, she must not know that I've been here with you. That would only start things off again. She must not think she is in competition with you."

Billie got up and reached for her hat and coat. Helena sat and watched her. Helena said, "There's something else that dogs me all day long. I know your mother wants to get rid of me as Rosenstein's manager. Does she also want to sell Rosenstein's? Everyone supposes that I know the answer."

"It's all tied together. If she decides to part with me, she will sell the store. If I win, she will keep it, and there will be a place for both of us."

Helena got up and went to her. "Billie, there's always a place for us, no matter what."

They reached again for each other.

Billie's heart beat fast with apprehension as she unlocked her door and stepped into her own apartment. The light was on in the living room. She had never turned it off. She stood still, gazing at the telephone. Had it rung while she was gone? Was her mother even now on the way over, having not had an answer to her call?

Finally Billie slipped off her hat and coat and flung them onto the nearest chair. How much longer, she wondered, could she stand this tension? But she must. In the end all her effort might go for naught. She longed for Michelle. Michelle's acerbic tongue and sardonic outlook would bolster her. But she could not appeal to Michelle now. Her mother had kept their quarrel a matter between the two of them. She must do likewise. She thought about Rachel. Michelle had said to her once that of course Rosalie knew about Rachel. But Rachel was not a Rosenstein and also Rachel was the soul of discretion. She would always avoid doing anything that Rosalie would have to take notice of.

The telephone did not ring. It was midnight before Billie was able to fall into a light sleep. Arriving at the store the next morning in the middle of the early bustle, while the saleswomen were readying their counters, she managed to maintain a calm cheerfulness. About midmorning Rachel came into her room.

"Billie, you're exhausted," Rachel said, putting her arms around Billie and kissing her. "This has got to be settled or you'll have a breakdown."

Billie kissed her cheek. "I think it will be settled very soon."

Rachel moved restlessly about the room. "You know that the store is alive with gossip this morning, don't you?"

"About what?"

"Moishe has gone back to Japan to set up an office for his father's firm. He says the opportunities

346

for investment banking there are very exciting. Lionel is enthusiastic. He has great faith in Moishe and he thinks he has been wasting his time playing around with Rosenstein's. He's washed his hands of us."

"Is all that true?"

"Of course it is. Moishe told me himself. But the gossip goes further. Moishe has gone to Japan because of unrequited love. Helena turned him down — the Rosensteins won't let him marry a goy — there are several versions. He would be disinherited if he did. So he's gone to Japan to drown his sorrows in making another fortune. The women are wondering if he likes Japanese girls. They're all in love with him, you know. They think Helena must be made of stone to turn him down for the sake of a career."

"Is that what they think?" In spite of herself Billie was smiling.

"Oh, more or less." Rachel was pleased that she had been able to lighten Billie's mood. Then, more seriously, she added, "It was Esther who gave me the news first, and she said something else. She hinted that Moishe left because the decision about Rosenstein's has gone against him."

Every nerve in Billie's body was stilled. "My mother has not told me that."

"Esther would not have said that to me unless there was some truth to it. There is to be a board meeting this afternoon, called at short notice. Have you been informed?"

"I know it now," said Billie, taking a breath.

"Esther is probably on her way here to tell you now, so goodbye. I'll see you later."

Billie reached the board room early and sat down in her usual chair at the far end of the long table.

When the others appeared she noticed that Lionel looked annoyed, as if called upon to waste time that he would rather be spending elsewhere. But it was Daniel who came in with a sheaf of papers and a pleased expression on his face. When the moment came he spoke briefly in a tone of satisfaction. He had to announce, he said, that the several shareholders whose interests he represented had instructed him to vote against the sale of the Rosenstein store to a conglomerate. Since these shareholders represented, as a group, the majority of the voting stock, this concluded the matter. The appropriate announcement was being made to the business community the following day, as soon as the board took formal action.

So, thought Billie, mamma decided and the rest followed her lead.

As Daniel finished his statement he raised his eyes to look across at Lionel, who sat tapping his fingers on the table. Billie saw the look of annoyance on his face deepen as he said that he was voting his son Moishe's shares in favor of selling the store but that the question was now academic.

Daniel seemed to pounce as he asked, "Are you going to challenge this vote?"

But Lionel shrugged his shoulders disdainfully and replied that he merely wanted the dissenting vote recorded. He got up as he said this and announced that he was leaving unless there was any other business that required his presence. Only matters concerning the store management, said Daniel mildly. Lionel sat down again as if to say, Get on with it.

As executive vice-president, said Daniel, he had concluded that the present management of the

348

Rosenstein Company was doing a good job, profitability was up, the morale of the employees was much better than it had been, he saw a successful year ahead. But the store itself needed a senior officer, someone who could revive the image of Rosenstein's as it was known to everybody, someone who had the vision to adapt the traditional store to modern circumstances. He looked in Billie's direction and smiled.

"We have her," he said, "in our midst."

This is mamma's doing, thought Billie, and the idea brought an upheaval in her emotions. What did this mean? Was it a bribe? A price to be paid for something she must do?

She managed to smile calmly as the others all turned to look at her expectantly. Of course they all knew that Daniel was Rosalie's mouthpiece. But even Lionel smiled at her in a friendly fashion.

"Couldn't be a better choice," he said, with a trace of indulgence in his voice.

There was a round of applause.

The meeting broke up. As Billie was leaving she found Esther at her elbow.

"Now that was a surprise, wasn't it?" she said, looking up happily into Billie's face.

Billie nodded. Had she known about this?

Esther went on talking. "You know, your mother has arranged this. You can't fool her. People think she hasn't any business sense, but that's a mistake. When she puts her mind to something, there's nothing she can't understand. She knows perfectly well what is wrong with Rosenstein's. And I'm so glad she stopped the sale. It would have been such a betrayal of your great grandmother."

"Yes," Billie murmured, walking to the door with Esther at her side. The big room was empty now except for the two of them.

"You're not surprised? You don't act as if you are surprised. Rosalie must have told you about this." Esther looked up at her expectantly, as if waiting for a revelation.

Billie did not answer. What she needed now was another session with her mother. Had Rosalie timed this carefully, after the first evening they had spent together?

When she got back to her office there was a message that Daniel wanted to see her. She found him seated at his desk, turned away so that he could lean his elbow on it. He was always the same neat grey man she had known all her life, so different from his brother the elegant Lionel, who characteristically looked over your head when you spoke to him.

Daniel said, "Sit down, Billie. I think we've got this business straightened out now. It's been pretty difficult these last few months, trying to deal with all this uncertainty. I'm just glad we're intact."

Billie wanted to say, "This is my mother's doing, isn't it?" but decided that this reality should remain unacknowledged. Instead she said, "What am I supposed to do, Daniel?"

"Well, I guess what you've always done, look after the store, only on a regular basis, not in and out. And you'll have some authority now, too." He paused and glanced keenly at her. "You won't have any trouble dealing with Helena, will you?"

Billie smiled. "You think two women won't get

350

along, is that it? No, I don't think I'll have any trouble with her. She wants to stay?"

"Yes. I was afraid she was getting fed up with all this — maneuvering. But no. At least, she hasn't told me that she wants to leave. I hope she hasn't been looking for another connection. A good deal of the success of this new plan depends on her. She has pulled the Company out of the doldrums, against the odds. But she can't run the store. She says herself that she doesn't have the feel for that. She's a fine manager for the Company, one of the new crop of trained managers. She's learning about retailing, about the women's apparel business. But, Billie, you're the one who knows what Rosenstein's ought to be. You've got an instinct for it."

Billie thought, Oh, yes. Mamma told him that. I'm the ghost of Old Leah. Aloud, she asked, "Are there any other changes?"

Daniel glanced down at a sheet of paper lying by itself on the polished desktop. "James Barton is leaving us. He's had an offer from one of the retail chains. He seems to think that will suit him better."

Billie smiled but made no comment. She knew Daniel was pleased that Barton had left but at the same time disgruntled at the idea that anyone would willingly leave Rosenstein's.

The board meeting, hurriedly called, had been held after the close of the business day. Billie walked through the empty store, somehow aware that Helena was not in the building. Daniel had hurried away, after her interview with him, ruffled because his usual fixed schedule had been disrupted, even for so important an event. She glanced about her, at the muted gleam of light in the great spaces, the shrouded glass cases of the counters. Only the watchmen were visible to say Goodnight to her.

The long spring evening light still lingered in the bottom of the street as she walked briskly uptown through the thinning crowds. She must act quickly before the fear that lay in her breast undermined her energy. She tried not to think of the pros and cons that gathered around the question of her mother's intention, tried only to prepare for whatever she would face when she stepped into her mother's boudoir. Surely her mother would not create this situation, would not make this gift to her, only to snatch it away with impossible conditions.

But finally, when she reached her parents' apartment, responded to Elise's Good evening, and stepped into her mother's room, she was astonished by her mother's greeting. Rosalie was dressed in a black boucle pant suit ornamented with a large gold orchid. It clung to her plump but still shapely body. She was standing across the room, her back turned. She wheeled around as she heard the sound of the door. Anger flashed from her eyes. She demanded, "Well, are you satisfied?"

Billie, stunned, stammered a few incoherent words.

Rosalie swept on. "You pushed me to the very edge, didn't you? One more step and I'd be over the precipice into — what? You'd have been there with me. But what do you care? You'd just walk away — with your shikseh — your —"

Billie put up her hand but Rosalie stopped before she could speak. They stared at one another. Billie saw the anger in her mother's eyes wane and then mix with another emotion. Was it anguish?

352

Rosalie said, "There's nothing more that I can do. You can say there's nothing more I could do. You've got the whip handle —"

Billie found her voice. "Mamma, I haven't got anything. I can't do anything to you."

"Except leave me, walk out of my life, make me an object of pity to everyone who knows me —" Rosalie grimaced as she said this. Yes, thought Billie, she'd hate that, she'd hate having to accept the sympathy of those who might feel a certain smug satisfaction at the spectacle of her distress.

Billie said, "I would not do any of that unless you force me to. I can't leave Helena. It would be a false thing to do. She is part of me now. She belongs in my life as much as you do —"

Rosalie interrupted impatiently. "It's you who are part of my life. You're my child. You've never been anything but part of me. Don't you realize that you can't cut yourself off?"

"I would never try."

Rosalie stared at her again and this time her eyes brimmed with grief. She sat down and dropped her face into her hands. Billie, harrowed, watched the light twinkle on the stones in her rings. Finally, unable to stand the suspense any longer, she asked, "Mamma, what am I to do? You know that Daniel called a directors' meeting this afternoon and said that the sale of the store is off and that I'm to be in charge of it. Everybody knows he is speaking for you, that it's you who have decided this. What does this mean? Is it an ultimatum to me? What am I to do? Daniel says that Helena will stay with the Company. What are you doing to us?"

Billie, watching her intently, nevertheless was

unprepared for Rosalie's sudden movement. She got up from the rose-satin loveseat where she had sat down and threw herself at Billie, seizing her by the arms in a surprisingly strong grip. She stared up into Billie's face, her own only inches away.

"What am I doing? I'm doing the only thing I can do: make you stay where you belong, keep you from going away out there, be an outcast like Michelle. Billie, Billie, you do love me, don't you? You are my daughter, my doll baby. You can't be cold-hearted —"

The tears were beginning to overflow her eyes. Billie, overwhelmed, caught her in her arms. "Mamma, don't you understand? It's because I love you that I've never been able to tell you about myself. I've known you would not want to believe what I wanted to tell you. I'm not a dreadful thing, mamma. If I could only make you understand that. Michelle is not a terrible person. I love her. She has always been my friend. The women who are her friends are not women who should be shunned. They are women like your friends, except for one thing, and that one thing is not something you should condemn. Think about it, mamma. Why is it so dreadful that I love a woman, that I can't love a man? It's what you've been taught all your life but you don't have to keep on believing it. You've never let a man dominate you, even papa. Why should you believe that there is only one way to live?"

She felt the tremors in Rosalie's soft body pressed against her own. Rosalie had buried her face in Billie's shoulder. The grip of her fingers with their brilliantly polished nails only gradually relaxed. After a moment she slowly raised her head and Billie saw that the tears had stopped and that the old shrewdness was back in her eyes. There was an ironical glint in them as she said, "You're not content with making me accept you and your weirdness. I've got to have Michelle and the rest of them." As she drew herself away from Billie she raised one hand and struck Billie lightly across one cheek. Billie's heart bounded with joy at the touch. It was the gesture her mother had always made when, as a child, she had been punished and then forgiven. An ache of remembrance succeeded the joy when she realized how long a winter the withdrawal by her mother from affectionate touching had been.

Rosalie sat down again on the satin-covered loveseat, this time leaning back and crossing her legs. "I told Daniel that I didn't want the store sold and I wanted you to run it. He said this new woman should stay with the Company. She had proved she knows how to make it profitable." Rosalie pointed to the place beside her. "Sit down here. I've a few things to say to you."

Billie obeyed.

Rosalie said, "I've been damned careful to see that nobody knows about this business. You know that. So far as anybody is concerned, you're good friends with this woman, you're going to be business partners. Everybody in the store is going to gossip about you — whether two women are going to be able to work together without jealousy and backbiting. She's your boss, since she is manager of the Company. Have you thought about that?"

"I don't think that's a problem, mamma. I know what to do about the store. Helena won't question that."

"And the other thing is: Are you going to let your personal feelings get in the way of your job?"

Billie laughed. "I don't think so. I know what Helena is like in her office — all business."

But Rosalie was still serious. "Nana was very astute in managing people. She could always foresee when emotional factors might get involved in management. She could always circumvent them. I think you could be like her when it comes to other people, but I wonder —"

"Don't worry about me, mamma. I've had a lot of training in disguising my feelings."

Her mother's eyes widened at her statement and then a burst of anger reddened her cheeks. "And I've always thought you were a little innocent I had to protect from life!"

She will never let me forget that I have deceived her, thought Billie. "Mamma, don't go on punishing me. I've always been wretched about deceiving you."

But Rosalie would not give up. "You've been pretty clever. Esther and Elise have never suspected anything — except your drinking. I've been stupid. I should have looked for a reason for that. I just thought you took after your father's side in that one thing. He's got several drunkards in his family. I never thought of Michelle. She knows all about you and this woman, I suppose."

"Yes. Michelle has known all about me since I was fifteen."

She was afraid that her mother would burst out again in anger but Rosalie merely looked at her in disgust. "Then I was right. It was Michelle who corrupted you."

"Michelle did not corrupt me. I used to go to her

356

house on my way home from school. She was kind to me and — and — well, it was a natural thing."

"Good God, Billie! What next do you expect me to believe?"

"The truth. Some time soon you must come with me to see Michelle. She doesn't hate you."

Rosalie stared at her incredulously. "Me? Go to see Michelle?"

"Well, she can't come to see you."

Rosalie said crossly, "One thing at a time. First of all, you've got to bring this new woman to see me."

"I've told you, mamma: her name is Helena."

"Well, Helena, then." There was a sudden trace of uncertainty in Rosalie's expression. "We didn't part on very good terms when I saw her last."

"She won't hold it against you."

Again there was an ironical gleam in Rosalie's eyes. "You'd better be careful about speaking for someone else, even her."

"She'll do it for my sake."

Rosalie seemed suddenly to relax. She sighed and said, "Billie, this is going to take a while. I know. I must take you as you are. I'll try to understand what you want me to feel. It goes against everything I've accepted all my life, everything I've taken for granted as the right and proper way to do things. But I am wondering now —" She broke off and put her arms around Billie. "Billie, Billie."

Billie said, "Mamma, I've been having a very hard time."

Rosalie kissed her on the lips. "Well, it's over now." She got up saying, "We're late for dinner. Be careful what you say at the table."

357

Billie followed her into the dining room. Her father was there already, being talked at by Esther.

Esther burst out enthusiastically, "I've been telling your father about the board meeting, Billie. I think it is perfectly wonderful."

Billie saw her father glance at her mother as if for confirmation. Rosalie nodded to him and then said in a satirical tone, "What's so wonderful about Billie running Rosenstein's? It's what Nana would have expected."

"But you're going to have to get along with Helena,'" said Esther slyly to Billie.

Billie shrugged. Her mother said to her father, "Alfred, we'll have to have Helena over to dinner," and her father nodded absently.

When dinner was over and Billie was putting on her hat and coat, her mother came over to stand close to her. Rosalie asked, "Are you going home?"

Billie nodded and they looked for a brief moment into each other's eyes.

Out on the street Billie walked slowly, aware of her own fatigue. The spring evening was mild and the sidewalks were full of people tempted by the fine weather to stroll. When she reached her apartment she dialed Helena's number and when she heard her voice said, "Will you come over now?"

There was a brief silence at the other end of the line before Helena said Yes. Within a few minutes she arrived at Billie's door. Billie closed the door behind her and they stood facing each other.

"What is it now, Billie?" There was an anxious note in her voice.

Billie, suddenly overcome with fatigue, walked into

358

the living room and sat down on the sofa. "I've won."

Helena, following her slowly, said, "Daniel has told me about the board meeting. I know all that part of it."

They sat together but separated by a certain stiffness. Billie, aware of this, reached out her hand to touch Helena. "But I've won with my mother."

Helena looked at her uncertainly. "What does she demand, Billie?"

"Nothing. She hasn't made a deal, honey. She says she cannot lose me, so she must accept you. You'll have to be patient with her, honey. But she will be as gracious about it as she can. I think her eyes are really open. You can meet her halfway, can't you? Eventually she'll accept you as a daughter."

Helena dropped her eyes and they were quiet for a while. When she raised them again she said, "I'll do anything you want me to do. I'll try to feel about your mother as you want me to. But there is a great distance between me and your family. I am sure you know that. It has nothing to do with prejudice. It is simply there. I'll always be a stranger to them and they will always be strangers to me, no matter how much difference familiarity and good feeling will make."

Billie moved to put her arm around her. "But you're not a stranger to me and you must never feel so. Yes, I know we have to live in a world that will accept us only on sufferance. It's not only my family. What people see from the outside will be what they accept or reject. Two women are going to run Rosenstein's. That's natural enough. It was a woman's creation. When they see us walk through the store together — I don't have to stay away from you any more — they will gossip. Will that matter to you? They'll soon think it was always that way."

Helena, aware that her own tense body was relaxing under the touch of Billie's hands, smiled wryly. "I'll have to take lessons from Rachel. No, it won't matter to me. Only you matter to me, Billie."

"Then we're safe — with each other," Billie murmured into her ear.

A few of the publications of
THE NAIAD PRESS, INC.
P.O. Box 10543 • Tallahassee, Florida 32302
Phone (904) 539-5965
Mail orders welcome. Please include 15% postage.

FATAL REUNION by Claire McNab. 216 pp. 2nd Det. Inspec.
Carol Ashton mystery.   ISBN 0-941483-40-1 $8.95

KEEP TO ME STRANGER by Sarah Aldridge. 372 pp. Romance
set in a department store dynasty.   ISBN 0-941483-38-X   9.95

HEARTSCAPE by Sue Gambill. 204 pp. American lesbian in
Portugal.   ISBN 0-941483-33-9   8.95

IN THE BLOOD by Lauren Wright Douglas. 252 pp. Lesbian
science fiction adventure fantasy   ISBN 0-941483-22-3   8.95

THE BEE'S KISS by Shirley Verel. 216 pp. Delicate, delicious
romance.   ISBN 0-941483-36-3   8.95

RAGING MOTHER MOUNTAIN by Pat Emmerson. 264 pp.
Furosa Firechild's adventures in Wonderland. ISBN 0-941483-35-5 8.95

IN EVERY PORT by Karin Kallmaker. 228 pp. Jessica's sexy,
adventuresome travels.   ISBN 0-941483-37-7   8.95

OF LOVE AND GLORY by Evelyn Kennedy. 192 pp. Exciting
WWII romance.   ISBN 0-941483-32-0   8.95

CLICKING STONES by Nancy Tyler Glenn. 288 pp. Love
transcending time.   ISBN 0-941483-31-2   8.95

SURVIVING SISTERS by Gail Pass. 252 pp. Powerful love
story.   ISBN 0-941483-16-9   8.95

SOUTH OF THE LINE by Catherine Ennis. 216 pp. Civil War
adventure.   ISBN 0-941483-29-0   8.95

WOMAN PLUS WOMAN by Dolores Klaich. 300 pp. Supurb
Lesbian overview.   ISBN 0-941483-28-2   9.95

SLOW DANCING AT MISS POLLY'S by Sheila Ortiz Taylor.
96 pp. Lesbian Poetry   ISBN 0-941483-30-4   7.95

DOUBLE DAUGHTER by Vicki P. McConnell. 216 pp. A Nyla
Wade Mystery, third in the series.   ISBN 0-941483-26-6   8.95

HEAVY GILT by Delores Klaich. 192 pp. Lesbian detective/
disappearing homophobes/upper class gay society.

                                         ISBN 0-941483-25-8   8.95

THE FINER GRAIN by Denise Ohio. 216 pp. Brilliant young
college lesbian novel.   ISBN 0-941483-11-8   8.95

THE AMAZON TRAIL by Lee Lynch. 216 pp. Life, travel & lore
of famous lesbian author.   ISBN 0-941483-27-4   8.95

HIGH CONTRAST by Jessie Lattimore. 264 pp. Women of the
Crystal Palace.   ISBN 0-941483-17-7   8.95

OCTOBER OBSESSION by Meredith More. Josie's rich, secret
Lesbian life.   ISBN 0-941483-18-5   8.95

LESBIAN CROSSROADS by Ruth Baetz. 276 pp. Contemporary
Lesbian lives.   ISBN 0-941483-21-5   9.95

BEFORE STONEWALL: THE MAKING OF A GAY AND
LESBIAN COMMUNITY by Andrea Weiss & Greta Schiller.
96 pp., 25 illus.   ISBN 0-941483-20-7   7.95

WE WALK THE BACK OF THE TIGER by Patricia A. Murphy.
192 pp. Romantic Lesbian novel/beginning women's movement.
                                        ISBN 0-941483-13-4   8.95

SUNDAY'S CHILD by Joyce Bright. 216 pp. Lesbian athletics, at
last the novel about sports.   ISBN 0-941483-12-6   8.95

OSTEN'S BAY by Zenobia N. Vole. 204 pp. Sizzling adventure
romance set on Bonaire.   ISBN 0-941483-15-0   8.95

LESSONS IN MURDER by Claire McNab. 216 pp. 1st Det. Inspec.
Carol Ashton mystery — erotic tension!. ISBN 0-941483-14-2   8.95

YELLOWTHROAT by Penny Hayes. 240 pp. Margarita, bandit,
kidnaps Julia.   ISBN 0-941483-10-X   8.95

SAPPHISTRY: THE BOOK OF LESBIAN SEXUALITY by
Pat Califia. 3d edition, revised. 208 pp. ISBN 0-941483-24-X   8.95

CHERISHED LOVE by Evelyn Kennedy. 192 pp. Erotic
Lesbian love story.   ISBN 0-941483-08-8   8.95

LAST SEPTEMBER by Helen R. Hull. 208 pp. Six stories & a
glorious novella.   ISBN 0-941483-09-6   8.95

THE SECRET IN THE BIRD by Camarin Grae. 312 pp. Striking,
psychological suspense novel.   ISBN 0-941483-05-3   8.95

TO THE LIGHTNING by Catherine Ennis. 208 pp. Romantic
Lesbian 'Robinson Crusoe' adventure.   ISBN 0-941483-06-1   8.95

THE OTHER SIDE OF VENUS by Shirley Verel. 224 pp.
Luminous, romantic love story.   ISBN 0-941483-07-X   8.95

DREAMS AND SWORDS by Katherine V. Forrest. 192 pp.
Romantic, erotic, imaginative stories. ISBN 0-941483-03-7   8.95

MEMORY BOARD by Jane Rule. 336 pp. Memorable novel
about an aging Lesbian couple.   ISBN 0-941483-02-9   8.95

THE ALWAYS ANONYMOUS BEAST by Lauren Wright
Douglas. 224 pp. A Caitlin Reese mystery. First in a series.
                                        ISBN 0-941483-04-5   8.95

SEARCHING FOR SPRING by Patricia A. Murphy. 224 pp.
Novel about the recovery of love.   ISBN 0-941483-00-2   8.95

DUSTY'S QUEEN OF HEARTS DINER by Lee Lynch. 240 pp.
Romantic blue-collar novel.   ISBN 0-941483-01-0   8.95

PARENTS MATTER by Ann Muller. 240 pp. Parents'
relationships with Lesbian daughters and gay sons.
                                               ISBN 0-930044-91-6   9.95

THE PEARLS by Shelley Smith. 176 pp. Passion and fun in
the Caribbean sun.   ISBN 0-930044-93-2   7.95

MAGDALENA by Sarah Aldridge. 352 pp. Epic Lesbian novel
set on three continents.   ISBN 0-930044-99-1   8.95

THE BLACK AND WHITE OF IT by Ann Allen Shockley.
144 pp. Short stories.   ISBN 0-930044-96-7   7.95

SAY JESUS AND COME TO ME by Ann Allen Shockley. 288
pp. Contemporary romance.   ISBN 0-930044-98-3   8.95

LOVING HER by Ann Allen Shockley. 192 pp. Romantic love
story.   ISBN 0-930044-97-5   7.95

MURDER AT THE NIGHTWOOD BAR by Katherine V.
Forrest. 240 pp. A Kate Delafield mystery. Second in a series.
                                               ISBN 0-930044-92-4   8.95

ZOE'S BOOK by Gail Pass. 224 pp. Passionate, obsessive love
story.   ISBN 0-930044-95-9   7.95

WINGED DANCER by Camarin Grae. 228 pp. Erotic Lesbian
adventure story.   ISBN 0-930044 88-6   8.95

PAZ by Camarin Grae. 336 pp. Romantic Lesbian adventurer
with the power to change the world.   ISBN 0-930044-89-4   8.95

SOUL SNATCHER by Camarin Grae. 224 pp. A puzzle, an
adventure, a mystery — Lesbian romance.   ISBN 0-930044-90-8   8.95

THE LOVE OF GOOD WOMEN by Isabel Miller. 224 pp.
Long-awaited new novel by the author of the beloved *Patience
and Sarah.*   ISBN 0-930044-81-9   8.95

THE HOUSE AT PELHAM FALLS by Brenda Weathers. 240
pp. Suspenseful Lesbian ghost story.   ISBN 0-930044-79-7   7.95

HOME IN YOUR HANDS by Lee Lynch. 240 pp. More stories
from the author of *Old Dyke Tales.*   ISBN 0-930044-80-0   7.95

EACH HAND A MAP by Anita Skeen. 112 pp. Real-life poems
that touch us all.   ISBN 0-930044-82-7   6.95

SURPLUS by Sylvia Stevenson. 342 pp. A classic early Lesbian
novel.   ISBN 0-930044-78-9   7.95

PEMBROKE PARK by Michelle Martin. 256 pp. Derring-do
and daring romance in Regency England.   ISBN 0-930044-77-0   7.95

THE LONG TRAIL by Penny Hayes. 248 pp. Vivid adventures
of two women in love in the old west.   ISBN 0-930044-76-2   8.95

HORIZON OF THE HEART by Shelley Smith. 192 pp. Hot
romance in summertime New England.   ISBN 0-930044-75-4   7.95

AN EMERGENCE OF GREEN by Katherine V. Forrest. 288
pp. Powerful novel of sexual discovery.   ISBN 0-930044-69-X   8.95

THE LESBIAN PERIODICALS INDEX edited by Claire
Potter. 432 pp. Author & subject index.   ISBN 0-930044-74-6   29.95

DESERT OF THE HEART by Jane Rule. 224 pp. A classic;
basis for the movie *Desert Hearts*.   ISBN 0-930044-73-8   7.95

SPRING FORWARD/FALL BACK by Sheila Ortiz Taylor.
288 pp. Literary novel of timeless love.   ISBN 0-930044-70-3   7.95

FOR KEEPS by Elisabeth Nonas. 144 pp. Contemporary novel
about losing and finding love.   ISBN 0-930044-71-1   7.95

TORCHLIGHT TO VALHALLA by Gale Wilhelm. 128 pp.
Classic novel by a great Lesbian writer.   ISBN 0-930044-68-1   7.95

LESBIAN NUNS: BREAKING SILENCE edited by Rosemary
Curb and Nancy Manahan. 432 pp. Unprecedented autobiographies
of religious life.   ISBN 0-930044-62-2   9.95

THE SWASHBUCKLER by Lee Lynch. 288 pp. Colorful novel
set in Greenwich Village in the sixties.   ISBN 0-930044-66-5   8.95

MISFORTUNE'S FRIEND by Sarah Aldridge. 320 pp. Histori-
cal Lesbian novel set on two continents.   ISBN 0-930044-67-3   7.95

A STUDIO OF ONE'S OWN by Ann Stokes. Edited by
Dolores Klaich. 128 pp. Autobiography.   ISBN 0-930044-64-9   7.95

SEX VARIANT WOMEN IN LITERATURE by Jeannette
Howard Foster. 448 pp. Literary history.   ISBN 0-930044-65-7   8.95

A HOT-EYED MODERATE by Jane Rule. 252 pp. Hard-hitting
essays on gay life; writing; art.   ISBN 0-930044-57-6   7.95

INLAND PASSAGE AND OTHER STORIES by Jane Rule.
288 pp. Wide-ranging new collection.   ISBN 0-930044-56-8   7.95

WE TOO ARE DRIFTING by Gale Wilhelm. 128 pp. Timeless
Lesbian novel, a masterpiece.   ISBN 0-930044-61-4   6.95

AMATEUR CITY by Katherine V. Forrest. 224 pp. A Kate
Delafield mystery. First in a series.   ISBN 0-930044-55-X   7.95

THE SOPHIE HOROWITZ STORY by Sarah Schulman. 176
pp. Engaging novel of madcap intrigue.   ISBN 0-930044-54-1   7.95

THE BURNTON WIDOWS by Vickie P. McConnell. 272 pp. A
Nyla Wade mystery, second in the series.   ISBN 0-930044-52-5   7.95

OLD DYKE TALES by Lee Lynch. 224 pp. Extraordinary
stories of our diverse Lesbian lives.   ISBN 0-930044-51-7   8.95

DAUGHTERS OF A CORAL DAWN by Katherine V. Forrest.
240 pp. Novel set in a Lesbian new world.   ISBN 0-930044-50-9   7.95

THE PRICE OF SALT by Claire Morgan. 288 pp. A milestone
novel, a beloved classic. ISBN 0-930044-49-5 8.95

AGAINST THE SEASON by Jane Rule. 224 pp. Luminous,
complex novel of interrelationships. ISBN 0-930044-48-7 8.95

LOVERS IN THE PRESENT AFTERNOON by Kathleen
Fleming. 288 pp. A novel about recovery and growth.
ISBN 0-930044-46-0 8.95

TOOTHPICK HOUSE by Lee Lynch. 264 pp. Love between
two Lesbians of different classes. ISBN 0-930044-45-2 7.95

MADAME AURORA by Sarah Aldridge. 256 pp. Historical
novel featuring a charismatic "seer." ISBN 0-930044-44-4 7.95

CURIOUS WINE by Katherine V. Forrest. 176 pp. Passionate
Lesbian love story, a best-seller. ISBN 0-930044-43-6 8.95

BLACK LESBIAN IN WHITE AMERICA by Anita Cornwell.
141 pp. Stories, essays, autobiography. ISBN 0-930044-41-X 7.50

CONTRACT WITH THE WORLD by Jane Rule. 340 pp.
Powerful, panoramic novel of gay life. ISBN 0-930044-28-2 7.95

YANTRAS OF WOMANLOVE by Tee A. Corinne. 64 pp.
Photos by noted Lesbian photographer. ISBN 0-930044-30-4 6.95

MRS. PORTER'S LETTER by Vicki P. McConnell. 224 pp.
The first Nyla Wade mystery. ISBN 0-930044-29-0 7.95

TO THE CLEVELAND STATION by Carol Anne Douglas.
192 pp. Interracial Lesbian love story. ISBN 0-930044-27-4 6.95

THE NESTING PLACE by Sarah Aldridge. 224 pp. A
three-woman triangle—love conquers all! ISBN 0-930044-26-6 7.95

THIS IS NOT FOR YOU by Jane Rule. 284 pp. A letter to a
beloved is also an intricate novel. ISBN 0-930044-25-8 8.95

FAULTLINE by Sheila Ortiz Taylor. 140 pp. Warm, funny,
literate story of a startling family. ISBN 0-930044-24-X 6.95

THE LESBIAN IN LITERATURE by Barbara Grier. 3d ed.
Foreword by Maida Tilchen. 240 pp. Comprehensive bibliography.
Literary ratings; rare photos. ISBN 0-930044-23-1 7.95

ANNA'S COUNTRY by Elizabeth Lang. 208 pp. A woman
finds her Lesbian identity. ISBN 0-930044-19-3 6.95

PRISM by Valerie Taylor. 158 pp. A love affair between two
women in their sixties. ISBN 0-930044-18-5 6.95

BLACK LESBIANS: AN ANNOTATED BIBLIOGRAPHY
compiled by J. R. Roberts. Foreword by Barbara Smith. 112 pp.
Award-winning bibliography. ISBN 0-930044-21-5 5.95

THE MARQUISE AND THE NOVICE by Victoria Ramstetter.
108 pp. A Lesbian Gothic novel. ISBN 0-930044-16-9 4.95

OUTLANDER by Jane Rule. 207 pp. Short stories and essays
by one of our finest writers.   ISBN 0-930044-17-7   8.95

ALL TRUE LOVERS by Sarah Aldridge. 292 pp. Romantic
novel set in the 1930s and 1940s.   ISBN 0-930044-10-X   7.95

A WOMAN APPEARED TO ME by Renee Vivien. 65 pp. A
classic; translated by Jeannette H. Foster.   ISBN 0-930044-06-1   5.00

CYTHEREA'S BREATH by Sarah Aldridge. 240 pp. Romantic
novel about women's entrance into medicine.
                                       ISBN 0-930044-02-9   6.95

TOTTIE by Sarah Aldridge. 181 pp. Lesbian romance in the
turmoil of the sixties.   ISBN 0-930044-01-0   6.95

THE LATECOMER by Sarah Aldridge. 107 pp. A delicate love
story.   ISBN 0-930044-00-2   5.00

ODD GIRL OUT by Ann Bannon.   ISBN 0-930044-83-5   5.95

I AM A WOMAN by Ann Bannon.   ISBN 0-930044-84-3   5.95

WOMEN IN THE SHADOWS by Ann Bannon.
                                       ISBN 0-930044-85-1   5.95

JOURNEY TO A WOMAN by Ann Bannon.
                                       ISBN 0-930044-86-X   5.95

BEEBO BRINKER by Ann Bannon.   ISBN 0-930044-87-8   5.95
         Legendary novels written in the fifties and sixties,
               set in the gay mecca of Greenwich Village.

VOLUTE BOOKS

JOURNEY TO FULFILLMENT   Early classics by Valerie   3.95

A WORLD WITHOUT MEN   Taylor: The Erika Frohmann   3.95

RETURN TO LESBOS   series.   3.95

These are just a few of the many Naiad Press titles — we are the oldest and
largest lesbian/feminist publishing company in the world. Please request a
complete catalog. We offer personal service; we encourage and welcome
direct mail orders from individuals who have limited access to bookstores
carrying our publications.